# THE CHILDREN OF LOCHANDEE

## GWEN KIRKWOOD

Published by Accent Press Ltd – 2013

ISBN 9781786151469

# Chapter One

Rachel felt an unexpected shiver tingle down her spine. Why, she wondered uneasily. Subconsciously her gaze was drawn to the slender, swaying figure of one of the young women from the teacher training college. Rachel had always had an uncanny instinct where the welfare of her family was concerned, but she was not given to dramatic flights of fancy. She gave herself a mental shake. Still, a frisson of unease lingered.

This was a happy occasion – a gathering of family and friends in the familiar surroundings of the Lochandee Village Hall. They were celebrating the coming of age of her youngest son and her granddaughter, Ewan and Lucy. They had been born within a couple of weeks of each other and a joint celebration had seemed a good idea. They were both at colleges in Ayr and consequently had several mutual friends.

It had been a shock when she first discovered Lucy was her granddaughter, the child fathered by her eldest son. Conan himself had never dreamt his wild moment of passion, kindled by his impending departure for the RAF, had resulted in the birth of a little girl. Lucy was almost 12 years old before her mother had confided in anyone.

Even then Beth had only divulged her secret because she knew she was dying. She had not wanted to leave her child alone, unprotected and without a mother's guidance. She had been beset with fears that the close friendship which Ewan and Lucy shared might blossom into a deeper relationship as they grew older. She dare not take her secret to the grave leaving Lucy unaware that her real father was not Harry Mason, the man who had adored her. Harry had died suddenly and Beth's grief had been deep, but she had been glad he had never suffered the heartbreak of discovering Lucy was not his child. He had never known she had committed that single fateful act of infidelity with his young friend, Conan Maxwell. Beth had worked at Lochandee and Rachel had known her most of her life. She had valued her help as a maid, but friendship and respect for each other had grown over the years.

We must have been blind not to see the family resemblance, Rachel reflected now, as she had done many times in the past. She watched with pride and pleasure as Ewan and Lucy circled the floor together, smiling, radiating the warmth generated by long-standing friendship and shared memories. Yet even in the family their true relationship to each other was rarely mentioned. She supposed it was what was known as a skeleton in the family's cupboard. Thankfully, it did not seem to have affected Lucy. She had grown into a pleasant, well-adjusted young woman, working hard at her music and her teacher training course, eager to fulfil the dream Harry Mason had cherished for her future. She was kind and thoughtful too. It was her kindness which had prompted her to invite the girl with the curtain of long blonde hair. Apparently Gerda Fritz-Allan was not one of her own particular friends but she had recently joined a study group at the teacher training college. All the others in the group had already been invited to the party and Lucy had felt it would be unkind to leave her out.

The girl had a rare beauty and Rachel frowned, wondering why she should have such an uneasy feeling about her. Was it her affectedly child-like voice and fluttering hands which irritated? She put such silly whims

2

out of her head. They would probably never see Gerda Fritz-Allan again after the young people returned to college tomorrow.

Rachel felt her heart swell with pride and she turned her attention to other members of her family as they joined the dancing. Bridie, her only daughter, and Nick, the son-in-law who'd earned her respect, and her affection. They danced well together, as they did most other things, including their singing and their work at Lochandee. Other young couples began to dance, fellow students of Ewan from Auchincruive Agricultural College and Lucy's friends from Craigie Teacher Training College. Rachel sighed. They all looked so happy and carefree. She hoped life would continue that way for all of them in a world free from wars.

Her eye was caught by Conan and Fiona. What a handsome couple they made, but what a pity they had not been blessed with children of their own. They had been married seven years now and Conan would be 40 in May. Fiona was 37. Secretly, Rachel was still a little in awe of her daughter-in-law. She was such a clever and capable young woman and she had proven a great asset and partner to Conan, helping him build up his business to a whole fleet of touring coaches and keeping his home so beautifully. She had excellent taste and the new extension to the house had made it a good investment, as well as a desirable residence. Far more important, Fiona had made a wonderful stepmother to Lucy. She would always have Rachel's heartfelt gratitude for that, and yet she almost envied the closeness of their relationship. They were more like sisters in spite of the years between them.

'Why are you frowning, lassie? You'll spoil your bonnie face.' Rachel looked up at the sound of her husband's deep voice and her heartbeat quickened. Even after all these years Ross's smile still had the same effect on her.

'I'm scarcely a lassie any more,' she chuckled. 'Watching all these young folks really makes me feel my age.'

'Och, we're as young as we feel, and you're as lithe as any o' them. I'm not 60 until November, remember, and I only feel half of that when I see that wee dimple in your cheek. Come on, let's show them how to dance. Some of the youngsters these days dinna know how to begin.'

'I know. Ewan was warning me that the second half of the party will be music to suit his generation. "Rock and roll", or something, he called it.'

'I think it's some sort of jiving they do nowadays. All the more reason for us to enjoy this half. Listen, they're playing the *Pride of Erin Waltz*.' He drew her on to the floor and Rachel felt her spirits rise, her fears and apprehensions forgotten, at least for the present.

A couple of hours later, Rachel, Bridie and Fiona cleared the remnants of the buffet meal away into the small kitchen at the back of the village hall.

'Well, they certainly enjoyed that!' Fiona exclaimed. 'I thought there were mountains of food but it's nearly all gone. I could never cook like you two,' she added with a wistful sigh.

'Och, Fiona, there's nothing to cooking when you've done it all your life,' Rachel reassured her. 'You can do so many other things that I've never heard of.'

'Yes, like organising,' Bridie grinned. 'I'd never have thought of setting the food out as a buffet but it worked splendidly.'

'Mmm. We'd never have managed to feed so many at a sit-down meal.' Rachel nodded agreement. 'Bridie, your father and I are going home as soon as we have seen Lucy and Ewan cut the cake. I got the impression Ewan thinks their friends will relax and enjoy it better if we are out of the way. I hope they'll not get too boisterous,' she added anxiously.

'Don't worry, Mum,' Bridie smiled. 'I think they only want some of the rowdy music that Dad calls a "hell of a din". Fiona and Conan will keep an eye on them. We'll stay on for a while, but I expect the twins will be ready for bed long before the finish.'

'I'm sure they will – after all, they're only seven. But it was good to see them joining in the dancing. Your father's sure they've inherited a good sense of rhythm from you and Nick. He says Alicia can sing beautifully.'

'Mmm, Max isn't bad either,' Bridie reflected. 'I wish we still had a choir at the kirk for him to get some practice. Nick thinks we should send him for piano lessons, but I'm afraid of putting him off, like Dad did with Ewan.'

'Oh, it wasna your father's fault,' Rachel protested. 'Ewan simply didn't have any musical ability and didn't want to be bothered. All he has ever wanted to do is farm Nether Rullion.' She smiled, the dimple flashing, making her look younger than her 57 years. It's almost a mischievous smile, Bridie thought affectionately. 'He can't wait to finish college and get on with breeding a cow good enough to beat your Lochandee herd.'

'Oh! Oh! That's what he thinks, is it! Nick and I will give him a run for his money then. We got a lovely little heifer calf from the Star family last week.'

'Well, Ewan seemed well pleased to get a brand-new tractor for his birthday,' Fiona remarked, joining the conversation as she deftly packed away the remains of the food.

'I'm afraid we were needing one anyway,' Rachel said ruefully. 'The old Ferguson had packed up, in spite of Nick's skill at keeping the machines in order. We did get Ewan a decent watch for something more personal though.'

'Well, according to Conan, Ewan's over the moon

about the tractor.'

'I overheard that beautiful blonde girl saying she thought it was a weird sort of a present,' Bridie chuckled. 'She thought he wouldn't get much pleasure out of a thing like that. I gather she doesn't know much about farming, or she'd realise what an essential piece of equipment it is for anyone as keen as Ewan. Are you and Dad taking him into partnership now he's reached the ... er ... age of discretion?' she asked.

'We had intended to, but your dad says he'll wait until Ewan leaves college and learns what real farming and hard work are all about.'

'Oh, I can just imagine Dad saying that!' Bridie laughed. 'Anyway that will only be another six months now. Ewan's course finishes at the end of June, doesn't it?'

'Yes, but one or two of his fellow students are talking about going abroad before they settle down.' Rachel frowned thoughtfully.

'And you think Ewan might join them?'

'He says not, but we'll wait and see. He seems younger for his years than you and Conan did at 21. I suppose the war made you both grow up too quickly. Ewan's still impressionable and there's no telling what distractions he might encounter.'

The three of them made their way back into the main hall but Lucy waylaid them at the door.

'Bridie, we're just persuading Nick to give us a song but he says he needs you to sing with him.'

'I'm sure your friends won't want to listen to our kind of music, Lucy.'

'Of course they will. I could listen to you both singing all night.'

'Yes, so could I,' Fiona said. 'Do sing, Bridie.'

'All right, if you and Dad will accompany us, Lucy? Do you have your accordion here?'

'No, but I could borrow one from Neville in the band.'

They had sung a couple of Scottish songs when Ewan called, 'Sing us some of the more modern songs please, Bridie?'

'What about *Que sera, sera*?' Nick responded. 'Isn't that appropriate for all you youngsters on the threshold of life?'

'That went down well,' Bridie said in surprise. 'For last, what about the one that young American lorry driver sings?'

'Elvis Presley? *Wooden Heart*? OK.'

When the song drew to a close they were greeted with enthusiastic calls for more, but Gerda Fritz-Allan did not join in. She was bored by someone else being centre stage. She wondered what had persuaded her to accept an invitation for a visit to the country when she could have been enjoying herself at a dance in Glasgow. Then she saw Nick stepping lightly down from the little stage and taking his small daughters gently by the hand. Margaret was shy but Alicia loved to sing. Lucy added encouragement and softly played an accompaniment while they sang *How Much is That Doggie in the Window?*.

Gerda was standing behind Fiona and Rachel.

'For God's sake,' she muttered. 'I didn't think I was coming to a Sunday school party!'

'I'm pleased not everyone thinks like she does,' Rachel whispered to Fiona, as the applause burst forth spontaneously making the twins hide their heads shyly.

'One more to finish then we'll leave you all to dance the night away,' Nick announced. 'How about, *I Could Have Danced All Night*?' He and Bridie exchanged a secret smile, which Gerda did not miss. The song was one of their special favourites.

They left the platform to loud applause as the bandleader struck up the dancing again, announcing a ladies' choice to get the ball rolling. Bridie was astonished when the girl with the long blonde hair made a beeline for Nick. She saw the surprise on his face, but then he was a fine figure of a man, she thought proudly, especially with his new fitted jacket with the split at the back. It accentuated his firm muscular figure and his long legs. Even so he was considerably older than Ewan and his friends. Nick and Conan had been 17 and had joined the RAF when Ewan was born – a big surprise to everyone, not least Ross and Rachel.

As soon as the dance finished, Nick extricated himself and crossed the floor to where Bridie waited with the twins. He was frowning slightly.

'There's home we'll go now.'

Bridie raised her eyebrows. She could always tell when he fell back into the Welsh lilt of his youth that something had upset or excited him.

Walking to the car he said quietly, 'A flirtatious piece, that one is. Too much experience, she has.'

Bridie nodded, knowing he meant the girl named Gerda Fritz-Allan. 'I think she's from the city. Fiona says she lives with her father. She doesn't know whether the girl's mother is dead or if the parents are divorced, but I got the impression Fiona felt she needed a mother's guidance. Perhaps she's had a go at flirting with Conan?' She grinned. 'Maybe she fancies older men – especially handsome married ones ...'

'Flattering me, are you, girl?' Nick chuckled softly and squeezed her hand.

'Why are you two holding hands?' Margaret asked innocently as they reached the car and turned to wait for Nick to unlock it. 'Hurry up, Daddy, I'm frozen.'

'So am I,' echoed Alicia.

'Well, sweethearts, it *is* February and we *did* tell you to wear your scarves and gloves,' Bridie reminded her small daughters. 'But you did look very pretty in your red velvet dresses.'

'Yes. Grandpa said we were the best-dressed young ladies at the party, except for Granny,' Margaret said solemnly.

'Blondie wouldn't have been too pleased to hear that,' Nick whispered in Bridie's ear. 'Thought she was the bee's knees, she did, in that revealing black dress. Far too old for her, it was, in my opinion.'

There had been a hard frost overnight and, as Bridie had feared, some of the dairy equipment was frozen and had to be thawed out with kettles of boiling water before the milking could begin.

'Thank goodness for the Aga and plenty of hot water,' she muttered, stifling a yawn and wondering what time the party had ended.

'I'll take the big kettle and thaw the dairy pipes if you can get the milking machines on,' Nick volunteered.

'Thanks, darling. Sometimes I'll bet you wish you'd never seen Lochandee.'

'Oh, I don't know, it has its compensations ...' He gave her a wolfish grin and slipped an arm around her waist. 'Like when I'm tucked up in a nice warm bed with this soft little bottom to cuddle.' He gave her rear end a gentle pat.

'I thought you'd had enough of that sort of thing last night, Nicholas Jones,' she retorted with mock severity.

'A-ah, there's never enough I get of you, cariad.' He gave an unexpected yawn. 'It's a pity cows can't milk themselves on Sundays though.'

It was later than usual when Bridie finally returned to the house when the milking was finished and the cows fed and cleaned for the day. The telephone was ringing.

'Hello ...' she answered breathlessly.

'A-ah, Bridie, I was just about to hang up. Have you had a bad morning with frozen pipes?'

'I'm afraid so, Mum. How are things at Nether

Rullion? Are you very tired after the party?'

'Not too bad. Ewan was up and out at the milking parlour with your father and Peter, but his friends are just surfacing so I'm waiting to dish up their porridge and cook bacon and eggs – at least for those who want it.'

'Mmm, that makes me hungry. We haven't had ours yet.'

'I mustn't keep you then. I just thought Fiona might need a helping hand. The girls want to see round the farm with Ewan's friends. I'm not sure whether it's the animals or the boys that's the attraction,' she added with a laugh. 'Anyway Conan is bringing them over here in about an hour and he says he is taking the whole lot of them back to his place for lunch.'

'Gosh! Fiona will be busy with the whole lot to feed.'

'Yes, I know but Conan thought it would save time. It gets dark so early and it looks as though it will be hard frost again. He says the bus doesn't hold the road like the Land Rover does so he wants to get them back safely and in good time.'

'Mmm, I can understand he'll not want to be too late on that road in the dark if it's icy. I'll go over and help. Nick will pick up the children from Sunday school and bring them over to Fiona's. Does she want any food? I could take some apple pies out of my freezer. You'll have to get one, Mum. They're wonderful for all sorts of things.'

'I'm sure they can't be as good as fresh pies,' Rachel said doubtfully, 'but I expect Fiona will be glad of any contributions.'

'I doubt if Ewan's friends will know the difference,' Bridie said drily.

'Maybe not. I cooked a big piece of ham to feed the boys so I said I would slice it up and send it back with Conan. Fiona sounded grateful for that. It's strange that she is so capable when it comes to making big decisions and dealing with all sorts of crises concerning the business, yet catering for a group of hungry students seems to worry her.'

'Yes, maybe I should persuade *her* to invest in a deep-freeze, then she can fill it up at leisure and always be prepared – even when her mother-in-law comes to tea!'

'Oh, Bridie! I'm not that bad, am I? I don't criticise, and I've always thought Fiona makes Conan an excellent wife.'

'I was only teasing, Mum,' Bridie chuckled. 'When the time comes I just hope Ewan gets a wife who fits into the family circle as well as Fiona does.'

'Yes,' Rachel sighed happily. 'I often think how lucky we are, your father and I. We felt so proud of you all last night.'

Fiona had worried about the sleeping arrangements for ten young women and only three bedrooms, but Lucy had assured her they were all used to making do with sleeping bags when the occasion demanded.

'We'll toss a coin for who gets the beds,' she had said cheerfully, but by mutual consent the girls had all agreed that Gerda should certainly have a bed. She was still new to their particular group and they were somewhat in awe of her beauty, fragile air and expensive clothes. It just didn't seem fitting to ask her to rough it as they were prepared to do.

They had thoroughly enjoyed the party and now looked forward to rounding off the weekend with a walk in the crisp, frosty air.

'It's such lovely countryside,' one of the girls remarked. 'You're really lucky, Lucy.'

'I know, I love it too,' Lucy smiled. None of them noticed Gerda's grimace of distaste, but Fiona did. She felt a surge of relief. The girl was not one of Lucy's special friends so it was unlikely they would see her again if she didn't like the country.

As though to confirm her opinion, Gerda demanded, 'Do we have to go looking at animals and trailing round a muddy farmyard?'

'Even if ye dinna want tae see the farm, Gerda, I'd hae thocht ye'd wanna hae anither wee flirt wi' yon birthday laddie,' one of the girls said in mock astonishment. She gave a wicked wink to one of her friends. 'Ye'll no want tae miss checking oot Ewan's inheritance,' she drawled, knowing full well her exaggeration of a broad Scots accent always annoyed Gerda.

'Inheritance?' Gerda frowned uncertainly. 'What inheritance? You talk as though he's a laird, or something.'

'Well, so he is. Laird o' his ain wee patch anyway.'

'Of course Ewan isn't a laird,' Lucy intervened quickly, alarmed by the sudden flare of interest in Gerda's pale blue eyes. 'Betty's only teasing.'

Betty grinned unrepentantly, little realising the seeds she had unwittingly sown in Gerda's mind.

# Chapter Two

Usually Gerda's questions would have exasperated Ewan in a very short time, but he was flattered by the interest she was showing in himself and the farm. He knew most of his friends were attracted by her so he basked in her undivided attention, answering even her most stupid questions with patient tolerance. He was aware of Lucy's eyes on them, amused, then amazed, her eyebrows raised incredulously. He knew exactly when her amusement turned to irritation and even contempt, and he felt uncomfortable. Lucy was usually the least critical of people.

Surely no one could be so ignorant of country life as to believe chickens popped out of an egg the moment it was laid, Lucy thought. Even more ridiculous was the prospect of bulls producing milk just as cows did. She wanted to ask Gerda if she would expect a man to suckle babies. Surely everyone knew a cow had to have a calf before she produced milk? These were things Lucy had known all her life, having spent most of her childhood with Ewan at Glens of Lochandee, but Gerda did not lack intelligence. Was she pretending, or trying to make a fool of Ewan?

Lucy realised she could barely conceal her irritation as Gerda continued to hog his attention, clinging to his arm and gesticulating theatrically, exclaiming in the high-pitched little girl voice she often used to gain attention. She had hoped Christine Greig, her best friend, and Ewan would be attracted to each other during the weekend here at Nether Rullion. Chris was so knowledgeable about animals, farming and the life they involved.

She and Chris had become friends as soon as they started at Craigie Teacher Training College. They were both country girls with interests in common. Chris was splendid with animals and children, but quiet and rarely made the most of her own attractions. She had three older brothers who teased unmercifully and a mother who seemed continually harassed with caring for her family, house and poultry. So people had to take Chris as they found her and impressionable young men never seemed to look beneath the surface, Lucy thought with a rare flash of anger.

'What they see is what they get with me,' Chris would grin merrily when the other girls tried to persuade her to use eye-shadow and mascara for the Saturday night dances.

Once, she had confided to Lucy, 'I would much rather have attended the agricultural college than trained as a teacher, but Mother insisted I must have a career that had nothing to do with farming. I couldn't stand a man who expected me to look like a film star all day.'

When Lucy embarked on her career she experienced a wider world away from the village of Lochandee, the farm and the garage. She had soon realised she had reason to be grateful for Fiona's guidance. She had advised her on her clothes and on the discreet makeup she wore, the expert styling of her curly hair, and even the way she walked and talked to suit the occasion. These things had given her confidence and an air of calm, particularly when she was feeling as quivery as a table jelly inside.

Lucy visited Chris's family quite often because their farm was only ten miles south of Ayr. She'd heard Mrs Greig's frequent comment, 'Three lads to be put into farms are more than enough. Our Chris needs to get hersel' a good job and earn some money. I dinna want her tae marry a farmer. It's all work an' no play.' Reluctantly, Chris had bowed to her mother's wishes, but Lucy knew her heart was as much in farming as Ewan's.

Ewan showed everyone round the milking parlour and the dairy. The huge tank not only held all the milk, but kept it refrigerated until the milk tanker arrived to take it to the creamery. Chris was genuinely impressed and interested. Her parents milked their cows in a byre and the milk was collected in ten-gallon churns which had to be carted to the end of the road every day in readiness for the milk lorry. She wanted to ask Ewan all about the various tubes and lines and how it all worked, but Gerda was clinging to him like a limpet.

'My brothers would love to see round here,' she murmured to Lucy. 'It must make the work a lot easier.'

'Yes, I suppose it does,' Lucy agreed. 'I know the local farmers all think Ewan's father was very far-sighted when he decided to go for a milking parlour and cubicle house instead of building a byre. There are quite a few springing up now, although Bridie still milks her cows in a byre at Glens of Lochandee. You'll have to come to stay for another weekend, Chris – just the two of us – then you can see everything. Bridie reckons she can give her cows more individual attention in a byre, but I've heard her say she thinks it would be better if they didn't need to be tied by the neck all winter.'

'Mmm, I can't believe that Ewan's cows can just wander around the shed freely and feed themselves at the silage pit. Don't they ever fight?'

'Sometimes, but you'll notice they've all had their horns removed so they can't do so much damage to each other.'

'A-ah yes, of course. I thought there was something different about them. I don't suppose Gerda would even know they'd ever had horns!'

'I'm sure she wouldn't. I wonder what's making her show such an interest. I can't believe it's genuine. She hates anything remotely smelly and she can't stand the smallest bit of mud.'

Chris gave her friend a knowing look and opened her mouth to tell Lucy exactly why Gerda was interested in Ewan and his farm, but Lucy was frowning and didn't catch her eye, so Chris closed her mouth and kept her opinion to herself. No doubt Gerda would soon lose interest in all things country, including Ewan. Even if the novelty lasted a while, surely Ewan would see she was only feigning interest?

In this she was wrong. Gerda made it her business to quiz Ewan's closest friends on his prospects as a farmer. Of all the girls they knew, Gerda was the least likely to make a farmer's wife, so they exaggerated his assets at every opportunity, teasing her unmercifully, never dreaming that Gerda would take them at their word. Mentally, she built up a picture of Ewan as a future country gentleman; so long as he had a wife like her to lead him, she preened secretly.

After the tour of Nether Rullion was over, Conan shepherded them all into the coach and back to Rullion Glen for lunch.

'We'll come over in the car and join you,' Ross said. 'We'll need the car to get home for milking.'

Fiona, with the help of Bridie and the twins, had already set out huge bowls of soup, with crisp buttery rolls and a selection of cold meats, to be followed by apple pie and cream. The crowd of young folk chattered happily as they ate.

'This has been the best weekend I've had since I started college,' one of the young men announced. There were cheers of agreement.

When they were ready to leave, Lucy turned to hug

Fiona.

'You've given me a lovely birthday, Fiona. I can never thank you enough for the way you look after me,' she said huskily. She turned to Conan and hugged him too. 'Thanks for laying on the transport and chauffeuring us all around, Conan.' She bent closer and whispered mischievously, 'And thanks for being such a generous daddy.'

'Och, you!' Conan gave an affectionate pat on her neat little rear. They rarely mentioned their real relationship and Lucy knew he still found it difficult to realise he had sired a child when he was little more than a teenager himself. It had taken her some time to get over the shock too, but now she liked to tease occasionally. Conan knew it was a mark of their deepening affection and a mutual respect which had grown with the years, but above all he knew he had Fiona to thank for helping Lucy come to terms with the shocks and changes in her young life.

As soon as they were all seated on the bus, Gerda lost no time in leaning forward and poking Lucy's shoulder.

'I say, it's a bit off to call your parents by their Christian names, isn't it?'

'I don't think so,' Lucy frowned, irritated by Gerda's sharp finger and equally probing stare. She was one of those people who seemed to sense when there was something different and she took a delight in delving into things which did not concern her.

'They're Lucy's adopted parents, as you know very well,' Chris said abruptly.

'Even so ...'

'Oh for goodness sake, Gerda, I knew both Conan and Fiona long before they adopted me. Anyway, Fiona is more like an elder sister to me than a stepmother.'

'I suppose it would make her feel old if you called her Mummy. So ... if they are only your adoptive parents you're not really Ewan's cousin? The two of you always seem so close? I thought there must be something going on between you ...?' When Lucy made no answer to the questions hanging in the air, she persisted. 'You look quite like each other, at least I've sometimes thought so, but then I thought you really were related. I couldn't help wondering ...?'

'Ewan and I were practically brought up together,' Lucy snapped. 'We've always been the best of friends, and I hope we always will be. Now will you sit back in your own seat and stop poking me in the back?'

Chris gave her a sideways glance and winked wickedly. She bit back a smile in case Gerda should see, but out of the side of her mouth, she whispered, 'She's jealous.'

'Heaven forbid Ewan should ever be tempted in that direction,' Lucy muttered with feeling.

'Mmm ... I can just imagine her tottering out to feed the chickens in her red toeless shoes with the three-inch heels,' Chris grinned.

As the cold weather of February turned to spring, and onward to May, the countryside burgeoned with new life and the scent of blossom filled the hedgerows. Ewan longed to be back home at the farm, but he worked hard at his studies. He wanted to gain his diploma now that he was so near to finishing his course. He was looking forward to helping with the crops and to working with the fine Friesian herd which his father had built up at Nether Rullion. Although they sometimes argued when he wanted to change to more modern methods, he was grateful for his father's wisdom and experience. Since he had been at college, he'd realised how fortunate he was to have the opportunity of returning home to Nether Rullion, with the prospect of farming it himself some day. Several of his fellow students were seeking employment, but some were going home to work with elder brothers, and wondering whether they would ever get a chance to farm on their own.

Ross was glad Ewan did not share the wanderlust of some of his fellow students. Although he did not feel his age, he knew he was not as fit as he had been when Conan was 21, or even a decade ago. He was looking forward to having Ewan to share some of the responsibilities and decisions. Most of all, he hoped he would take over some of the increasing piles of paperwork attached to their pedigree herd. All the calves were black and white, and each one had to be carefully sketched and coloured in with its respective markings. All this, plus the sire, dam and grandparents, together with their registration numbers, had to be done in duplicate and submitted to the breed society within a month of the calf's birth. It was not a side of farming which Ross enjoyed and the older he got, the more he resented using up his valuable time and energy. Rachel dealt with all the farm accounts and paid the bills and he was grateful for that. Sometimes she relented and helped him sketch the calves and fill in the pedigrees, but it was not a chore she wanted to add to her own busy life on a regular basis.

'I'm getting older too, you know,' she remarked from time to time when she felt her husband needed a gentle reminder. 'There are no maids to help in the house these days as there were before the war, and I like things to be clean and tidy for when the milk recorders arrive.'

Every month, a young woman came to stay at the farm overnight – sometimes two nights when there were a lot of cows milking. She weighed the milk from each cow at the evening and morning milkings, recording the results in ledgers and calculating the records for the month. In addition, she tested the butterfat from each animal, using special Gerber tubes and a portable centrifuge. These records were an essential requirement for a pedigree dairy herd. At the end of each lactation, the records helped in the selection of the best breeding animals, as well as adding value to a cow and to her progeny in the sale ring.

'You could get rid of the hens then you'd have more time to do the pedigrees,' Ross suggested on one occasion when he was exasperated with the number of calves he needed to draw.

'Get rid of my poultry!' Rachel was indignant. 'They pay for the housekeeping, Peter's wages *and* the petrol. Besides, I like having the chickens and hens – it's better not to have all our eggs in one basket ...'

Ross exploded with laughter and his ill humour vanished.

'You know what I mean,' Rachel chided, but the dimple at the corner of her mouth could not be hidden and she grinned at him. 'Seriously, Ross. What if we had another outbreak of foot-and-mouth and lost all our cows again?'

'Don't even think about it!' Ross growled in mock horror.

'No, it's too terrible to contemplate, I know. But about the pedigrees – I'm sure Peter would help you with sketching the calves and filling them in, if you asked him. He's proven himself capable of most things we've asked him to do since we took over Nether Rullion, and he's conscientious.'

'Aye, you're right there. I've never regretted taking a chance with Peter. I'm glad he decided not to return to Poland when the war was over. He keeps his wee cottage as neat and clean as a new pin too.'

'Yes, it would have been nice if he'd met a suitable girl for a wife, but he seems content with his garden and vegetables in the summer and his wood carving in the winter.'

'Aye, a wife might have led him astray. Did he tell you he was thinking of buying a second-hand car for himself?'

'No, he's never mentioned that to me. I did hear Conan telling him he could get a new Mini for four hundred and ninety-five pounds, nineteen shillings and threepence, now that the Chancellor has cut the purchase tax.'

'It's still a lot of money,' Ross said gravely. 'Peter was just asking Conan for advice. I think he's keeping a lookout for a bargain for him.'

'Maybe he'll go out more if he gets a car.'

'He might. I think I'd better wait for Ewan to come home and take over the pedigrees. He's familiar with most of them already.' He smiled reminiscently. 'I reckon there's going to be some healthy competition between Nether Rullion and Lochandee when Bridie and Ewan start showing and selling in the same ring at pedigree sales.'

'So long as it stays as friendly rivalry it will be all right,' Rachel grimaced. She did not welcome a family feud between her daughter and son. 'Anyway half of Bridie's cattle are still pedigree Ayrshires. She's loath to change over to Friesians completely.'

'I know.' Ross grinned down at her and his eyes crinkled at the corners. 'And I suspect you agree with her,' he teased.

'We-ell ... Yes, I shall always have a soft spot for a good Ayrshire cow, and if you would admit the truth I suspect you do too, Ross Maxwell.'

'They take a bit of beating for appearance, but we've to think about the economics these days. The Friesians do give better yields and eat more roughage. I'd hate to get too complacent, but I reckon we've been jolly lucky that things have gone so well for us since we bought Nether Rullion. I never imagined we'd get the loan for the land paid off in record time. It's a great relief.'

'Well, so far, the government have made sure we get a fair price for our produce since the war, even though they say the price of food in the shops is the lowest in Europe.'

'It's government policy to pay us a subsidy to encourage home production and keep the price to the consumers in check at the same time,' Ross mused. 'The

21

idea is that the workers will be less likely to strike for higher wages if they can afford to eat well.'

'I suppose that's what Mr MacMillan meant when he said we had "never had it so good",' Rachel nodded, 'but from what Fiona says, people want to afford more than food and clothes these days. She says some holidaymakers book for next year's holiday as soon as this year's is over. Perhaps *we* should think about having a little holiday once Ewan comes home …?'

'A holiday! We …' Ross stopped suddenly and stared at his wife, his keen glance searching her face. 'You're not feeling ill, are you, Rachel?' he asked anxiously.

'No, of course not, silly! I just thought it would be nice to have a few nights away together, just the two of us.' She sighed wistfully. 'We've never been on a holiday. Conan says the people who go on his buses really enjoy seeing all the sights and having their meals set before them every night.'

'I think I'd be bored to tears riding around on a bus all day,' Ross scoffed, 'and so would you. Now, I'd better go and start the milking. The parlour's made that job a lot easier so we should be thankful for that.'

'It has,' Rachel sighed, 'but the milking still has to be done twice a day. I don't suppose they'll ever invent self-milking cows!'

At Glens of Lochandee Nick's thoughts were running on similar lines to his mother-in-law's.

'I wonder whether your parents will take a holiday from the farm when Ewan comes home from college?' he remarked as he and Bridie walked behind the ambling cows, bringing them in from the field for milking. 'I think your mother has looked unusually tired recently.'

'I can't imagine my father on holiday,' Bridie said, 'but I'm sure it would do them both a lot of good if Conan could persuade them. By the way, did I tell you Lucy's been offered a job at a school in Ayrshire when she finishes college?'

'No! Are Fiona and Conan disappointed she'll not be working nearer home?'

'If they are, they would never say so,' Bridie mused. 'Fiona says that lovely blonde girl has been pestering Lucy to invite her down for a weekend, but they're not particular friends. I think she irritates Lucy a bit.'

'No wonder! Irritate me she would, that one. Dramatic, she is.'

Bridie's eyes widened. Nick was not given to criticism and a return to his Welsh accent always reflected his feelings.

'I thought *all* men automatically fell for beautiful blondes?'

'Not this one, bach.' He stepped closer and slipped an arm around Bridie's waist. 'All the woman *I'm* wanting, you are.' He squeezed affectionately and she laughed up at him.

'I'm glad to hear that, for I've no intention of letting you go, Nicholas Jones. Let's see, how many years have we been married now …?'

'September 1949, it was; 13 years this year and not a single regret have I had.'

'That makes two of us, then. I think Fiona and Conan are well- matched too, in spite of the resistance they both put up when they were younger. I just wish they'd had children of their own …'

'Maybe they don't want any. They work so hard at the business. I believe that's Conan's baby.'

'Yes, he's always been ambitious, I know,' Bridie sighed. 'And they do everything together. That wouldn't be possible if they had a family – not the travelling part, anyway.'

'So is the blonde beauty coming down to stay, then? I must say I prefer Lucy's friend from Ayrshire. Christine, isn't it?'

'Yes, Christine Greig. Her father bought a Lochandee bull at the Castle Douglas sale a few years ago. He said he wouldn't mind another, if it was going cheap!'

'A satisfied customer then.'

'Chris has three brothers, all keen on farming. Lucy told me they're trying to rent another farm a few miles away. I have a sneaking feeling that she has a soft spot for the eldest brother. His name's Donald but he gets called Don for short.'

'She'll not be thinking of getting married until she's established herself in teaching, though, if I know Lucy?'

'I shouldn't think so. She's a sensible lassie, and she listens to Fiona's advice. Conan is thinking of buying her a wee car of her own if she passes all her examinations. I think both Conan and Fiona miss Lucy's lively company about the house. And her music, of course. Perhaps they think she'll come home more often if she has her own transport.'

'I expect Ewan will be wanting a car of his own, then? The pair of them were always like twins – except for the music, of course,' Nick reflected.

'I hope Ewan has grown up enough not to want whatever Lucy gets.' Bridie frowned. 'Anyway he'll be living at home and use Dad's car when he needs one, I suppose.'

A little while later, Nick helped Bridie fasten the chains which kept the cows in their own stall along both sides of the long byre.

'I wonder why Gerda Fritz-Allan wants to come down here again?' he asked. 'She didn't seem like a country girl to me.'

'I don't know. She and Lucy are not exactly bosom pals.' Bridie frowned. 'I don't think she has a very happy home life. Her mother went off with someone else when Gerda was 11. She was killed in a cable car accident soon

24

afterwards. Apparently her father spends most of his time at his office. That's what Lucy told Fiona anyway. I think she was feeling mean for not wanting to invite Gerda for another weekend.'

'There's kindly, she is, our Lucy,' Nick said warmly. 'But she's not a bit like the blonde siren.'

'No-o. I think Ewan must be feeling sorry for Gerda as well. He's been putting on the pressure with Lucy to invite her down once the exams are over.'

'Sorry? Feeling sorry, is it!' Nick gave a mocking guffaw. 'That's not how I'd describe Ewan's feeling for Miss Gerda Fritz-Allan, from what I saw of them.'

Bridie frowned, but she didn't reply. Nick was a shrewd judge of people and situations but in Ewan's case she hoped fervently he was wrong.

# Chapter Three

'You don't seem too sure about bringing Gerda Fritz-Allan home with you when college finishes, Lucy?' Fiona suggested shrewdly when she telephoned to finalise the arrangements for clearing her possessions out of her college accommodation.

'We-ell ...' Lucy frowned at the receiver in her hand. She was talking from the payphone in the corridor and one never knew who might overhear.

'Has Ewan anything to do with it?'

'He's keen to have her down again,' Lucy admitted. Fiona guessed by her tone that the idea had been Ewan's. 'But sometimes I do feel a bit ... well, sorry for her. I've been so lucky to have a home with you.'

'Och, away with you,' Fiona laughed softly, but her voice was a little husky and she was touched, as she always was, by Lucy's appreciation of herself and Conan. 'We're the ones who've been blessed.'

Lucy considered her own good fortune again as she and Gerda carried their suitcases upstairs at Rullion Glen.

'Lucy, you don't know how well-off you are to live in such a lovely house.'

'It wasn't always a lovely house,' Lucy chuckled. 'You should have seen it when it was just a poky little flat tucked onto the end of the garage. Conan and Nick built it up from absolutely nothing but a bare piece of land after they came home from the Air Force. They worked terribly hard.'

'Did they fall out?'

'No. They just wanted to do different things so they each took out their share and went their separate ways. Nick's done very well with his own business. He has more trade than he wants sometimes with his livestock transport. His real love is repairing machines and adapting them, seeing how they work, and of course spending time at Glens of Lochandee with Bridie and the children too. He couldn't have done that if he'd stayed in partnership here.'

'No, I suppose not. The Conan Maxwell Coach Company must be getting well-known. I'm always seeing their coaches on the road.'

'It expanded quite fast after Conan and Fiona got married, I think. They work so well together.' Lucy sighed. If ever she married, she hoped she would be a real partner to her husband as well as a wife and, hopefully, a mother.

'A-ah but I expect Fiona knew she was on to a good thing when she married him?' Gerda remarked smugly and Lucy's irritation returned at the thinly disguised bitchiness in her tone.

'Neither of them knew what the future held then,' she said sharply. 'They've both worked jolly hard. Fiona used her own money to expand the business and she built the original house so we could all live here, near the garage. The land used to be part of Nether Rullion so that's why they named the house Rullion Glen. They only extended it fairly recently and made the garden.'

'If you say so,' Gerda shrugged, 'but your foster mother, or whatever she is, certainly looks after herself. I mean, the clothes she wears for a start ... you never see her in anything cheap or shabby.'

'A-ach!' Lucy choked in disbelief. 'I reckon that

27

description fits you even better than Fiona! And at least Fiona earns the money to buy her own. Besides she needs to be smart and efficient when she's dealing with a whole lot of men. She says they judge her by appearance, but they never seem to expect we women have brains as well.'

'Some have brains!' Gerda corrected grimly. 'I don't know whatever possessed me to train as a teacher. The long vacations, I suppose.' She stifled a yawn. 'I can't say I'm looking forward to keeping a class of spoiled brats in order, but my old man says he's supported me long enough.'

'Well, you'll be independent once you get a salary,' Lucy said cheerfully. 'I'm sure not many of the children are spoiled brats. I'm really looking forward to teaching. I love the younger children.'

'Maybe that's because you've been pampered yourself,' Gerda muttered with more than a hint of jealousy. 'You don't know how lucky you are.'

'Oh, but I do,' Lucy said fervently. 'I never forget how much Conan and Fiona have done for me, and still do.'

'My mother went off and never even said goodbye. I don't think my father cares whether I'm in the house or not. He's always working – or so he says,' she added darkly.

'I'm sure he must care,' Lucy said, 'or he wouldn't buy you all those lovely clothes. You have twice as many as anyone else at college. And jewellery too.'

'Oh that!' Gerda screwed up her small nose. 'He says he has to work such long hours so that he can afford all the things I need, but I think he just buys me things to ease his conscience.'

'His conscience?'

'Well, he must feel guilty, mustn't he? Mum wouldn't have gone off if he'd made her happy. Then I wouldn't have been without a mother. It's his fault, so he deserves to buy me what I want, to make up for it.'

The evening meal was barely over when the telephone rang.

'That's my kid brother wanting to speak to Gerda,' Conan said drily. His expressive eyebrows rose as he met Fiona's glance. 'He seems to be badly smitten by her,' he muttered when Gerda had left the dining room. Lucy bit her lip and Conan's eyes moved to her. 'Was it Ewan who persuaded you to invite her for the weekend?'

'Mainly.'

'Well, don't worry about it. He's old enough to know what he's doing. Just don't let either of them use you. If they try it again and you want an excuse, just tell them I need you to work in the office with the bookings …'

'Do you really?' Lucy's eyes lit up and Conan looked surprised.

'Do you want a holiday job then? I thought you'd want a rest before you take up your new teaching post in September.'

'But that's weeks away … Anyway, I want to earn my keep.' Her mouth set in the stubborn line which both Conan and Fiona had learnt to recognise.

'Well, I'd be glad of some help in my office,' Fiona nodded at them both.

'Right then,' Conan said with satisfaction. 'We're certainly busy enough with all the summer trips. There's always something being cancelled or rearranged. If it's not a hotel that's overbooked, it's a driver going off sick, or a coach needing an emergency repair. We could use someone with initiative to help over the busy time.'

'You really mean that? You're not just making a job for me?' Lucy said eagerly.

'I would really appreciate having you to help, Lucy,' Fiona smiled.

'Right then,' Conan said, assuming a stern businesslike manner as Gerda returned to the room, 'you'll start work on Monday, Lucy. Nine o'clock prompt. There's no allowance for family when you're on my payroll. Don't you forget that, young lady.' Lucy met his eye briefly and bit back a smile.

'Yes, sir!' she said promptly. 'You can rely on me.'

Gerda looked from one to the other and her dismay was obvious.

'Ewan was hoping I'd be able to stay a few days longer ...' she said. 'Maybe until Thursday, or ... or even until after next weekend. Surely you don't have to work during your vacation, Lucy?' She looked accusingly at Conan.

'Money doesn't grow on trees, young woman. If people want to eat they need to work first. Doesn't your father tell you that?'

'Och my father! He's aye lecturing about the cost o' things.' For a moment Gerda forgot her airs and graces and her native Glasgow accent was more apparent. A faint smile hovered on Fiona's lips. She had met several Gerdas in her life.

'Well, you may as well make the most of your weekend then, girls. I'll deal with the washing-up for tonight. You two can help tomorrow.' Her eyes rested briefly on Gerda's surprised face. It was clear she had not expected to do anything other than enjoy her weekend. 'Has Ewan persuaded his father to lend him the car tonight?' she asked pleasantly. 'Is he coming to take the pair of you into Dumfries?'

'Er ... er, yes.' Gerda's eyes sought Lucy's, frantically trying to convey a message, but Lucy was busy collecting the dirty dishes to take to the kitchen. A little while later she went upstairs and found Gerda hovering by her bedroom door.

'Couldn't you pretend you have a headache, Lucy?' she said impatiently. 'Ewan will be here soon and I want to get changed.'

'Well, what's stopping you?' Lucy asked.

'Do you mean you intend to come with us then?'

'Mmm ...' Lucy put her head on one side as though considering the matter. 'We-ell, I can see I shall be very welcome as a third ...'

'But ...'

'Don't worry, Gerda.' Lucy grimaced. 'I think I really would end up with a headache if I had to watch the two of you mooning over each other all evening. There is just one thing, though ...'

'What's that?'

'Don't involve me in any of your schemes, and most certainly don't expect me to lie for you – either of you.' She watched as Gerda's colour rose under her pale skin. Lucy's eyes narrowed. 'I mean it, and you can tell Ewan that too. I would never lie to Mr and Mrs Maxwell, not even to cover up for Ewan. I've too much respect for them.'

'Respect! They're stuffy old fogies!' Gerda muttered angrily. 'Ewan says the whole family go to church on Sundays and they're insisting he must be home before midnight. They only agreed to let him have the car because they think you're going as well.' Turning on her heel, she flounced off to her own room. Lucy sighed. What an exciting weekend this is going to be, she thought morosely and wished she had accepted Chris's invitation to spend it with her family in Ayrshire. At least she and Don would have had some time together, even if it was only helping him finish hoeing the turnips or starting on the hay.

During the summer holidays Gerda twice wangled an invitation to stay with Lucy. On both occasions she used the excuse that she was lonely because her father was away on business and Ewan added his own persuasion.

'I'm surprised she doesn't try getting a job for the

31

summer,' Fiona commented.

'I don't think Gerda likes work. The trouble is, we don't really have anything in common except the course we shared,' Lucy admitted. 'I've never heard her mention missing her father before, though. I didn't think his job took him away from home.'

'I expect it's an excuse to invite herself.' Fiona nodded. 'But this time we'll leave her some chores to do.' She smiled. 'After all, we both know she's just using us. It's Ewan she really wants to see. I do hope he gets rid of his moonstruck blinkers soon, for his own sake, I mean.'

'Oh, so do I!' Lucy agreed fervently. She had a growing feeling that, for the first time in their lives, Ewan wouldn't want her opinion on Gerda and her stomach gave a sickening lurch. She wished she'd never invited Gerda to her birthday party.

# Chapter Four

Rachel suspected Ewan and Lucy had quarrelled and she guessed it had something to do with his increasing obsession with Gerda Fritz-Allan.

She had believed Ewan's main ambition in life was to farm at Nether Rullion and to breed even better Friesian cattle than his father. She couldn't believe he could become so infatuated with a girl like Gerda who had no interest in animals, or in the countryside. She had looked forward to welcoming Ewan's wife when the time came, just as Alice Beattie had welcomed her to Glens of Lochandee when she was young and newly married to Ross. Her heart sank and she felt cold all over at the thought of the beautiful blonde girl becoming such an important part of her family. If only Gerda did not have such a superior and sophisticated air, such a petulant mouth and dramatic manner. If only she had some character, some substance ...

It was the middle of harvest and the last week before the new school term started. Reluctantly Rachel had given in to Ewan's pleading and invited Gerda to stay at Nether Rullion for the few days before she started her teaching career.

'They're far too young to be serious,' Ross grumbled. 'And we're far too busy with the harvest. It looks as though we're encouraging them if we invite her to stay here.'

'I think Lucy would agree with you. I suspect they've quarrelled over her refusal to invite Gerda down again. Anyway, Ewan reminded me that he's 21 now, and we were even younger,' Rachel said unhappily. 'And I've always said we would welcome his friends.'

'We were already living under the same roof and we had both been working since we were 12 years old. Our circumstances were different,' Ross insisted stubbornly. 'Neither of them has earned a penny yet.'

'Everyone is so busy, my dear,' Rachel said, doing her best to instil a warmth into her voice. She felt a hypocrite because she could not feel any warmth in her heart when she looked into Gerda's cold blue eyes. 'Please make yourself at home. We have to make the most of the good weather to get the harvest in. Ross – that is, Ewan's father – thinks it will break soon and he's usually right about such things.'

Gerda sniffed. A common countryman couldn't possibly tell what the weather was going to do. She had expected Ewan would be at Lockerbie station to meet her, even though he had told her where to get the bus. She had been feeling annoyed all the way to Nether Rullion, but her anger had given way to a feeling of triumph and satisfaction when she saw the surprise on his mother's face as she stepped out of a taxi. Rachel had been more dismayed than surprised when the girl asked where she could find Ewan so that he could pay the taxi driver. She had paid the man herself, but her heart was troubled. It was better that Ross shouldn't know about such extravagance.

'So where is Ewan then?' Gerda demanded petulantly.

'He's driving the tractor. I expect he warned you he'd be baling straw if the weather was good?'

'Oh, he mentioned something about harvest, but surely

he can stop for the weekend now I've arrived?'

'They barely stop long enough to eat, I'm afraid. He'll not be back at the steading until dark. They all work as long as the daylight lasts when the weather is so good. If you'll bring your luggage, I'll show you your bedroom, and make you a cup of tea. Then, if you'll excuse me, I must go and bring in the cows ready for milking. You can come with me if you like, dear ...?' Rachel suggested uncertainly. She had never met a young person before who made her feel as awkward and unsure as Gerda did. The girl stared at her as though she had taken leave of her senses.

'Bring in cows! Me? Not on your life.'

'Very well. Make yourself comfortable while I attend to things outside. I have the eggs to collect and the hens need their afternoon feed. You wouldn't like to ...?'

'No, I would not.'

Rachel sighed as she left the house and called for Tess, the ageing collie. The dog rose languidly in the afternoon heat and trotted at her heels. She bent to pat her head.

'You're always ready to help, aren't you, lassie ...?' The dog wagged her tail, knowing she was being praised. As they walked down the leafy lane towards the pasture where the cows were grazing a wave of relief washed over Rachel. Gerda's presence would have brought a strain to the blue and gold of the late summer afternoon. She breathed in deeply, relishing the scents and sights of the hedgerow. The blackberries were ripening fast now, clusters already hanging, luscious and glistening, ready for picking to make bramble and apple jelly. Ewan and Lucy had always helped her gather brambles from the hedgerows. She wondered whether Ewan would help this year. He loved homemade jam.

The whole world seemed to be still, as though waiting. Even the leaves barely rustled. The gentle cooing of a wood pigeon added to the soporific effect and Rachel felt herself relax for the first time in the past few days. She had not looked forward to Gerda Fritz-Allan's visit and it troubled her that she should feel so inhospitable towards any of Ewan's friends, and especially to one who was clearly so important to him. She had made an extra effort to make the guest bedroom clean and pretty. She'd cleaned, swept and washed, and done more baking than usual so that the girl would surely find something to please her.

'The house is always clean and tidy, lassie,' Ross had remonstrated. Rachel smiled to herself as she walked between the hedgerows. She was 58 now, but Ross still called her lassie when he was being affectionate, or when he was concerned. She pondered his suggestion to buy a freezer chest for storing food. Bridie had told him it would keep fresh beef and lamb for a year and her scones and cakes would keep for months. She frowned, wondering whether the food would be safe to eat afterwards. Ross seemed quite enthusiastic.

'The man who supplied the tank for storing the milk says his firm have sold quite a few to farmers' wives.' He hadn't told her how much these new contraptions cost. She frowned. After a lifetime of careful budgeting, Rachel found it impossible to accept that they could live comfortably now they had paid off the Nether Rullion land and built modern buildings for housing the dairy herd, and a parlour for milking them. It was hard to believe that a chest run by electricity could be better than the cold slab in the pantry or the little refrigerator where she kept the milk and butter. It would be wonderful if she could bring out scones as good as freshly baked ones without having to bake every day. Maybe she would consider it.

She swung open the field gate and called for the cows. Most of them looked up and began to move towards the open gate, knowing it was nearly milking time. A few lay still, chewing their cud contentedly and one or two were intent on snatching a bit more grass to chew while they waited for their turn to go into the milking parlour. Rachel was still amazed at how quickly they had learnt the new routine of using the parlour instead of finding their own stalls in the byre. They had their own order of precedence too. Old Star was always the first in to be milked, with Belle a close second. They were the oldest cows in the herd and they led the way and the rest followed as obediently as a class of children under the supervision of a strict headmaster.

Tess, the collie, began to move slowly around the stragglers, urging them to follow the herd, yet knowing instinctively that she must not hurry them when their udders were full of milk. Rachel leaned on the gate and looked up at the sky. She was sure this weather would not last much longer.

'Wouldn't be surprised if we have thunder, old girl,' she murmured, bending to pat the dog as the last of the cows ambled through the gate. Tess looked up at her with trusting liquid brown eyes. She hated thunder. She rarely came into the house but whenever there was a storm she scratched urgently at the door and darted under the scullery table the moment someone let her in, cowering there until the storm died away.

As they walked slowly behind the herd of cows Rachel whisked ineffectively at the flies and dust which inevitably surrounded the animals in the summertime. She broke a branch from a nearby elderberry bush and wafted the offending insects away. She wondered whether they really disliked the smell of elderberry leaves, or whether it was one of those stories she remembered from her childhood. Most of the farmers who brought their horse to be shod at her father's smithy forge had adorned their bridles with bits of elderberry when the flies were biting.

Just as well Gerda did not come, she thought. That beautiful blonde hair would have been coated in dust by now.

Ross was waiting for her at the gate into the farmyard. He smiled gratefully.

'I wondered whether you'd have time to get the cows in for me when you had yon lassie to entertain.' His blue eyes crinkled at the corners and the appraising look in their blue depths deepened the colour in cheeks already flushed with the heat of the afternoon. Even after all these years, Ross could still make her pulse race and she knew he still found her attractive. They had been so lucky to have each other, to work together as they had and still be in love. She had always felt Bridie and Nick shared the same sort of union and she was truly thankful. She had believed Conan was too proud and independent to have such a deep and loving relationship, but as the years passed she had realised that Fiona was the perfect partner for him in every way. She brought out both gentleness and respect in him. Rachel hoped it would be the same for Ewan one day.

'The flies are really biting today. I think you may be right about a thunderstorm. I asked Gerda if she wanted to come but it's just as well she declined,' she said brushing away the flies with the elderberry branch.

'Aye, I've seen her. I asked if she'd like to make a cup of tea for both of us until you returned with the cows.'

'Oh good, I'm sure she must be ready for one and I ...'

'Good? It's not good at all. She said she didn't know where anything was and, in any case, she hadn't come as a servant!'

'Oh dear!' Rachel stared at Ross's face in dismay. She knew by the furrow between his brows and the grim set to his mouth that he and Gerda had not got off to a good start. 'I suppose she's just not used to country ways,' Rachel soothed.

'Well, I hope Ewan soon realises that, then. He needs a wife who'll support him, not somebody good for decoration and nothing else.'

'Times are changing, dear.' Rachel sighed. 'A lot of wives have careers of their own now and they don't give up work when they marry as they did before the war.'

'I get the impression she's not even keen to follow her career. Anyway it's different for farming folk. A man still needs a wife who will understand when his work comes first, lend a hand when he needs one …'

'I know, I know, dear. Not every woman is cut out for milking cows and feeding poultry. You …'

'I'm not saying she needs to milk cows these days, not with milking machines and parlours,' Ross conceded, 'but there's still a lot a good woman can do to support a man, inside as well as out. I'd certainly expect her to keep accounts, make the meals, rear the poultry and clean the eggs. Aye, there's plenty to be done. I can't imagine Ewan will want to come in and start cooking his own breakfast if he's been up since five o'clock milking cows, can you?'

'Do you think he's serious about Gerda, then?'

'I don't know, but I think she sees farming life through very rosy spectacles if you ask me.'

'Time will tell,' Rachel murmured. 'Did you have a drink of tea then? I sent a basket out to the field. I thought you would have it there.'

'Oh, I did, but I could have drunk another one and I thought the lassie might be glad of one herself. I was trying to be sociable and make her feel at home, but I didna get much response.'

The men worked on at the harvest long after the milking was finished. The storm clouds were gathering and the rumble of thunder could be heard in the distance.

As soon as milking was finished Ross had hurried back to the field, taking with him a basket of rolls and scones to keep the men going until they finished for the day and could sit down to a proper meal. Rachel and Gerda had eaten together, but as soon as the meal was over the girl had draped herself over the settee in the living room and turned on the television.

The rumble of thunder was growing louder. Rachel grimaced. She hated storms. As a child she used to think it was God riding his chariots across the floor of Heaven. When the noise was very loud and near she had always thought He must be very angry and she hoped his chariots would not fall through the floor and kill them all. Even now her imagination ran riot when the thunder seemed to be right overhead. A sudden flash of lightning made Gerda come running through from the living room.

'Where's Ewan? He should be here. I hate thunder ...'

'I know, dear. They'll all be in soon.' Rachel was standing at the kitchen door. She was just as anxious to see the men and their machines safely home. 'There's the rain coming,' she said, watching the first huge drops plop into the dusty yard. Another crash of thunder drowned out her words and Gerda screamed. Tess made a dart for the house, tail between her legs, head down. Her damp coat brushed Gerda's long, bare legs and she aimed an angry kick at the collie. Rachel frowned.

'It's the only time poor Tess comes indoors. She's petrified of thunder. We think it's loud enough but dogs' hearing is far more acute and sensitive than ours.' She watched Tess squeeze beneath a low table and she went to pat her gently. 'Poor lamb. You feel safe there, don't you? It'll soon pass over ...'

Gerda watched scornfully. How could anyone call a dog a poor lamb? Rachel moved back to the open door where the rain was now splashing onto the tiled floor of the back porch. She didn't like to feel shut up inside when there was thunder. Another terrific rumble seemed to come from above their heads.

'I think you should turn off the television now, Gerda. I believe it can conduct the lightning or something. A-ah, I hear the tractors coming home. Ewan will be here soon.'

'About time too ... oh, my gawd! See that bloody lightning? It's forked. That's bloody dangerous!'

'Ye-es.' Rachel stared anxiously through the arrows of rain, vaguely conscious that she preferred Gerda's native Glasgow speech, even with the expletives. 'A-ah, the men are all in from the field.' She sighed in relief. 'I see them sheltering under the barn beside the tractors ...' She broke off as lightning lit the sky and Gerda screamed. Rachel put an arm around her slim shoulders, trying to offer comfort, but the storm was a bad one – far too close for her own peace of mind.

The rain slackened briefly and the three men ran across the yard to the house. Ewan and Peter, long-legged and young, covered the distance in no time, and tumbled laughingly into the porch, shaking their wet hair from their eyes like a pair of young puppies. Rachel handed them each a towel, but her eyes were fixed on Ross a few yards behind them. He would be 60 in November and was still lean and fit, but no match for a son of 21. The rain was pelting down again, faster than ever.

'Where's young Billy?' she asked, as he stepped into the porch beside her.

'We came home by his cottage and dropped him off. Thanks, lassie.' He grinned at Rachel as he accepted a towel, rubbing vigorously at his hair, still thick and mainly dark except for a few silver streaks above his ears. 'Phew! That's better. Peter had better wait here a while. He'll get drenched just running to the other end of the steading.'

'I've some soup heating on the Aga and there's a beef casserole with dumplings in the oven. Change your clothes while I set them out.' She moved through to the large kitchen. Ross followed on his way to the stairs, but his eyebrows rose when he saw Gerda perched on Ewan's knee, her arms draped around his neck.

'Peter, you'll eat with us tonight,' Rachel said firmly.

41

'Oh no, Mistress Maxwell ...' Peter rose to his feet.

'I insist. Just for once.' Rachel smiled and pushed him gently back onto the kitchen chair. 'You're much too independent, laddie. It's late and you'll be too tired to start cooking after such a long, hard day.'

'But you've kept us well supplied with the harvest baskets at the field ...'

'Och, nothing but sandwiches and scones, and a bit o' apple pie. Now you need a proper meal. Anyway you've all earned it and there's plenty.'

Peter bit his lip. He always tried not to take advantage of the kindly folk who had given him work and a place in the world. He often thought he was the most fortunate man alive to have found a family like the Maxwells when he was a young prisoner of war, lucky too with old Mrs Forster. She had given him lodgings in the old farmhouse and mothered him as though he was the son she had lost. He had missed her terribly when she died, but Mr Maxwell had agreed he should take over the house and Mrs Forster had left him her meagre savings and her furniture. Now he had a home to call his own and a lovely garden and he asked for nothing more ... He almost jumped out of his chair. A terrific thunderclap exploded overhead. Gerda screamed and clung even more tightly to Ewan. The electric light sputtered and died.

'Oh well, at least the meal is cooked and ready to eat,' Rachel said philosophically. 'I think there's still enough light left for us to manage ...'

'It's creepy!' Gerda protested.

'I'll get a candle,' Ewan offered, drawing her arms from his neck. 'I'm a bit damp,' he laughed ruefully, shaking the legs of his trousers away from his skin. 'How about you, Peter?'

'Just a bit. I'll probably be worse before I get home.' His dark eyes twinkled. His hair had dried into a mass of black curls, Gerda noticed. She had barely looked at him earlier. After all, he was just a labourer and she didn't think Mrs Maxwell should have invited him into the house. Now she saw that he was a handsome man, even in his working denims. Moreover, he had an air of aloof pride; a certain dignity which she felt was out of place for a man in his position. She frowned. She would soon bring him to heel and keep him in his place when she was in charge at Nether Rullion.

They were halfway through eating their meal when Tess scrambled out from her refuge, barking hysterically.

'Poor dog, she's terrified,' Rachel said, pushing back her chair and moving to soothe the shivering collie. The back door was still ajar and the porch floor was wet but Rachel preferred it that way. As a child, someone had once told her that if the devil got into the house with the lightning, he needed a way to get out. She knew it was silly but she had never been able to dispel the feeling that it was safer to leave the door ajar. Now the dog seemed to share her fear as she darted to the open door and back towards her, barking furiously, gazing up at her with anxious brown eyes, then darting back to the door, as though beckoning her to follow.

'She's mad!' Gerda muttered, picking desultorily at her food.

'Come into the kitchen then, old girl,' Rachel soothed, reaching for the dog's collar, but Tess darted away, back to the door, then to Rachel and back again to the door in a frenzy. Ross frowned and set down his knife and fork reluctantly. The beef and dumplings were delicious at the end of a hard day's labour.

'I think she's trying to tell us something,' he said.

'Yes.' Peter nodded and followed Ross and the dog to the door. They peered through the driving rain, but there was little to be seen except rivulets washing through the farmyard and gutters overflowing.

'Thank God we got the straw baled and the stacks

covered,' Ross said fervently. 'Any corn not cut will be flattened by this lot. Come on in, Tess.' He bent to grasp the dog's collar but she refused to budge from the doorway, her ears pricked. She looked up at Ross, whining in agitation. 'I wish I knew what you were trying to tell me, old girl ...'

'Anybody would think the bloody dog could talk,' Gerda muttered with contempt, but Ewan did not smile; he was not even looking at her. He was sitting up tense and alert, his eyes on Peter.

'What is it? Can you smell something?' he called, watching the man wrinkling his nose.

'Fire! Yes, I think Tess smells fire ...' Even as he spoke he was pushing his feet into his Wellingtons and dashing into the farmyard, oblivious of the pouring rain. Halfway across, he turned to yell. 'The barn! It's the barn. Struck by lightning ...'

'We left the tractors there!' Ross and Ewan were already pulling on their own boots.

'There's four calves penned in there, as well.' Ewan gasped as a tongue of flame leapt into the leaden sky.

'Phone the fire brigade, Rachel!' Ross called as he followed the two young men down to the barn.

'Ross! Be careful, oh, please be careful ...' Rachel's voice trailed away as she ran to the phone, her face ashen.

Gerda grimaced. She was still sitting at the table. She pushed away her plate with a look of distaste. Some weekend this was turning out to be. She had had every intention of bringing Ewan to a major decision.

Rachel dashed back into the kitchen, pulling on her coat, her feet already in her Wellingtons.

'The fire brigade is on its way. Phone, Bridie. If the fire spreads ...' She caught her breath on a half-sob.

'What's her number?' Gerda asked. Rachel called the number over her shoulder.

'Conan too. The numbers are on the yellow card.'

It was Nick who answered. Gerda was pleased to have someone to talk to and she chatted, without urgency.

'Were you phoning for anything in particular?' Nick asked, puzzled. Gerda usually showed little interest in anyone except Ewan.

'There's a fire outside. It's the lightning.'

'A fire?' Nick didn't think he'd heard correctly.

'Yes. Mrs Maxwell asked me to tell Bridie. Don't know what she can do about it,' Gerda shrugged carelessly. 'She's phoned the fire briga–' Suddenly there was another loud crash and the phone seemed to jump out of her hand. The line was dead. Gerda began to whimper with shock. Ewan had no business rushing out and leaving her on her own. She lifted the candle to go back to the kitchen but a sudden gust blew out the flame. She swore and groped her way back to the big cooker.

She was still standing there in the gloom, clinging to the steel rail, when Bridie, Max and the twins burst into the house 20 minutes later.

'For goodness sake, why are you in the dark, Gerda?'

'The candle went out.'

'Well, there are matches on the shelf there.' Bridie reached for the box herself, as well as a second brass candlestick gleaming dimly in the gloom. Impatiently she lit them both. 'Where's Mum?'

'Outside, I expect.'

'She's out there! We followed the fire engine in. Nick's gone to help. I'll go and bring Mother in. I pray to God they can stop it spreading ...' Bridie's face was white, but as she glanced at the table, still littered with dirty dishes, she frowned.

'They'll all be soaked to the skin and cold. Fill up the big kettle and put it on the hot plate ...'

'Which one is that?'

'Max will show you. Girls, help Gerda clear the table and wash the dishes will you, please? Then ...'

'Hey, I'm not here to take orders!' Gerda protested. 'Or to skivvy …'

'Then you should go back to where you came from.' Bridie snapped, her face strained with worry. 'I'm going to find Granny and Grandpa. Margaret and Alicia, you know how to lay the table. Be good. No, Max, you can't come with me. It's not safe.'

'But, Mum …'

Bridie waved away his protest and hurried outside. The thunder seemed to be farther away now but flames were leaping into the sky. The rain was still lashing down and Bridie prayed silently that it would stop the fire spreading. They had seen the light in the sky and sparks as they sped along the road.

Another car drew up.

'We saw the fire! What's happened?' Conan demanded urgently.

'Thank goodness you've come,' Bridie breathed. 'Will you keep Max indoors please, Fiona? And get some order into the kitchen if you can? Everyone will need hot drinks but Gerda's useless. I'm going to bring Mum in.'

'She's out there?' Conan gasped incredulously, immediately loping away without waiting for a reply.

'I'll come with you, Bridie,' Lucy said. 'Maybe I can help with something, if there are animals to be moved … or whatever.'

'OK, you might be better at persuading Mum to come in than I am. Ah, here's someone else come to help,' she said gratefully, as she recognised a neighbour's car.

Rachel struggled valiantly with the ropes which had been used to make a temporary pen for four young heifer calves. They were not quite old enough to be turned out to the fields and yet they needed the fresh air during the recent humid weather. Ross had made the pen in the open sided barn, but it was one of the poles supporting the roof which had caught fire. Ross, Peter and Ewan were busy trying to get the tractors and machinery well away from the flames and Rachel wished she had brought her penknife.

At last she managed to loosen one side and she yanked the gate open. The calves did not understand. They refused to move from their huddle in one corner. The smoke was increasing and Rachel coughed violently, her eyes streaming as she tried to usher the animals to safety. She could no longer see the figures of the men as the smoke thickened, but she knew there would be an inferno if any of the tractors caught fire. The only thing she could do was to stick her fingers into the mouths of two of the calves and coax them out of the pen as they sucked. It was the only thing they understood. She had rescued three calves and was just going back for the smallest when she heard Ross shouting her name. He was rushing towards her, just a few feet away. Rachel blinked frantically, trying to clear her streaming eyes. There was an almighty crash. She gasped in horror. Ross was lying face down. A thick beam was pinning him there, across one arm and his leg. Everything seemed to happen at once. Rachel did not know she had screamed as she struggled to Ross's side and tried to lift away the beam. Then Conan was beside her, drawing her away.

'Let me go! Your father's trapped. He'll be burned alive! Please God ...'

'Leave him, Mum. Nick and I will carry him. Get out of here. Now!' Reluctantly Rachel obeyed. She knew Conan and Nick would do their best to get Ross out. She remembered the calf but she could barely see it in the smoky darkness. Then she felt it nuzzling against her and thrust her fingers into its mouth, leading and pushing it as quickly as it would move to join the other three in the open field adjoining the stack-yard. Behind her she heard Conan and Nick and saw they were carrying Ross between them.

'We'll lay him out in the open, well away from the fire,' Conan decided.

'Ross, oh, Ross,' Rachel cried and ran to kneel beside him. 'You can't leave him here! We must get him inside ...'

'No, Mum. He's hurt. Better not to move him any more until we know how badly. Go back and phone the doctor ...'

'No! I can't leave him ...' She turned at a slight tug on her arm.

'Come, Mrs Maxwell, I'll help you back to the house. You must help me find blankets to keep him warm.' Lucy's voice was calm and firm. Rachel went with her as meekly as a child and Conan knew he had never been so proud of the child he had sired as he was amid the smoke and danger. Bridie took her place and knelt beside her father.

'Can you hear me, Dad?'

'Aye ... Can't move my leg ...'

'No, I-I think it's broken. We darena move you until the doctor comes. Lucy has gone to fetch blankets ...'

'Where's Ewan? Have you seen Ewan?' His voice rose urgently.

'Ewan will be fine ...'

'No! He couldna get his new tractor out. Tell him to leave it. Not worth his life ...'

'The firemen are getting things under control.' Bridie tried to sound reassuring. 'I don't think it will spread to the house now, or to the cattle sheds.' There was no reply. Bridie realised her father's eyes were closed. His breathing sounded laboured.

# Chapter Five

Dawn was breaking by the time the firemen were ready to leave and even then two of them were left to keep watch in case the smouldering timbers should be fanned into flames again.

The ambulance had arrived promptly considering the stormy night and the flooding on some of the side roads. Bridie watched anxiously as her father and Ewan were carried to the waiting vehicle. They were both too shocked or in pain to protest, but her mother had only agreed to go because she couldn't bear to leave her husband and son. At the hospital, the doctor had checked up on her breathing and insisted she should stay in hospital at least for the remainder of the night.

Bridie could scarcely wait until morning to phone for a report.

'We are keeping your mother in for observation, but she'll probably be allowed home later today.' The nurse had informed Bridie briskly. 'Your father has a fractured fibula and we think he has fractured a bone in his arm. Unfortunately the doctors are unable to operate as he is suffering from smoke inhalation. Dealing with his breathing is our first priority. Meanwhile we have given him something to ease the pain.'

'And Ewan? My brother?'

'He has sustained a nasty burn on his forearm, but he'll probably be allowed home after the doctor has seen it again tomorrow.'

'At least they are all alive,' she breathed with relief as she turned to face Fiona and Conan. 'Nick, I think I should stay here to help Peter with the milking, and there's the calves to feed, and the hens to attend. He can't do everything himself and the poor laddie must be as exhausted as we are.'

'Milking time already, it is,' Nick reminded them wearily. 'I'll tell Emmie and Frank what's happened when I get back to Glens of Lochandee. I'll give them a hand with the milking before I go to the garage. Shall I leave the children here?'

'We may as well let them sleep.' Bridie nodded. 'I'm glad you were here to take charge inside, Fiona, and persuade the twins to go to bed.'

'I'm glad I was able to help,' Fiona said simply. 'The men appreciated copious quantities of hot tea once they had things under control.'

'Not to mention sandwiches and toasted cheese,' Lucy said wryly, stretching her arms above her head and smothering a yawn.

'Yes, thank goodness you thought to bring some bread, Bridie. The freezer is a blessing sometimes. I just hope everything else will turn out as well.' She looked at Conan.

'You'll let us know when there's any news, Bridie? We'd better get off home now and snatch a hot bath. How about you, Lucy? You worked hard, outside as well as in. We're proud of you.'

'Perhaps I should wait here, if Bridie is helping Peter with the milking. Someone ought to be here in case the twins wake up. Anyway Mrs Maxwell might need someone to bring her home.'

'Yes, Lucy, you're right,' Bridie agreed with relief. 'But you should try to have a nap while you can. Where's Gerda, by the way?' she asked suddenly.

Fiona raised her eyes heavenward.

'She went to bed,' she said flatly.

'When?'

'Oh ... more or less as soon as we arrived. But it's probably just as well,' she added wryly. 'Your seven-year-old twins have more idea about setting to work than Gerda has. They were really good, and so was Max, once he accepted that he couldn't go outside.'

'Oh dear,' Bridie sighed. 'You'd have thought Gerda would be anxious about Ewan, at least. Still, you never know, this may have put her off the idea of living in the country,' she said hopefully.

As the weeks passed, Ross chafed against his inability to work. The corn harvest was all safely undercover but there were still turnips to lift. He grew them for winter feed, in addition to the pit of grass silage. He was reluctant to cast off the old methods in spite of Ewan's arguments that turnips were out of date and silage was easier handled.

'I know Bridie still grows turnips and hay at Glens of Lochandee, Dad,' Ewan argued earnestly, again and again, 'but she still has her cows in a byre. When you have a milking parlour and cubicle shed you should move on to more modern feeding methods.'

'Turnips are damned good feed and it's a good crop this year,' Ross insisted, 'So it's up to you and Peter to get them in and properly stored. Gerda will have to get used to farm life if she's as set on marrying you as she seems to be.'

Ewan flushed. Since the fire he had been tied to the farm due to his father's incapacity, but his parents seemed to have accepted Gerda as his special friend and she came down to Nether Rullion most weekends. He knew they didn't feel she was suited to the life of a working farmer. In his heart, he knew they were right, but he wanted her – needed her. His body ached for her. She excited him as no other woman had. He had said this to one of his college friends but Gus had given a mocking guffaw.

'How many women do you know at your age, Ewan?' he had chuckled. The answer was none, but he knew he longed to make Gerda his, and she had made it clear that marrying her was the only way he was going to get her, in spite of her flirting and teasing. It troubled him when she refused to accept the demands of farm life and the time needed to care for the animals. She railed continually because he had work to do at weekends.

'We're not all lucky enough to be teachers,' he laughed. 'The cows don't leave on Friday nights and come back on Monday mornings as your pupils do.' Patiently, he tried to explain that life was more hectic than usual at Nether Rullion while his father was incapacitated. The situation was aggravated because they had a lot of cows calving to increase their winter milk supply. The price was better than milk produced in summer, but it meant longer milking times and more calves to rear and this routine work was the same on Saturdays and Sundays as every other day.

He had never known either of his parents to be ill and he had begun to realise how hard they both worked. Since his father's illness his mother had spent more time indoors keeping him company. Although she still fed the newly born calves she left the older ones to him and Peter. She usually fed the few pigs which they still kept and she always attended to the hens and pullets. She regarded them as her particular responsibility. They depended on the sale of her eggs to pay Peter's wages and his own spending money, as well as the household expenses and petrol for the car. This left any profit they could make from the cows and sheep for major expenses: buying cattle cake; maintaining and renewing machinery, buildings, fences and drains – as well as buying in the seeds and lime for the spring crops.

Ewan had been proud to show his college friends around Nether Rullion and he knew some of them had envied him. His father kept the whole farm clean, tidy and well-maintained. Every spring the buildings were thoroughly cleaned and lime-washed and the wooden doors freshly painted. Moreover his father was coming round to the idea of using more fertiliser as a regular routine on the grassland too. Ewan knew this was partly due to his own reports from college lectures, but he was beginning to appreciate that his father must have adapted many times during his lifetime according to the changing demands made on farming.

'You're young and impatient, laddie,' his mother remonstrated when he thought his father would never see his point of view, or make the changes he considered modern. One thing Ross and Ewan still disagreed upon was the use of chemical sprays. Ewan insisted this would soon be the only way to grow cereals, according to his lecturers. Ross remained wary, and stubbornly refused to use them.

'A few thistles in the corn will do you no harm. That's all part of harvesting.' Ewan had argued that there were other weeds which spoiled the yields of the corn. Secretly, he sometimes felt a bit overwhelmed by the decisions his father had to make. Every year there were more regulations coming into force to control the quality of food sold to the public. Even poultry keeping was changing. There was talk of fierce competition from businessmen who knew nothing of traditional farming methods. They were intent on breeding hens which would lay eggs for 360 days of the year. The idea was to keep these hens in tiny individual cages, feeding and watering them via conveyor belts.

Where his mother looked after 300 hens at Nether Rullion, these men would have 3,000 or more. Where his mother had six wooden huts dotted around the farm steading and paddock, these new methods would house them all in one large building. His mother had laughed at the idea of a hen laying an egg almost every day of the year. She simply couldn't visualise hens being kept in cages all day, being fed and watered at the touch of a button on a time switch, instead of scratching around in the earth.

'It's unnatural,' she insisted. 'How could they lay eggs or stay healthy if they never have any fresh air!' Ewan was not so sure, but he didn't argue. His mother knew as well as anyone how farming had changed since the war.

During his time at college he had listened to innumerable lectures and discussions concerning modern trends in farming. Some of the lecturers believed the public wanted cheaper and cheaper food and the majority of people didn't care how it was produced. His father, on the other hand, believed the price of food to the consumer would go up if the discussions concerning a European Common Market bore fruit. Higher prices to the general public would mean demands for higher wages, he maintained, and that would lead to spiralling costs for everything. Ewan smiled, knowing how opposed his father was to any marketing agreement with Europe, since it would mean restrictions in trade with Commonwealth countries and possibly an end to New Zealand lamb and butter.

Ewan had tried to talk to Gerda about his way of life and the future of farming, the changes which were coming to them all, but she was all in favour of cheap food.

'Why should I care how you farmers produce food? I'd have more money for clothes if I didn't have to pay so much for food and digs. Just think, Ewan, we could go away at weekends, instead of slaving away milking cows. We could go abroad in the winter …' He had laughed at her. She was like a child sometimes, with her wild enthusiasms, and at such times he wanted to give her the moon if it would make her happy. She simply didn't understand that cheap food didn't mean cows only needed milking five days a week. If anything it would mean breeding cows to give more and more milk every day.

Ross often sat in brooding silence, his eyes watchful. Rachel worried about him. He had never been a moody man, but then he had never been so confined to the house as he had been in the weeks since harvest and the fire. His broken arm prevented him hobbling around on crutches and he questioned Ewan constantly about the cattle and the sheep. Peter too was summoned to answer questions, but usually the pair of them ended up with a lively discussion on woodwork, or some other topic which was nothing to do with farming and Rachel welcomed Peter's visits warmly, assuring him that they were both happy for him to come in whenever he had time to spare.

Rachel had always known when Ross was hatching some plan or other and she was almost certain there would be some changes made as soon as he was out and about again. She prayed that his plans would not upset Ewan, or the fragile peace which existed whenever Gerda came to stay.

A few days before Christmas, Fiona telephoned.

'Lucy telephoned us last night,' she said excitedly. 'She asked me to tell you that Donald Greig has asked her to marry him ...'

'Lucy? To marry? So soon?' Rachel echoed faintly, and saw Ross sit up straighter, listening intently.

'They're not getting married for another 18 months, but Donald has bought her an engagement ring and she wanted to tell us. They mean to have a quiet wedding sometime in the summer of 1964, after Lucy has completed her probationary teaching. She sounds so happy and excited ...'

'And so do you, Fiona.' Rachel smiled at the

telephone. It was unusual for Fiona to show her feelings so clearly.

'Yes, well, we're both pleased for Lucy. She has known Donald almost since she started college. Chris invited her to stay for a weekend with her parents and I suspected there was a mutual attraction between Lucy and Donald from the beginning.'

'Yes, you could be right when I think about it. Chris seems a nice girl. I hope the rest of the family are the same.'

'So do I,' Fiona echoed fervently. 'I did wonder whether Mr Greig might be a bit ... thrifty though,' she said carefully.

'We're all thrifty. Do you mean a bit stingy, Fiona?'

'Perhaps. I don't really know, of course. Just one or two comments Chris has made occasionally. I expect the Greigs have had to be careful with three sons wanting to farm and Chris to be educated. We're sorry Lucy will not be settling nearer to us but Conan says it will not take us long to drive up to Ayr in the car.'

'Didn't Lucy mention the Greigs were hoping to rent another farm?' Rachel said. 'Has it materialised?'

'Yes, I think that may have precipitated the engagement. The laird has agreed but only on condition that the tenant lives there and occupies the house. Lucy says it's very dilapidated but the laird has promised to do some basic repairs. Don's going to live there on his own until they get married.'

When Rachel broke the news of Lucy's engagement to Ewan, he smiled widely.

'Well, that's no surprise. Don Greig never looked at any of the other lassies after Chris introduced him to Lucy. He came into Ayr most Saturday nights to take her out. I'll phone and congratulate them after supper.' Rachel nodded, aware that Gerda had greeted the news with a scowl and a tightening of her mouth. Was she jealous?

'Did you know Donald Greig, Gerda?' she asked gently.

'Of course. We all knew him. I don't know what Lucy saw in him, or in his sister,' she added waspishly. She shuddered with distaste. 'You should've seen how rough her hands were, and her fingernails were always broken.' Rachel resisted looking down at her own work-roughened hands. She said nothing.

Gerda had made it clear that she intended spending the Christmas holiday at Nether Rullion. Rachel was surprised that she was leaving her father on his own, but perhaps he had other friends – maybe even a woman friend. Gerda revealed very little about her home life.

Rachel was as unprepared for the second surprise in the days leading up to Christmas. Gerda had travelled down to Nether Rullion as soon as the school closed for the holidays.

'There's only one shopping day left with Christmas Eve being a Sunday,' she announced, 'so Ewan will need to take me Christmas shopping tomorrow.'

'I've done my shopping,' Ewan protested, 'and I've a lot of extra work to do getting everything organised for the holiday. We only do the essential work at Christmas. It'll be like three Sundays in a row this year.'

'Sundays!' Gerda exploded. 'You *always* work on Sundays, even though I come to see you. Sometimes I wonder why I bother!' she pouted.

'We only do milking, feeding and mucking out,' Ewan defended. 'You wouldn't expect us to leave the animals to starve, would you?'

'It wouldn't bother me,' she shrugged.

Ewan had not considered getting engaged yet but Gerda made straight for the Midsteeple and the jeweller's shop nearby. He soon realised that an engagement ring was the thing she had set her heart on.

57

'You're just wanting to keep up with Lucy,' he teased, but Gerda was furious at such a suggestion.

'I don't need to keep up with anyone, but if she can get engaged so soon after leaving college, then so can we.'

'A-ah, but there's a difference. Don is five years older than we are and he's been working since he was 16. His father wouldn't let him go to agricultural college. He said he needed him to work at home.'

'What difference does that make?'

'It probably means he's earned a bit more money than I have,' Ewan said drily. 'Anyway, we should have consulted your father ...'

'Oh, Ewan, don't be so old-fashioned. He'll not care.'

'Well, I should've discussed it with my parents. After all, it will affect them if we get married and ...'

'Ewan Maxwell, I've given up my Christmas holiday to spend it on your bloody farm, with you! The least you can do is forget about your family and buy me a decent engagement ring.' She saw Ewan's brow darken. She knew he loved the farm and the way of life. Before he could argue, she purred softly, 'You have to prove your intentions are honourable when you keep pestering me for ... you know what!' She fluttered her thick darkened lashes provocatively and edged closer, hugging his arm against the rounded softness of her breast. He felt the familiar stirring in his loins.

'Oh, all right then. There's loads of time before we need to discuss serious plans. Let's go inside and see if they have anything I can afford which pleases you.'

Rachel was surprised when Gerda flashed the diamond ring in front of her nose the moment the two of them returned from town. She glanced anxiously at Ross but he didn't seem as surprised as she was.

'We-ell now,' he said slowly, 'so you're keeping up with Lucy, eh? It will be a long engagement, I suppose ...'

He caught the venomous expression in Gerda's narrowed eyes and broke off, his eyes moving to Ewan.

'Oh, we're not getting married for ages ...'

'The wedding will be at the end of June,' Gerda cut Ewan short, flashing him a beaming smile. 'Ewan doesn't want to wait, do you, lover boy? We've no need to wait as long as Lucy. I'm quite willing to give up my career for Ewan. If we have the wedding at the end of June we shall have the long summer holiday in front of us.'

'You might.' Ewan grimaced. 'I shall probably be making hay by July.'

'You will need a place to live before you make serious plans,' Ross intervened firmly. 'I imagine that's your first priority.'

'But surely you and Mrs Maxwell will be mov—'

'There's a cottage coming vacant,' Ross cut in abruptly. 'Ewan, did young Billy tell you the laird is planning to sell off the cottages where his parents live?' Billy Smith lived quite close to Nether Rullion and had recently come to work for Ross after leaving school.

'No, he didn't mention it,' Ewan said puzzled. He'd expected his father to be angry and present them with a list of reasons why they couldn't possibly get married yet. Indeed, he felt things were getting out of his control.

'A house would be a good investment for the future. If we could buy the one next to the Smiths for a couple of thousand it would be big enough for the pair o' you. That's if you really are planning to get married so soon, Ewan?'

'I hadn't consid—'

'What sort of cottage?' Gerda demanded belligerently, her eyes straying round the big farm kitchen as though already making plans for it.

'Well, of course, it's your decision, laddie,' Ross said.

'It's my decision too!' Gerda interrupted. 'What sort of a cottage are you talking about? I'm not going to live in any old shack'

'Oh, the cottages aren't shacks!' Ewan said, almost impatiently. 'Billy's home is quite comfortable. I've seen it.'

'Well, it's that or nothing,' Ross said firmly, looking Gerda in the eye. 'If you take my advice you'll both wait a few years before rushing into marriage.'

'We don't want to wait, do we, Ewan?' Gerda fluttered her eyelashes at Ewan and moved closer.

'Well, if that's what it has to be, we could probably get a grant to modernise the cottage,' Ross mused. 'They have large gardens at the back – a relic from the time workers all kept a pig and a few hens and grew their own vegetables.'

'As Peter still does,' Rachel said.

'Yes, he does, but I was thinking about the future,' Ross said. 'When ...' He glanced wryly at Ewan. 'When you've both earned some money, and can afford it, there would be plenty of room to build a garage, or an extra bedroom for your children ...'

'Children!' Gerda almost screeched. 'I see enough kids at school every day. I don't intend to have any squawking little brats.'

'Well then, a small cottage should suit you fine,' Ross said and closed his mouth firmly. He was well aware what Gerda Fritz-Allan had in mind. He'd seen her glancing critically around his home many times, having had plenty of opportunity to observe her during his convalescence. In his heart, he hoped fervently Ewan would see her true colours and change his mind in the months ahead, but he had no intention of alienating his son by thwarting his plans outright. It was Ewan's life. It had to be his decision and even Ross admitted Gerda was a beautiful girl. He just wished he didn't feel so uneasy about her. He had tried to like her.

Ross had never spent so much time in the house in his

life before. It had made him appreciate Rachel's hard work more than ever, but in contrast it had shown him that Gerda was lazy and often ill-tempered during the weekends she had spent at Nether Rullion. He suspected she wanted the best from life but with the minimum of effort on her part. He had noticed the way her mouth drew into a thin line whenever her plans were thwarted. Now he watched her glowering at Ewan, clearly longing to state her opinion, while he seemed quite oblivious to her displeasure.

'That's a splendid idea,' he said now. 'Thank you, Dad, for ... well, for understanding, and for being prepared to help us find a place to live.'

'Do you think your father would like to join us and share your news, Gerda?' Rachel asked. 'Or perhaps he knows already?'

'No.' Ewan flushed. 'I didna know myself until we went to town, so ...' He grinned at Gerda but she returned his look with an angry scowl.

'Then you must tell him immediately. Ask him if he'll join us. We don't want to leave him out. We'll have a family gathering to celebrate. Ask him to come on Boxing Day, if he is free, and he could stay overnight.'

'He'll never trail down here to the country,' Gerda said ungraciously. 'I'll tell him we're engaged next time I phone.'

As soon as they were alone she turned angrily to Ewan.

'Why did you agree? You needn't think I'm going to live in a poky little cottage! I'm ...'

'We shall be as happy as a pair o' skylarks,' he chuckled seizing her around the waist and swinging her round gleefully. 'I never thought they'd take our news so calmly, let alone help us make plans for a place of our own. I can't wait ...' He kissed her passionately.

'Well, I can!' Gerda pulled away from him. 'I'm not going to any horrid little hovel.'

'Oh, Gerda,' Ewan laughed merrily. 'We'll do it up like a wee palace. You'll not know it when it's finished. Dad always makes a good job of things once he starts. You'll enjoy choosing your own furniture and colour schemes. You know how you enjoy shopping for new things ...'

'I thought we'd live in *this* house. After all, you're the farmer now ...'

'You'd better not tell Dad that!' Ewan chuckled. 'I hope he has plenty of years left yet. He's still the boss and he makes the decisions so you'd better keep on the right side of him.'

'Hmph.' Gerda pouted. 'I still think you could have suggested they should move out and let you take over.'

'Oh, I expect they'll move when they're too old to work.' Ewan shrugged. 'Meanwhile, I'm glad Dad's still in charge. It'll give us a few years without so much responsibility. It's the Young Farmers' Christmas Dance tonight. How about getting into your slinky red dress so that I can show you off and make the lads envious?'

Gerda looked at him and her eyes brightened. There was nothing she loved better than getting dressed up and dancing. Ewan was a handsome partner too and she loved it when he showed her off to his friends.

'But before you make plans for tonight I want you to phone your father. I don't think we should keep him in the dark. It makes me feel uncomfortable. Anyway, it was good of Mum to invite him, so the least you can do is pass on her invitation.'

No one was more surprised than Gerda when her father readily agreed to come to Nether Rullion on Boxing Day, and even to stay overnight.

As soon as the festive season was over, Ross made an appointment to see Jordon Niven, the solicitor who handled all his family's legal affairs and who had given sound advice over the years. He did not confide his real reason for seeing his lawyer and Rachel assumed he was arranging the purchase of the cottage, and perhaps enquiring about a grant.

Ross had no wish to worry Rachel with his own misgivings. In his heart he felt providing a home for Gerda and Ewan might be the least of their problems. Yet the girl made Ewan happy and what more should he ask than a lifetime of happiness for the youngest member of his family. Moreover he and Rachel had taken an immediate liking to her father when he had spent a couple of nights at Nether Rullion to celebrate the engagement.

John Allan had spoken frankly with Rachel and himself, telling them that he owned his own wee house but he was not a wealthy man. He had put aside money to provide Gerda with the sort of wedding he believed she would want, but he had little else except his works pension. He confided he had only moved into a blue-collar job ten months ago. Previously, he'd been a welder in the shipyard where he had spent all his working life. This had been something of a surprise considering Gerda's version of her father's employment. They had appreciated his honesty and sincerity.

They both sensed there was more he wanted to say, yet he had kept his own counsel on whatever matter troubled him. He had an air of weariness which had aroused Rachel's sympathy, and some concern. Several times, when he thought he was unobserved, Ross had caught him shaking his head as though in despair. Ross could not know that the older Gerda became the more he wondered whether she bore any relation at all to himself. He knew her mother had been an outrageous flirt, but he had adored Gerda as a baby, spoiled her as a pretty toddler and indulged her as a demanding teenager. But he could no longer deny her selfishness and the inherent discontent which reminded him painfully of her mother. It had destroyed their marriage, and ultimately taken her life.

Ross guessed nothing of John Allan's doubts and fears when he promised to help the young couple find a home, and happiness. Yet every instinct made him wary.

When Ewan had started at college they had paid an allowance into his bank for textbooks, fees and a little extra for pleasure. He had never overstepped his budget. The arrangement had continued in the months since Ewan had come home to work, except that Ross had promised to make him a full partner in the farm and he knew it was in his own interests to plough back any spare cash into the business. He had the use of the car and his food and clothes. Ewan had his own dreams for the future and until recently they had all revolved around Nether Rullion and the pedigree herd. Ross knew most farmers' sons were treated in a similar fashion, though some accepted the old ways more willingly than others. Many of their contemporaries in other work could earn big wages and few of them thought of setting aside money for the future. Consequently they enjoyed riotous weekends.

Ewan seemed content but Ross realised this arrangement would have to change once his son had a wife. The time had come to make him a partner as he had promised. He was a good son and a hard worker, so why, Ross asked himself, did he feel so wary about giving him half of the land and stock on Nether Rullion? It was what he and Rachel had worked for since the day he secured a bank loan and bought the run-down farm. They had worked hard together and put everything they could back into the land and the buildings until it was one of the most fertile and modern farms in the county. When he died the whole farm would be Ewan's. But there was Rachel's future to consider too.

Ross felt he would like to talk over his plans with Fiona but she was part of his family now. It would be unfair to involve her in his judgement. When she had worked for Jordon Niven, before her marriage to Conan, he had taken her advice on more than one occasion and he valued her common sense and wisdom. Conan had been fortunate indeed in his marriage to Fiona.

'What's worrying you, Ross?' Rachel asked softly, as they lay side by side in the big bed. 'You're twitching and turning. Why are you so restless?' It was the night before his appointment with Jordon Niven.

'I'm not worrying – well, not exactly,' he said slowly. 'I need to make plans for the future. It's time to make Ewan a partner in Nether Rullion. He'll need a bit more money every month when he marries. But I worry about your future too.'

'You don't need to worry about me! I have my hens and ...'

'But when we're too old to look after hens, and milk cows, Rachel, we shall be dependent on Ewan to support us then ...' Ross frowned in the darkness. He prized his independence and he had never considered his own mortality or infirmity until the fire. The doctors had warned him the smoke inhalation had damaged his lungs and he would have to take care. He wasn't afraid for himself but he worried about Rachel being left on her own. He couldn't explain his uneasiness. He couldn't imagine Gerda being very patient, or even very kind, to an old lady – even one who had worked all her life for the benefit of her family. 'Almost everything we have is tied up in the farm. We'll need to use some of our capital to buy one of the Bevendale cottages and do it up for Ewan and Gerda ...'

'I'm sure Ewan appreciates you're giving him a fine start in life. He'll see we're all right if ever we need him.' Rachel chuckled. 'After all, we've taken good care of him all these years. Everything we've worked for at Nether Rullion has been for Ewan. He'll not forget that. Surely you've no fears on that score, Ross?'

'No-o. Not really, I suppose, not as far as Ewan is concerned, anyway.' He hesitated. 'At the market I heard a couple of farmers discussing pensions for their old age. It sounded like a good idea but we never heard of pensions when we were young. Besides, there was never any money to spare. We put it all into buying land and then improving it.'

'Surely you've no regrets, Ross?'

'Not so long as I can always take care of you, Rachel. I could never have managed without you. You know that, don't you?'

'We've been fortunate indeed, Ross.' She laid her cheek against his broad shoulder. 'So fortunate to have each other. So there's no need for you to worry about silly things. You've done well for all our children. Go to sleep now or you'll be falling asleep in Mr Niven's office. It's always as hot as an oven in there.'

Ross paid several visits to the lawyer's office over the next few months and he considered his advice carefully.

'You seem to have some doubts, Mr Maxwell. Do you feel you can't trust your younger son?' Jordon Niven frowned. 'You have every reason to be proud of your family and the way you have brought them up.'

'Yes, I am.' Ross nodded. 'And I'm pleased you've managed to buy the cottage and arrange the grant for modernising it. We shall have to keep on at the builders or it will never be ready in time. The wedding is at the end of June.'

'Yes, but I sense you have other reservations about the future?'

'I don't know. Ewan and his future wife are so young. I wish they hadn't been in such a hurry but, as he keeps reminding us,' Ross gave a wry smile, 'we were just as young. I'm just not sure Gerda understands what farm life is like. I don't think she realises how we have to budget for the rainy days. Her father admits he spoiled her and I get the impression she believes farmers who own their land are made of money.' Ross grimaced. 'The only time we're worth anything is when we die, unless we have no sons and can sell up to retire.'

'I can't see you retiring, whatever your circumstances, Mr Maxwell.' Jordon smiled. 'If she is an intelligent woman, Ewan's wife will realise her living depends on keeping the land, surely?'

'I'm not sure she understands anything at all about farming, or about living in the country. The only thing I am sure about is Ewan is besotted with her. She makes him happy, and she certainly wants to marry him, so who am I to judge?'

Jordon Niven put his fingers together in a pyramid and frowned thoughtfully.

'Leave it with me,' he said at last. 'I think I may have a suggestion to make regarding the land, but I'd like to discuss it with my father first.' He grinned suddenly. 'He may be retired but he likes to be consulted occasionally when the interests of his former clients are concerned.'

'Very well, but meanwhile you'll draw up the papers to put half the business in Ewan's name? Then draw up my will leaving the rest of the Nether Rullion business to him when I die. I've promised it will be his since he was a schoolboy. He never wanted to do anything else but farm. He is the opposite of Conan.'

'You're sure about your will?' Jordon asked with a frown.

'Yes, for the present anyway. I suppose I can always rearrange my affairs as time goes on. You don't think of taking a wife yourself, Mr Niven?' Ross asked curiously. He had known the young lawyer since old Jacob Niven first took him into partnership. 'I expect your father would like to see his grandchildren.'

'Your son, Conan, stole my ideal woman, right from under my nose.' Jordon smiled disarmingly. 'Fiona has everything – a good brain as well as looks. She's a great asset to any man, but she always kept herself aloof. I don't know how the Maxwell charm succeeded in breaking down the barriers when I failed.'

'Aye, Fiona's a fine lassie. She has helped Conan a great deal and they always seem happy together. We're thankful for that.'

'But you're not so happy about young Ewan's choice of a wife?'

'I don't know. I just don't know,' Ross said slowly. 'They seem too young to be settling down for a lifetime. Neither of them have any money, but they have plenty of ideas for modernising the cottage – as long as I'm paying,' Ross said drily.

'A-ah, then you should give them a set sum – reasonable but not over generous. Then leave it to them. Insist they must get their priorities right. Don't be persuaded to hand out more if they run short. I see a lot of problems over money in my business. In my opinion, a man is better off without a wife than having one who can't budget her money.'

'Mmm, that's not a bad idea ... The sooner they realise I don't have a bottomless purse the better. Well, Ewan understands that anyway, but he's in love and he wants to give Gerda the world. Maybe I'll take your advice.'

'You may not be very popular if they overspend on the wrong things and end up sleeping on the floor because they can't afford a bed.' Jordon Niven grinned wickedly. 'But it is a lesson better learnt early. Perhaps you can see now why I have never taken a wife myself. Most women would find me much too hard, I fear.'

'Maybe you're wise,' Ross smiled.

'Maybe. Come back and see me in a week. I'll give you my advice for dealing with the Nether Rullion land and let you have my father's opinion – though we may not be too popular with your son, or your future daughter-in-law.'

# Chapter Six

Ross told Ewan and Gerda he had opened an account for them with the money they could use to modernise and furnish the cottage. Ewan was overwhelmed by his parents' generosity and support. Even Gerda seemed satisfied.

'Just remember that's all you're getting, in addition to the grant,' Ross warned sternly. 'If you don't budget for the essentials you must make do until you've earned enough to pay for the rest yourselves.'

'You've been more than generous, Dad,' Ewan said happily. 'Gerda will enjoy choosing the furniture and curtains and things, won't you, sweetheart?'

'I shall, but I've no intention of scrubbing out after the filthy workmen.' She looked defiantly at Rachel. 'You'll have to get someone else as your slave.'

'Well, that's between you two now. Paying someone to do your work will all be part of your budget. It's up to you how you spend it,' Ross said. Silently he thanked Jordon Niven for that bit of advice. Gerda had made it clear already that she had no intention of helping with anything to do with the farm, not even the poultry. She called the hens 'feathery fleabags'.

She would be leaving the school in Ayrshire at the end of the summer term, and she had talked of giving up her teaching career altogether. Ewan had persuaded her to apply for the vacancies at two village schools near Nether

Rullion so that she could complete her training. She had seemed surprised when she was successful in gaining one of the posts, but Ross had the impression she was not thrilled at the prospect. He suspected Ewan would not find his beautiful bride the easiest of people to share his life. If only he could have been persuaded to wait until he had more experience of life. But did the young ever listen to advice? Had he? He shook his head. His heart was heavy. He sensed Rachel's foreboding too, but they had offered their opinion and they could not run their children's lives. Ewan was a man now – young and not worldly wise perhaps – but old enough to make his own decisions.

'We wondered whether you would like one of those new washing machines as a wedding gift from us?' Rachel suggested.

'One that does everything?' Gerda asked, her pale eyes gleaming.

'I think they do,' Rachel said uncertainly. 'Fiona says you put the clothes in, and washing powder, then you switch it on and leave it. You don't need to rinse the clothes or put them through the ringer as I do. Fiona is thinking of getting one herself. Her twin tub keeps breaking down. You just hang them out on the line to dry when the machine stops, or so she says.'

'Doesn't it dry them as well?' Gerda frowned. 'I thought that's what automatic meant. After all, if I'm working at school all day I shan't have time to mess about with Ewan's dirty farm clothes.'

'All day?' Ross teased with a chuckle. 'We've done half a day's work in the milking parlour before you start at your school, lassie.'

Gerda scowled. She was never quite sure when Mr Maxwell was teasing and when he was criticising her.

'Your father has been extremely generous, Gerda.' Rachel smoothed away the tension. 'You will be able to buy other things which will make everyday work easier.'

'You know how much my father is – is giving us?' Gerda's blue eyes widened in surprise and swivelled accusingly to Ewan. But she had not told Ewan the exact amount. She had no intention of telling him. She had her own plans for that money. After all, it was supposed to be *her* wedding, she thought defiantly. Her father must have told Mrs Maxwell in one of the letters they exchanged. She coloured hotly, wondering what else he had said.

She had never mentioned the furious quarrel with her father, not even to Ewan. Apparently he had been saving up for years to give her a traditional wedding with all the trappings her heart desired. It was to be his final gift to her and she knew he really meant final this time. She shivered inwardly as she recalled their heated exchange.

How often she had dreamed of herself sailing down the aisle in a beautiful gown and veil with a church crowded with admirers, but she had certainly never envisaged her father's friends and neighbours being a part of that crowd. She had been dismayed when he insisted Jim and Mary O' Docherty, Fran Bristow and her father, and Willie and May McBurnie and their brood must be invited, and that was only some of them from the Avenue where she had been brought up.

'They're common! I'm not having them at my wedding!'

Gerda had been unprepared for the anger which had darkened her father's brow, the purple colour which had suffused his thin face, then drained away to leave him ghostly pale. She had never seen him like that before.

'They are my friends – and yours,' he said very quietly, very distinctly.

'They're loud, and when they're drunk they're – they're just slobs and ...'

'And they have hearts of gold. Where do you think I'd have been all these years after your mother cleared out, leaving me nothing but a pile of debts and a four-year-old bairn?' He almost snarled in his contempt. Gerda was shocked by the change in the mild little man she had always known. He even seemed taller as he drew himself up. 'Well? Who looked after you when I went to work? It was May McBurnie. She's been more of a mother to you than your own mother ever was – even when she was here. Who did the washing for us and cleaned the house? Have you forgotten how Mary slaved after you, and the tantrums you threw when you didn't have a clean white blouse every day and you wouldn't wash or iron a single thing for yourself, even when you were old enough? Well? Have you really forgotten our real friends? Where d'you think I'd be while you're away at college, spending every penny I can earn on your clothes and your pleasures? Who would I have talked to every evening without Jim and Willie and the rest o' my friends?'

'They may be your friends, but they're certainly not mine!' Gerda snapped. 'And it is my wedding. *Mine*, Father!'

'Oh, aye, and who's to pay for it?'

'You, of course. It's your duty as my father ...'

'Duty? You know nothing about duty! Or loyalty.' He almost spat the words at her. 'Anyway, I've often wondered whether I am your father, or whether I'm the silly bugger who was landed with you. Your mother played the field, but I never knew what a whore she was until a few years ago.'

'You shouldn't speak ill of the dead! You can't mean that ...'

'Can't I? I've searched for a bit of me in you often, even a resemblance to my mother, or my father, or even our Ginny – God rest her soul. I've seen nothing in you to remind me o' any o' them. You're your mother's bairn all right – her looks, aye, but ye've inherited her discontented nature too, now you're a grown woman. Only God knows who sired ye.'

Gerda sat down heavily. She was stunned by his outburst. This was the man she had thought adored her – the man she had twisted around her little finger all her life.

'So,' he said more calmly, 'Who are you going to invite to this grand wedding o' yours? We've no close relations left since your Aunt Ginny died. Where are all your fine friends? I've never met any o' them …'

Gerda opened her mouth to answer. But who were her friends? She hadn't kept in touch with any of the girls she'd known at school. Those she had known at college were just fellow students. Lucy had befriended her, but in a rare flash of honesty Gerda admitted she had only used Lucy to capture Ewan. Slowly she closed her mouth. Who *would* she invite to her wedding to fill the church, and *which* church? Neither she nor her father attended church. Tears welled into her blue eyes. John Allan turned away. He had never been able to resist her tears, but this time he could not – would not – deny his own friends. That would be like Peter denying Jesus Christ before the cock crowed.

In the end he had relented, but only so far. There would be no wedding without his friends and neighbours. If Ewan agreed to a civil ceremony he would give them the money he had saved to pay for her wedding. It would help to furnish their new home. Gerda had stared at him as her dreams melted away. When John Allan admitted he'd saved a thousand pounds for her wedding day she was astonished. So he really had planned to give her a grand send-off. For the first time genuine tears filled Gerda's eyes, but she was the one who turned aside. They were tears of self-pity.

Ewan had been shocked at the idea of a wedding which was not in church. In the end it was Rachel who had found a compromise after an exchange of letters with John Allan. Gerda's father agreed to come down to Nether Rullion for a night. The wedding ceremony would be held in the Lochandee Kirk which Ewan had attended all his life. Their parents would be the only people present, except for Ewan's friend Gus, who had agreed to be best man, and his witness. Reluctantly Gerda had asked Lucy to be her witness, and even more reluctantly Lucy had agreed. In her heart she knew she was only doing it for Ewan. Twice they had quarrelled when she had tried to persuade him not to rush into marriage with Gerda, and they had never had a serious quarrel in their lives before.

After the wedding they were to have lunch in a hotel near Lockerbie, for which John Allan insisted on paying.

Bridie was surprised and saddened that Ewan was not to be married with all his family and friends around him, whether in Glasgow or Lochandee, and the twins were bitterly disappointed they could not be bridesmaids.

'Conan and Fiona had a quiet wedding and they are supremely happy,' Rachel reminded her. 'Apparently Gerda doesn't have many relations and her father feels they'll probably make better use of the money putting it towards their home. Neither of them has worked long enough to have much in the way of savings.'

After her conversation with John Allan during his first visit she guessed this was only part of the truth, but she liked Gerda's father so she had not asked questions. 'He may be right, you know, Bridie. All the pomp and ceremony in the world will not guarantee a lifetime of happiness.'

Ewan's thoughts were preoccupied with the cows he was getting ready for the Dumfries Show and, as it drew nearer, he was relieved Gerda was not planning a big wedding. Her demands on his time seemed endless as it was, and there was so much to do at Nether Rullion in the summer, even without preparations for the show. He had agreed to most of her plans, but he had insisted the wedding must not be arranged until after the show. He had great hopes of winning at least one class this year. The rivalry between himself and Bridie was friendly but Ewan longed to prove himself as a first-class stockman and he was determined to have his cows in superb condition. Each evening, after milking was finished, he and Peter haltered them and walked them round and round the yard to train them in readiness for the show ring. It took a lot of time and patience.

Gerda grew more and more exasperated with this evening ritual.

'It'll only be for another week,' Ewan said, but she would not be placated, and absolutely refused to do any of the cleaning at the cottage. Instead, she had asked Billy Smith's mother to do it. As she had always done when she felt resentful or neglected she went on shopping sprees, oblivious of the fact that their budget was dwindling rapidly and the builder and the plumber still had to be paid. They had worked extremely hard to please her and to get the cottage finished in time for the wedding.

Ewan was dismayed and angry when he realised how much money had been drawn from the account for the cottage renovations.

'You'll have to stop buying things until we have paid the tradesmen,' he insisted.

'We have to have carpets and a bedroom suite,' she said sullenly.

'We'll manage without a carpet in the bedroom if we can't afford one,' Ewan said. 'And we'll leave the front room empty for now. Why did you buy all those mirrors and ornaments, Gerda? And those carvings you asked the joiner to make for the built-in cupboards.' He looked around the hall and up the narrow staircase in exasperation. 'I can't see where the money has gone.'

'Oh, don't worry so much!' Gerda said impatiently. There was no way she could tell him she had spent 42 guineas on a radiogram if he was going to be like this. 'I've chosen the carpet for the sitting room. We need a good one for our best room so I've bought a lovely thick Axminster. You'll love it when you see it. The three-piece suite was a bargain at £71, 19 and six.' Ewan opened his mouth to protest but she snapped accusingly, 'You were too busy to come with me last weekend so it's your fault if we've overspent.'

'Gerda, you'll have to cancel them. You must have realised we don't even have enough left to pay the tradesmen.'

'A-ah, but you don't know how these things work, Ewan. We can get them now, but we don't have to pay everything immediately. There was this lovely salesman in Simmons. A handsome, dark-haired young man ...' She looked archly at Ewan but he was frowning and only half-listening. She raised her voice angrily. 'He has arranged everything specially for me. I've paid a deposit on the big items of furniture and the carpets. It's only two shillings in the pound. Then we pay the rest over two or three years ...'

'You've what!' Ewan stared at her in disbelief, but he could see she was deadly serious. 'We don't do that sort of thing, Gerda! You'll have to cancel them. We don't buy things until we can pay for them. You'll end up paying twice as much as ...'

'Of course you don't!' Gerda snapped. 'I'm not stupid. It's only a shilling in the pound.'

'That's five per cent. You're paying more than the goods are worth! Don't you see ...?'

'For goodness sake, Ewan that's not much to ask!'

'It's £20 extra if you spend £100. How much did you spend, Gerda?' Ewan looked at her, saw her guilty flush and his heart sank. 'Well,' he sighed heavily. 'We don't work that way at Nether Rullion, and at a guess I'd say your father doesn't buy things until he can pay for them. You'll just have to use his money to pay Simmons' account. We'll try to save and put it back as a nest egg for you, as I expect he intended.'

'Indeed I shall not. I've used that money to buy a dress for the wedding and some clothes for our honeymoon.'

'What honeymoon?'

'A-ah, that's a surprise.' She fluttered her eyelashes and edged closer. 'Very romantic, though you're the one who should be planning romantic surprises for our honeymoon.'

'And how do you know I haven't?'

'You haven't, have you?' Gerda asked, her eyes widening.

'I'd planned to have a few days on our own, touring down south. Dad says I can borrow the car.'

'Oh, that's all right, then. Nothing that can't be changed. We're going to Paris, lover boy.' Her voice deepened huskily and she trailed her fingers down his cheek, down his neck, and down inside his shirt, pressing her body along the length of his until she felt him respond as she had known he would. It was a heady sensation to discover she had such power over men. As a child, tears had always worked with her father, but the power she was discovering as a woman was far more exciting. She would soon wean Ewan away from the old ways of Nether Rullion and his parents.

'Your father must be sitting on pots of money!' she said softly against his cheek, her lips moving tantalisingly close to his. 'You'll have to tell him we need a bit more.'

'No!' He jerked his head back, looking down into her lovely face. She bewitched him. 'Father has been more than generous to us already. We must cut back. Farmers don't have money to throw away on fripperies, even with the guaranteed prices and the marketing boards. We still ...'

'Who do you think you're kidding?!' Gerda scoffed. 'Don't take me for a fool, Ewan. I can read, you know. I read in one of your farming papers – *Scottish Farmer*, I think it was – it said an Aberdeen Angus bull had sold for 60,000 guineas! One bloody bull. You've got lots of bulls at Nether Rullion so ...'

'Oh, Gerda!' Ewan half-laughed, half-groaned in despair. 'That was a pedigree Aberdeen Angus from a famous herd, with excellent breeding. Even so, I can't see how he was worth all that myself, but ours are nothing like that kind of value.'

'Oh, don't give me that, Ewan. I don't believe it. Isn't that why you're spending all this time preparing your cows for Dumfries Show? Isn't that why you're so desperate to beat Bridie so that everyone will want to buy them?'

'We-ell, it helps a bit if you win ...'

'There we are then. You'll just have to sell a bull, or two.' She reached up and kissed him full on the mouth, a lingering, passionate kiss as she twined her arms around his neck. She didn't want any arguments, at least not any which prevented her getting her own way.

Even to herself, Gerda would never admit she was jealous of Lucy. It was Lucy's close friendship with Ewan which had first drawn her attention to him, and made her determined to win him away from Lucy. She hadn't believed the two really were only friends and, even now, she sometimes wondered when she saw them together. She knew Lucy was determined to complete her two years in teaching and gain her parchment before she married Don Greig and it pleased her to learn they were only planning a small wedding for members of their respective families too. She couldn't have borne it if Lucy was going to have a big affair. In her heart, Gerda still yearned for a fairytale wedding, with lots of admiring people and herself as the beautiful bride.

She was determined on one thing: her own house would be a palace compared with the old barn of a farmhouse where Lucy and Don Greig would have to live. Don was staying there by himself because the landlord had insisted the tenancy depended on the place being occupied. The previous tenants had been elderly, old-fashioned and reluctant to have changes. Consequently, the house did not even have piped water, electricity or a water closet. Gerda had overheard Mrs Maxwell telling Bridie that the landlord's promised improvements consisted of little more than a hot water system in the house and installing a bathroom. The news filled Gerda with smug satisfaction. Her little cottage would be far superior to anything Lucy would have, if Don had to make any other improvements himself. His father had refused to spend money on the house and had insisted on controlling everything as one business, along with the Greigs' Home Farm. He was sending 20 cows for Don to milk, some sheep and one of his tractors, but Don would get a wage instead of sharing the profits.

Mrs Greig had insisted on buying paint and wallpaper to make the place more habitable for Don, but it was Lucy and Chris who spent most of their weekends scrubbing and painting. Gerda, gazing around her own newly decorated home, with the expensive flock wallpaper in the small dining room and the heavily embossed paper in the sitting room, gave a smirk of satisfaction. She had lots of ideas which would make Lucy's home look like a slum in comparison.

The day of Dumfries Show arrived. Ewan was up at the crack of dawn to get the milking finished and set off to the show with the five animals he had selected for various classes. He and Ross had disagreed on his choice of two of the animals, but in the end his father had accepted that it should be Ewan's decision now that he was a partner, and because he had worked so hard to prepare the animals. Gerda simply couldn't believe Ewan was serious when he told her they would be shampooed from the tips of their tails to the end of their noses on the day of the show.

'Well, we do trim their hair first,' he said seriously. 'And they'll probably need to be washed again when they arrive at the show. After that, someone needs to stand guard and wipe their bottoms if they make a mess, as well as keep polishing up their horns, if they have any, and brushing their hair to keep them smart.'

'You're pulling my leg!' Gerda said accusingly.

'I wish I was!' Ewan grinned wickedly. 'But no, I'm serious, Gerda. It's a lot of work presenting cattle at their very best, honestly. I'm hoping you'll come to the show a little later. Mother has packed a huge basket of sandwiches, scones and flasks of coffee or tea. If you come to the cattle lines you'll see us all there. And if we win plenty of prizes you could lead one of the cows around the main ring for the parade, if you like.'

'Me? Lead one of those huge, smelly beasts! I hope you're joking, Ewan Maxwell ...'

'I wasn't actually.' Ewan frowned and hid his disappointment. He thought Gerda would have enjoyed parading a prize animal around the ring where everyone could admire her, as well as the animal he hoped she would be leading. 'Even the twins can lead a cow around the ring,' he told her. 'All Bridie's family help on show days, and Max is getting as keen as Bridie. I hope we can beat them or the young wretch will never let me hear the end of it.'

'I don't understand what all the fuss is about.' Gerda pouted. 'I hope you haven't forgotten we're supposed to be getting married in less than a week?'

'As though I would forget that!' Ewan chuckled. 'It's the most important day of my life ... we-ell after today!' His eyes twinkled and he ducked his head as Gerda swiped out at him. 'You will come to the show, Gerda, won't you? I want to show you off too.'

'But I thought we were going to the show dance at

night?'

'So we are, but it doesn't take you all day getting ready. Besides I'd like you to understand what it means to me, showing the Nether Rullion cattle. I'm really proud of them.'

# Chapter Seven

Ewan's pride and joy were boundless when his favourite cow won the overall dairy-breed championship, beating one of the Lochandee Ayrshires into reserve. Bridie was genuine in her congratulations and hugged him warmly.

'You've done well, little brother,' she teased, then more seriously, 'I thought you'd be showing the heifer out of the Star family. Is she out of condition?'

'No-o.' Ewan grimaced ruefully. 'Dad preferred her. We were third with the Jenny heifer, so I expect he'll say we would have won that class too if I'd listened to him. He could be right, I suppose, but we've had a good day.'

'You certainly have ...'

'Can't you two talk about anything else but cows?' Gerda interrupted, tottering to Ewan's side and clinging to his arm.

'You'll get used to it, Gerda.' Bridie laughed. 'And at least you'll have two silver cups to show for all Ewan's effort. They'll look lovely in your new house. I'm quite envious.'

'But you have to keep cleaning them with that awful polish,' chirped Alicia.

'It makes your hands all dry and nasty,' Margaret nodded.

'You two are just jealous,' Ewan teased, aiming a playful fist at them. They grinned back at him, nodding vigorous agreement.

'We'll beat you next year though, Uncle Ewan,' Max threatened with an irrepressible grin. 'Hey, did you see Peter has won a cup in the crafts classes with one of his marquetry pictures?' he asked. 'It's a ship in all different woods. It's great! I heard a man saying it was really good and he wondered whether he could commission one.'

'What's commission mean, Dad?' Margaret asked.

'The man would like Peter to make one specially for him,' Nick told her. 'I just had time for a quick look at the pictures and the walking sticks, but I thought Peter's was outstanding.'

'I didn't have time to go round,' Bridie said regretfully. 'Did you enjoy the craft tent, Gerda?' she asked, trying to include her and banish the impatient frown from her lovely face.

'I didn't look.'

'Oh. I thought you might have enjoyed that sort of thing.'

'I prefer the stalls where you can buy. What's the use of goggling at other folks' stuff? I bought this. Look.' She held out a brown leather handbag, beautifully embossed and hand sewn. Bridie's eyebrows rose.

'It's lovely,' she murmured, and wondered how Gerda could afford such an expensive accessory when there must be lots of things they needed for their new home. 'I hope you're both coming back to Lochandee tonight for supper? Mother and Father are coming with Conan and Fiona. I think Lucy and Don will be there too, but he has to get back to Ayrshire tonight.'

'All right,' Ewan nodded eagerly. 'It will be good to see Lucy and have a chat with Don ...'

'We can't,' Gerda intervened. 'We're going to the show dance. You promised, Ewan.'

'That doesn't get going until about ten o'clock unless times have changed since I was young,' Nick chuckled. 'Plenty of time to join us for a meal before you go.

83

Anyway Bridie has some wedding gifts for you, haven't you?'

'Yes.' Bridie nodded. 'Do come ...'

'No!' Gerda stared challengingly at Ewan. 'I've suffered the talk and preparations for your bloody show for weeks. I've had enough. We'll go back to Nether Rullion and get ready for the dance.'

Bridie looked down at the crestfallen faces of her children. They loved family gatherings and above all they loved Ewan. He and Lucy had so often teased and played with them. She looked up at her brother and saw the disappointment in his eyes too.

'We'll come another time,' he smiled ruefully.

Everything about Gerda and Ewan's wedding was expensive, from the bride's cream lace dress and veiled hat to the bouquet, which she had insisted upon, even though the wedding was not the traditional grand affair. She had made an appointment for studio photographs and the lunch had so many courses Rachel could not even nibble at the last three. She hid her doubts and concentrated on Ewan's happy expression. She was glad Ross had been so understanding about the honeymoon in Paris.

'I hadn't intended to leave you and Peter for more than four days, Dad,' Ewan had explained, 'but Gerda arranged a surprise honeymoon in Paris. It would mean being away ten days if we go ...?'

'Oh.' Then after the faintest hesitation Ross nodded. 'You must go if it's all arranged. Aye,' he sighed. 'You only get married once. Things are different now to what they were in our day, but there's no doubt you'll have to settle down to plenty of hard work when you get back.'

'You're sure you can manage?'

'We managed well enough until you left college, laddie!'

'Yes, but that was before the fire and you were fitter then.'

'Fitter? I'm like a new man after all those weeks of sitting around the house,' Ross growled, but they all knew this was not true. 'Peter and I will manage fine. The hay is all in and the first cut of silage is in the pit. We'll start mowing the second cut ready for you coming back if the weather is good. That should just be about the right stage.'

'All right.' Ewan grinned in relief and gave his father a friendly thump. Rachel often watched the two of them discussing the farm, the crops, the breeding of the cattle. It was their life and they loved it. She was thankful now that Ewan had been born in their later years. It had been a shock at the time to find she was expecting another baby when Conan was already old enough to fight for his country – old enough too to sire a child of his own, she recalled wryly, though none of them had realised it then.

So, they waved Ewan and Gerda away with goodwill, and John Allan set off back to Glasgow immediately afterwards. Suddenly the day seemed flat.

'Your turn next, lassie,' Ross said, turning to Lucy.

'Mmm, not for a year though. It seems ages away.'

'It will not be long in passing,' Rachel comforted. 'Beth and Harry would have been proud that you have done so well and waited until you have finished your teacher training, Lucy. No one can take that away from you, lassie, and things are changing now, even for farmers.'

'Aye, they buy fancy washing machines and vacuum cleaners, then they spend half the week curling at the ice rink,' Ross nodded, tongue-in-cheek. 'At least you'll bring in some money if you're teaching children.'

Lucy laughed. 'I suspect Don's father hopes I'll bring in some money *and* be able to help Don milk the cows as well. That might be possible in the summer holidays, but during term time we have a lot of preparations to do for lessons.'

'I'm sure Don will understand that,' Rachel said.

'Oh, he does. And he knows I love the children.'

'Aye,' Gus chipped in. 'He was real jealous of me being best man today,' he grinned. 'He needn't worry though, I like my freedom. I don't envy Ewan being tied down with a wife. I can spend enough money myself without needing the help of someone like Gerda.' He laughed but Rachel had an uneasy feeling there was criticism beneath his banter.

'Ewan was saying you plan to go abroad?' she remarked.

'Yes. I'm bound for Canada for a year. I leave in a fortnight. Well, Lucy, I'm ready to set off home now. Do you want a lift back to Ayrshire and that jealous swain of yours?'

'Did anyone ever tell you you're mad as a hatter, Gus?' Lucy laughed. 'But yes, I would like a lift back, since you brought me down here.'

Ewan enjoyed the experience of visiting Paris, but he was eager to get home when they landed at Dover. He was astonished when Gerda seriously expected they would take several days touring around on the way back to Scotland.

'We have to get back. I said we'd be home tonight,' he insisted. 'Father and Peter will have the grass cut ready to start making silage tomorrow. Anyway we have the car. I expect they'll be needing it.'

'I don't see why. Your mother does all her shopping from the vans. I never knew there were so many butchers, bakers and grocers. She even has a fish man to bring her fresh fish.'

'Well, that's what they do for a living. It's their business. They are pleased to have new customers. I expect they'll call on us once they know we are settled in at the cottage.'

'They needn't bother! I shall go to Dumfries and choose my own shopping. I do think you ought to tell your father we need another car now you are married, Ewan.'

'Oh, I don't think we can afford two cars,' Ewan said in alarm. He was beginning to feel Gerda's demands were never-ending. He frowned as he remembered her father's advice just before they said goodbye. He had been deadly serious. Ewan glanced at Gerda in the seat beside him. Her full red mouth had a sulky droop and there was a tiny frown between her eyes.

'Cheer up, sweetheart,' he urged, patting her knee gently. 'It'll be good to get home and have some peace in our own wee house.'

'Will it?' she asked plaintively. 'Maybe for you it will. I can't see what difference it will make if we just have another night, or two, on the way up north.'

'No, Gerda.' Ewan's tone was firm. 'I promised to be back to work by tomorrow. That's the end of it.' Gerda's scowl grew and her mouth set in a thin line. She was beginning to realise Ewan was not as easily swayed as she had thought, nor as her father had been. Ewan had genuinely enjoyed Paris, particularly the gardens and visiting the Louvre. He would have stood for hours watching the pavement artists or watching the world go by from the outdoor cafés. Gerda was surprised to find Ewan so interested in art and history, and she had grown bored with sightseeing. She wanted to be part of the nightlife of Paris. She had enjoyed dining late in the evening, but Ewan had grumbled about being hungry and even a cup of coffee was expensive. But it was not just the sights of Paris which had caused minor disagreements; Gerda knew their honeymoon had not been the greatest success. She was Ewan's wife now and he didn't expect to have to buy her favours each time he wanted to make love to her. Nevertheless she kept up a morose silence as they drove mile after mile.

Ewan seemed content to concentrate on his driving, at least until they had left the busy roads behind. Eventually they stopped for an early lunch and he smiled and talked pleasantly. Gerda realised she could either sulk or return to normal but, whatever she did, Ewan was not going to change his mind, nor was he going to make any effort to humour her. She looked at his profile.

'You're just like your father,' she muttered involuntarily. Ewan looked down at her, his dark brows arched in question. 'Oh, never mind,' she said impatiently. 'Let's eat. I'm famished.'

'Suits me,' Ewan smiled. 'That was the general idea. Why did you say I was like my father just now?'

'Stubborn. I can just imagine him being the same.'

'It's not being stubborn, Gerda. It's keeping my word. I said I'd be back and I shall. My father would never let anyone down if he could help it. That's why so many of the neighbours come to him when they need help or advice. I hope I'm as well respected when I'm his age.'

'But you still argue with him and disagree.'

'We don't argue,' he laughed. 'We discuss things and sometimes we have a different opinion. I suppose it's because I'm a different generation.'


Ross was pleased to see Ewan back. He hadn't realised how much work and responsibility his son had taken over in the year since he left college. Worse he had been dismayed to find how much less fit he was himself after all those weeks without hard physical work, or how breathless the dust made him when shaking out straw to bed the calves – such a simple task, yet it had left him wheezing for breath and his heart thumping.

Peter had already mown the grass ready for silage and it was wilting in readiness for gathering into the pit.

'I'm glad you're home, Ewan,' Ross greeted him.

'We're all ready and needing you to drive the silage chopper. Even young Billy is eager to get on while the weather holds.'

Ross did not enjoy silage making himself. He was getting too old for changes and modern methods with new – and ever more complicated – machinery.

'Nick has promised to come over tomorrow and lend a hand on the buck rake,' he told Ewan, 'but he'd like us to send Peter over to Lochandee to give them a help when they start the harvest.'

'That's fair enough.' Ewan nodded and began to ask questions about the cows and various other matters.

'For goodness sake,' Gerda snapped in exasperation. 'We've only been away five minutes. Nothing much can have changed in such a short time. Let's go home. You've kept saying that's what you wanted.'

'I *am* home. The farm is home. You go down to the house, sweetheart. I'll not be long. You still have some wedding presents to open. I want to see Peter's gift so that I can thank him properly when I see him.'

'Oh that! You went on enough about it before we went away. It won't be anything much. He's just a labourer ...'

Ross frowned and looked into Gerda's pale blue eyes. He took a deep breath, but before he could say anything Ewan intervened, his own mouth tighter than usual.

'Whatever it is, Peter has given it to us – probably chosen with great care too, from what I know of him. We shall both thank him for it. I'm sure he'd appreciate a short letter from you, just like everyone else.'

Gerda scowled but didn't reply as she flounced out of the house.

'I think Gerda's a bit tired after the long journey,' he said, proffering a feeble excuse on her behalf.

'Mmm ... well, I think she's in for a surprise. I've seen Peter's gift and it's beautiful – quite unique, in fact. I'd be proud to own it.'

'That's praise indeed!' Ewan said in surprise. 'I'll go and see for myself as soon as you've given me all the news.'

When Ewan arrived at his new home an hour later, Gerda hadn't opened Peter's neatly wrapped parcel, or the two small parcels which lay beside it on the new settee. Instead Gerda had opened one of the suitcases and was trying on a pair of new red shoes with ridiculously high heels. She also had on a very short, very straight skirt. It was obviously new too, but he hadn't been round the Paris shops with her. He shook his head. She'd already bought a pile of new clothes for their holiday. Gerda's father was right; she just couldn't resist buying more.

'I'll open Peter's parcel, shall I?' he offered.

'You're more interested in Peter's bloody present than you are in me! How d'you like my new outfit?' She twirled around, swaying this way and that between him and a long mirror at the end of the hall.

'You look fine. Gerda, I do wish you wouldn't swear …'

'Swear? Good God, Ewan, that's not swearing. You wait until I really get started. And at the rate you're going that'll not be long!' She strode through the door and snatched Peter's parcel out of his hands and flung it back onto the settee. She didn't throw quite far enough and it slid onto the floor. Ewan's mouth tightened and he bent to pick it up and carried it into the kitchen to open it at the table.

He stood and stared at the picture in silence for several minutes. He couldn't believe his eyes. Gerda strutted in to see what had caught his attention.

'Well!' she sneered. 'You'll see what I mean now. Some wedding gift your fine Peter has bought us. It's homemade – a bloody picture made with bits of wood.' She gave a hollow laugh. 'Well, if you think that's going to hang in my house you can think again. You can stuff it in the rubbish bin.'

'Gerda!' Ewan was horrified. Before she had joined him, he had felt tears prick the back of his eyes. He could visualise the hours and hours Peter must have worked painstakingly cutting out each tiny shape and contour, even designing the picture himself, for no one else could have captured Nether Rullion like that. 'See the ripples in the sky,' he said softly, 'the darker shape of the hill in the distance, the golden sheen of a harvest field,' his finger reverently traced the beautifully inlaid pieces. 'And the farmhouse, the exact outline, and the steading ... It must have taken for ever just drawing it all out – and then to find so many different woods, so many grains and shades,' he breathed incredulously.

'For goodness sake!' Gerda snapped. 'It's rubbish. He's made it himself, I tell you. It's certainly not hanging in my house ...' Ewan turned to stare at her. He felt cold fury bubbling up inside him. He wanted to shake Gerda. He wanted to knock some sense into her silly little girl head. He forced himself to breathe in deeply, several times. Stupidly, Gerda took his silence for acquiescence. She reached for the picture.

'I'll put it in the bin. He'll never know ...'

'You're a heartless snob!' Ewan shouted, and his fingers tightened on the frame of the beautifully polished picture. 'You haven't even looked at it properly. Have you any idea of the hours Peter must have spent – no, not hours, months and months! It's a work of loving care, and he did it specially for us. My father is right – it's unique.'

'I'm not a snob! I'm not having that bloody monstrosity in my house. And ...'

'This picture will leave this house only over my dead body.' Ewan's face was white. His eyes were narrowed slits, and they gleamed more green than blue in his anger. Gerda stared at him.

'D-don't look at me like that! You frighten me.

Ewan …' She began to whimper and her eyes filled with tears. Ewan ignored them. He looked at his wife and wondered how she could look so beautiful and yet have no soul. 'You have no soul,' he said aloud. 'I don't understand how anyone could fail to appreciate the skill and love that Peter has put into that picture. We'll hang it on the long wall in the sitting room. You wait and see, all your friends will admire it.' Ewan was calmer now, his voice even again, but Gerda recognised the thread of steel in it. She wouldn't dare defy him, at least not yet. This was their first real quarrel. He could hang his picture, but she would see to it that he paid for his outburst.

It was November when news of President Kennedy's assassination rocked the world. It was announced on radios and televisions of every nation. Rachel was busy ironing when the radio programme was interrupted to make the announcement. The shock upset her more than she would have believed. He'd been so young and handsome, so vital and full of energy, with a lovely wife and young family – everything to live for … He was a leader, strong and trustworthy. He hadn't given in under the pressure of the Cuban crisis. He'd stood his ground with confidence and the most powerful nation in the world behind him, trusting him to make the right decisions. Another war had been avoided. Who could possibly take his place? Rachel almost felt she had known him after seeing him so often on the television. She felt shattered and alarmed. She prayed fervently that the peace of the world would not be threatened now that he was gone. She thought of the words of the poet, Robert Burns:

Man's inhumanity to man

Makes countless thousands mourn!

How true. Rachel switched off the iron and went outside to find Ross, to share the news and seek his comfort, as she had always done when she was troubled.

# Chapter Eight

As Rachel had predicted, the months passed swiftly and it seemed no time before preparations were being made for Lucy's wedding to Don Greig.

'I can't believe Chris and I – and Gerda too, of course – will soon have been teaching for two years,' Lucy said, shaking her head in disbelief.

'You've lost weight, lassie,' Ross told her, eyeing her with affection. 'Have you been working too hard?'

'We've been pretty busy. I wanted to get most of the rooms made habitable,' Lucy admitted, 'and there's only Don in the house so he has to do his own cooking as well as the work outside. He has 50 cows milking now, and another 20 to calve before mid-September.' She smiled at Ross. 'Of course, it would be a lot easier if he had a lovely modern milking parlour like yours but there's no hope of that. Even the byres are a bit old-fashioned and inconvenient, but I think he'll be able to improve them in time. He does have a woman from one of the cottages who washes the milk cans and keeps the dairy clean, but she has a large family so that's all she can manage. It's all Don can pay for, or rather all his father considers necessary. Mrs Greig is sending a hen house and some of her pullets over as soon as we get settled after the wedding.'

'You'll have a little bit of money for the house then, lassie, if you have to give up the teaching,' Rachel said. 'I don't know what I'd do without the egg money.'

'That's what Don's mother intended,' Lucy said ruefully, 'but his father has other ideas. He says the hens will have to be fed so any money must be pooled for the good of the family. He keeps reminding us that he has another two sons to set up in farms. He runs everything as one business so all the income goes to the Home Farm and he pays all the bills from there. He gives Don an allowance, when he remembers, but it's little more than money for his food and clothes.' She frowned. 'I'm not meaning to criticise but even Mrs Greig thinks it's not enough. She says I'll just have to keep a bit of egg money back and say nothing. I'll hate having to be deceitful but I do feel sorry for Don. He works so hard and it is his brothers who benefit. There are two of them, as well as Mr Greig and a boy, but they only help Don when it's hay time or sheep shearing. None of them came to help with the turnip hoeing. They milk 70 cows, but that's as many as their byre will hold so they're sending all the heifers to Don, and Mr Greig has started dealing in dairy cattle. He goes to market two or three times a week. Of course they have a hundred ewes and Don only has 40.'

'Surely one of Don's brothers could lend a hand more often?' Ross asked. 'It's only a couple of miles between the two places, isn't it?'

'Two and a half to be exact.' Lucy grimaced. 'Don wouldn't like to think I was complaining, and I'm not really, except that I feel he works too hard.' She smiled wryly. 'Chris says her father has always been tight-fisted when it comes to parting with money. She says Jake and Willie take after him, but Don and herself take after their mother. I must say Mrs Greig does what she can to help Don.'

'I'm glad to hear that,' Rachel said, with some concern. What sort of life would Lucy have, she wondered?

'There's a boy who comes to Skeppiehill during the

holidays and at weekends. He wants to work on a farm when he leaves school. Don says he's a good help already, but Mr Greig refuses to give him anything for working. Mrs Greig gives Don a few shillings from her egg money every now and then, and sometimes a dozen eggs for the boy's mother, to encourage him to keep helping. His name is Richard Green. As a matter of fact, his elder brother Adam is a dairyman on a big dairy farm about ten miles away. It's not far from the school where Chris teaches and they've become very friendly. In fact, they're more than friends but Chris's father doesn't approve. He says Adam has no prospects.'

'Some of the good dairymen earn more money in a year than many farmers,' Ross commented. 'I expect Mr Greig thinks Chris should marry a farmer?'

'Yes, he does. Adam has ambitions to be a farmer himself, even if it is only a smallholding, but Mr Greig doesn't want to hear about his dreams. He doesn't know Adam already rents three small fields from a neighbouring farmer. He and Chris have bought four pedigree heifer calves between them. They plan to sell them as heifers, after they have had calves.'

'Good for them!' Ross whistled. 'They'll get another four calves to rear if they're lucky, then?'

'Yes, Adam's really keen on his stock. You'd like him, and so would Ewan. He studies the Friesian pedigrees and the sale catalogues and he knows all about the Nether Rullion and the Lochandee herds. Mrs Greig and Don know about Chris's plans, but she doesn't talk to her father about them any more. She feels a bit bitter because she can't even take Adam home. He's trying to buy a couple of dilapidated cottages with some outbuildings so they can house the calves in the winter and they plan to get a pig and some hens. If he can get the cottages at a reasonable price, he and Chris hope to get a grant to renovate them. I think they will get married eventually, but

Chris knows that wouldn't please her father at all, so no one mentions it.'

'All right,' Rachel smiled at Lucy. 'We'll not say a word out of place when we meet Mr Greig at the wedding, shall we, Ross? Are you listening?'

'I shall be Mr Tact himself,' Ross promised. 'Is your friend Christine bringing her boyfriend to the wedding, Lucy?'

'Yes, would you like to meet him?'

'I would indeed.'

'Shall I arrange to seat him at your table then? He would enjoy that and hearing about your herd. He'll not know many people except Chris.'

'Then we'll look after him,' Rachel promised.

'I – er – I haven't mentioned Don's father to Fiona or Conan – I mean, about him being a bit – er – mean …' Lucy said suddenly, and her cheeks flushed guiltily. 'I shouldn't have talked so much to anyone …'

'Don't look so worried, lassie.' Rachel laid a comforting arm around her slim shoulders. 'We'll not breathe a word and it does you good to confide sometimes. I'm sure things will work out for you both eventually.'

'Aye, and we can understand both sides,' Ross nodded. 'Sometimes I feel we keep Ewan on a tight rein – he gets £15 a week and that's a lot more than Peter and more than we've ever taken for ourselves.'

'Don would think he was rich if his father paid him half that every week!' Lucy said incredulously.

'Well, Ewan's a partner now and he'll have to learn to share the responsibilities and decisions before long, including doing the accounts …' Ross frowned. 'I'm just not sure he and Gerda are ready for that yet. The lassie seems to spend money like it's flowing past her door. Still,' he shrugged. 'I suppose she earns it herself so there's not much I can say. We bought a little van to have two vehicles between us, but she's not satisfied with that

96

arrangement. She's bought a brand-new car of her own. She didn't get it through Conan, or take Nick's advice either, so she must know what she's about.' He winked at Lucy. 'You teachers must earn even more than I thought, lassie. Now I'll need to go and do some work or Peter will be looking for me ...' As Ross walked away he didn't see Lucy's wide-eyed surprise. She knew Gerda was no better paid than she was herself, yet she certainly wouldn't have bought a car. She knew she was lucky Conan had given hers for her 21st birthday.

'Come and have a cup of tea, lassie,' Rachel said and ushered Lucy into the big cosy kitchen. 'Conan said he would be over this afternoon, about three, he thought.' She glanced at the old Wig Wag clock on the wall. 'He'll be here in time for tea. I'll set out some scones and a bit of gingerbread. They're still his favourites, I believe?'

'Yes, I'll have to ask you for some of your recipes,' Lucy smiled. 'Don loves home baking.'

'Ah, here's Conan now. You're just in time for tea, laddie, as I should have known you would be!'

'Of course,' Conan grinned. 'I wanted a word with Dad too. Will he be in for tea?'

'He'll be back soon when he sees your car.' Rachel frowned. 'He's trying not to eat so much baking. He thinks if he puts on weight it'll make him more breathless.'

'Weight? Dad?' Conan laughed. 'He's as lean and fit as he ever was ... isn't he?'

'Yes,' Rachel said seriously. 'But don't you see, he must feel short of breath or he wouldn't be thinking about it? Anything with dust aggravates his lungs since the fire. Ewan and Peter do their best to keep him away from those sort of jobs, but I expect he does things automatically because he's done them all his life.'

'Mmm, I see what you mean,' Conan nodded, 'and, knowing Dad, he wouldn't take kindly to being wrapped in cotton wool, or told he should keep away from his animals.'

'No,' Rachel agreed. 'I'm learning to accept that there may be some risk to his health, but he has to have some pleasure from life too, and farming has always been his joy as well as his work, especially the cows.'

Looking at the woman who was her grandmother, Lucy couldn't suppress a small shiver. She knew how deeply they loved each other, and how much they would each miss the other's companionship when the inevitable parting came, but they were relatively young and she prayed they would have many years together yet.

'Anyway,' Rachel said briskly changing the subject. 'You said you wanted to talk to Lucy about the wedding ...?'

'Yes, I do ...' Conan flushed. 'But I meant to lead into the subject tactfully.' For a moment both Lucy and Rachel saw the vulnerable uncertainty of a small boy with his hand caught in the sweetie jar, and both laughed aloud. This was not the Conan Maxwell, successful young businessman, they both knew.

'It sounds ominous,' Lucy chuckled. 'You'd better tell me now.'

'All right, but don't take offence or argue until you've heard me out?'

'Agreed,' Lucy promised solemnly, but her green eyes – so like his own, so like Rachel's – twinkled.

'Well, Fiona and I know how independent you like to be, Lucy, and we respect you for it. We also know you didn't want us to spend a small fortune on a big wedding for you and Don. We agreed to that, mainly because we believe it would send all the wrong messages to the miserable soul of your prospective father-in-law and ...'

'Wh-what did you say?' Lucy gasped.

'Sorry! Sorry,' Conan held up his hand. 'It's just the impression he gave us when we had a talk, but maybe he's just ... well ... careful. Anyway, we've arranged for a marquee to be erected in the small paddock at the bottom of the garden at Rullion Glen. Fiona has got it all organised with caterers and decorations, and heaters if the weather turns cold ...'

'Oh, but ...'

'Hush ...' Conan held up his hand to silence Lucy's protest. 'Fiona is really enjoying organising it. In fact, Lucy, I want you to know what a lot of pleasure you have brought to both of us. Fiona has no other family at all, as you know, and she thinks of you as more than her daughter – she regards you as a sister and friend. Whatever she does for you, I can assure you she probably gets more pleasure and satisfaction than you do. So don't hurt her by being too independent, or too proud to accept her generosity. She thinks this may be the last time we shall be able to do anything, once you have a husband. Anyway, now that the wedding is to be in a marquee it won't matter if you invite a few more guests than you intended. If Don's brothers want to bring their girlfriends, for instance, and the two cousins he often mentions. So you're happy with all that?'

'Well, yes. In that case, I'd like to invite Carol too. She was such a good friend to Mum when we were all at Lochandee. Wendy and Joanne, as well. Mum often said how she loved them when they came with Carol as young evacuees, but ...'

'But nothing. I'm glad you thought of them. Carol and your mother helped each other a lot during the war. Right, that's the reception then. Now, we know Don can't get away from the farm for more than a night, so Christine has an idea. Her boyfriend has agreed to take a few days of his own holidays and milk the cows for Don. We're just tagging on a few more days to his wedding day. It's probably the last holiday either of you will get for years. Fiona and I want you to make the most of it. I've booked you into a hotel in Jersey. You fly from Manchester. One

99

of our drivers will take you down to the airport, so it's all arranged.' Conan was talking quickly now, anxious not to let Lucy interrupt or have time to consider.

'B-but ... I don't know what to s-say,' Lucy gasped. Then suddenly she was in Conan's arms. 'Y-you've both done so m-much for me already,' she stammered, trying to brush away the tears.

'No more than you deserve, lassie,' Conan said huskily. Watching them, Rachel wished with all her heart that Conan and Fiona had been blessed with other children, but it was not God's will and at least they were supremely happy with each other.

'Er ... there's just one more thing, Lucy, but this is supposed to be a surprise. I'm giving you warning so that you don't refuse it. Fiona wants to buy you something special for a wedding present – something you would not buy yourself. I know you might think it's an extravagance but please ... please accept it. It's what she wants to do. It was her own idea.'

'But ...' Lucy looked puzzled. 'I already know. Fiona told me you're buying us one of those automatic washing machines and I can't tell you how much it will be appreciated ...'

'No, lassie.' He looked across at Rachel. 'Mum and Dad want to buy that for you – the same as they bought for Ewan and Gerda.'

'Oh!' Lucy turned open-mouthed to look at Rachel. 'That's such a big present ...'

'We wanted to make you and Ewan just the same, lassie, just as you've always been in our eyes.' Lucy knew they were talking about relationships and love as much as wedding presents and her chin trembled. Rachel simply opened her arms and hugged her. 'We wish you all the happiness in the world, Lucy.'

'Am I to hear what this special gift is then?' Lucy asked tremulously.

'No, that really is Fiona's surprise,' Conan grinned. 'All I ask is that you accept it and don't argue about it being too much. She would never buy anything she couldn't afford, but you know that, lassie.'

'Yes,' Lucy nodded, 'but I'm really intrigued now.'

'You know that Bridie and Nick and the children want to buy you a deep-freeze?' Rachel asked. 'Bridie thinks they're wonderful. She keeps trying to persuade me to get one too.'

'Everyone is being so generous ...'

'Ewan wanted to buy you a vacuum cleaner but Gerda refused. She said you probably wouldn't have any carpets to clean.'

'Well, she's right there,' Lucy smiled ruefully. 'We'll get some eventually. Meanwhile, Don and I have made a huge rag rug for the kitchen from everybody's scraps. I remembered how Mum, a-and H-Harry used to make them. I've made two rugs with wool ends for our bedroom. I got a huge bag from one of the woollen mills for three and sixpence and they look really nice in shades of pink and blue and green.'

'I'm planning to have one of those carpets which go from wall to wall for our sitting room, like Gerda has in all her rooms,' Rachel said suddenly. She caught Ross's look of surprise. He had heard no mention of such plans. She sent him a green-eyed warning and a small frown which he interpreted as "Keep quiet, I'll explain later". 'If you and Don wouldn't mind having a second-hand one, you're more than welcome to ours ...'

'Your rust carpet, with the lovely border?' Lucy said in surprise.

'Yes,' Rachel nodded quickly. 'I think one of those fitted from wall to wall would be warmer for our old bones; not so many draughts round the edges, you know? Of course, Don may not want my second-hand offerings ...'

'Oh, Don wouldn't turn his nose up at a gift, and I've always liked the warm rusty colour. Are you sure? We would have to pay …'

'Indeed you will not, lassie,' Ross intervened quickly. He understood what Rachel was about now. They all knew how fiercely independent Lucy was. He was all in favour of her getting the carpet. 'Just you ask Don if he'll cart it out of our way or we'll end up with an attic full of junk.'

The twins could scarcely contain their excitement as the wedding drew near. They were to be bridesmaids along with Chris and they had new dresses almost down to their ankles in a beautiful pale blue. Lucy was borrowing Bridie's wedding dress, but it had needed a few extra tucks since she had lost weight. In the end, Lucy had invited most of the girls who had been at college with her and they were all bringing their various partners.

'It'll be almost like a college reunion,' Chris said excitedly. 'What does Gerda say about the wedding growing bigger and bigger?'

'I have hardly seen either Gerda or Ewan,' Lucy confessed. 'But she'll know most of them, so I expect she'll enjoy seeing them again.'

'You don't really believe that, do you?' Chris scoffed. 'The only person Gerda enjoys seeing is her own reflection in the mirror – unless she's changed since she married Ewan, of course. I wonder if he's still as besotted with her?'

'I expect he is,' Lucy chuckled. 'It's barely a year since they were married.'

It was true, Gerda could still drive Ewan wild with desire when she set her mind to it. She had a slim figure with curves in all the right places and no one could deny that she was beautiful with her long silver blonde hair, her blue eyes and finely boned oval face. When she heard that most of the people she had known at college would be at the wedding her first reaction was one of jealousy that Lucy was to have a proper celebration.

'You'll be the belle of the ball in the dress you wore for our wedding,' Ewan told her. Gerda's pale eyes narrowed thoughtfully.

'Yes, I will ...' But it would not be in a dress she had already worn. She would have a brand-new outfit. She would go to Glasgow or Edinburgh. A new hat, gloves and handbag all to match she would have, as well as some new shoes. Maybe one of those really sexy Mary Quant fashions? Perhaps she should have her hair cut too ...

'Ewan, you should let your hair grow and have a style like the Beatles,' she said aloud.

'I'm not a teenage pop idol!' he laughed.

'Well, you could at least try to be a bit more modern.'

A few days later, Gerda was filled with resentment. She could barely wait for Ewan to come in from the hayfield, but when he did, he was hot and tired, ready for his evening meal and then bed. Gerda had not prepared a meal.

'I thought you'd have it in the hayfield with Peter,' she said sulkily.

'Oh, we had sandwiches at six o'clock but that's three hours ago and I'm ready for my dinner.'

'Well, you'll have to make do with bread and cheese then. That's all there is.'

'What did you get a freezer for if you've nothing in it?' Ewan asked irritably.

'Don't you snap at me. You didn't tell me your parents had given Lucy and Don Greig a carpet, as well as buying them a washing machine for a wedding present.'

'They didn't buy her a carpet. Lucy is just taking the carpet square that Mum had in her front room.'

'They didn't offer us a carpet! She's not even part of the family.'

'Of course she is ...' Ewan said wearily. 'Where's that

103

bread and cheese you were getting ...'

'Get your own! She's only adopted. Why should they give her a carpet and not us? You went on and on about the money I had spent and ...'

'Well, you did spend far too much! We're still paying most of my wages every month for the things you bought, and we'll be paying for them next year at this rate. Anyway, you wouldn't have accepted a carpet square from my mother even if she'd offered it to you.'

'You're dead right I wouldn't!'

'Well then? What are you going on about, Gerda? I'm tired and hungry. It's been a long day ...'

'It's the principle of the thing. But you've always stuck up for Lucy. You can't see past her. It's a wonder you didn't marry her yourself,' Gerda taunted.

Ewan frowned. Several times he had been on the point of telling Gerda that Conan was Lucy's real father and he was really her uncle, but something always held him back. In some way, he felt he had to protect Lucy from Gerda's spite, and his family too ... There ought not to be secrets like that between a man and his wife, but he knew instinctively Gerda would use such gossip at every opportunity. He wondered whether Lucy had confided in Don and Chris, and their parents.

Lucy had told Don about her true parentage. She felt there should be no secrets between them. As she had guessed, it made not the slightest difference and together they had told Chris and Mrs Greig one Sunday afternoon.

'Well, lassie, it's none of our business who your parents are,' Mrs Greig smiled, reassuringly. 'All I ask is that you make my laddie happy and I can see you do that already. I reckon he's a lucky man.'

'Mmm. I agree with that,' Chris said, 'but I don't think you should tell Dad that Conan Maxwell is Lucy's real father. You know how funny he is about some things, and he would ask all sorts of awkward questions.'

'Aye,' Mrs Greig frowned thoughtfully. 'Aye, well, maybe you're right, lassie. Maybe we'll just keep it between the four o' us, then.' No more was said about it until Chris and her mother had departed, then Don took Lucy in his arms and kissed her tenderly.

'You know how much I love you,' he said huskily. 'It wouldn't make any difference to me if the devil himself was your father. I doubt if he'd be any tighter than my old man,' he added with a rueful grin. 'As a matter of fact, I really like Conan and Fiona. They both seem more like an elder brother and sister than prospective parents-in-law. I had expected them to be a lot older the first time I met them at your 21st birthday party.'

'I couldn't have wished for a nicer couple if God had made them specially,' Lucy said with feeling, 'so I don't really mind who knows. It's just that we never talk about it in the family because it would have caused such a scandal locally.'

'It would still cause gossip if it happened now,' Don nodded, 'but I suppose everything was more strict during the '40s. Dad often grumbles about young folk having neither morals nor manners since the war, so Chris is probably right about not telling him.'

'Well, you know your own family best,' Lucy acknowledged. 'You know when I went to the hospital to collect Mrs Maxwell after the fire she introduced me to the nurse as their granddaughter.'

'Well, so you are, and would be if Conan was your adoptive father, in a manner of speaking anyway.'

'I know, but even since then there's been a difference ... just a subtle change, a firmer claim to kinship or something. I can't quite put my finger on it because they have both been kind to me all my life – both before and since they knew the truth. Whatever it is, it makes me feel warm and ... och, I don't know.' She hid her face against Don's broad shoulder. 'I expect you think

I'm crazy.'

'I think you're wonderful,' Don said huskily, stroking her chestnut hair with a gentle hand. 'And I don't blame Mr and Mrs Maxwell for being proud to claim you as their granddaughter.'

Lucy looked up into his face and smiled. 'You always reassure me.'

'I can hardly wait until the wedding and I know you're really my wife,' Don said and his arms tightened.

# Chapter Nine

It was a beautiful day in early July and Lucy looked almost ethereal as she moved gracefully down the aisle on Conan's arm followed by Chris and the twins, their dark curly heads lowered shyly as they clasped their posies of pink and white rosebuds. The little Lochandee church was full and the village people crowded outside, waiting to see the bride and guests as they entered and pass on their good wishes to the bride and groom when they appeared as man and wife. Most of them had known Lucy and her mother all their lives. Some of them even remembered her great-grandfather, old Mr Turner and his bicycle shop – the man who had taught Conan all about cogs and wheels, and greasy hands.

The good wishes were many and they were sincere. Lucy had already been overwhelmed by the generosity of these people when she arrived at Rullion Glen to find a room full of wedding gifts, large and small. Now she felt a lump in her throat at the warmth of their greetings and for a fleeting moment she wished with all her heart that her mother could have been here to see this day and all their friends. Her eyes were bright with love as she raised her face for Don's kiss on the steps of the church. The people cheered with delight. Gerda did not smile. In her heart, she knew she was jealous of Lucy's effortless popularity.

It brought her satisfaction to know she was the most fashionably dressed of all the women at the wedding. She had already seen some of the young men eyeing her appreciatively and the trendy short skirt showed off her shapely legs to perfection, with her new stiletto heels with their sling backs. Knowing how much the Maxwells loved music, she knew the wedding reception would not be complete without some sort of entertainment. Surely Fiona Maxwell would have organised a wooden floor for the marquee so that they could dance.

Fiona had not only organised a wooden floor but she had arranged for a small band as well. The young fruit trees and bushes in the Rullion Glen garden were adorned with coloured fairy lights. She was determined that the whole affair should be as perfect for Lucy and Don as she could make it. Lucy still didn't know what she had bought for their wedding present. It was to be a surprise when they returned from their honeymoon and, with Chris's co-operation, it would be delivered and waiting for them on their return to Skeppiehill Farm.

The catering firm was first class. Conan had spared no expense and the drinks flowed freely. He knew most of the members in his own family would enjoy the evening with or without the beer and spirits, but he and Nick had seen more of the outside world so had agreed that most of the younger men would enjoy free beer. What neither of them had anticipated was the amount of wine which Gerda and two of her companions imbibed. The young men flocked around her, seeking every opportunity to hold her close, whether the dance was a frenzied rock 'n' roll number or an old-fashioned waltz.

Soon after the bride and groom had departed, Bridie gathered up the tired twins and a reluctant Max.

'Och, young Max, we workers must go home to bed,' Chris told him, smilingly. 'Adam and I must leave now if we are to be up in time to milk Don's cows in the morning.'

'But Dad's not coming home yet ...'

'He's helping Uncle Conan serve the drinks and that's no place for youngsters like you, young man,' Bridie told him firmly.

Ross and Rachel, along with Mr and Mrs Greig retired to the relative quiet of Fiona's lounge for a friendly chat, leaving the younger guests to dance the night away.

Eventually the caterers departed, leaving Nick to take one more tray of drinks to a noisy group at the far end of the marquee. Ewan, leaning against a tree near the entrance to the marquee, reached out and lifted one of the glasses, drained it and reached for a second before Nick could pass on.

'Steady on, Ewan,' Nick frowned. 'You'll not know whether you're at the cow's head or its tail tomorrow morning. In fact ...' He drew up his arm and peered at his watch. 'It is morning! No wonder your mother and father, and Don's parents, have all left.'

'Pass me 'nother.' Ewan slurred and lurched toward the tray.

'I think you've had enough. It's that wife of yours who's keeping the party going. You'll have to get her home. Mind you, she's no more fit to drive than you are. If you wait until I've taken this tray of drinks to that noisy bunch I'll drive you home.'

'Doan wanna go h-home,' he hiccupped. 'Ge-er me 'nother ...' He blinked foolishly at Nick. 'Lucy sh-should've married me ...'

'There's talking nonsense, you are!' Nick said, consternation accentuating his Welsh accent. 'Know well enough, you do, Lucy was never for you, boyo.'

'Sh-sh-should've been mine. Bloody Conan. M-messed everything up.'

'There's rubbish you're talking! Drunk you are, Ewan. I will be getting the pair of you home right now.' Nick hurried away.

He found Conan in the kitchen brewing some coffee.

'There's young Ewan out there. Needing some of that, he is. Drunk and miserable he is, poor devil.'

'Bad as that?' Conan raised his brows.

'There's home I'm taking him,' Nick said grimly. 'That wife of his too.'

'Watch her then, Nick. The way she's carrying on tonight, she reminds me of some of the worst women who used to hang about the RAF camps.'

'Mmm, taken her jacket off she has for the dancing. Not much left to cover her. Her dress now, up it is where it should be down, and down where it should be up. No wonder is it, our Ewan is drunk.'

'They could stay here for the night,' Conan said. 'We've plenty of room.'

'Better if I get them home,' Nick said darkly and hurried away to get his car. He had no difficulty persuading Ewan to drink the coffee. He kept a firm hold of his elbow though to guide him in the direction of the car. Once he was safely in the back seat he went to fetch Gerda. She was enjoying herself in a wine-induced haze.

'Time you were going home, it is,' Nick said loudly in her ear. Some of her fellow dancers fell back a little.

'Go'way,' Gerda brushed a hand at him as though he was a persistent fly. Nick was tired and more than a little concerned for Ewan in his present state.

'There's leaving we are. Now.' Nick grasped Gerda's arm but she began to struggle, wriggling her hips as though going on with the dance. Irritably Nick waved to the band, indicating it was time to stop. 'Past midnight, it is, boys. There's coffee for you, and food, in the kitchen up at the house. You'll find Mr Maxwell there.' The band began to pack up. Gerda swore loudly and crudely at Nick.

'It's time we were all going home,' one of the men announced peaceably.

'Wish I was going home with you,' another one told Gerda drunkenly. She reached out an arm towards him, but

110

Nick caught her and held out the small bolero jacket which matched her tangerine dress and almost made it decent.

'Put this on. There's cold it is out there now.' Gerda shrugged it away.

'Please yourself,' Nick muttered grimly. He had never liked Gerda and tonight he almost hated her. He grasped her arm none too gently and half-led, half-dragged her to the car, ignoring her foul language and drunken hiccups. He almost pushed her in beside Ewan.

It was Nick who unlocked the cottage door and helped Ewan inside, before hustling Gerda after him. He gave her no time to protest or try out a drunken flirtation – something he dreaded more than her filthy temper.

It was cool inside the cottage and Ewan sobered up enough to throw off his jacket and help Gerda up the stairs. Automatically he washed his face, cleaned his teeth and drank a glass of water, unaware of his actions. Back in the bedroom Gerda lay sprawled across the bed, singing tunelessly. He helped her undress, feeling all the thwarted passions of the day rising in him as her naked flesh was displayed. She made no effort to cover herself.

Astonishingly, she responded with a desire which more than matched his own. In truth, Gerda was as intoxicated by the admiration she had received during the evening as she was by the copious quantities of wine she had drunk. She didn't know, or care, whether she was making love with her husband, or any one of the young men who had been so eager to partner her. Neither did she raise any objections to Ewan's almost insatiable desire. Indeed, she seemed more than ready to meet passion with passion.

It was a few days after the wedding when Bridie called in at Nether Rullion to have a chat. The children were enjoying the summer holidays and they had accompanied her, eager to see Ewan and follow him around as he

111

worked.

'Nick said Ewan got a bit worse for wear after we left the wedding reception.' Bridie grinned. 'Has he quite recovered?'

'He has now,' Ross said darkly, 'but he missed the milking on Sunday morning. Peter went to call him up when he didn't turn up but he couldn't even make them hear.'

'We didn't see him until four o' clock on Sunday afternoon,' Rachel said, 'and he still looked dreadful. I'm surprised at Conan supplying so much drink,' she added reproachfully. 'Beer has gone up to two and a penny a pint.'

'Oh, Mum!' Bridie chided. 'Conan was doing his best to be the perfect host. He would expect his guests to know when they had drunk enough. I thought Fiona made a super job of organising it all. I was quite sorry I had to leave so early, but Alicia and Margaret were really tired – not that they would admit it, of course.'

'Children never do.' Rachel smiled.

'I had a grand talk with Chris's boyfriend, Adam Green,' Bridie said. 'He seems really keen on cattle and he knows a lot about the Friesian pedigrees. The four heifer calves he's bought are really well-bred. Their pedigrees all go back to Adema 88. One of them is out of a first-class cow too. I told him I wouldn't mind buying a bull calf out of her. He seemed surprised. It's a shame he can't get a farm of his own.'

'Well, his own parents aren't farmers and they have no money to help him get a foot on the ladder,' Ross said. 'I had a good talk with him and Chris too. They deserve encouragement. Ewan and I would buy a half share with you if he breeds a decent stock bull, Bridie. You never know where he and Chris will end up if the right opportunity comes along. They're both prepared to work hard.'

'Yes, but Chris says her father would never help them,' Rachel said. 'He only considers his sons apparently. I thought he seemed quite intolerant where Chris is concerned. He even disapproved of her bringing Adam to the wedding.'

'I got the impression he favours his youngest son. Jake, isn't it?' Ross frowned. 'He seems to have made up his mind he's the one who will get the Home Farm eventually. That wouldn't be so bad, but he doesn't seem to treat Don very fairly. Apparently Mr Greig deals quite a bit at local markets and he's started sending cows and heifers to Don's place if he hasn't a buyer waiting, but all the pedigree cows are at the Home Farm and he leaves Don with the ones he doesn't want.'

'But I thought it was Don who was most interested in the breeding and the pedigrees when he was at home?' Bridie said.

'So I believe, and it was Don who did the milking and started grading up their own cows to pedigrees. When I mentioned that, Mr Greig just shrugged and said Don's day would come soon enough but he'll need to work for it. Meanwhile he's the boss and he'll make the decisions.'

'Don couldn't work much harder from the sound of things!' Bridie said indignantly.

'No-o,' Ross said slowly, 'he'll not have an easy time. It's not much fun being landed with half a dozen extra heifers to milk without warning. By the time he's got them nicely quietened and settled down to milking, his father takes them off to another market to sell them on at a profit.'

'Oh! I'd hate that!' Bridie said vehemently.

'Mmm. I gather Don doesn't like it much either and it's only since they got Skeppiehill Farm that Mr Greig has dealt much in dairy cattle. Before that he just bought and sold sheep and a few bullocks.'

'It sounds as though Don and Lucy will have a hard

time dealing with Mr Greig,' Rachel said. 'But I do like Mrs Greig. I think she'll do her best to see Don and Lucy get fair treatment.'

'I wonder what they'll all say when they see Fiona's wedding gift?' Bridie chuckled. 'I'll bet Mr Greig says it's a waste of money.'

'It's really generous of Fiona, and such a thoughtful gift too,' Rachel said warmly. 'Lucy loves her music and it would be such a pity to let all her hard work go to waste, particularly if she gets a family and has to give up teaching.'

'Aye.' Ross smiled. 'Fiona is a wise lassie. I wouldn't mind betting she's looking to the future. Lucy and Don may have a struggle as long as Mr Greig insists on controlling all the purse strings and treating Don like a labourer.'

'You think that's the reason for her choice of gift?' Bridie asked puzzled.

'Oh, I'm sure she bought it because she knows how much pleasure Lucy gets from her music and the lassie couldn't have afforded to buy a piano of her own – even a second-hand one. But she is qualified to teach piano and it crossed my mind she may be able to take a few pupils for piano lessons if she needs a bit of spare cash. I'd be surprised if Fiona isn't thinking along those lines.'

'A-ah, I see now ...' Bridie nodded. 'Good old Fiona. Either way I'm certain it is a gift Lucy will appreciate for life. She just loves her music.' She stood up and stretched. 'Well, I'd better see what my offspring are up to. I have a feeling they'll be telling Ewan we're going to beat him at the show next week. It doesn't seem like a year since he won the championship, does it?'

'No.' Rachel sighed. 'Time goes so fast these days, or seems to.'

'He hasn't had much time to prepare the cows for the show this year,' Ross said with a slight frown. 'I think I must be getting old or I'd have given him more help.'

'Oh, you can't blame yourself, Ross,' Rachel said quickly. 'Ewan has had Gerda to consider this year. But at least they seem happier and more settled since Lucy's wedding.'

'I expect Gerda is enjoying the school holidays too,' Bridie said. 'It's a pity she hasn't any interest in the farm. I'm sure they'd have been happier working together.'

'Not everyone is as lucky as you and Nick, or me and your father.' Rachel smiled. 'But I must say it's a relief to see Gerda more content. I thought her father might have come down to stay for a little while but they don't seem to keep in touch very often.'

Ewan too felt more relaxed and happy. Gerda was less restless and she had not been on any more shopping frenzies since Lucy's wedding. He had no idea she had already committed her salary, as well as his wages, to various hire purchase agreements. Even her wedding outfit was to be paid off over the next six months.

Money, or lack of it, was not the only reason Gerda stayed at home. She felt content and relaxed for the first time in her life. She even pottered in the garden and experimented with her new cooker.

Even when Bridie won the championship at the Dumfries Show and Ewan didn't even get reserve, Gerda felt none of her usual jealous spite. She smiled serenely at everyone. The twins responded by taking her hands and leading her off to see their favourite ice-cream van. She rather enjoyed being introduced as the young Mrs Maxwell of Nether Rullion and it was easy to be gracious when the men offered extravagant compliments about her appearance, while the women viewed her slim figure and long blonde hair with envy.

Even when the long summer holidays were over and Gerda had to return to work she didn't resume her usual grumbling as Ewan had anticipated. He was delighted and

115

went out of his way to help with household tasks whenever he could. Long days at the harvest meant this was not always possible but Gerda remained placid.

It was a particularly cold day at the beginning of October and Gerda decided to put on a pair of warm trousers for her Saturday shopping trip into Dumfries. She had never got used to having her groceries and butcher meat delivered by the vans which came round all the farms, and without which Billy Smith's mother could not exist. Mrs Smith didn't have a car and could not have driven one anyway. She rarely went to town at all. Even the clothes for herself, Billy and his father were ordered from one of the two travelling tailors who called every quarter at the farms and cottages. Gerda's one concession was to patronise the baker's van which came round three times a week with fresh bread and scones and cakes. Recently, she had developed a craving for fish and Mrs Smith was delighted to get it for her from the van which called on Wednesdays, bringing fresh fish all the way from the east coast.

As Gerda tried unsuccessfully to fasten the waistband of her trousers that October morning, she was dismayed to find she must have put on weight since she had last worn them in the spring.

'It's eating so much fish!' she wailed at Ewan who was just finishing his breakfast. 'I've put on so much weight I can't fit into my clothes!'

'You look as lovely as ever to me,' Ewan reassured her, and he meant it. It was true Gerda did enjoy better meals these days, but she seemed so much happier and contented, Ewan didn't care if she put on weight. She still had plenty of curves to satisfy him. He grinned wickedly at her.

'Do you want me to help you dress?' he asked.

'That's all you think about, Ewan Maxwell,' she pouted prettily. 'How is it you're not rushing back to the farm this morning?'

'I'm going soon, but the rush is over for now. The harvest is all in and we haven't started the turnips yet. Anyway I've already milked a hundred cows while you were getting your beauty sleep.'

'I must be eating too much ...' Gerda muttered returning her attention to the offending trousers. 'I'll go and change into a winter skirt.'

'It's not that cold,' Ewan told her. 'This is just a crisp autumn morning. The sun will get out soon and it will probably be hot by afternoon.'

'I'll be back by then and I can change into something cooler if it is.' She soon discovered she couldn't button any of the skirts she had worn last winter. She had been eating more lately, and enjoying her food too, but she didn't want to get fat! Anyway, she couldn't afford new clothes. Her heart sank at the thought of all the money she owed to various firms. She would never dare to tell Ewan. She sensed his shadow in the bedroom door and turned to face him, still struggling with the button of her skirt.

'Don't look so distressed, Gerda,' he said softly. 'It's not the end of the world if you've put on a bit of weight. I love you like this.' He moved closer and ran his hand down the length of her body, drawing her closer. 'And I like you better still without your skirt, or any other clothes, come to that,' he said huskily, beginning to remove her blouse.

'It's not often you have time for this so early in the day,' she laughed throatily. 'You'll have to wait a second while I go to the bathroom. Must take my usual precautions, you know ...' She broke off, staring at Ewan, her eyes wide with shock.

'Gerda! What's wrong? Are you ill?' He moved to draw her close again but she shrank away and sat down on the edge of the bed. Her face had drained of colour.

'It can't be ...' she whispered faintly. 'I can't ... I

117

always ...'

'Gerda! What is it? What's wrong? Tell me ...'

Her eyes narrowed and she stared at him, but her mind was calculating dates. Suddenly she jumped up.

'I don't want a baby!' she screamed. 'I never, ever want a baby. I won't have it! I tell you, I ...'

'Gerda!' Ewan caught her flailing arms and sat her down again on the side of the bed. He turned her towards him. 'What's wrong? What are you trying to say?'

'It must be a baby! Don't you see? I haven't ... I haven't had ...' She began to cry. Tears rolled down her pale cheeks and sobs shook her body.

'Do you think you are having a baby, Gerda?' Ewan asked softly, incredulously, and there was no doubting the hope and happiness in his voice. Gerda stopped crying and stared at him.

'It's your fault!' she screamed. 'I told you I didn't want a bloody baby! Not now! Not ever! It's all your f-fault!' She began beating his chest with small clenched fists.

'Well, if you are expecting a child, I should hope it is mine!' Ewan said, trying hard to stop the smile which wanted to stretch his mouth all the way across his face. He felt a bubble of happiness inside him. Gerda had told him she didn't want a child, but he had always hoped she would change her mind some day. She had asked the doctor for a birth control pill. He had sent her to a family planning clinic, but after her first visit she had changed her mind about the pill. She had said there were precautions she could use and she would see to it that there were no babies.

'Are you sure, Gerda? Are you expecting a child?'

'I d-don't know ...' She had stopped fighting and screaming now and she flopped against him, her head under his chin. He could smell the scent of her silky hair. 'Oh Ewan, I d-don't want a baby. I never want a baby. It's horrible. The thought of it makes me feel ill ...' She grimaced and clung to him. Then she pushed him away, staring wildly into his face. 'I shall get rid of it. You can, you know. People do ...'

'No, Gerda! No, you can't think of such a thing! Anyway we don't know for sure. You must see the doctor ...'

'I won't have it! I will *not* have a baby!' she screeched through gritted teeth. She began to pull clothes from the wardrobe, flinging them over the bed, the chair, the floor. 'See! Nothing fits me! Already I'm fat. Babies make you fat and ugly and horrible.' She began to sob, but when Ewan tried to take her in his arms and comfort her she threw the hairbrush at him and picked up a glass scent spray. 'Get out! Leave me alone! This is all your fault. Get out ...' She threw the heavy glass bottle but Ewan ducked in time and closed the door behind him. He was deeply troubled. If Gerda was expecting a child, surely such emotion couldn't be good for her? He went slowly downstairs. Supposing it was not a baby? What if it was something terrible ...? Almost without being aware, Ewan pulled on his Wellington boots and made his way to the farmhouse and his parents. His mother would know what to do to calm Gerda. Surely she would be able to help her?

Rachel listened attentively to Ewan's garbled account.

'I expect it's the shock if Gerda thought she couldn't have a baby ...'

'It's not that she couldn't. She d-d ...'

'Well, for whatever reason, it seems to be a shock to her,' Rachel soothed. 'Would you like me to go down and talk to her? She may be wrong after all. But that could account for her appetite, her new serenity and ...'

'Serenity! She's anything but serene, Mother. She's talking of getting rid of it, if it is a baby ...' There was a catch in Ewan's voice and Rachel found herself wanting to hug and comfort him as she had when he was a little boy, but it was his wife who needed the comfort and support right now. 'You wait here. Make yourself a cup of tea to steady you. I'll bring Gerda back with me if I can persuade her.' She pulled on a cardigan and set off down to the cottages. It was not far if she cut through the orchard and the small paddock, but by the time Rachel got to the lane she saw the taillights of Gerda's little car speeding away from her, amid a screech of tyres and a cloud of dust. Her heart sank. 'Please God, don't let her do anything foolish!

# Chapter Ten

Gerda returned from town filled with anger and deep dismay. She blamed the doctor, she blamed Ewan, she even blamed his parents. She convinced herself they wanted a grandchild. They had wished this horrible fate upon her. Furiously, she bought new winter clothes, running up her account to the limit in Binns, before moving down to Buccleuch Street. She had long desired a fur coat. She was oblivious of the cost now. She had already opened an account in Barbour's – one of the most expensive shops in town – but now she didn't care who would have to pay the bill. Certainly it would not be her.

She knew Ewan and his family, notably Bridie and his mother, disapproved of running up accounts. Ewan had flatly refused to get one of the new credit cards called American Express. He said he didn't earn the £2,000 a year you had to have before you could get one.

'You could tell them you do,' she had pleaded but he just shook his head emphatically.

Now she felt an obscure feeling of triumph as she swirled in front of the long mirrors and drank in the lavish compliments of the well-dressed sales assistant. The woman was experienced and knew exactly which customers could be influenced by insincere flattery. Moreover, she had heard of the Maxwells of Nether Rullion. Her brother-in-law had a small farm and she had heard him speak highly of them. Even so she was taken aback when Gerda asked if she might try on the mink coat which had arrived that very week. The squirrel fur at £400 was expensive, but there was a world of difference between it and a mink. You could buy a house for that money.

'It's the only one we have had in. It *is* very expensive, madam,' the sales assistant demurred. She knew farm workers earned about £10 a week and she resolved to quiz her brother-in-law about the Maxwells. They must be very wealthy landowners.

'Yes, I know ...' Gerda agreed. Suddenly she knew how she would use her hateful condition to her advantage. She leaned towards the woman conspiratorially. 'My husband is hoping for a son and heir,' she whispered, and patted her flat stomach. 'He is so delighted he would buy me the moon.'

'Then madam must certainly try the mink – £2,190, ten shillings, it is.'

Gerda winced inwardly, but she heard the awe in the woman's tone, and saw the way she stroked the sleeve so lovingly. Having tried the coat she knew it was what she coveted more than anything else. What was to stop Ewan selling a bull to pay for it, she thought defiantly. God knows he seemed to have plenty of them. She thought defiantly of Bridie and Mrs Maxwell. Neither of them spent a lot of money on clothes. Their maxim was if you couldn't afford a new dress you made the old one do. Well, they all deserved to suffer, she decided resentfully.

'Perhaps madam would like a new hat to go with it? And we have a lovely calfskin handbag at £50. It would go perfectly with the mink,' the woman purred. Gerda readily agreed.

On the way home she argued her case for her wild spending spree. What if she *had* run up a huge debt? Ewan deserved to pay. Nothing could be as bad as her suffering, the humiliation of her slender waist expanding, the gross bulge which would distort her slim figure – not to mention the pain and degradation of giving birth. She shuddered with horror at this last prospect and almost drove into a ditch.

In the weeks which followed, nothing Ewan could say or do could make Gerda see reason. In desperation, he sought Rachel's advice, thinking she might understand the ways of women in Gerda's condition. Rachel did her best to convince Gerda there was nothing to worry about but her sudden outburst, her foul language and uncontrollable temper surprised and dismayed her.

'Dear child, please try to be calm,' she said in consternation. 'You'll harm yourself, and your bairn.'

'I don't give a damn! I wish it were dead. The doctor refused to get rid of it ...'

'Then think of your own health.'

'What the hell does that matter! I shall be ugly and fat and ... and ...'

'Of course you won't. As soon as the baby is born you will soon...'

'Shut up! Don't talk about it!' Gerda screamed and clamped her hands over her ears like a child. 'Why don't you go and tell Conan and his precious Fiona you want another generation of Maxwells! That's all you're bothered about! And whether we have another war and your darling boys have to go!'

'Well, the world *is* rather a troubled place just now,' Rachel agreed. It was true she had mentioned her fears to Ewan when the Indonesian troops had invaded Malaya. A state of emergency had been declared. Britain, New Zealand and Australia had all agreed more defence and economic aid must be provided. 'Now there's all this trouble in Vietnam,' she said speaking her thoughts aloud, hoping to channel Gerda's attention away from her own concerns. 'President Johnson has declared, "The world must never forget – that aggression unchallenged is aggression unleashed." I think it's a warning that war will follow.' She trembled at the thought. She remembered the shock and devastation of the last war. 'If Russia and America go to war, the Americans would expect Britain to help, and people like Nick and Conan would all be required to sacrifice their lives once again.'

'Well, if people like me weren't forced to have babies, there wouldn't be any people to fight!' Gerda shouted unreasonably. Rachel sighed. It was clear Gerda could think of nothing but herself.

'But you're keeping in good health, dear, aren't you?'

'What do you care about my health? All you're interested in is another Maxwell to carry on farming your bloody land! Get out! Get out!' she screamed.

Deeply troubled by such hysteria, Rachel left the cottage. That evening she sat down and wrote to Gerda's father, expressing her concern for his daughter's health and for their unborn grandchild. She pleaded with him to come and visit Gerda.

*I will do anything I can to help*, she wrote, *but Gerda will not confide in me. Perhaps she is frightened. Perhaps you can make her understand that childbirth is perfectly natural, and infinitely safer than it used to be. Please come if you can help her.*

John Allan wrote by return, thanking her but declining her offer of hospitality. He feared his presence would aggravate Gerda even further and Rachel's heart sank as she read.

'He says her mother reacted in just the same way,' she told Ross. 'He says she was the most unnatural mother he ever knew, even after the baby was born. She never wanted to look after her. He says she seemed incapable of loving her. Poor Gerda. No wonder she's so distraught and so ... so ...'

'Selfish!' Ross finished the sentence curtly. 'Don't waste your sympathy on her, and don't you be worrying about her.' He had little patience with Gerda's histrionics. As far as her health was concerned, she looked better than she had ever looked, positively blooming, if it weren't for the miserable droop of her mouth. 'Let me see the letter?' He took it gently from Rachel's fingers and read on. 'A-ah ...' He expelled a long breath. 'Even her own father is advising Ewan not to give in to her demands. He says whatever he tried, it didn't make her mother any more human. She just made more and more demands ... Poor Ewan! I fear he's married a siren, if Gerda takes after her mother, and it sounds as though she does. He's already given in to her over ...' Ross bit back his words, frowning. He hadn't meant to tell Rachel yet ... He didn't want to worry her, or upset her.

'Given in over what?' she asked. 'He has to humour her at a time like this,' she reasoned anxiously. 'Surely you agree ...'

'Not to the tune of paying nearly £3,000 for the debts she's run up – and all that on top of the money we gave them for the house. Ach! Rachel, I didn't mean to tell you so bluntly, but you would have had to know eventually. She hasn't spent all that money because of the baby. She hasn't known about it very long ...' He turned to face his wife and saw Rachel's face had drained of colour.

'£3,000?' she whispered hoarsely. 'B-but I d-don't understand. She hasn't bought anything for the baby yet. I-I mean a cot or pram, or – or anything ...' She sat down heavily. '£3,000!' It was three times as much as she spent in a whole year on herself and Ross and keeping house. 'That's far, far more than Peter earns in a year ...'

'I know, I know.' Ross sighed. 'I didn't mean to blurt it out. Ewan was forced to tell me. It seems they've had letters threatening to send in the bailiffs.'

'What! B-but how ...? When ...?' Suddenly Rachel bowed her head and clasped her hands to her temples. She felt sick and dizzy. How could Gerda and Ewan have got into such debt? Ross had been more than generous. And Gerda had earned her teacher's salary until recently. How would they manage without it? She'd blamed Ewan for having to give up her career. Even without her job, she didn't do any of her own housework or cooking. She had employed Mrs Smith to go in to the cottage three days a week and Ewan had to pay her wages. Now this ...

'Please, Rachel, drink this ...' Ross was kneeling beside her, holding a glass of water, his face, so close to her own, was filled with love and concern.

'B-but what shall w-we do?' she asked hoarsely. 'It's such a lot of money!'

'I've drawn it out of the money I was saving for our old age,' Ross admitted. He shrugged helplessly. 'I told Ewan I must tell you. He understands it must never happen again. It can't happen again. But I don't think he knows how to deal with Gerda in her present state. He's thrilled to bits about the baby himself. I suppose that makes him more tolerant with her. He says he'll repay us, but I can't think how ...'

'We'll manage, dear.' Rachel reached up and stroked Ross's cheek. 'We're both in good health and, so long as we have each other, we'll manage.'

'I know,' Ross said huskily. 'So long as we have each other ...' he repeated. He shivered suddenly, looking down into Rachel's pale face. 'I couldn't live if anything happened to you, my love. We've been so lucky.'

'I know, I know. We'll get by.' Rachel got to her feet, but she felt suddenly old – old and very tired. Deep in her heart she knew this wasn't the end of the problems Gerda would bring to them, and to their family.

The contrast between Lucy's new life and Gerda's could not have been greater. Don worked hard and without complaint; his father's promise made their labours seem worthwhile. One day, Skeppiehill Farm would be his, and the stock would be of his own choosing; fine pedigree cattle and a small flock of sheep for breeding. Stockmanship was Don's great asset and sometimes Lucy felt he ought to have been a vet.

'You seem to have an instinct – a sort of sixth sense where animals are concerned,' she told him. 'You sense they're falling sick almost before they do.'

'That's just regular observation.' Don grinned. 'I'm pretty certain Bridie has it, and your grandfather too. Most farmers only call in the vet when the animals are already sick, so my sixth sense, as you call it, wouldn't have been much good. Anyway farming is what I love, and what I've always wanted to do.' He hugged her. 'And I'm the luckiest man in the world to have a wife like you,' he said softly.

Lucy fed the calves and hens each morning before she set out for school, and frequently helped Don with the milking when she returned in the afternoon, especially during hay and harvest when he worked from dawn to dusk to get the crops safely in. Usually his father sent one of his brothers and a hired man over to help at such times, so Lucy made meals for them too. She often blessed the modern appliances which made her life easier than it would have been without her family's generosity. She clearly remembered the wash house and boiler at Glens of Lochandee where she and Ewan had helped to turn the mangle to ring out the clothes when they were children. Bridie telephoned occasionally for a chat and Lucy often expressed her appreciation to her, and her grandparents, for the washing machine and deep-freeze.

As for the piano, it was pure luxury. Something she could never have afforded, or justified to Don's father. It brought her the greatest pleasure. Time was precious but in the evening before they went to bed, she usually played for a little while, feeling the tensions of the day seeping away as she wove the magic of her music. Often Don would wash and prepare for bed then creep into the room and sit in the big armchair, sipping his glass of cool milk and listening contentedly. Sometimes he would request some of his favourite melodies. Greig's *Morning* from *Peer Gynt*, and the tune he called *The Trout*, were two of his regular requests, but mostly he was content to listen as the music rippled like soothing balm, quieting his fretful thoughts and calming the stresses of his day, as it did her own.

It was Fiona who passed on the news that Gerda had given up her teaching and was expecting a baby.

'I believe Ewan is having problems trying to keep her calm, but Conan says he's privately elated with the news.'

'Oh, I'm sure he must be,' Lucy said joyfully. 'Do please pass on our congratulations. Gerda always said she would never have a baby when we were at college, but I'm so glad she has changed her mind. She knew far more about birth control than the rest of us,' she chuckled. 'She always said she would take the contraceptive pill if she ever got married. I'm a bit surprised she changed her mind so soon, but I don't think she really enjoyed teaching.'

'Mmm, I don't know about that,' Fiona said dubiously. 'Apparently the baby is due about March. Nick has a theory it happened after your wedding. He drove them both home that night because they were so drunk.'

'Oh, well, so long as they don't blame us!' Lucy laughed, then added more seriously, 'I'm sure it will be for the best. Gerda will have a baby to love and care for, instead of thinking so much about herself, how she looks and what she should wear.'

'I hope you're right, for Ewan's sake. Some people don't know how lucky they are.' Lucy heard the wistful note in Fiona's voice and changed the subject. She knew the greatest disappointment in Fiona's life was that she had been unable to give Conan a son, but it didn't seem to trouble him. More than once Lucy had heard him say what a disappointment he had been to his own father because he didn't want to follow in his footsteps.

'If we'd had a son he would probably have wanted to be a farmer, and follow in my parents' footsteps instead of mine!' he chuckled. 'Then I'd have been as disappointed as my father was.'

Fiona had enough sense to know this was perfectly true but still regretted her childless state. Now that she was married herself, Lucy understood. She longed for children of her own – certainly more than one. Although she had been an only child, she'd had Ewan as her constant companion, so had never been lonely. Even now she regarded him as a dearly loved brother. Fiona had been an only child too and had once confided that she'd often felt alone. As always when Lucy thought about children, she worried about giving up her work. She earned considerably more than the allowance Don's father paid them and she wondered whether he would increase it if she gave up teaching to care for a family.

She had mentioned this to Chris during one of their discussions.

'I wouldn't bet on it,' she had answered darkly. 'All Dad thinks about is our Jake and Will and a farm for them. He was always harder on Don and me.'

Lucy and Chris had become even closer friends since they had been sisters-in-law, but it made Lucy uncomfortable when Chris spoke bitterly of her father. They were barely on speaking terms these days. He disapproved strongly of her friendship with Adam Green and it made Chris all the more determined to support Adam in whatever he decided to do. She loved him and she willed him to be a success, if only to prove her father wrong.

'We had an awful argument,' she confided on one of their visits to Lucy and Don. 'Dad was ranting on telling me I shall never be anything but the wife of a farm labourer with Adam. I told him Adam's a well-respected stockman and he earns twice as much as the pitiful allowance he pays Don. And that's only for looking after a dairy herd, not for having the responsibility for the whole farm, as Don does. Of course, Dad blustered furiously. He says Don has to make sacrifices now if he wants to farm on his own in the future.'

'Oh, Chris, you shouldn't quarrel with your father on our behalf,' Lucy said. 'Your mother is very kind ...'

'I know she is. She feels as bad as I do that Don works so hard and gets so little to keep for himself. I don't see our Jake economising much, and he has girlfriends galore. He's ruined! And Willie is nearly as bad now that Don and I have left home. At least I'm working for myself, but Don is working to support them!'

'Never mind, lass,' Don placated. 'We'll get by, you and Adam, Lucy and me. How about the four of us meeting up for the Christmas Eve dance in Ayr?'

Don had turned Chris's thoughts away from their father and they all looked forward to the dance.

'I shall really miss all the family on Christmas Day,' Lucy sighed. 'We always had a family gathering. Mind you, I think Bridie will be making it this year. My grandparents are not getting any younger and I think Gerda makes their life more difficult with all her moans – at least that's what Nick says. Your mother has invited us to the Home Farm for Christmas dinner. Will you be there, Chris?'

'Nope.' Chris pursed her lips into a determined line. There was an unforgiving expression on her pleasant face. 'Adam's not invited, so I'm not going either.'

'Come and join us on Boxing Day then,' Lucy urged. 'Fiona and Conan are coming up, if the weather's OK. I think they might bring Max and the twins too. Max is longing to see round the farm with Don, and Alicia and Margaret always like an outing. I'm really looking forward to making little parcels for them to open.'

'That's because you're so good with children, Lucy,' Chris said warmly. 'But we'd love to come. Wouldn't we, Adam?'

'Yes, so long as you understand we'll have to be back for the milking.'

'That's all right. Don will have to milk anyway. I know the cows don't just dry up for Christmas, Adam,' she chuckled.

'Aye, well, that's more than some of Chris's fellow teachers realise,' Adam said with a wry smile. 'They think I'm mad getting up at five o'clock every morning, but I was forgetting you spent most of your childhood at Glens of Lochandee.'

'I did, and I loved it there.'

'Aye, and she can milk cows with the best o' folk,' Don said proudly.

'I expect that's why you and Chris get on so well.' Adam smiled at Lucy. 'You share the same interests.'

'Yes.' Lucy nodded gravely. 'We do. I can't help wondering whether Ewan and Gerda will ever develop common interests. I think she's leading him an awful dance now that she's expecting a child.'

'He was a fool to marry her,' Don said with feeling. 'It was so out of character for Ewan, but he seemed to have a blind spot where Gerda was concerned.'

It was the onset of morning sickness one February morning which alerted Lucy to the fact that she was expecting a child. In spite of the discomfort and inconvenience, she and Don were delighted at the prospect, but they resolved to keep their secret to themselves as long as possible.

During the cold weather Gerda treated herself more than ever as an invalid, often spending most of the day in bed, or lying on the sofa watching the new colour television she had bought. The result was a large baby, and this, coupled with her hysteria at the slightest pain, made her labour long and difficult, culminating in an operation to save the baby.

Ewan gave Gerda all his sympathy. He was delighted and deeply moved by the sight of his baby son when he viewed him first through the glass panel in the hospital special care unit.

'He's a sturdy wee fellow,' the doctor assured him. 'We're just making sure he's all right but we'll have him out of here in no time. Your wife ...' The doctor hesitated, frowning as he chose his words with care. 'She has not seen him yet. She ... er ... she says she doesn't want to see him. It does happen sometimes after a traumatic birth ... but ... well, we would like to be sure there will be someone to keep a close eye on both mother and child when she gets home. Of course, that will not be for about 10-14 days and hopefully her natural mother's instinct will have overcome the experience of giving birth when she holds him in her arms.'

'Y-yes, I'm sure it will,' Ewan said uncertainly. How could he tell this kindly looking doctor that Gerda had made up her mind she didn't want anything to do with the baby. She was adamant that she would not feed him herself. In spite of his worries over Gerda Ewan was filled with pride and deep satisfaction at being a father. 'We have a very good neighbour who helps my wife around the house,' he assured the doctor, 'and my parents live near too, if we need any advice.'

The doctor nodded and looked relieved. He had heard of mothers who refused to care for their own babies, but he had not yet experienced such a situation himself. He observed Ewan carefully. He was young to have the responsibility of a wife and baby but at least he seemed happy about his new status.

At first, Gerda refused to talk about the baby, but when

the nurses kept asking if she had chosen a name for him she suddenly gave them the first thing which came into her head. That evening when Ewan visited she told him the baby was to be called Ringo. He stared at her in disbelief.

'Ringo! What sort of a name is that to call my son?' he demanded angrily. Gerda's mouth formed the familiar sullen pout which he had come to expect.

'It's after a young singer I saw on the television. He's part of a group. He might be famous one day.'

'More likely here today and gone tomorrow,' Ewan answered caustically. 'Isn't he one of the lads from Liverpool who call themselves The Beatles? You can't burden a child with a name like that.'

'Why not? It's different ...'

'Of course it's different. Why can't we name him after your father, or my father, or both if you like?'

'No! I'm going to call him Ringo.'

'No son of mine will have a name like that,' Ewan said stubbornly and Gerda recognised the green glitter in his eyes. She knew he meant it. Suddenly she felt too tired to argue and her eyes filled with the tears which came all too readily.

'Choose one of the other names then,' Ewan said more gently, 'if you must have someone from the television. What are they ...? Let's see, there's one called George, and a John, and one called Paul. At least they are ordinary names. Or your dad's surname: Allan? Don't you like any of them? We'll have to arrange a christening at church and you'll be able to wear your smart clothes again.' Ewan was learning how to channel Gerda's thoughts from divisive subjects. True enough, the tears dried and she brightened visibly at the thought of standing up before the congregation in Lochandee Kirk.

'Mmm ...' She began to try out each of the names with Maxwell. 'Paul Maxwell sounds all right ...'

'Yes, it sounds quite good,' Ewan agreed, with a flash

133

of relief, and resolved to register the birth of his son without delay. Unbeknown to Gerda, he registered the baby as Paul Ross Maxwell and, although she was annoyed at the change when he told her on the morning of the christening, she was too absorbed in grooming herself for the role of beautiful young mother to make a fuss. The gravity of the service and the vows she and Ewan made on behalf of their small son washed right over her head, but she accepted the adulation and admiring glances of the congregation as her right.

Afterwards, the family gathered at Nether Rullion for a buffet lunch. Even Gerda's father had agreed to come down for the christening, bringing with him a lady friend whom Gerda had never met before. Daisy Wright was a plain, homely woman who did her best to fit in with everyone, but Gerda and her father were wary of each other and Rachel could only guess at the bitter quarrel which must have come between them.

'I don't think we shall be receiving any invitations to visit from Gerda,' he told Rachel wryly before he left, 'but I'd appreciate a wee bit o' news about the wee fellow when ye have a minute to drop a line.' He looked her in the eye and shook his head bravely. 'Dinna let her tak advantage o' your kind heart. The bairn is hers. She should be looking after him, but I can see for masel' that ye're more used tae him than she is.'

'I love him dearly already,' Rachel smiled, looking down at the infant in her arms. 'We both do. I'm just helping out until Gerda recovers her strength.'

'Aye, well, that will be a good while if she's like her mother,' he warned.


Shortly after she had eaten, Lucy had to make a dash for the bathroom. When she came out Gerda was waiting on the landing.

'I saw you hurrying upstairs,' she said. 'You're looking

pale.' She eyed Lucy shrewdly. 'Sick were you?'

'Just a bit of an upset,' Lucy said lightly. 'I'll be all right in a wee while. Don and I will have to be leaving soon to get back for the milking, but I'm glad we came. You have a lovely baby, Gerda. You must both be very proud of him.' Lucy was sincere but Gerda's pale eyes glittered angrily.

'He might be lovely but just look what he's done to me!' She glared down at herself in disgust.

'But you're almost back to normal already, Gerda, and surely it was worth it to ...'

'Worth it! Just you wait another few months. I guessed that's what's wrong with you when I saw you rush to the bathroom − not that I ever had that bother. You'll soon look like an overblown balloon and ...'

'But that's only for a few months and I'm sure it must be worth any discomfort to have a baby of one's own,' Lucy said.

'It's awful. It's degrading the things you have to suffer in hospital. Do you know what they ...'

'I don't want to hear, Gerda,' Lucy interrupted firmly, seeing the malice on Gerda's face and knowing how much she would enjoy recounting all the worst aspects of giving birth. She pushed past her and ran down the stairs to join the others, but Gerda followed her and announced loudly,

'Lucy's going to have a baby!'

Silence fell on the room as the chatter stopped and everyone looked towards Lucy with Gerda behind her. Lucy's eyes sought Don's across the room and he hurried to her side, putting a protective arm around her shoulders.

'Thank goodness we told your parents,' he whispered softly, then he turned to face the room. 'It's true but we didn't want to steal the limelight from Gerda and Ewan,' he said smoothly. 'Now that you all know, I must say we're delighted and ...'

'When, Lucy? When is it due?' Bridie asked excitedly.

135

'October.'

'Oh, I'm so pleased for you. You and Don will be super parents.'

'I'm pleased for you too, lassie,' Rachel said, giving Lucy a warm hug. 'But I hope you'll take care and not be working too hard ...'

'She never said that to me,' Gerda muttered angrily to Ewan.

'She knew you did take care,' Ewan said. 'Lucy is farther away and there's none of her own family near enough to help.'

'There was none of my family near me!'

'Lucy, Lucy.' The twins tugged at Lucy's hands. 'Can we come and stay in the holidays and help you nurse the baby? We know how. We help Granny to look after baby Paul, and we rock his pram when he cries.'

'I'm sure I'll be pleased to have your help,' Lucy laughed, 'but we shall not have a baby for ages and ages yet.'

'How long is ages?' asked Alicia.

'Four months at least. That will be after your summer holidays. You will be back at school.'

'But we'll have a week in October for potato picking. We could come then,' Margaret insisted eagerly. Bridie raised her eyes heavenward.

'We'll have to see how you two behave, and if you've learnt to tidy your room by then,' she told her offspring, and received the usual groan in perfect unison as a reply.

# Chapter Eleven

Ross was secretly delighted when he heard the baby was to bear his name, albeit as a secondary one and Peter Forster rejoiced in the news of another generation of Maxwells at Nether Rullion. He had long since decided he would never marry and have a family of his own. The Maxwells had befriended him when he most needed friends and, except for the kindly Mrs Forster, who had treated him as her own son, they were the dearest people in the world to him. So his pleasure in the birth of Ewan's son was sincere. The future of Nether Rullion was assured and he felt deeply satisfied and content with the world. He rarely saw Gerda so he had no opportunity to express his congratulations in person.

As time passed, he was surprised to see the baby spending several hours every day with his grandmother and yet Gerda herself rarely came near the farm. He knew young Billy Smith had neither liking nor respect for her.

'She's a lazy bitch,' he confided to Peter, 'and she thinks she's Lady Muck, the things she expects my Ma to do. The extra money's useful, though, since we bought the cottage, so Ma puts up wi' her queer ways. She drives into Dumfries most days as soon as Ewan brings the bairn up here to his granny. She reckons the bread and the groceries frae the travelling shops are too dear, but Ma says it's just an excuse to gang gallivanting. It costs her more in petrol than the odd ha'penny on a loaf. When the bairn is at home Ma always has tae change his nappies. She washes them all tae. She says there's aye a stinking pile waiting for her tae clean after the weekend.' He wrinkled his freckled nose in disgust, then grinned his infectious gap-toothed grin. Peter, who was intensely loyal to the Maxwells, instantly forgave him for telling tales. '''Tis a pity bairns are not born like wee calves wi' their clothes already on and just lifting their tails when they want a pee!'

'We should all be as hairy as cavemen then,' Peter chuckled. 'And that young lady who works at Mr Conan's garage wouldn't fancy you like that,' he teased, laughing aloud at the flare of colour in Billy's cheeks.

It was a Saturday afternoon a few weeks later and Peter was bathed and changed into his second-best suit, preparing to drive into Dumfries for a haircut. He was surprised to see Gerda pushing the pram towards the farm house. The baby was propped against his pillow, chortling merrily to himself and waving his chubby fists at the world in general. Gerda seemed oblivious to his charms but Peter paused to speak, as he always did when he saw Mrs Maxwell pushing Paul in his pram. The child recognised a familiar face and gave one of his wide gummy smiles. Peter grinned down at him, pleased that the baby was beginning to remember him. He resolved to carve him a wooden tractor for Christmas, a sturdy toy on little wheels with a pull-along string.

'He's a lovely boy, Mrs Maxwell. I must congratulate you on producing such a fine son,' he said sincerely. Gerda would have walked on by but suddenly she stopped scowling and stared at Peter. She rarely saw him when he was clean shaven and smart. His black wavy hair was thick and shining. He was smiling down at her and, for the first time, she noticed how white and even his teeth were against his tanned skin. Paul crowed and waved his fist and Peter turned to look down at him, poking him with a gentle finger. He loved children and animals. Recently, he had acquired a collie pup of his own which he hoped to train to work the cattle and sheep. But Gerda didn't want him to turn his attention to Paul – she wanted his admiration, even if he *was* only a worker. Gerda couldn't bear to be in the company of a man if he didn't give her all his attention.

'Are you going into town? I don't suppose I could beg a lift? There's something wrong with my car and Ewan has gone off to one of the fields – something to do with getting ready for harvest. He wouldn't even take time to bring his own son to visit his grandparents,' she added in an aggrieved tone. There was nothing wrong with her car. It was a sudden whim that had made her ask for a lift from Peter, a determination to make him notice her.

Ewan had refused to wake baby Paul from his sleep just to bring him to his grandparents.

'Surely you can stay at home and look after him yourself for once,' he had said irritably. 'Mother has him far too often as it is. She's not getting any younger, and this hot weather tires her out.'

'She likes having him. It won't do any harm to waken him. I need to go to Dumfries.'

'No, you don't, Gerda. You went yesterday, and the day before, and probably the day before that, for all I know. It's just become a habit.' Ewan had not even waited for her to agree. He simply strode away up the track to the fields, expecting her to do as he asked. Gerda scowled, remembering the set of his shoulders. Ewan was no longer a college boy; he was broadening out into manhood – strong and straight like his father – but he had no right to give her orders as though she was one of his workers. She would teach him a lesson and she would use Peter Forster to do it.

'Right then, Peter, I'll just dump the pram up at the farmhouse and call to Mrs Maxwell. I'll be back in a second.'

'B-but I'm only going in to the barber's. I promised Ewan I'd be back to get the cows in for milking ...'

'That's fine. You can drop me off at the bottom of Friars' Vennel and pick me up when you're ready,' she called over her shoulder, allowing him no opportunity to protest further.

It didn't take Peter long to get his hair cut and buy the few things he needed. He was waiting on the Whitesands, impatient to get back to the farm as he had promised but there was no sign of Gerda. She was deliberately testing his patience as well as Ewan's. If Peter was late back, Ewan would know she had been with him. She saw him sitting in his little Morris Minor, drumming his fingers on the steering wheel and frowning anxiously.

The windows were wide open and holidaymakers strolled along beside the River Nith, watching the water cascading over the salmon leap. Normally Peter would have enjoyed watching them but today he felt tense and uneasy. He barely knew Ewan's wife. He had never been alone in her company before. Usually she scarcely passed the time of day when she saw him. So why was she being so different today – surely it was not just because he had admired her baby ...

'Here I am! Not too late, I think.' She leaned against him deliberately, drawing in her long legs slowly, taking time to smooth her skirt before she shut the car door. She turned to look at him.

'Mmm, the barber has certainly cut away your lovely curls,' she gurgled throatily, and to Peter's consternation she reached out and ran her fingers seductively through his hair, allowing her fingertips to trail down the side of his neck. He jerked away sharply.

'We're half an hour late,' he said shortly and started the car, driving away with several bumpy jerks. He cursed silently and felt the tell-tale pulse beating beneath his jaw.

He prided himself on his driving. Gerda leaned forward to place a carrier bag on the floor between her feet, showing an expanse of thigh as her skimpy skirt wrinkled up. She made no effort to tug it into place, well aware that Peter had noticed, even though he was making a good show of keeping his eyes on the road.

Once they were out of town and cruising along the Lockerbie road, she turned towards him, a smile hovering on her full red lips. He glanced at her and wondered if she had any idea how much more beautiful she looked when she lost her sullen pout. He could understand why Ewan had suffered such a fatal attraction.

Gerda laid a hand on his thigh. He almost swerved into the grass verge.

'Don't do that!' But she didn't remove her hand. He brushed it away roughly.

'Why, I do believe you're shy, Peter?' she said softly and edged closer so that her shoulder touched his. 'Have you ever had a woman ...?' She blew gently, right into his ear. He shivered. He could smell her perfume and feel the soft brush of her hair. Her hand moved back to his thigh and this time her fingers splayed out, far too probing for Peter's comfort. He put his foot down on the accelerator and the little car shot forward, but that didn't stop her searching fingers and he pushed her away.

'Yes, I've had women!' he told her coldly. 'They are two a penny. A wife is different. Or ought to be,' he added pointedly.

'Being wives doesn't mean we're not still women,' Gerda murmured. She lifted her hand to brush her fingertips over the newly cut hair at his temple. 'Being married has not changed me ...'

'Then it should have done!' Peter said harshly, and knocked her hand away, none too gently.

'So what would *you* want in a wife then, Peter?' Gerda purred, undeterred by the grim set of his mouth and the frown which creased his brown forehead. She knew she was making him feel uncomfortable, disturbing him. She enjoyed teasing. He changed gear as they turned off the main road and he did not answer. Gerda persisted. 'Don't you want to get married? You're getting old,' she taunted.

'Old?' He glanced at her.

'Well, you must be at least ten years older than Ewan.'

'Ewan is just a boy,' he snorted. 'He should be enjoying life, not tied down with a wife and children.'

'Tied down!' Gerda was indignant. 'I'm the one who is tied down. I'm the one who's had to bear his brat!'

'It was your choice. No one forced you to marry him.'

'So! You haven't told me what you want in a wife? I think I can guess though. You'd want a woman who put your slippers to warm every night and did …'

'I can tell you what I wouldn't want in a wife,' Peter said fiercely. They were almost at the cottage now he realised with relief. He turned to face her as he drew the car to a halt. 'I wouldn't want a slut for a wife, a woman who flirted with every man she met.'

'Why, you!' Gerda's pale eyes were like ice as she raised her hand. Peter pushed it down.

'I wouldn't if I were you,' he said quietly, and she saw the contempt in his expression. Over Peter's shoulder she saw Ewan approaching, a look of surprise on his face at the sight of his wife in Peter's car. Her own car was still standing at the door of the cottage and he'd thought she was inside looking after Paul. Suddenly Gerda leaned towards Peter and pressed her mouth to his, then climbed out of the car. 'Thank you so much for a lovely afternoon, dear Peter,' she said loudly. Peter's eyes widened in shock and he brushed a hand angrily across his mouth. He was unprepared for the door opening on his own side, even less to find Ewan's furious green eyes staring down at him. He knew at once Ewan had witnessed the kiss – knew too that had been Gerda's intention.

'Sweet Jesus!' he muttered and brushed a hand across his eyes.

'What the hell do you think you're doing with my wife? Who asked you to take her out?'

'She did.' Peter felt at a disadvantage sitting in his car with Ewan standing over him. 'She said her car wouldn't start and ...'

'Don't tell me lies! There's nothing wrong with her car. You're using that as an excuse to go jaunting with my wife. My wife! You ...' Peter pushed him away and clamoured out of the driver's seat. He stood straight, the same height as Ewan now. They faced each other.

'I'm talking to you man to man, Ewan,' he said quietly, 'not as your paid employee. If you can't control your wife then don't blame me. I didn't ask her to come with me today, or want her for that matter ...'

'Oh no?' Ewan gave a harsh laugh. 'That's not what it looked like to me. What would you have done if I hadn't arrived, I wonder.'

'Possibly slapped her face,' Peter said evenly. He sighed heavily. He had always got on well with Ewan, but in some ways he was still so young, even though he was a husband and a father. 'I'd hate to see you hurt, Ewan. Surely you must know if I wanted a woman I could get one any Saturday night on the Whitesands in Dumfries.' He saw Ewan's eyes open wide and realised Ewan had probably not known that sad little fact of life. How sheltered his life had been. 'I would never take another man's wife, Ewan – least of all that of my boss. I'm happy here. You know that too. What you don't seem to know is how to handle a woman like the one you've chosen for a wife – and what's more I can't advise you in that. But I'm telling you now, just keep her away from me in future.' Ewan stepped back automatically and Peter got into his car and drove away, but he had a sick feeling in the pit of his stomach. Somehow he knew that wouldn't be the end of the matter.

Ross was tired. It was always a busy time of year but now that they had both silage and hay to gather in each crop seemed to run into the next without respite. As soon as the sheep were sheared, and sometimes even before, the first of the silage was ready to cut. The state of the grass was important to get protein for winter feed for the cows, and the right amount of sugar in the leaf to encourage a good fermentation. Ewan was adamant that it had to be at the right stage. Day after day they carted the heavy loads of fresh grass to the pits, levelling it and rolling it to get the ideal conditions, enough heat but not too much, and there had to be no air pockets. They wanted only the beneficial bacteria to multiply.

Then the pits had to be covered and weighted to make them as air- and watertight as possible. Ewan would have liked to erect roofs over the silage pits to keep them dry but Ross felt the cost was more than they could afford. As soon as the grass had grown again, the routine began once more, topping up the pits so there was plenty of silage for the winter. No sooner was that done than the hay was ready. True, they didn't make as much hay since Ewan had left college because he preferred the silage, because they already had a milking parlour and cubicle sheds which he had adapted for easier feeding. He had influenced Bridie with his ideas too. She was considering converting the Lochandee byre into a milking parlour, but that meant she would need to build a huge shed for cubicles to house the cows in winter. It would cost thousands of pounds.

One of the officers from the government buildings in Dumfries had advised her about getting a grant to help pay for it. Expansion was what the government wanted.

Ross sighed heavily. Everything seemed to move at a pace faster than he could keep up with these days. No sooner was the hay in than they would be making a third cut of silage and even before that was finished the corn harvest would be ready.

He frowned. Rachel was tired and irritable these days too. He was sure she was doing too much, looking after Ewan's child every day. It was not as though Gerda went to work, or came and helped with the hens, or the calves. She did nothing. He wondered how she filled her day.

When they were busy with seasonal work, Bridie always sent Frank Kidd and his father over to help. Sandy was getting too old for hard work now but he still liked to come for the hay and harvest. He always said no one made a harvest tea like Mistress Maxwell, but Ross realised it was all extra work for Rachel too. The busier the men became the busier she was too. Of course, Peter went over to help with the hay and harvest at Glens of Lochandee in exchange but that did not lessen Rachel's workload.

Max and the twins loved to come to Nether Rullion if they were on holiday from school. Max was 12 and a useful young worker, and already as good with the tractor as Frank, although it made Ross uneasy to see him in charge of the big machines.

'I'm careful, Grandpa,' he insisted. 'I do exactly what Dad's taught me to do, and he says so long as I do that, I'll be safe.'

Alicia and Margaret loved to help with baby Paul, but that was a mixed blessing for Rachel. They were ten years old and sensible. They helped her collect the eggs, then clean and pack them into boxes ready for the packing station. They entertained wee Paul and took him for walks in his pram. She loved them dearly and enjoyed their company, but they had healthy appetites and enjoyed their granny's cooking – particularly her rhubarb pies and gingerbread.

Ross resolved to have a word with Ewan. Gerda was the only member of the family who didn't pull her weight. Ewan was irritable and tired too, and there was a tension between him and Peter which Ross had never noticed before. Indeed the whole atmosphere troubled him.

At Skeppiehill, Lucy often felt hot and tired as the summer progressed. The baby was not due until October and she did most of the milking herself while Don worked at the hay and harvest. The rest of her time was spent feeding the calves and hens, as well as making teas to send to the harvest field for Don and his brother, and young Richard Green who had recently left school and become a full-time worker.

Don's father had succeeded in his ambition to buy the farm which neighboured Home Farm. He had decided it should be for Jake, his youngest and favourite son. Neither Don nor Lucy could feel much enthusiasm. They were afraid it might make Mr Greig even more mean with money. Don had already spoken to his father about needing an increase in his weekly pay, now that Lucy needed to give up teaching, and with a baby soon to be fed and clothed. Mr Greig flatly refused. Lucy knew Don's mother had quarrelled with her husband about it. In fact, the relationship between Don's parents was decidedly strained and it troubled Don when he felt he was the cause. The only time Mrs Greig spent any time with Chris was when she came over to see Don and Lucy and arranged to meet her mother too.

As soon as Lucy had recovered from the baby's birth, Chris and Adam planned to be married. Her mother was aware of her plans, but it grieved her that her only daughter was to be married so quietly and without her father to give her away.

'Oh, Ma, he gave me away the minute he knew I was a lassie!' Chris exclaimed impatiently, then hugged her mother when she saw how hurt she was by the whole affair. 'I'm not bothered about a fancy wedding, Mum, honestly. Adam and I know we love each other. We know

146

we're right for each other. Surely that's what matters?'

'I know it is, ma bairn, but I canna understand your father being so bitter about Adam. He's a hard-working young man and he's a fine stockman. He might even get a farm one day ...'

'Oh, he will, Ma. He certainly will,' Chris said, pursing her lips with determination. 'We're not doing so bad already – just that the land we rent is spread out, with a bit here and a bit there, and the animals take more looking after. But we'll show Dad. One of these days he'll realise Adam is just as good as any of his sons. Except our Don ...' she added softly. 'Nobody works as hard as he does, nor for so little. I don't know how he puts up with Dad. Surely he's given them more money now that Lucy has had to give up her job?'

'Not yet he hasn't. If he doesn't, I've told Lucy she must keep as many hens as she can manage to look after, so long as she can sell the eggs. She'll have to keep the money.'

'But then Dad will stop paying Don altogether, or cut down the pittance he allows him.'

'Surely he'll not do that?' Mrs Greig said with troubled eyes. 'He'll drive Don away if he goes on being so mean. You know he has it in his head that if he keeps Lucy short of money she'll go whining to her parents. He thinks they're made o' money and they'll just keep handing over to her.'

'But that's terrible! Lucy would never ask anybody for anything. She's too proud. Anyway, Don would hate that. Besides ...' She frowned. 'I don't think the Maxwells *are* wealthy. They work hard and seem to be making a success of the tourist buses, but they earn their money, just like farmers do, except it's a different kind of business.'

'I know that, and I've tried to tell your father, but he doesn't want to listen.'

'No, he's getting more thrawn as he gets older. I never

remember him being this mean and miserable when we were all young.'

'Oh, he's always been a bit tight with money,' her mother said wryly, 'but he never grumbled about me keeping a bit o' egg money to myself so we always got by. The thing is, he's real proud o' the way Don runs the farm. When the neighbours compliment him and Lucy as a pair o' hard workers, he laps up all the praise. "Aye," he says, "I brought up ma lads we-el," and takes all the credit!'

'Mmm. Well, Don's not that soft. You wait, the worm will turn one o' these days if Dad doesn't treat him fairly. After all, he's got a farm for each o' his sons now. Willie will get the Home Farm, and Jake will have the new place. He can't expect Don to go on handing over all the profits from Skeppiehill, just so that Jake can act the gentleman. It's time his blue-eyed boy got down to some hard graft, like everybody else.'

Her mother nodded, but her eyes were troubled. She didn't like to hear Chris sounding so bitter, even on Don's behalf. She'd always been such a happy, cheerful girl, and had worked as hard as any of the boys, but her father had taken her for granted.

# Chapter Twelve

Lucy's baby was born with the minimum of fuss on 4 October 1965. Don was thrilled with his baby son, and felt a deep surge of love for Lucy as she looked up at him, pale and tired, but supremely happy, a tender smile curving her soft mouth.

'I do love you, so very much,' he whispered huskily. Silently, he vowed he would make their lives happy and provide well for them. Surely now his father must see he had to have his independence, to make his own decisions or mistakes and, above all, provide a decent living for his wife and child.

'What shall we call him?' Lucy asked. The birth had been nothing like as bad as Gerda had threatened. She was thankful her baby was perfect, but for now she was exhausted and relieved it was over.

'Chris wants to come to see you both tomorrow,' Don said. 'She can hardly wait to see her new nephew.' He grinned wickedly. 'We'd better think of a really shocking name, before she dreams one up for us. I think we should keep away from family names and then we don't offend anyone. What do you think?'

'We-ell, all right, but I would have liked to call him Harry for a second name. I always thought of Harry Mason as my father, and he *did* love me. He was a good man.'

'I'm sure he was,' Don said gently. 'Of course we'll

call the wee fellow Harry. How about Zacharias for his first name?' he suggested solemnly, making an effort to keep his face serious. Lucy's eyes flew open.

'You wouldn't ...' Then she saw the twinkle in Don's eyes and knew he was teasing. 'What about Alexander?' she asked, 'Or Niall ... Or Fearcher – that's Gaelic for Farquar, I think. It means "very dear one".'

'Mmm,' Don said doubtfully. 'Don't you think it should be short – easy to spell for the wee fellow? What about Ryan?'

'Ryan ... Ryan Greig ... Mmm, I think that sounds all right. I'll try it out on Chris, if she does manage to visit us tomorrow.'

'Oh, she will. And I think Conan and Fiona and Mrs Maxwell are hoping to drive up to see you on Wednesday, if you feel well enough.'

'Oh, I'll be fine once I've had a good sleep. It will be lovely to see them, Don.'

'Yes. I expect Mum will pay a quick visit tomorrow. She can't wait to see her first grandchild.'

He bent and kissed her tenderly. 'I'll leave you to rest now, my darling. I hate going home without you ...'

'I know. I wish I were coming with you. One of the nurses says it will be a week before I can get home.'

'You've done a splendid job. Babies are so helpless,' Don said, looking down at the tiny dimpled fists of his sleeping son. 'When you think how calves and lambs just get up and walk and feed ...'

'I know,' Lucy smiled. 'That's what I said to the nurse, but she said cows don't have to wash nappies and iron little nightgowns. She's advising me to rest while I get the chance.'

'She's right, and you're almost asleep now, so I'll let you have peace. I'll be back tomorrow night.'

Rachel stared now at the helpless infant, sleeping so

peacefully with his hands above his head. She felt tears prick her eyes and had to struggle to keep them back. This was her great-grandson. She could scarcely believe it. She'd had her 60th birthday in May but still didn't feel like a great-granny.

'He's a beautiful baby, Lucy,' she said, and her voice trembled. She swallowed hard and looked at Conan. He knew exactly what she was thinking. He gave a wry grimace.

'No, I don't feel like a granddad, so don't ask!' But he grinned widely. 'You've done well, lassie,' he said looking down at Lucy, watching them anxiously.

'You have indeed,' Fiona agreed and Lucy was surprised to see her eyes fill with tears. 'He's so lovely, and he looks so helpless ...'

'He certainly knows how to feed,' Lucy told her with feeling. 'I'd be glad if you could come up and stay for a day or two when I get home?'

'Oh, I'd love that,' Fiona agreed instantly, and looked at Conan. He shrugged.

'It's OK with me. Things are easing off a bit now the summer bookings are over. Of course, it would be better still if you could come down and stay with us, Lucy, but I don't suppose there's much chance of that?'

'No,' Lucy said regretfully. 'I'm afraid not. Don could have done with a wee break. He works far too hard, but there's not much we can do about it at present.'

'Your mother's cottage at Lochandee is for sale,' he said suddenly. 'Fiona and I thought of buying it ...'

'Whatever for?' Rachel asked in surprise. 'I didn't even know it was on the market.'

'Oh, it was just a whim. The old couple who were in it have neglected it rather, and the garden is overgrown. It seems sad to see it like that and I don't think it'll make much money, although there's plenty of ground at the back. It's a good site. It would be a good investment if I thought Lucy and Don would ever have any holidays to spend there ...' He sighed. 'It was just a thought. We really miss you, lassie. I wish I could have afforded to buy a farm nearer to us for you and Don but we can't manage that.' He looked down thoughtfully at the sleeping child. Rachel followed his gaze. Was he thinking of the baby's future?

She never knew exactly what was in Conan's mind, but so far he seemed to have made the right decisions as far as his own business was concerned. In fact, she had to admit she was proud of Conan and Fiona's achievement, building up a completely new business from nothing. It always gave her a thrill these days when she saw one of their buses on the road, heading for places she had barely heard of.

Conan was not sure himself why he wanted to buy Beth's old home, except that he knew Lucy had been happy there as a child. Indeed, he'd spent many happy hours himself in the bicycle shop with her great-grandfather, old Mr Turner. It was just a gut feeling he had that he wanted to buy it. Of course, he wouldn't consider it without Fiona's approval. She agreed it might prove an asset, so long as the asking price was reasonable, but she knew it would never be worthwhile as a holiday home for Lucy and Don, much as she would have loved the idea. Don simply didn't have time for holidays.

Back at Nether Rullion, Ross was tired and irritable. He couldn't bring himself to make the effort to go with Rachel to visit Lucy, much as he longed to see her and the baby. Conan had tried hard to persuade him to take a day off and accompany them. The thought of getting ready, and the long drive, seemed like a huge effort. Now with Rachel gone and the house quiet, he wished he had gone. He felt lonely and dispirited.

In his heart, Ross knew it was his own lack of energy

which depressed him, but he also knew he must have words with Ewan. Things could not go on as they were. Rachel had too much to do and Gerda took advantage of her love of children, and baby Paul in particular. He spent so much of his time with them now, it was almost as though he was their son instead of their grandson. He was a bright, happy baby. Ross loved him almost as much as Rachel did, but he didn't have the extra workload of caring for him.

So instead of taking his usual rest after lunch, Ross went out to wait for Ewan's return.

'Come into the house, Ewan,' he said as soon as he saw him walking up the track from his own home. 'There's things we need to talk about.'

Ewan's heart sank. He could see by his father's grim expression that this was serious and not just the farm his father wished to discuss.

As soon as they were indoors Ewan turned to him. 'If you're wondering about Peter and me ...'

'This has nothing to do with Peter,' Ross interrupted, 'but since you mention it, I've noticed he doesn't seem as happy as he was, and there's tension between the two of you which I don't like. I've always run a happy ship and Peter's a grand worker, an honest and reliable man, so whatever is wrong between you, you'd better put it right.'

'I will. It was a stupid misunderstanding on my part anyway.'

'Good. It's Gerda I wanted to talk about. She doesn't pull her weight. It's bad enough that she neither wants to work at her own job or help with anything here, not even the hens. Most farmers' wives are glad to look after the poultry.'

'She's just not used to country life. Besides, I didn't think Mum wanted to give up her hens ...?'

'She doesn't, but she can't do everything. You knew Gerda would have to live in the country before you married. We did try to tell–'

'I know! I know!' Ewan snapped, then quickly, 'I'm sorry, Dad.' He rubbed a hand over his brow. 'She – she doesn't seem to want to adapt …'

'Well, she should at least look after her own bairn!' Ross said shortly. 'Your mother has far too much to do.'

'I thought she liked having Paul?' Ewan looked hurt.

'She does. She loves the wee fellow. We both do. I know she'd rather look after him than spend time doing the accounts, but they have to be done as well, and it's all too much. And don't tell your mother I've been discussing this with you.'

'Of course not,' Ewan nodded. 'I'd be willing to take over the bookkeeping, if you think Mum would agree. Would that help?'

'We'll ask her. Don't think she's been grumbling about having Paul. She loves him, but he's your bairn. I'd have thought Gerda would've wanted to care for him herself.'

'I expect she'll be better with him when he can walk and talk. She hates changing his nappies …'

'From what Billy Smith says his mother does that more often than Gerda – *and* does all the washing. I think if you bring him up here a few hours each afternoon that should be plenty.'

Ewan had expected another quarrel when he conveyed the gist of his father's comments to Gerda. Surprisingly, she seemed to consider them seriously and later that evening she offered to help with keeping the farm accounts. He was surprised and pleased. Maybe she had found an interest in Nether Rullion at last, he thought with relief. Certainly he had more than enough work to do himself.

Ewan was increasingly aware how easily his father became breathless and how quickly he seemed to tire, even when attempting light tasks. He wondered whether his mother had noticed the changes, and whether it was really his father who was tired of Paul. He'd certainly seemed irritable today and that was unusual – and why hadn't he gone to visit Lucy?

Gerda was less pleased the following day when Ewan insisted she must take care of their son more often herself.

'I suppose your mother will only have time for Lucy's baby now!' she snapped.

'Lucy's …?' Ewan stared at her. 'Don't talk daft,' he laughed. 'Mother only went for the day, to see her and the baby. They're too far away to visit very often. And I can't see Lucy and Don having much time to come down here. Don seems to be even more overworked than I am.'

'That's what you think. I know your mother has been knitting for Lucy's brat. Even the woman who works at Lochandee knitted two pram suits for him.'

'Emmie?'

'If that's her name …'

'Emmie is Frank Kidd's wife. She's known us all our lives. She and Lucy's mother were close friends. Anyway, she knitted two jackets for Paul when he was born, didn't she? How do you know she knitted for Lucy, anyway?'

'Bridie was going on about it.'


It was a long winter for Ross. He had several bouts of severe bronchitis and each one seemed to leave him more prone to the next infection. He refused to stay in bed.

'People die when they take to their beds,' he insisted stubbornly. 'Anyway, I can breathe better when I'm sitting up.' More than once he'd added softly, 'And I like to be near you, Rachel.'

She knew this was true, and indeed she felt easier in her own mind when she could keep an eye on him as she worked, peeling the vegetables, making broth, just cooking and baking or cleaning the eggs. They talked when he had the energy and he dozed when he was tired. She kept the kitchen as cosy as she could, thankful for the constant heat of her Aga cooker. It was rare for the doors and windows to be closed at Nether Rullion, but Rachel watched over Ross diligently, constantly afraid of draughts or anything which would give him a chill.

She was thankful she no longer had the responsibility of paying the bills and keeping the books. The government were becoming ever more watchful for things like income tax, especially where they thought businesses avoided it. They had to keep accurate accounts and obey more regulations than ever before. She'd heard Bridie telling Ewan one of the conditions of accepting a government grant was the presentation of her accounts to the Department of Agriculture inspectors.

'It's to prove we're worthy of the grants we've been given for building the new milking parlour and cubicle shed,' she explained. 'We're supposed to prove we've made Glens of Lochandee more efficient with the money.'

'I'm glad I've kept the hens myself, then,' Rachel said, as she listened to their discussion. 'I always keep a cash book. Just in case any of the inspectors want to take a look.'

'You'd be lost without your hens and chickens, Mum,' Bridie grinned. Ewan said nothing. Gerda and he'd had an almighty quarrel when Gerda discovered she was not to handle the cash from the egg sales. He couldn't understand it because she didn't want anything to do with the hens themselves.

'I'll be back to see you tomorrow,' Bridie said to her father. She followed Ewan outside and they talked for a little longer before Bridie drove home.

'I think Ewan's a bit worried about the way Gerda looks after wee Paul now that Mother doesn't have him so often,' she said to Nick when they were snuggled up together in bed later that evening.

'Why? I mean she's nothing else to do and surely even Gerda wouldn't neglect her own baby?'

'You wouldn't think so,' Bridie agreed slowly, but Nick could tell she was frowning, even in the darkness. 'Maybe it's just Ewan being over-anxious. He thinks the world of wee Paul. What did he say exactly?'

'O-oh, he was just asking me if babies always got red cheeks when they were getting teeth. They often do, of course ... But – but he seems to think Gerda slaps Paul across his face when he cries. Apparently she hates changing his nappies so she just leaves him until Ewan gets home, if Mrs Smith isn't there to attend to him.'

'And Ewan changes the nappies?' Nick asked incredulously. 'More fool him then when Gerda's sitting around all day twiddling her thumbs.'

'Well, what would you do if your baby was crying and miserable, and your wife refused to attend to him? You wouldn't just leave him. You're too soft-hearted for that.'

'I'd spank my wife's backside and tell her to get on with it.'

'Oh, would you indeed!' Bridie said. 'You and how many men?'

'Just me, cariad,' Nick said softly and drew her closer. 'The best wife in the whole world, I have.'

All thoughts of Ewan and his wife were forgotten.

Ross's health seemed to improve, and once or twice he even made the effort to travel into Lockerbie, which surprised Rachel as he rarely went to town except to the market.

The New Year was barely over and Ross had done his usual work helping with the milking and the calves to relieve Peter and Billy Smith over the holidays. Gerda alternately sulked and grumbled because Ewan couldn't take a break.

'Even if I could leave the cows to milk themselves, where would either of us want to go in the middle of winter?' he argued.

'I've heard some of the young farmers are going off on a skiing holiday,' Gerda said, 'but we never go anywhere exciting.'

'We're not exactly young, free and single any more either. We're a married couple with a son to care for.'

'We could leave him with your mother now that your father is keeping better.'

'Oh no, we couldn't,' Ewan said angrily. 'Paul is our responsibility. Anyway, my mother has him often enough as it is, since father's chest improved.'

'Well, we could take him with us then ...'

'No! I'm not going anywhere at this time of year. All we need is a frosty spell and there's frozen pipes to thaw every morning before the animals can drink, not to mention the roads to clear to get the milk tanker in if we get snow. I can't leave my father to cope with all that.'

'I wish I'd never married you, you miserable bastard! Even *my* father was going abroad for Christmas.'

'Was he?' Ewan's eyes widened in surprise. 'I didn't know you'd heard from him. You said you'd quarrelled ...'

Gerda flushed guiltily.

'I haven't heard from him,' she muttered. 'Nor do ever I want to hear from him again. One of his old neighbours sent me a Christmas card, if you must know. He's gone and married that – that woman!' Gerda's red mouth curled contemptuously.

'Daisy? He's married Daisy and never said a word to anyone?' Ewan laughed aloud. 'Well, good for them. I hope you've written to wish them happiness? We should send a wedding gift ...'

'Over my dead body! Anyway I don't know where they are.'

'What d'you mean?'

'It seems Daisy owned her own house as well and they've both sold up and taken off. According to Mary

Docherty they're thinking of settling abroad somewhere where it's warmer. She only sent a card because she'll be crowing over me!'

'Why would she be doing that?' Ewan frowned. 'She probably thought you'd want to know ...'

'Don't be so bloody stupid! She'll be laughing up her sleeve because she knows I'll not get his house now – not when he's got another wife. I'll bet it was her who persuaded him to sell it. She'll be spending the money and enjoying herself.'

'They both will, and why not?' Ewan reasoned. 'Your father has worked all his life. Anyway, I liked Daisy.'

Gerda stared at him as though he was mad, then uttered a stream of oaths and slammed out of the house. He heard the car start and raised his eyebrows at his small son, playing on the hearthrug at his feet. Paul raised his own dark little brows in perfect imitation and Ewan laughed and scooped him up, cuddling him close.

'You're all the compensation I need for putting up with a bad-tempered wife,' he whispered, knowing Paul was still too young to understand or repeat his words.

It was the middle of January when Ross developed another severe chest infection. There was great anxiety for several days and Fiona telephoned Lucy with news every evening. Suddenly the weather took on a brief spring-like spell and Ross's health seemed to take a turn for the better too.

'I have a terrible urge to go and visit,' Lucy confided to Don that evening. 'You know, he's never seen Ryan yet. Would you mind terribly if I drove down to Nether Rullion now the weather's improved a little? I thought we could stay overnight with Fiona and drive back again in daylight.'

'All right,' Don agreed. He leaned forward and pulled her close, kissing her gently. 'You know I'd feel happier if I was coming with you both, but I really can't get away at this time of year.'

'Oh, Don, I know that.' She reached up and touched his cheek. 'I wouldn't expect you to go. I'm not sure why I suddenly feel the need to go myself but I have this sudden urge to see them all … Silly, isn't it?'

'No, sweetheart, it's not silly at all. They're your family and we didn't even get to see any of them at Christmas this year. You go while the weather's reasonable.'

'All right, I'll phone Fiona now and we'll go tomorrow if it's convenient.'

Although the days were short, a pale sun broke through the February chill as Lucy drove down the twisty road towards Dumfriesshire. She enjoyed the familiar glimpses of the river and Drumlanrig Castle as she drew nearer Dumfries, before cutting across country in the direction of Nether Rullion. There were still pockets of snow behind the hedgerows and on the hills, but Lucy felt a surge of happiness as she approached the familiar countryside and the warmth of welcoming faces.

There were even more welcomes than she had anticipated by the time she reached Nether Rullion. All Bridie's children attended Dumfries Academy now. She'd collected them straight from school and driven over so they could all see baby Ryan. Rachel hugged her warmly and took the sleeping baby from her, holding him down for Paul to see. The lad was 11 months old now and pulling himself up at every chair or ledge. He poked gently at the woollen bundle in his grandmother's arms and looked up enquiringly. 'Bay-bay …?' he enquired, round-eyed. Margaret and Alicia both wanted to hold Ryan at the same time. Obscured by the general hubbub, Lucy managed to regain control of her own emotions. She was overwhelmed by their warmth, but shocked at the sight of her grandfather's haggard face, so pale and thin. He'd always had such a healthy outdoor look and it smote her heart to see how frail he seemed, how ready to take a seat by the fire.

'Tea's all ready,' Rachel smiled, reluctant to relinquish her hold on the baby who was smiling at all and sundry after his long sleep in the car.

'He'll probably show me up tonight by not sleeping at all,' Lucy smiled ruefully.

'Don't worry about that, lassie. Fiona and Conan will want to make the most of him.'

'Yes,' Bridie agreed, 'and Nick will be popping over there to see you both later this evening.' She glanced towards her father and lowered her voice. 'We thought it better not to have everyone here at once.'

Lucy nodded her understanding and bent to talk to Paul.

Ewan stood in the doorway, silent in his stockinged feet, unobserved. Lucy's love of children, her gentle voice and smiling face were all such a contrast to his own wife, he thought, with a touch of sadness. His small son was doing his best to chatter in response to Lucy's baby talk, holding out his favourite toy motor to her.

'You're a beautiful boy, aren't you?' Lucy laughed and picked him up in her arms, catching sight of Ewan's wistful face as she rose to her feet. Paul saw him too and chortled even more merrily, holding out one chubby arm. 'Da-da, Da-da,' he announced triumphantly. Ewan came forward then and kissed Lucy on the cheek, enquiring after her health and how her journey had been.

'How's Gerda?' she enquired in return, but she couldn't miss the shadows which darkened Ewan's green eyes, so like her own. It had always been like looking at a mirror image.

'Gerda is ... she's in good health. She – she needed to go into town. She'll be sorry she missed you ...'

Lucy nodded. She knew Ewan far too well. Gerda had not wanted to be here. And Ewan was not a happy man.

'Conan was telling me Gerda has joined the amateur dramatics club? Is she enjoying it?'

'I reckon so. She was there several evenings a week before Christmas, helping with the pantomime. She works behind the scenes – makeup and costumes and things, I think.' He spoke without rancour and Lucy wondered if he found it a relief to have peace from Gerda's constant company now they were married. She had always found the other girl's carping and criticism very wearing herself. On the other hand, Ewan loved her or, at least, he had loved her when they married and she had no reason to suppose that had changed – had she? She looked at him more closely. There was no doubt he looked strained and tired but his father's health and the extra responsibilities of Nether Rullion could account for that.

Later Conan and Fiona welcomed her and baby Ryan just as warmly. Fiona was reluctant to put Ryan down to sleep for the night. She had bought a second-hand cot and Bridie had brought over some baby blankets which had been left from the twins' baby days. A little later, Nick called in, but when the news and weather came on Lucy saw his laughing face sober dramatically. The announcer was forecasting the end to the brief spell of fine weather with the threat of hard frost with snow in places, particularly Scotland. He and Conan exchanged frowning glances.

'Do you have to return tomorrow, Lucy? Are you sure you couldn't stay a few days with us?' Conan asked, knowing what her answer would be, even before he asked.

'I must go home tomorrow!' Lucy said in consternation. 'I promised Don ...'

'Aye, well, I think you should stick to the main road then,' Nick advised solemnly. 'It'll be busier, but you'll be less likely to get stranded if there's other traffic about. The gritting lorry will have been out if there's much ice or snow,' he added quickly at sight of Fiona's anxious expression. 'I'll be getting back to Lochandee now then and let you get a good night's sleep.'

Conan went with him to the door and Lucy knew by their low voices they were concerned for her. She turned to Fiona with a reassuring smile.

'We'll leave straight after breakfast and be home by lunchtime, so don't worry. I just had a feeling that I wanted to see my grandfather again, after he has been so ill. I – I got rather a shock though. I'm glad I came. I'm pleased he's seen Ryan.'

'Ye-es.' Fiona looked at her oddly, noting her pensive face as she stared into the leaping flames. 'We're all truly happy to see you Lucy, but I'll not rest easy until you phone to let us know you're safely home.'

# Chapter Thirteen

Nick returned to Rullion Glen the following morning before Lucy had even started to eat her porridge.

'I know there's no sign of snow here yet, Lucy, but it's been a hard frost and Bridie thinks there could be snow up by Cumnock. I've a spare set of wheel chains here so I'll pop them in the boot if that's all right with you? Do you know how to fit them?'

'I-I think so,' Lucy frowned. She hadn't had time to listen to the weather forecast and it was still dark outside, but she guessed it was going to be one of those bleak February days when it never seemed to be proper daylight. She felt her stomach begin to churn. Perhaps she shouldn't have come to visit at this time of year after all. Then she remembered the shock she'd felt at the sight of her grandfather and knew she was glad she'd made the effort. He had been touchingly pleased to see her and Ryan, his first great-grandson. She thanked Nick for his trouble and summoned a wavering smile. 'You're very thoughtful, Nick. I do appreciate it.'

'A pleasure, it is, Lucy,' Nick said gruffly. 'We wouldn't like the car to skid with the baby and you. There's too precious, you are.'

'We'll hope the chains aren't needed,' Conan said, 'but they're a big help if the roads are bad. I'll put a shovel in too. I see you've already got a spare travelling rug. If you're prepared, you'll not need anything.' He grinned. 'I

164

think I'm beginning to sound like my mother. Remember how she worried about us, Nick, when we were home on leave from the RAF?'

'Indeed I do. Kind she was too. Packing up food for the journey, in spite of the rationing.'

Lucy hastily swallowed her own breakfast, feeling a sudden urgency to be safely home again with Don. She wasted no time in preparing Ryan for the journey, tucking him warmly into his carrycot as soon as he'd been fed and changed. He had slept most of the way down, as he usually did when the car was moving, but today he seemed to sense her own tension and whimpered fretfully. Conan insisted on securing the cot to the back of the rear seat with two raincoat belts, in case the car should skid. Fiona had filled a large flask of hot coffee and packed sandwiches.

'Just in case you get delayed,' she smiled wanly, wishing Lucy didn't have to make the journey on her own.

'We know you're a careful driver, Lucy,' Conan assured her, 'but you can never be sure what sort of problems other drivers might cause. Best to be prepared, and if you've any doubts turn round and come back here. I'm sure Don would prefer that, rather than have an accident.'

'Yes.' Lucy nodded, swallowing the lump in her throat with difficulty. She hugged them both warmly and climbed into her car, blinking back tears. How blessed she was to have two people who loved her so much, when they could both have resented her. In spite of the bitterly cold morning she felt an inner warmth, kindled by the love of her friends and family.

The house telephone rang at Rullion Glen Garage. Fiona answered and gave the number, feeling a strange quiver in her stomach.

'Hello, it's Don Greig here.' The line crackled

abominably. 'Can I speak to Lucy, please?' he shouted.

'Hello, Don. Lucy left here about an hour ago ...'

'Oh, hell! I didn't expect her to leave so early. Straight after lunch, she said yesterday ... Should've phoned sooner. Hello ...? Can you hear me?'

'Yes. Is everything all right?'

'Weather's terrible here ... I wanted Lucy to wait with you ...' A loud crackle drowned the rest of his words.

'Phone us when she gets home!' Fiona called quickly, but she didn't know whether he'd heard her or not. The phone in her hand was burring but there was no connection. She tried to call him back, but without success.

She pulled on her coat and boots and made her way down the icy path to the bottom of the garden, oblivious for once of the snowdrops peeping through beneath the sheltering rhododendrons which she and Conan had planted together. As she made her way to the garage to find Conan, the sky glowered ominously overhead. She shivered. There would certainly be snow before night. How quickly the weather could change at this time of year. She wondered what instinct had urged Lucy to drive down to see her grandfather at this time of year now he seemed to be recovering at last. Yet it had been like spring yesterday and the day before. Who could blame her for wanting him to see her son?

Gerda was irritable and short-tempered. She had no excuse to go to the drama club until preparations started for the next play. Some of the players had been given parts, but so far the costumiers and stagehands had not met to discuss their plans for the production. She couldn't wait for the next meeting. Hubert, the new stage manager, thought she'd made some good suggestions towards the last production. Although she had been one of the poorest students in the music group at college, her basic training was proving an advantage now and she'd discovered a hidden talent for devising dance steps to suit the music. Gerda glowed when he expressed his appreciation so openly.

Hubert Boyd-Hill was relatively new to the area, as she was, and this forged an additional bond between them. She basked in his admiration. More than once he'd offered to drive her home. She had been forced to decline because she had her own car, but she knew from his expression that he was disappointed by her refusal. If he asked again, she would explain that she was only refusing because she didn't want to leave her car in town. She shuddered at the thought. Her car was the one thing which made life at the farm bearable. She would feel like a prisoner without it. Besides, what explanation could she give to Ewan? He'd been furious with her for begging a lift into town with Peter when there was nothing wrong with her own car. She couldn't use that feeble excuse again.

Even so, she resolved to find some reason for getting better acquainted with Hubert. He was at least five years older than Ewan – maybe more – and had lived in London, so was clearly a man of the world. He told her he'd come back to Dumfries when his elderly mother was ill. She had since died, leaving him her house. He'd decided to stay in the north for a while until he had sorted out her affairs. Dick Bone, one of the main actors, hinted that was not true. He said Hubert had lost his job and come to stay with his mother because he was short of money. He said she'd been frail for years and Hubert had never been near when she needed him. Gerda preferred to think Dick was jealous. She had seen Hubert driving away in a sleek black Jaguar so that proved he wasn't short of money, didn't it? Most of the women in the little company hung around him, including Dick's girlfriend, so she guessed he resented Hubert's charisma and good looks.

Paul had been playing on the rug in front of the fire,

but he began to demand attention, and then to cry. Gerda frowned and swore under her breath.

'What's wrong with you now!' she snapped, exasperatedly. 'You've had your dinner. You can't possibly need changing again, you sodden little pee-bag!'

'Gan-gan ... want Gan-gan.' The little boy began to cry in earnest. Gerda glared at him, then her eyes narrowed thoughtfully. She glanced out of the windows. Big flakes of snow were still swirling from the leaden sky but they were melting almost as soon as they landed. Why shouldn't she drive into town? If the snow did settle, she might be a prisoner here for days. Why shouldn't she grab a little time to herself, while she could? That's what she needed to cheer her up: a little jaunt into town. She hated winter and the short dark days. The idea had no sooner entered her head than she was bundling Paul into his coat and leggings. She would drop him off with his grandmother then she could smarten herself up in peace before she set off for town.

Rachel had stopped asking where Gerda was going or when she would be back, only to have her head snapped off. But today she looked anxiously at the lowering clouds and ventured her opinion.

'The snow's falling faster now. I think we'll have a fair covering before dark,' she said anxiously.

'I need to go into town to get stuff for him,' Gerda muttered, glaring towards her small son, whose chubby arms were clasped around Rachel's neck as though he would never let her go. 'I'll be back before the roads get bad. Send him home with Ewan after he's finished milking his bloody cows.' She turned on her heel and hurried back to the car without waiting for Rachel to agree.

Rachel pursed her lips. She hated to hear Gerda swear, especially now Paul was picking up words and trying them out for himself. She sighed. It never occurred to her daughter-in-law to ask if it was convenient to leave the child for the afternoon. She hugged him tightly. She loved him, of course she did, and she knew he loved being with her, but today it was too cold and wet to take him outside with her to gather up the eggs. She would have to leave him with his grandfather while she hurried round the hen houses on her own. She frowned briefly. Ross tired so easily still, although his chest was much improved. When he was tired, he was easily irritated – even with Paul, much as he loved his small grandson.

Gerda donned the fur coat which had caused such anger and dismay when she'd been threatened with the bailiffs. She snuggled into the soft fur and preened herself before the mirror. She had regained her slender figure and felt elegant in her high-heeled, thigh-length boots. She paused a moment, frowning angrily as she remembered Alicia remarking that she looked like Dick Whittington in the pantomime at Carlisle. It was bad enough when the twins dissolved into giggles, but she caught the look which Nick and Conan had exchanged and the suppressed smiles on their faces. She'd been furious, but now she twirled before the mirror and admired her own reflection. What could they know about fashion? Nothing! She looked good. She felt good. They could snigger as much as they wanted. She arranged the matching fur hat on her blonde head and fixed it at an attractive angle.

The roads were still clear, although the snow was coating the fields and hedgerows with white and the windscreen wipers were kept busy clearing snowflakes. The town was quiet but the shops were well-lit and Gerda's spirits rose. She'd keep away from Barbour's today. Her account was already overdrawn and she had a feeling some of the staff had been warned. Having opened accounts at two of the shops in Carlisle recently, she determined to go down there to view the new spring fashions when the weather cleared. Meanwhile, she'd have a browse around Binns and perhaps buy herself a new perfume. It was warm and bright inside the department store and her spirits rose. She still couldn't get used to Dumfries being such a small country town after being used to such a wide choice of department stores in Glasgow. Not for the first time, she wondered whatever had possessed her to tie herself down to a life in the country. Ewan's adoration had cooled and she couldn't twist him around her little finger with the promise of sex any more. There was no excitement in her life …

She dabbed perfume on the inside of her wrist from the sample which the smiling assistant offered.

'Let me buy that for you,' a deep voice said behind her left ear. Gerda spun around, looking up into the dark, handsome face, with a shadowy outline of stubble around his jaw.

'Why, Hubert! I didn't expect to see you today.' Her pleasure was evident in her shining eyes and parted lips. If she'd been a cat she would have purred loudly, Hubert thought cynically. 'I can't decide which of these two perfumes to buy.' She dabbed a more expensive perfume on her other wrist and held them out for him. He bent his head and she was surprised to see a faint sprinkling of silver at his temples. It added maturity and increased his desirability, she decided. If he was going to buy the perfume she would choose the most expensive one. He said he preferred the first one, being wise to the ways of women, and well-versed in the price of such fripperies. Gerda was not so kittenish underneath and she insisted she would really prefer the second. She made a good pretence at displaying shock when the assistant stated the price.

'Let me take you for a cup of tea in the restaurant,' she smiled winningly. 'That's the least I can do, since you have been so generous.' She linked her arm through his as he tucked his wallet firmly back into the inside pocket of his jacket and buttoned up his overcoat. She drew him unresisting towards the lift.

They lingered a long time over tea and cream cakes. The restaurant was quiet with few shoppers willing to linger more than necessary in such uncertain weather. The waitress hovered in exasperation. She wanted to clear the table and be ready to leave as soon as the manager gave permission. She glanced anxiously out of the tall windows which overlooked the street. The snow was beginning to lie now and the road below was white, even where the car tyres had left tracks. At last, she breathed a sigh of relief as the couple rose to go.

Gerda smiled with satisfaction. It had been a profitable afternoon. She'd made all her explanations to Hubert Boyd-Hill and he'd offered to collect her at home and drive her to the drama club meetings so that he could see her home afterwards.

'Indeed, why wait until the meetings start officially,' he said softly, looking directly into Gerda's pale blue eyes. 'We could start our own discussions as soon as the weather clears. It sounds as though your husband is too busy to ask questions.'

'How right you are! Ewan's far too preoccupied with his cows to bother about my arrangements.' She gave a tiny pout. 'I'm really looking forward to sharing our mutual interests.'

'And so am I. So am I,' he said as they stepped into the lift. They were alone as the metal doors slammed shut. He turned and drew her into his arms, kissing her expertly, until her lips parted. He lifted his head with a small smile of satisfaction. He wondered if her husband's family was really as wealthy as she pretended. The mink coat she was wearing must certainly have cost a pretty penny. He would see for himself when he collected her.

They were both surprised at the changes on the streets when they emerged from the warmth and brightness of the store to snowflakes swirling all around them and pavements thickly coated.

171

Gerda drove slowly and carefully. She had no wish to damage either herself or her car. Inside she felt a bubble of excitement as she recalled her meeting with Hubert. It didn't occur to her to wonder why he was not at work in the middle of the day like most other men in midweek. The snow was thicker as she turned on to the narrower roads where there had been less traffic. She peered through the windscreen. She ought to wear glasses for driving, but she hated the thought of anything which would mar her beauty. She was later than she had meant to be and wondered whether Ewan would be home before her. She hoped he was attending to Paul. She frowned at the thought of her small son. He was a burden she'd dismissed while talking to Hubert. Her mind was going over the afternoon's conversation when the offside front wheel of her car caught the grass verge, hidden by snow. It skidded across the narrow road and tilted sideways, half in a ditch. Gerda panicked. She revved violently but the wheels spun uselessly. It was really dark now. She fumbled in the glove compartment for her torch and switched it on. No response. The battery was flat. Why hadn't she checked? She hated the dark.

What was she to do? Should she wait for Ewan to come and search for her? But no, if he was home he would be looking after Paul, and he would probably be angry because she was not there to look after him herself. She pushed open the car door with an effort, and scrambled out. Her feet were already frozen and damp from the short walk in town. The soles of her fashionable boots were thin and not meant for trudging down a country road where the snow was now well over her ankles. Her fur coat, her beautiful mink, was getting wetter by the second and she tried to hurry, blinking the snow from her eyelashes. Before long, she reached the end of the short lane leading up to the two cottages and even from here she could see the light streaming out from Mrs Smith's kitchen window, but her own house was in darkness. She tried to see her wristwatch but it was too dark. Surely it must be after six o'clock though, so why wasn't Ewan home and getting Paul his supper, preparing him for bed …?

The reality was Ewan felt extremely harassed and angry. In her haste not to leave Paul too long with his grandfather, Rachel had hurried round the hen houses as fast as she could, while taking care not to break any of the precious eggs. They were always scarce at this time of year. The days were so short, with the weather damp and cold, so the hens couldn't be blamed for wanting to stay inside all day. On days like this they were settling down to roost for the night by three o'clock in the afternoon. Rachel was coming out of the last wooden hut when her foot slipped on a patch of ice beneath the virgin snow. She tried hard to hold on to the basket of eggs but in doing so she twisted her ankle, making her wince with the hot shooting pain. She could have wept with frustration. At least half the eggs would be cracked or chipped and she had barely enough to keep her regular customers supplied at this time of year. She hated to let them down. Her ankle throbbed painfully as she turned to secure the wooden door, and for the first time in her life Rachel forgot to close the little trapdoor which the hens used.

She was hobbling painfully across the farmyard when Peter Forster came round the end of the tractor shed. He hurried to her side at once, his face filled with concern. He took the basket from her frozen fingers and gave her his free arm to lean on as he helped her back to the house. Rachel felt embarrassed as he helped her off with her wet coat and proceeded to ease her Wellington boot from her swelling foot. Peter had infinite patience but, in spite of his gentleness, Rachel couldn't help but wince.

'Thank goodness it's not broken,' she said shakily.

'This is almost as bad.' Peter frowned anxiously. 'It's swelling rapidly. Sprains need a cold compress and a crepe bandage for support. You'll need to rest it.' He kicked off his own snowy boots. 'Let me help you into the kitchen where it's warm, then I'll bring Ewan to help you and to make a cup of hot tea.'

'Thank you, Peter,' Rachel said faintly. 'You're a good laddie.' Peter smiled to himself. He would always be a laddie in the eyes of Mr and Mrs Maxwell. He settled her by the Aga and reassured Ross that nothing was broken. Paul would have climbed on her knee to kiss her better but Peter forestalled him, explaining gently that his Gan-gan was hurt and couldn't cuddle him just now.

When Ewan saw what had happened, he realised his mother had probably been hurrying too much. His lips compressed. As soon as he had bound up her ankle and placed it on a low stool he made tea for her and for his father. Then he hurried out to find young Billy.

'Go down to the cottage and tell Gerda to come up here at once. Tell her my mother has injured her ankle,' he said brusquely.

Billy returned, as there was no reply at Mrs Maxwell's cottage and the car was away.

'Ma would come and help if I tell her what's happened,' Billy suggested. Ewan thought for a moment.

'All right then, Billy. Take the tractor down and bring her on the back of it, if she's willing. Explain what's happened. Maybe she could make the evening meal and keep an eye on Paul until I've finished the milking, or until Gerda returns,' he added grimly. 'And Billy ...'

'Aye?'

'Ask your mother if she would help up at the farm instead of working for my wife at the cottage. My mother will have more need of her until her ankle is better. Gerda can do her own housework, aye, and look after Paul. It'll give her more to do than driving off to Dumfries every day,' he muttered angrily, more to himself than for Billy's hearing, but the lad had sharp ears and he repeated Ewan's words to his mother.

'Aye, it's time the laddie saw sense.' Her eyes gleamed with satisfaction. 'Time he stood up to that lady wife o' his like the man he is. Spoiled her he has, frae the very beginning. I'd rather help up at the farm any day. At least Mistress Maxwell appreciates what folks do for her, and that's more than ye can say for her ladyship.'

'Hurry up then, Ma. Ewan said I was to give ye a lift on the back o' the tractor. Can ye hold on?'

'Aye, laddie. Better than walking up tae the farm in this snow. Thoughtful laddie he is, Ewan. Just wait while I get ma coat and scarf, son, then I'll be with ye.'

Don tried to telephone Fiona and Conan shortly after two o'clock but he couldn't even get the operator. Why, oh why wasn't Lucy home by now, he fretted, pacing restlessly around the kitchen, reluctant to go back out to work, yet knowing there was nothing he could do if the phone lines were down.

Back at Rullion Glen, Fiona was just as worried. She tried to phone Don for the umpteenth time.

'Lucy will be safely home by now,' Conan reassured her. 'They can't let us know if the phones aren't working.' Even so he had come home early. There was little to keep him at the garage today, but his thoughts had been continually with Lucy and his own baby grandson.

'Ours are working,' Fiona said irrationally, and Fiona was never irrational. 'Br-Bridie ph-phoned.' To Conan's consternation, she began to weep, silent tears rolling down her pale face.

'Hey!' he said softly, dismayed. Fiona never cried. She was always in control of her emotions – well, except for some things, but that was passion and this was real distress. He drew her gently into his arms. 'There's no need to get so upset. Lucy is an excellent driver.'

'I-I know. B-but Bridie was worried too. Sh-she had

heard the tail-end of a radio announcement. The r-roads are bad up by Sanquhar. Th-there's been an accident somewhere near C-Cumnock ...'

'An accident? When? What did it say?'

'A c-car ...' Fiona's voice was barely audible and she hid her face against his chest and clung to him. Conan's arms tightened. He felt suddenly tense.

'What did they say?'

'A c-car and two lorries. One ... one person k-killed. No n-names y-yet. It mustn't be Lucy. It c-can't b-be Lucy! But ... b-but ...'

'Oh God.' Conan breathed. 'Oh dear God, please don't let it be Lucy ...' He sank down onto the settee, taking Fiona with him. They clung to each other, each needing the other's comfort and reassurance. Conan rarely showed his deepest feelings but Fiona felt his cheek damp with tears against her own.

'Lucy's all we have,' she sobbed against his chest. 'I've never been able to give you children.'

'Ah, Fiona, my darling girl. I don't need children. You know I love Lucy, and I know you do too. You've been a wonderful mother to her – a sister, a friend and confidante – but you mean more to me than anyone, or anything, in the world. I don't tell you often enough how deeply I love you. How much I need you. So long as we have each other, we'll get through this – together.' His voice cracked and he held her tightly, stroking her hair, even while his own heart was breaking at the thought of Lucy and their baby grandson, possibly still trapped in the car somewhere. 'I must not – we must not – let out imagination run riot,' he murmured against her cheek. 'We're fearing the worst but, so long as we're together, we'll face whatever has to come,' His arms tightened around Fiona's shivering body. 'Meanwhile, my darling, we must have faith. We must hope and pray Lucy and wee Ryan are safe.'

176

# Chapter Fourteen

Don Greig heard a tractor and tugged on his coat and boots, thinking one of the neighbours must need help. He was astonished to see his father chugging slowly into the yard.

'What's wrong?'

'That's a fine way to greet your old man!' He switched off the engine. 'Your mother's been nagging me since 11 o' clock. She can't get through on the phone.'

'It's out of order. Is yours on?'

'Aye. It's only yours, and the few cottages along this road, I reckon. Somebody must've run into the telegraph pole at the junction. The line's down.'

'So it'll be on in the village?' Don asked eagerly. Why hadn't he thought to go down on the tractor and try the call box?

He half-turned away, but his father asked abruptly,

'Is that wife o' yours back wi' the bairn? That's what I've come to find out.' His face was grim, and Don knew he hadn't come of his own accord.

'No, they're not back yet. I'm just going ...'

'She's a silly bitch going visiting at this time o' year. And you're a silly bugger for letting her go.'

Already tense as a fiddle string with worrying about his beloved Lucy and their baby son and the worsening weather, Don's anxiety boiled into anger. Furious anger. Suddenly uncontrollable.

'You're right, Dad! I *am* the silly bugger! Staying here, working for you like a bloody slave. Getting paid a pittance for my trouble. Why *should* Lucy have to stay away from her family when they're ill? I should've been with her, but I can't leave your bloody farm. Yes, yours! It's not mine, is it? Not one blade o' grass, not a single piece o' straw, not even the muck I barrow to the midden every day. Adam and Chris are better off than we are, yet you despise him for not being the son o' a farmer! I've no say in how things should be run. I can't employ a man. I've no money to pay one. And there's Jake, a farm bought for him, in his own name, no less! He hasn't a single bloody cow to milk, but he's got two men running after him, while he twiddles his thumbs. Lucy and me, we're slaving here to pay their, yes *their*, wages ...'

More and more words tumbled out of Don in a fast and furious torrent. He was powerless to stop them. All his pent-up frustrations poured forth, but his anger was fuelled by his anxiety for his wife and son. Even when he paused for breath his father stared at him open-mouthed. Don, his eldest, had always been the easiest to manage – the quiet, hard-working son. He had the patience of the true stockman. He rarely swore, never lost his temper ... Even when Don swung away from him he couldn't speak. Don, white faced and tight-lipped, stared up at him coldly. 'Now you can bed your own bloody cattle. They're yours, after all. Everything's yours! I'm going down to the phone box.' He strove for a calm he could not feel. 'And I'll tell you another thing! Don't send me any more of your dirty dealing heifers to milk, because I'll send them right back to you!' Yet, even as he strode towards his own tractor he noticed one of the lights on his father's needed a bulb. His father was a hopeless mechanic. He would see if he could get a spare bulb at the machinery repair shop on the way back.

Fiona was relieved to hear Don's voice but her spirits

sank when he told her he was calling from the call box in the village and there was still no sign of Lucy.

'I-I'd hoped to hear they had returned to Rullion Glen,' Don said dully, and only now did he realise how much he had pinned his hopes on hearing Lucy was safe. Fiona could not add to his worry until they knew more about the accident at Sanquhar and one person killed.

Lucy drove steadily, negotiating the twists and turns on the road to Thornhill, and on past Drumlanrig Castle, through Sanquhar, her spirits rising as the miles to home and Don grew fewer. The wipers were still managing to keep the windscreen fairly clear, but she could see the snow was getting thicker and faster. Ryan had slept almost all the way down and she hoped fervently he would do the same most of the way home.

The thought had barely entered her mind when she came upon a line of traffic. The driver two cars in front got out to pass on the news that a car had skidded on a patch of ice while turning into a farm road.

'We'll not be held up long though,' he said reassuringly, his eye on the carrycot as Ryan began to stir. 'Two young fellows in a van are manoeuvring it out o' the way. There's nobody hurt.'

'Thank you.' Lucy summoned a smile and wound up the window, but the cold blast of air and the man's voice had been enough to disturb Ryan and he began to whimper. Lucy sang softly, hoping the sound of her voice would soothe him as it usually did, but she could feel her own tension mounting as the snow blotted out the world while they waited.

Eventually, the vehicles began to move again and she breathed a sigh of relief. Surely the movement of the car would put Ryan back to sleep. But her baby son had other ideas. He was nearly five months old now and blessed with a fine pair of lungs when he decided to exercise them. Nothing Lucy could say, or do, while driving would pacify him and she felt her own tension growing with the noise and his obvious distress. Normally, when the roads were clear, she would have been at least three-quarters of the way home by now. In front of her, a large articulated lorry slowed. Another lorry coming in the opposite direction stopped and the two drivers held a brief conversation. Lucy risked a quick glance round at Ryan and saw his small fist waving furiously, one woollen mitten already off. His woolly hat was lopsided, covering half his face at one side and stuck behind his ear at the other, as he writhed and struggled.

He couldn't be cold. Fiona had filled a small hot-water bottle and tucked it under the mattress of his carrycot and he was warmly clothed. Perhaps his struggles and yells had made him too hot, or probably thirsty. Lucy frowned. At least she could give him warm milk and a reassuring cuddle, but where? About five minutes later the lorry in front indicated he was turning off into a lay-by. Instinctively, Lucy seized the opportunity to follow in the tracks he was making in the smooth white snow. She drew to a halt close behind the lorry.

She squeezed into the back of the car and wrestled with the straps Conan had used to secure the carrycot in the car. Obviously he had reckoned without her needing to undo them before she reached home. Eventually she lifted out her gasping baby son, opened her coat and snuggled him inside before she opened her blouse for him. He sucked greedily and Lucy smoothed his hot little brow with a gentle finger, relieved by the blessed silence.

'Anyone would think I was starving you, little one,' she murmured. She felt her own stomach churning but she knew it was more nerves than hunger. Even so she wouldn't mind a drink of hot coffee from the flask now she'd thought about it. She glanced at the lorry anxiously, praying he wouldn't leave until she was ready to follow.

Another lorry drew in behind her, the bonnet so close to her bumper she knew he must be nearly touching. She felt shut in between the two huge vehicles. She saw the vague shape of the driver going past her window to talk to the driver in front. She was startled a few minutes later when her car door opened and a man's head was thrust inside. She stifled a scream.

'Ooh, I'm sorry, lass. Didn't know you was- was ...' He nodded towards the suckling baby, his own face red. Lucy was quite decent but she felt acutely embarrassed.

'What do you want?' she asked tensely.

'Me and my mate there ...' He nodded towards the other lorry. 'We just wondered if you're all right, see? Didn't know as y'ad a baby.'

'I'm f-fine. Th-thanks ...' Lucy stammered.

'I stopped 'cause me mate stopped. Same firm, see.'

'Oh.' Lucy wished he would go. She wanted to move Ryan to her other breast. He began to whimper.

'I've kids back 'ome. Wouldn't let 'em out in this weather,' he ventured with a note of criticism.

'I'm on my way home now. I've been visiting a sick relative,' Lucy said defensively. 'Now if you'll excuse me ...' Another head appeared.

'Did y'tell 'im, Bill? Ooh! It's a woman. You all right, love?'

'She has a kid. She's feeding it.'

'Oh. Sorry, love. We wondered if you wanted a hot drink? I 'ave a flask and a spare cup. Me wife allus sends me off OK in this weather.'

'Thank you. I have a flask. Will you be staying here long?' Lucy ventured anxiously.

'Naw, not long. The lorry back there, 'e stopped to tell us there's a bit of an 'old up further up t'road. Lorry slipped 'is load or summat. We'll wait till you're ready. You follow in my tracks and Bill 'ere'll watch you from behind. Peep yer 'orn when yer ready t'move on.'

'Thank you. Y-you're v-very kind.'

The journey seemed to Lucy to get slower than ever from then on. The snow was falling faster now. Suddenly the brake lights in front flashed urgently and they ground to a halt. After about five minutes, the two lorry drivers climbed from their cabs and met at the tail of the first lorry. One of them tapped on her window. She was reluctant to open it in case the cold air wakened Ryan again. She wound it down the merest crack.

''E's gone to see what's wrong. We'll let yer know, love.'

It seemed ages before the two men came back. It was like being alone in a white closed-in world, just her and Ryan. Lucy grew more and more agitated as the snow piled up beside the road. She wished she could telephone Don. But even if she could have reached a phone in this wilderness, he wouldn't be in the house. He was probably thawing out water bowls so the cattle could drink, or collecting the eggs instead of her. Her heart sank even further when the lorry drivers returned. She could see by their solemn faces they were getting anxious too, though they spoke cheerfully enough.

'Looks like we'll be 'eld up for a good while yet, lass. There's trouble up ahead. I could bring yer one've me sandwiches ...'

'No, no thank you. I have a pack somewhere.' Lucy looked round vaguely. 'B-but how long? I mean, why ...?'

'Seems there's an accident. Take a while to clear. You get that rug round yerself, lass.'

'Get your feet up off the floor.' The other driver advised. 'Further away from t'snow. You'll keep warmer snuggled up. Nothing else we can do but keep warm and wait. We're going into the cab in front. Peep if yer want owt.'

''Ave a bit of a nap if yer can, love. Looks like being a slow journey, even when t'road's clear.'

'Where yer 'eading anyway, love?'

Lucy explained the way she usually took across country to Skeppiehill.

'Y'd be better staying wi' us, love. Follow me up as far as yon big roundabout, then double back.'

'It's a bit further but y'd be safer, lass,' his companion nodded. 'I'll knock on t'window when we're ready t' move. Don't you worry? D'ye want owt from yer boot?'

'Er ... no thanks. I've got the baby's things in here. I have chains in the boot? Perhaps I should put them on now the snow is getting deep?' She hoped she could remember Nick's instructions.

'They wouldn't do any 'arm, love. We'll just put 'em on now for yer, if yer like?'

Lucy accepted gratefully. 'You've been very kind, but you must be wet and cold, and I don't even know your names ...?'

'Bill Rowbottom.'

'Johnny Greenhough,' they said in unison and grinned cheerfully.

Don was subdued and deeply troubled as he drove back from the village, but he'd remembered to get a bulb for his father's tractor and as soon as he got back he fixed the light. His father appeared at one of the shed doors, fork in hand. He came across and clapped a hand on Don's shoulder.

'Ye're a good lad, Don. I'll think on what ye said and we'll come to an arrangement. About you managing things here.'

'Right,' Don nodded, but his mind was on Lucy. It would be dark in less than an hour today, what with the snow and heavy clouds. 'You'd better be getting home. Mother will be worrying about you. Remember to put your lights on.'

'What news o' your wife and bairn?'

183

'They haven't returned to Dumfries. Lucy must be on the way here.' His father nodded, and frowned up at the glowering sky. 'Let us know if ye can. We'll report your phone out of order.'

'I did that from the call box. They'll not repair it until the weather improves though.'

When his father had gone, Don collected the egg basket and hurried round the half dozen hen houses, collecting the eggs. Most of the hens were already perching for the night and he shut them all in to save returning later. He had begun to realise what a lot of work Lucy did outside, between her hens and rearing a few capons and geese for Christmas, as well as feeding the calves for him. For two summers now she had kept two hives of bees and done quite well with the honey from them. She and Chris had both decided it would be a worthwhile sideline for a bit of extra cash. He hoped his father would remember and keep his word about making changes, but he knew what a control freak his father had become – how reluctant he was to hand anything over. Knowing this had made it all the more of a shock when he had bought the farm for Jake and put it in his name. The hurt had been greater because Jake was the youngest of the family and had done least to build up the family business.

Lucy couldn't believe she had half-dozed. It was the sound of tapping on her car window which alerted her.

'We're ready to roll, lass. You OK?'

She nodded, blinking her eyes and stretching her stiff, cramped limbs. She longed to go to the toilet and to stretch her long legs outside but this was neither the time nor the place. She realised the two lorry drivers had been busy shovelling away snow from her car and helping other vehicles in the line. She was tremendously grateful to have met up with such good Samaritans. Mercifully, Ryan was still sleeping peacefully, snuggled up in his cot. She wished she had a radio in the car to hear the news and weather. She had forgotten to wind her watch this morning in her haste to get away. She'd told Don she would be leaving soon after lunch, so hopefully he wouldn't be too anxious yet.

Both the lorry drivers tooted their horns at her when they reached the roundabout. Lucy tooted back as she veered off on the last leg of her journey home to Don. She had made a note of the name of the Yorkshire firm on the back of the first lorry, already resolving to write and thank both the drivers. She knew the road well now, but the snow was deeper with less traffic and the side roads were the last to be cleared and gritted. She was glad of the chains helping to grip the packed surface but it took her twice as long as usual to reach Skeppiehill.

As she drove into the yard she could see the lights streaming from the byre making yellow paths across the snow, and illuminating the dancing snowflakes. She gave a huge sigh of relief and thankfulness. Before she went into the house, or even lifted Ryan from the car, she ran to the byre door to tell Don they were safely home.

Afterwards, young Richard Green told his elder brother and Chris, 'I thought he'd never stop hugging and kissing her, he was that pleased to see her.'

'Just you wait until you fall in love, kiddo,' Adam grinned. 'I expect poor old Don was worried sick having his wife and bairn out on the roads on such a night.' His expression sobered. 'And it was a nasty accident that held them up. It could easily have been Lucy.'

'Thank God it wasn't,' Chris said seriously. 'I was worried sick and, according to Mum, even Dad was relieved when Don phoned from the call box to say they were safely home. I see in the newspaper one of the other people who was injured has died, as well as the driver.' She shuddered. 'Yes, I can imagine our Don just about wetting his breeches with worry. Lucy and young Ryan are his whole world.'

Spring came with a flourish of primroses on the grassy banks and beneath the hedgerows. Shy wild violets peeped out from their secret places and Ross was thankful to be alive. He was able to get outside again without fear of the cold, blustering winds which had robbed him of his breath and wrapped iron bands around his chest until he could scarcely move. Rachel was relieved to see him looking so much happier. She knew nothing of his difficulties with the wind and the iron bands, but she had sensed how tense and unhappy he had been. His mind so often seemed to be concentrating on other things as he sat brooding beside the fire, or shooting questions abruptly at Ewan. He came in regularly to keep his father up to date with the progress of the spring sowing, or newly calved cows, the lambing and all the other farming developments. She suspected Ross had too much time to think and his thoughts had magnified into anxieties during the long periods he had been forced to spend indoors. They had both felt it was a more drawn-out winter than usual, though in fact it had been just another season.

Ross had insisted Ewan should employ another man, which concerned her, thinking he was giving up on life. Common sense told her he would never be fit to do the full day's work of a healthy young man again, but his brooding troubled her. So it was a relief to see him outside again, taking an interest in the stock, the newborn lambs and, surprisingly, even the garden. In truth, Ross felt as though he'd been away for a long time and was seeing everything through new and appreciative eyes.

Rachel was surprised when he insisted on driving to Lockerbie, even though it was not a market day. Usually they discussed everything connected with the farm and family. She wondered whether these visits had something to do with his health, but no doubt Ross would confide in her when he was ready.

Her own spirits rose with the spring sunshine. She'd taken delivery of a new batch of day-old chicks and they were chirping merrily in the electric brooder which Ross had bought for her two years earlier. It had taken her some time to get used to buying in chicks ready-hatched instead of setting broody hens on clutches of eggs. Now they came in boxes, little balls of yellow fluff, already sexed. She still marvelled at this, as it was a blessing not having twice as many cockerels as she wanted. Even so, she still liked to rear a few ducklings from the odd broody hen.

There were still days of blustery showers, more like March than May, but they didn't usually last more than a day or so. Ewan had only a few ewes left to lamb, stragglers which were late for one reason or another. He had penned them in a small field on the other side of the farmyard and taken the rest of the flock to new pastures farther away. Ross enjoyed keeping an eye on the few remaining ewes. He felt he was doing something worthwhile while Ewan and Peter got on with other work in the fields.

It was on one of these afternoon checks around the ewes that Ross saw one with a lamb hanging. Ewes could be notoriously stupid and the moment she saw Ross she set off at a run across the small paddock with the half-born lamb still dangling, obviously needing a little help to ease it into the world. At the same time, Ross was aware of the clouds gathering beyond the barns. He guessed another sharp shower was on the way and, with it, the increasing bite of the spring winds so typical of his native south-west Scotland. He sighed. He ought to hurry towards the barn and shelter until it passed, but by then the lamb would be dead and he hated to see death in any young animal when it could so easily be prevented. The little group of sheep had gathered together again and were circling closer.

He waited, still and silent, feeling the first cold drops

of rain on his cheeks. The ewe came with the rest, obviously feeling safer as part of the group. Ross waited until they were near the corner of the little field, then he made a grab for the ewe. He had years of experience of the ways of sheep and he caught her, grabbing her thick fleece and drawing her down, struggling to hold her until he could reach the lamb with his other hand. But the ewe was well grown and heavy and in her stupidity she resisted and struggled with all her might.

Ross hung on grimly and succeeded in helping the lamb, willing it to live as it lay slimy and bedraggled. He wanted to rub it dry before the wind and rain chilled it, but his breath caught in his throat and the familiar iron band tightened around his chest, holding him on his knees. He bent forward, gasping against the restriction in his chest. Warily, the ewe came closer to investigate the feeble bleating of her offspring. She licked it dry, nudging it to get onto its feet and follow her away from the figure of the man who now lay sprawling on the grass, one hand outstretched.

'Rachel ...' he breathed on a last, long sigh.

The rain came in piercing silver darts, cutting, wetting, driven by the sharp gusts of wind. Moments later the sun reappeared, the wind sighed gently. A rainbow arched across the sky.

# Chapter Fifteen

Only three weeks earlier, Fiona had been rejoicing with Lucy over the news she was expecting another baby in November. She knew how much Lucy had always hoped to have more than one child, being an only child herself. Now she feared the shock of her grandfather's death, baldly reported over the telephone, might affect the mother-to-be, or the baby, so it was a relief when Don's deep voice came over the wires. He would break the news gently and he was there to comfort Lucy.

Don himself was shocked to hear of Mr Maxwell's death. They had believed he was making a good recovery. Sixty-four was not so very old, surely? If only the fire had not damaged his lungs. Even in his agitation Don thanked God that Lucy had followed her instinct to visit him in February. He shuddered remembering how nearly he had pleaded with her not to make the journey to Nether Rullion. She would never have forgiven herself, or him. At least she could be glad her grandfather had seen their baby son, his first great-grandchild.

Rachel was too stunned to fully appreciate all that Ross's death would mean to her, or to those around him. All she knew was that she had lost her lifelong friend and companion, as well as her husband and the father of her children.

At his funeral, the little church at Lochandee had been

packed but she was overwhelmed by so many faces. Afterwards the memory was no more than a blur. She could not even recall the reassuring words of Jordon Niven, the young lawyer, when he had talked with her after the funeral. In her heart she felt nothing he, or anyone else, had to say could make the slightest difference. For the present she could think no further than coping with each day, and even worse, each long night.

Ewan felt the full weight of the burden of running Nether Rullion now. He was 25 and responsible for the employment and welfare of two men older than himself, as well as young Billy. He must use them well, treat them fairly and pay their wages promptly. This had been his father's maxim, and now it must be his. His mother, his wife and his young son were all dependent on him alone now, and the income he must make from farming of Nether Rullion.

In response to Jordon Niven's brief letter, he had visited the lawyer in his office in Lockerbie, as he had requested. He was surprised and puzzled by some of the provisions his father had made. It was evident his mother had known nothing of the most recent changes and neither did she want to discuss them. Had his father had a premonition of his own death? What else had he seen of their future as he sat by the fireside? He must have observed more of the minutiae of all their lives than he had ever had time to see when he was out milking cows every day. Ewan felt no resentment about the changes. Indeed he felt an obscure relief.

After some reflection he decided not to tell Gerda the details of the provisions his father had made and of his discussion with Mr Niven. He knew there should be no secrets between a man and his wife but he sensed she wouldn't understand his father's decision. One thing she would certainly question was the legacy of £1,000 to be paid to Lucy. He hadn't yet brought himself to tell her of

Lucy's true relationship to his family. His intuition told him Gerda would be even more spiteful towards Lucy than she was already.

'Aah, Lucy …' He sighed softly. He could not forget her tear-drenched eyes, or the way she had clung to him after the funeral, understanding and sharing his memories and his grief. There had always been a close relationship between her and his father, even before any of them had understood she was one of the family – certainly before his father had arranged the music lessons when she was still a child, and later shared a mutual love of music. He was glad the bond he himself had shared with her remained as strong as ever in times of trouble. Theirs was one forged by more than the ties of blood; they had genuine respect for each other and shared a true friendship, which had grown and strengthened throughout their childhood and teenage years.

How gentle she had been with his mother. In contrast, Gerda had seemed almost callous. Fiona, ever shy of showing emotion, had seemed embarrassed in the face of his mother's grief, while Bridie had been in need of comfort herself. As always, she'd turned to Nick, as he should have been able to turn to Gerda, but Nick had proved a tower of strength to them all.

Gerda had offered no words of comfort to anyone. When he broke the news of his father's death later that afternoon, her first words, and her selfishness, had shocked him.

'Now Mrs Smith can return to her proper duties.'

'What do you mean?' He had been bewildered by her train of thought.

'She'll be working for me again, of course. Your mother doesn't need her now.' He still felt sick and ashamed for her.

'Mrs Smith will stay where she is.'

'You mean we're moving to the farmhouse?' Gerda's

eyes gleamed in anticipation. 'When?'

'No! For God's sake, Gerda, my father died less than three hours ago and you're already wanting changes. Have you no heart? No feelings?' He had not heard what Jordon Niven had to say then. 'Leave things be. Mrs Smith will be company for my mother in the days ahead, even if she doesn't need her help. Let her decide.'

'All you think about is your bloody family and your animals. Why don't you think about me, for a change?'

'Because you're hardly ever here.' Suddenly he was angry and disillusioned and the whole world seemed to be crashing around him. 'All you think about is yourself and your drama group! And that fancy spiv who calls on you – Hubert Hill, or whatever he calls himself.'

'Hubert *Boyd*-Hill,' Gerda corrected haughtily. 'At least he's civilised and knows how to treat a woman.'

Ewan didn't answer. He felt drained with grief, utterly alone. Only the chubby arms of his small son brought him comfort and hope for the future.

On 15 November Lucy gave birth to another baby boy, and Don knew he was the result of their passionate loving after the anxieties of the snowbound roads on that February night.

Chris, who was to be godmother, looked down wistfully at her small nephew.

'It's time you had a baby of your own.' Lucy smiled gently at her dearest friend.

'Adam and I would both love to have children, you know that. We're not quite ready for them yet, though. It would mean me giving up teaching. We've nearly paid for the cottage and at least it's habitable now. Maybe next year, when Adam sells his heifers …'

'Are they doing well?'

'Very well,' Chris said proudly. 'Bridie thinks they should leave a good profit, if they all calve without problems. She has her eye on one of them herself. She likes the breeding of it.'

'You're almost as enthusiastic as Adam, and Bridie herself,' Lucy teased.

'Well, it's our bread and butter. If we can't have quantity, we must go for quality, Adam says.'

'You've done so much in such a short time. I think you'll soon have quantity as well. At least you own your own home, which is more than we do. I hope your father is proud of you?'

'He'll never admit it, if he is. I don't think he'll ever approve of Adam. That's why we need to prove ourselves and get established before we have any children,' she said vehemently.

'Well, to be honest,' Lucy blushed, 'we didn't mean to have another baby quite so soon ...'

'Maybe not, but he's here and he's lovely,' Chris crooned, giving the white woolly bundle a hug. 'How about you and Don, then? Are you managing OK? Is Dad sticking to his agreement? Mum says he still refuses to put the tenancy in Don's name, even though Don pays for the rent.'

'That's true, but at least the rest of the decisions are up to Don now and I think we shall end up with a small profit this year, and hopefully a better one next year. It's been a big relief since your father stopped sending those lorry loads of cattle from his dealing. We can budget for the feeding and fodder now, so the work is more even. Don was always afraid the dealers' cattle might bring tuberculosis or abortion, or some other disease to infect our own cows. Now we know where we stand, he's grading up some of the better cows to pedigree status and we've started milk recording.' She grinned. 'We'll soon be in competition with you and Adam, and with Bridie and Ewan.'

'You'll need a spare bed for the milk recorder to stay

overnight then?'

'Yes. We're going to decorate the back bedroom as soon as I can find the time and energy again. It's a tremendous boon having a regular man to help with the field work, now I shall have two wee Greigs to keep me busy. Not that Richard isn't turning into a good lad,' she added quickly lest Chris should think she was criticising her young brother-in-law.

'Oh, I'm sure he's a good laddie but he's just a boy. He's like Adam though – he prefers working with the cattle rather than tractors. It suits him fine now that Ted Black is working at Skeppiehill. Dad should have let Don have a full-time man from the beginning.'

'I know,' Lucy said quietly. 'It was impossible to do it all. He still works too hard, but I don't think he can help himself. There's always another job to do.'

'Aye, Don was always the most conscientious of my brothers.' Chris smiled wryly. 'I can't imagine how Jake will run a farm of his own. He always managed to slide out of the jobs he didn't like when we were all at home. As for our William, he'll work hard enough when he has to, but he's like Mum; he'll do anything for a peaceful life, even when he knows Dad is being unfair – as he was to you and Don.' She gave Lucy a mischievous smile. 'That's two good things which came out of the February storms.'

'Two?'

'Yes, this wee cherub and Don losing his temper and standing up to Dad at last. He was so worried about you and wee Ryan he didn't care what he said to Dad. Have you decided on a name for him yet?'

'We're considering Cameron Donald – what do you think?'

'Mmm.' Chris repeated the names. 'Yes, I think that will suit you, wee fellow,' she crooned down to the sleeping infant. 'Though you'll probably get called Cam or Ron or Don …'

'Oh, don't say that!' Lucy pleaded, chuckling when Chris pretended to do a little dance as she sang the names.

The christening was just before Christmas. The weather was usually worse after Christmas anyway and Bridie had thought it might take her mother's mind away from the first Christmas without Ross.

'Mother has always made the Christmas dinner and had all of us around her. This year I've persuaded her to let me make it at Glens of Lochandee. No fuss, just Nick, me and the children.'

'What about the rest?' Lucy asked.

'Oh, Gerda never wants to come to family gatherings. Nick can't stand her anyway, so it's just as well. Ewan will probably enjoy playing Santa Claus this year. I expect Conan and Fiona will be coming to you if the weather is suitable?'

'Yes, I think they will, so long as the rest of the family don't mind?'

'No, better for Mother to have a quiet Christmas this year, I think. But if you're willing to have the christening, Lucy, that would be a good excuse for a family gathering, but without the emotional nostalgia this Christmas will hold for Mother. I'll make the christening cake if that would help.'

Lucy agreed, so the Greigs and the Maxwells were duly invited. At the last minute, Gerda said she felt unwell and decided it would be better if she spent the day at home in bed.

Chris came over early to help. They had arranged a christening luncheon after the morning service at the local kirk. This would allow the travellers to get home before it was too late, if the roads were icy. Rachel found it hard to join in the celebration but she was content to nurse the baby – another great-grandson – and listen to the conversation. She liked Don's mother. She was a homely woman who cared deeply about her family and clearly loved her two small grandsons, but Rachel had never felt easy about Mr Greig. She noticed the way he ignored Chris's husband, although it was obvious that Adam was very knowledgeable about cattle and pedigrees. She could hear Bridie and Ewan having a good discussion with Adam. Mr Greig's voice rose above the others and she half-listened as he quizzed Don about a bull he had bought the previous week.

'That was a fair price you paid – 480 guineas, I heard.'

Don quirked an eyebrow at Lucy and she smothered a smile. They had guessed his father would criticise.

'Well, he doesn't need your permission any more,' Mrs Greig defended her son. 'And he was always a fair judge o' a good beast.'

'Aye, I'm not doubting that. I'm just wondering where he got that kind o' money.'

'He didn't come and ask you for it anyway,' his wife retorted.

'Not yet he hasn't, but there's time.'

'Don't worry, Dad,' Don said drily. 'I wouldn't have bought him if I'd thought I would need to ask you for the money.' He refused to satisfy his father's curiosity.

Afterwards, while Chris helped Lucy with the washing up, she said quietly, 'I knew Dad would quiz about the bull. Don told me you'd given him half of the money your grandfather left you. I'm sure you won't regret it though. Adam says he has a fine pedigree and he should leave some good stock.'

'Yes, that's what Bridie thought. I'd have given Don all the money but he wouldn't take it. It was a struggle to persuade him to use half, but he really needed a bull and it's such an important part of the herd. I remember my grandfather telling Bridie a good bull was half the herd, though we do use more artificial insemination now. Don insisted we put the rest of the money in the bank in case of emergencies.'

As soon as Ewan and Paul had left, Gerda climbed out of bed and enjoyed a leisurely bath, generously perfumed with the new bath salts she had bought. Then she dressed in a new red woollen suit and high black suede boots. She flung her mink coat and leather bag carelessly onto a chair to wait for Hubert but she couldn't resist a last little pirouette before the mirror.

As time wore on, Gerda's anticipation and excitement turned to irritation, then to anger. Hubert had promised to collect her by 11 o'clock and take her out to lunch. He'd promised more than that and she felt a small quiver of guilt and apprehension for he'd made his meaning all too plain. Still, she shrugged, she was taking the contraceptive pill now so who was to know? There'd be no more mistakes as there had been with Paul. She grimaced at the thought. She would rather die than go through all that again.

Then at last she saw Hubert's car turn into the lane and her annoyance evaporated.

'I had thought we might have a bite of lunch here before we set out,' he said, 'but I saw that old bitch next door peeking from behind her curtains, so we'd better not linger.'

'But you said you were taking me out to lunch,' Gerda pouted.

'I know. I was waiting for the postman. I expected one of my clients to send me a nice fat cheque this morning but it hasn't arrived. So I'm a bit short of ready cash. I don't suppose you could bring a few pounds? I'll pay you back when I've been to the bank'

'I'll see how much Ewan has left in the drawer where he keeps the money for the wages,' Gerda said with a little frown. 'Now that bread's gone up to one and threepence ha'penny, I can never make the housekeeping last. Imagine, the doctors and dentist getting a 35 per cent pay rise, up to 4,000 a year! I keep hinting at Ewan that he should give me more money but he ...'

'Oh, don't go on so much about money!' Hubert said irritably. 'Just get some and let's be off.' Gerda frowned but she rarely argued with him, in case he stopped coming. He often mentioned clients these days, but she could never quite discover what sort of clients he had, except that they were supposed to be in London.

'I've booked us in for bed and breakfast in a ...'

'I can't stay for bed and breakfast!' Gerda gasped. 'Ewan will be back tonight.'

'Well, we know it's bed then dinner we really want, but I could hardly book for that, could I!' He sounded impatient. 'Not where we're going, anyway. It would be different in London, of course.' Hubert gave her one of those looks which promised so much, and yet made Gerda feel almost gauche. She was a little in awe of his confidence and sophistication. Sometimes she sensed a restlessness in him and wondered if he was bored and wearying for the bright lights of city life. Twice he had returned to London and she had missed his company badly. They often met when Ewan thought she was with friends, or at an evening class, or curling.

Hubert drove straight back into Dumfries. Gerda was surprised. As soon as they had parked the car he led her into a long, narrow café where they often met. As usual they went right to the back. Hubert ate heartily then immediately went off to the toilets, leaving Gerda to pay the bill and meet him outside. She was a little put out by this, even though he had warned her he was short of cash. Presumably he would pay for their bed and dinner with a cheque. She hoped so because Ewan didn't keep much cash in the house these days. She flushed. He must have realised she often helped herself. He had never said, but he hated quarrels, especially if Paul was around.

At the thought of actually going to bed with Hubert, Gerda's insides went into spasms of desire and tension. So far they had indulged in some rather heavy petting but she had always called a halt. This time he had made it clear they must seize this opportunity to sleep together while they had the chance. She knew part of the attraction was because Hubert was forbidden fruit, but she did enjoy the way he made her feel feminine and desirable. Her stomach clenched with anticipation. Wasn't she supposed to be an honourable married woman? A slight smirk lifted her mouth as she thought how shocked the Maxwells would be if they knew she was dishonouring their respectable name. Things had been grim enough when Ewan's father had needed to settle her debts after she bought her fur coat and a whole new wardrobe. Mr Maxwell was no longer in charge now though, and she could handle Ewan, or rather his finances, since he had entrusted her with the farm accounts. She had found it wasn't too difficult to hide one or two minor expenses, now Ewan was preoccupied with additional responsibilities. Again, she felt a twinge of guilt at her impending betrayal of her husband. Ewan did trust her, in spite of their frequent arguments.

She would have been surprised had she known of the problems, and potential scandals, each generation of Maxwells had faced and overcome with dignity. She would also have been furious to learn she had been kept in the dark about their family secrets, particularly where Lucy was concerned. She had always been jealous of Lucy.

'Where in the world are we going?' Gerda asked, sitting up straighter as they crossed the border into England.

'I've never been to this place myself,' Hubert admitted. 'It was recommended to me as suitably remote and they serve excellent food apparently.'

'I see ...' Gerda frowned as the shadows lengthened. 'It will be quite a long drive home. I'd like to be back and tucked up in bed when Ewan returns, remember?' Hubert gave her a sideways glance.

'Would it be so terrible if he discovered ... us? The worst that could happen would be divorce.'

'Divorce? I don't want a divorce!' Gerda sat up straighter. Hubert's lip curled slightly. No, you little goose, he thought, you want to have your cake and eat it, but I fancy a nice big slice too. His voice was silken smooth however.

'Just imagine the pleasures we could enjoy together, sweetheart,' he said softly. 'You could spend your money as you wished, without having to ask your husband.'

'Ewan never has that much spare money. His family have always ploughed everything back into improving the farm or the stock or the land. It's all tied up. They live well enough when it comes to food. They never skimp on anything in that line, but when it comes to clothes!' She raised her eyebrows and pulled a face. 'Bridie and her mother make a new outfit last about ten years! They've never heard of fashion. Even Fiona Maxwell is growing like them.'

'Fiona? She's the one who lives at Rullion Glen Garage?'

'Yes. Ewan reckons she has as much money, and as much influence in running the business, as Conan does, but she ...'

'She's very attractive, and she was very smartly dressed the day I saw her. Women like that don't need to follow fashion. They have style.' Gerda looked at him sharply. Was he trying to make her jealous? No, his admiration seemed genuine, but she still felt put out.

'You wouldn't find her very warm in bed, I'll bet. She's never given her husband a child.'

'Not like you, eh, my pet?' He patted the hand in her

200

lap. Suddenly he frowned. 'There's no chance you'll have more babies, is there?' he asked sharply.

'You bet there isn't! I've taken the pill ever since Paul was born.'

'Good. I wouldn't want that sort of problem.'

'Neither would I! Where in the world are you taking me?'

'I'm beginning to wonder whether we're lost. I knew the place was remote but this is beyond a joke,' he muttered as he negotiated the narrow twisting roads. There was little sign of habitation anywhere and darkness was falling fast now. Had the supercilious Humphrey Jacobs played a nasty trick on him when he recommended this place? But no, he'd telephoned and they had taken his booking, though he'd not given his own name. Had he taken a wrong turning then?

'There's lights, look! Away down there ahead of us,' Gerda said suddenly.

'A-ah, so there are,' Hubert said with relief. Even so, he had to follow the narrow road around several sharp bends as they wended their way downhill towards the welcoming lights ahead.

'This will be an awful road if it snows,' Gerda said nervously.

'You're telling me!' Hubert's expression was grim, but it lightened as he reflected, 'but we'll not be here long enough for that. Just don't let on we don't intend using the bedroom once dinner is over.'

'But surely they'll realise ...? I mean...' Gerda frowned. She felt unaccountably nervous. She'd lived most of her life in town, as Hubert had, but swiftly learnt that if you wanted to do anything secretly it was easier to do it among the crowds of folks who never noticed you than it was in the country where everyone knew everyone else – even in remote places like this. However, she kept silent, sensing that Hubert would not thank her for her opinion.

The building was long and low but already the lights glowed in welcome from almost every window and a spacious courtyard spread out before them. Raised flowerbeds flanked the entrance, though they were almost bare now except for hebes and some cyclamen.

'Gosh, it's cold.' Gerda shivered as they climbed out of the car. She wondered why Hubert had not parked nearer to the entrance. He was about to lock it, then he paused.

'You'd better leave your coat in the car.'

'Leave my coat!' Gerda pulled the warm fur closer around her slim figure.

'It'll be safe enough locked in the boot. We don't want them to think you're Lady La-la, do we?' He couldn't tell her he had every intention of slipping away without paying the bill. He would say they were coming to collect their luggage, but they would just drive away. 'Just hand your coat to me and you run inside. I'll be with you in a second.' It would never do if she had to leave her coat behind, he grimaced.

He remembered Gerda didn't know what name he had booked under. She might give his real name. He sprinted after her and was in time to usher her indoors. 'You go to the fireside,' he said softly. 'I'll get the room key.'

Gerda obeyed but she couldn't calm her nerves. She'd never felt like this before. 'But then you've never cheated on a decent husband like Ewan before.' She almost stopped in her tracks. In her head, she could hear those words quite clearly. It was her father speaking them. But when had she ever paid attention to her father's advice? She tossed her fair hair defiantly and seated herself beside the blazing fire in the small lounge which opened off reception. Moments later Hubert joined her, swinging a key triumphantly between his thumb and forefinger.

'I told them we'd bring our luggage in later,' he whispered. 'I said we wanted to freshen up before we ate

202

our evening meal. They've agreed to start serving at 6.30 p.m. tonight because there aren't many other bookings. The young woman on reception says there's snow forecast for the hills and that always makes a difference to their trade at this time of year.'

'I see ...' Gerda said feeling suddenly breathless. If there were not many people in, they would be more conspicuous, but surely there couldn't be anyone who knew Ewan, or any of the Maxwells, in a place like this? Even so, she hurried up the staircase in front of Hubert, reluctant to be seen for once.

The room was warm and clean and comfortable, but not the sort of elegant place Hubert expected to use in London. The chintz curtains and bedspread were pretty though and suited the character of the old building and the small en suite bathroom provided everything they needed for their short stay.

Gerda heard him turn the key in the lock and turned to face him. He opened his arms wide. She went into them with less urgency than he had expected and he frowned slightly, but he was confident he could rouse a passion in her she had probably never experienced in her life so far.

# Chapter Sixteen

Ewan often wondered where his day had gone. He missed his father more than he had believed possible considering Ross had been getting less active and involved in day-to-day running of Nether Rullion.

'It's all the little jobs he did,' he confessed to Rachel, 'and the bits of advice I took for granted.' He sighed. 'There were so many things he had accumulated from a lifetime's experience.'

'I know, laddie.' Rachel nodded. It was three years now since Ross died but she still found herself turning to speak to him, to ask this or that, or to tell him some detail about her day. 'But you're doing all right, aren't you? You're not worried about the farm, are you?'

'No-o, not really.' He frowned. 'The small expenses always seem to add up to more than I expect but we've a lot to show for our big expenditure. I keep trying to explain to Gerda that the cows have to be fed, and kept bedded and warm if we expect them to produce milk and calves. She seems to think I'm being extravagant when the big feed bills come in during the winter, or when the accounts arrive for new grass seed or cereals in the spring. She doesn't understand that nature needs a helping hand and doesn't just produce abundance unaided.' He grinned ruefully. 'Except for weeds, of course. All the sales reps are keen to sell sprays to kill this or that, but I'm not so sure they can all be as harmless as they claim.'

'No, nature has its own strengths and weaknesses, though I must say it must make life a lot easier now that you don't handle all those thistles in every sheaf of corn.'

'Yes, buying the combine has proven a great benefit, but I'm afraid that's another expense Gerda doesn't understand. She seems to think every time I buy something like that for the farm, *she* should have some luxury or other for herself or the house.'

'I don't suppose she understands that's the way businesses run.' Rachel nodded. 'I must say I'm very glad I still have my few hens to keep my independence. But surely Gerda must be getting used to the way the cash flows in and goes out again at different times of the year, and that it's essential to budget for the lean times? She is still doing the farm accounts for you?'

'Oh yes. She does them, but she has no interest in what they mean.' Ewan frowned and changed the subject. He didn't want to be disloyal to his wife, and yet ... 'At least we have moved on a bit. Not like Polish farmers – still milking half a dozen cows in a wee wooden byre.'

'A-ah, yes. Peter was telling me about his trip to his homeland. He seemed rather disappointed, I thought.'

'Yes, he was, but then it's such a long time since he lived there and none of his close family survived after the war. He's glad he's been back to see but he says this is where he belongs now. I was relieved to hear it. I don't know what I should do without Peter.'

'He's a good man, but Billy is almost a man now and he must be proving quite useful, isn't he?'

'Oh, he is, but I don't think he's got over the shock of his mother's death yet.'

'Well, it was so sudden, I can't blame him.'

'Are you sure you don't mind giving him his dinner every day? It's not too much work for you?'

'Not at all. I'm glad to do it. He's a nice laddie and it makes it more worthwhile cooking for myself too.'

'But you have Paul most days as well ...?'

'He's a grand wee laddie.' Rachel's face softened. 'And a born farmer. I shall miss him when he starts school. There's not much he doesn't know about what you're doing each day and what all the machines are used for. He loves to talk to Billy over lunch. Billy tells him the names of the cows and which ones have had a calf.'

'Yes, he has a good memory for one so young. I'm often surprised,' Ewan admitted proudly.

'It's a wonder Gerda doesn't miss his company ...'

'She seems pleased to be rid of him,' Ewan said frankly. He often wondered what his wife did all day at the cottage now that Paul was getting more independent. He had long since accepted she needed a drive in the car every day on some pretext or other. She had joined a badminton club in Dumfries and still went to the drama group. She still saw Hubert Boyd-Hill whenever he was up in Scotland, even though she knew he disliked the man intensely.

His name was never mentioned since that December night, three years ago. He had returned from Lucy and Don's after the christening, expecting to find Gerda in bed recuperating from her illness. After dropping his mother off at the farm he had come home to find his own home cold and in darkness. Snow had begun to fall on the way home and it was settling fast. Paul had fallen asleep not long after leaving Lucy's, worn out by the day's excitement and his play with Ryan. The two little boys were almost the same age and played well together. Even his mother had relaxed a little and smiled at their antics, forgetting her own grief for a little while.

He carried his sleeping son into the house and put him straight to bed. Then he had lit the fire, made himself a hot drink and settled down to await Gerda's return. He was annoyed that she had ventured out on such a night, after claiming she was too ill to attend the christening. She'd not even left a note to say where she had gone.

He must have dozed fitfully, for he woke with a stiff neck. It was well past midnight. The minutes ticked into an hour, and then two. Ewan's anxiety grew. Had Gerda gone gallivanting with the actor fellow? Ewan had no idea whether Hubert Boyd-Hill really was an actor or not, but he always seemed to be acting a part any time they had met. Ewan felt an instinctive distrust of the man.

He had been relieved when Gerda joined various evening classes, but none of them interested her as the drama group did. Her father had been right to warn him, he decided sadly; she was born to be restless. He was learning to live with that for the sake of Paul. He shuddered, remembering their confrontation in the early hours of that bleak December morning – and her ultimatum. He had no doubt she would carry out her threat.

His tension and anxiety had grown as the minutes ticked into hours, but it had turned to impotent fury when Gerda eventually waltzed nonchalantly into the house, with Boyd-Hill following as though he belonged there. There was no explanation, no apology. They both looked like cats that had swallowed the cream. Ewan rose from his chair, white faced with weariness and anxiety, but – at the sound of their empty laughter – anxiety turned to fury. He couldn't help himself. He strode to the door, taking Boyd-Hill with him by the neck of his overcoat. The oily smile died on Hubert Boyd-Hill's face. He was taken aback to find Gerda's husband still up at that hour. At the sight of green eyes glittering with anger he offered no resistance. He breathed in the frosty night air with a gasp of relief.

Gerda began to sulk but Ewan was too angry to choose his words.

Even now, three years on, he could still see the malice in her pale eyes when he told her she must choose between himself and her actor friend. When she saw he meant it she had used her trump card. She knew Ewan and she knew what would hurt him most.

'If I go, I take the boy!' Her voice was a whining screech, filled with spiteful venom. She didn't love Paul. She didn't even want him. But the child was the best weapon she could have wished for. His love for his son was Ewan's Achilles heel, and she knew it. She exploited her advantage to the full. It was moral blackmail.

Ewan had no love left for Gerda. She had destroyed it. But he loved Paul with all his heart and he could not bear to be parted from him. Even less could he consign his child to Gerda's callous treatment. As time passed they developed an uneasy truce. On his part, it was for Paul's sake alone. As far as he was concerned, his marriage was over and he no longer cared. He threw himself into his farming, striving for success and an inheritance Paul would be proud to own.

It surprised him that Gerda continued doing the farm accounts when she steadfastly refused to do anything else to co-operate. She didn't like cooking or mending, she hated housework, she was not fond of children and had no desire to go back to teaching. She showed not the slightest interest in the farm or the animals. Yet the only time she grumbled over doing the accounts was when he remonstrated with her over her extravagant household expenses, and that was becoming a serious bone of contention. She never failed to remind him of the huge bills for the farm.

'Will you never understand, Gerda, that's the way business works? You have to spend a little to make a little. The things you spend money on don't earn us anything.'

Ewan appreciated any help, but not at any price. He had become more involved in the British Friesian Cattle Society and the National Farmers' Union and attending meetings took up precious time, but he was seriously considering taking over the accounts himself. He and Bridie also gave a fair amount of time to help the local young farmers' club with their competitions and coaching evenings. They'd benefited themselves in the past and felt they owed something in return.

Gerda grumbled incessantly about any activities which took him away in the evenings, but he knew it was only because she wanted to go out herself and he wasn't always available to look after Paul.

There were the records to be kept for the pedigrees and the milk recording. He wished Gerda would agree to take over the registrations of the pedigree calves. Each one had to be sketched meticulously within a month of birth, and its pedigree registered, and all in duplicate too. As with the Lochandee herd, the good breeding and pedigrees added a substantial bonus when selling the surplus heifers. All this he explained patiently to Gerda, trying to capture her interest, if only for the benefit of their son. Ewan still held a glimmer of hope that Gerda might settle down and be a worthy mother, even though he knew beyond doubt that she could never be the wife he had dreamed of.

At Skeppiehill, Lucy and Don were expecting their third child and Don was longing for a little girl just like Lucy.

'You're the best thing that ever happened to me in my whole life,' he smiled, squeezing Lucy's thickening waist. 'I love our bonnie laddies but I hope this one is a wee girl just like you.'

Lucy smiled down at him from her perch on the arm of his chair. She stroked the hair back from his temple.

'We'll just take what God sends us and love the little mite just the same. I think Chris and Adam are hoping for a wee boy.'

'I can't say I blame them. Adam's done well since he got the tenancy of Wester Hall. It was a good move buying the cottage and doing it up. Selling it gave them the capital to stock the farm just when they needed it. Even Dad must be impressed with his son-in-law but I'll bet he'll never admit it.'

'No, I don't suppose he will.' Lucy frowned, tracing the lines etched prematurely on Don's craggy face. 'You work far too hard, my love,' she murmured softly. 'If you have any more sleepless nights, you'll be worn out.'

'I know. But it's not really a bad toothache ...' Don yawned. 'Anyway, you'll be pleased to hear I've made an appointment to see Mr Munro, the dentist, on Friday morning.'

'Oh good! At last.' Lucy grinned, standing up and stretching wearily. 'I'll make us a drink of cocoa then we'll get to bed. This little person may have been kinder to me over the morning sickness business, but he's making up for it now the way he kicks! I think he's going to be a rugby player.'

'No. I'm sure this one will be a wee girl and she's already practising her piano scales,' Don quipped, but his smile was weary and he smothered another yawn.

When Fiona telephoned to enquire how she had got on with her check-up at the clinic, Lucy told her Don had made an appointment to see the dentist.

'I don't know whether his teeth can be solely responsible but Don is so exhausted by night. I'm getting really worried about him.'

'You shouldn't be worrying, Lucy,' Fiona said. 'It's not good for you, or the baby.'

'I know, but Don works so hard ...'

'He always has. That's why he's making such a success. Bridie's really proud of you two. She was telling Conan what a good stockman Don is proving.'

'Well, he loves his cows, but I don't want him to kill himself over them.'

'He won't. I'm sure he has more sense than that, Lucy,' Fiona comforted. Even so, Lucy stared hard at the phone when she had replaced it on its rest. She shuddered. Maybe tuberculosis was less common these days, but it could still occur and Don's father had been one of the last to get his dairy herd attested. Don and his brothers all drank raw milk when they were children. Oh, stop it, Lucy! She admonished her inner self sternly. Your imagination is running riot.

Strangely enough, Don was more cheerful and less exhausted than he had been for weeks when he set off for town. Lucy sighed with relief. So it had just been her imagination and, of course, Don had not the faintest sign of a cough, as Chris had been swift to remind her.

On Friday evening, as Fiona cleared away their evening meal, she put a hand on Conan's shoulder.

'You wouldn't phone Lucy, would you, darling? Enquire how Don got on at the dentist?'

'The dentist!' Conan laughed. 'Don's a big strong man and as tough as they come! Of course I'm not phoning. Anyway, you usually enjoy any old excuse for a chat with Lucy ...'

'I know. I don't want her to think I'm fussing though. It's just that she seemed extraordinarily worried about Don the other day and it's not like Lucy to exaggerate or get things out of proportion. Of course, I tried to brush her worries aside, but after I put the phone down I couldn't help wondering ...'

'You're worse than Lucy,' Conan teased. 'Hurry up and clear up, then we'll take a run over to see Mum, unless there's anything else you want to do?'

So it happened that the telephone rang in an empty house when Lucy tried to contact Fiona later that evening. By the next morning, in the bright sunshine of a new day, she had succeeded in calming her fears. She decided not to bother Fiona. After all, Mr Munro had probably sent Don to the doctor because there was nothing wrong with his teeth.

'He just said it was a medical matter,' Don had said.
'But why did he insist you see the doctor immediately?
I mean, he didn't even give you chance to come home
first.'

'He probably guessed how much I hate wasting time
getting changed into my good suit just to see the likes o'
him.' Don grinned. 'Anyway, he telephoned Doctor
Mackenzie himself, so I didn't have much option but to go
straight over to the surgery. At least it saved me waiting.
Doctor Mackenzie saw me straight away. He asked how
you were keeping, by the way.'

'Did he say what your blood tests were for? Maybe
you're anaemic, like I was before Ryan was born? Maybe
that's why you're so tired ...'

'Maybe.' Don frowned. 'Let's forget about it,
sweetheart. Just you worry about yourself and that wee
princess o' mine.'

'All right.' Lucy nodded. But she didn't find it so easy
to set aside her concerns over her family, and especially
Don. He was the light of her life – her reason for being.
Every instinct told her something didn't add up. But what?

Rachel was always pleased to see her family and she
welcomed Conan and Fiona warmly.

'And how's Lucy keeping? Did she say when the baby
is due?'

'She seems to be keeping well.' Fiona smiled. 'The
baby's not due until August. She seemed more concerned
about Don than herself. He's getting ready to start making
silage next week, but she thinks he's far more tired than he
ought to be.'

'Mmm, well, this *is* a busy time of year, and he does
the milking himself, as well as working in the fields all
day.'

'Lucy says young Richard's an excellent man,' Conan
intervened, 'and Don gets support from his neighbours
when he's busy with silage.'

'That's true,' Fiona conceded. 'But then he has to help them in return, so that makes it last twice as long.'

'Would you like to take a run up to visit Lucy next week, Mum?' Conan asked. 'We could take young Paul with us, if you like? He and Ryan seem to get on well. I suppose it's because they're about the same age.'

'And both crazy about cows and tractors!' Fiona chuckled.

'Would you have time to go?' Rachel asked doubtfully. 'I mean, isn't this the start of your season, what with the tours and everything? People keep telling me they see your coaches wherever they go.'

'We have to take a day off now and then so midweek suits better than weekend, especially if we're both away from the depot.'

'All right, that would be lovely,' Rachel agreed. 'So long as Lucy isn't too busy. I could do a good baking for her to put in the freezer,' she added with enthusiasm.

'Oh, Mum! You never stop looking after us all, do you?' Conan laughed.

'But I'm sure Lucy would appreciate that,' Fiona added quickly. 'Especially if she's providing extra food for the men at the silage. I'll give her a ring tomorrow night and see whether it'll be convenient. I – er – I'd like to see her for myself ...' Fiona couldn't dispel her own feeling of uneasiness, yet neither could she explain it.

There had been no word from the doctor about Don's blood tests when the family arrived for their visit on Tuesday. As Don said, with the weekend in between, there hadn't been much time. He didn't mention the phone call from the surgery asking him to go in. He was glad he'd taken the call himself. He didn't want to worry Lucy, or spoil the time with her family. Such occasions were rare enough for her. Even so, he could have done without wasting precious time going down to the surgery so soon, and at such short notice, when they were just getting into

213

the swing of silage making, but the doctor had phoned himself and been insistent. Maybe it would be worth it, if he could prescribe something to dispel the awful feeling of lethargy.

# Chapter Seventeen

It was a beautiful day, so typical of early summer with the fields and hedges a verdant green. Ryan and Paul played happily together in the garden at Skeppiehill with three-year-old Cameron tagging along behind them, joining in when he could. Rachel had brought a bountiful supply of scones, fruit pies and buns for the freezer, as well as gingerbread and a fruit loaf. Lucy appreciated her grandmother's thoughtfulness.

'You must have been busy preparing for a week!' she smiled, giving Rachel a spontaneous hug, in a way the rest of Rachel's family never quite managed.

'It's a pleasure, lassie. I remember what it used to be like when there were extra men to feed at Lochandee. Of course, we had no freezers then to prepare in advance, but your mother was always there to lend a hand.' She sighed. 'Poor Beth. I don't know what we'd have done without her.'

'She certainly made lovely apple pies,' Fiona agreed. 'She used to bring me one regularly when I first moved to Lochandee.'

Looking back afterwards, Lucy felt that was the last day of true, carefree happiness.

Fiona knew immediately there must be something seriously wrong, when Lucy telephoned in the middle of the following afternoon. She could hear the tension in her

215

voice and knew she was striving to hold back tears. Then it was Fiona's turn to sink onto the hall seat. She felt someone had hit her in the chest.

'Leukaemia! Oh, Lucy! I-I c-can't believe it ...' Fiona knew her own face had drained of colour and wondered how Lucy must be feeling, and in her condition too. 'What ...? How ...?' She couldn't even frame the questions tumbling around her brain. 'Sh-shall I come up? Could I ...?'

'Don has to see a consultant,' Lucy said dully. 'Doctor Mackenzie's arranging it. He-he said there'd be no delay.'

'How's Don taking it?'

'Well, he only heard this morning. I-I think he's blocking it out. He's gone outside to organise the silage team. Oh F-Fiona ...' Lucy could no longer stifle her tears. 'I'll ph-phone when there's more n-news.' She put the phone gently back on its rest, knowing Fiona would understand.

Fiona did. She clearly recalled how stunned and frozen she'd felt when she heard the doctor's diagnosis for her own mother. This was far, far worse. Don was a young man, father of two young sons – and another child not yet born.

She pulled on a jacket and ran to the office at the depot to find Conan. He saw at once that something had upset her. He dismissed the young man who was taking his instructions. Even so he was as stunned as Fiona by Lucy's news.

'I pray to God they can do something for Don,' he breathed raggedly. 'They're so young ... There are different kinds of leukaemia, aren't there?'

'I-I believe so.' Fiona nodded, her voice little more than a whisper. 'Poor Lucy. They were doing so well together, since Don felt he was running the farm, a-and w-with their little family and everything ...' She bit back a sob. Conan strode round the desk and took her in his arms.

216

Fiona rarely showed her emotions and he knew how deeply distressed she was. So how much worse must Lucy feel?

'We must wait and see what the consultant says. What sort of treatment they can offer. If only ...' Conan bit his lip. He felt small and helpless in the face of this problem. No amount of hard work or money could help, even supposing he had thousands of pounds to spare.

The consultant explained to Lucy, as gently as he could, that this form of leukaemia was particularly virulent, and even more so in the case of younger patients. Moreover, he suspected Don had probably been fighting against it longer than they realised.

In the days and weeks which followed, Lucy maintained an outward calm but inside her heart and mind rebelled against the unfairness, the cruelty of life. In that summer of 1969, the world seemed to be holding its breath until one man could set his foot upon the surface of the moon. In Britain, it was almost four o'clock in the morning on 21 July when Neil Armstrong uttered his famous words, '... One small step for a man, one giant leap for mankind.' While the world rejoiced at this momentous achievement, all Lucy asked of God was one small miracle to help Don overcome the disease which was eating away at his life's blood.

The silage was finished, the grass had grown again. Ill though he was, Don organised the men to bring home the second cut. Only when both the silage pits were full and stored for the winter did he give in. Don's remaining strength ebbed away.

He was laid to rest in the cemetery beside his grandparents. Lucy knew she had to be brave for the sake of her two small sons, then at the end of August, she gave birth to a baby girl; the little princess Don had yearned for and would never see. Her control snapped. Lucy gave way to the well of grief. Fiona was with her. She watched helplessly, her own heart heavy. There was nothing, absolutely nothing, she could do to comfort Lucy at a time like this. All she wanted was her husband at her side.

Following Don's death, all the neighbours rallied round to help at Skeppiehill, well aware of Lucy's burden and the need to regain her own strength. Surprisingly, Don's brother Willie came over most days to help Richard with the milking and feeding the calves and sheep. Lucy knew she could not go on accepting charity. She had to organise the work now. She needed to employ another man to help Richard. When she was stronger, and the baby more settled, she would do the milking herself if the two men were busy with other work, now that their neighbour's daughter, Biddy Norman, had agreed to lend a hand with the children for a year.

Don had insisted on discussing the future with her and Lucy knew they could just about afford to pay another man now and still eke out a living for herself and the children. She wasn't afraid of hard work. Indeed, it would be a relief to throw herself into labours which would send her to sleep at night. She would plan for the future of her children. Adam would advise her about breeding and which bulls to choose to keep the pedigrees.

Having thought through her plans, she told Willie, expecting him to be relieved. She asked him, as she had also asked Richard, if he would keep a lookout for a good, trustworthy man she could employ. Willie avoided her eyes and scuffed the ground with the toe of his boot.

'I'll mention it tae faither,' he muttered.

The following morning, Mr Greig arrived himself. He didn't beat about the bush, but neither could he look Lucy in the eye. His tone was brusque.

'Farming's no sort o' a life for a woman on her own,' he said. 'There's no need for ye tae hire a man. The wages are going up to £13, three shilling a week. Ye'd never manage. I've decided oor Willie will take over Skeppiehill. It's time he'd a place o' his ain. There's a wee cottage in the village would do for you and the bairns.'

Lucy stared at him. The colour drained from her pale face and for an awful moment she thought she might faint.

'B-but Don and I ... We talked it over, planned the future, before ... before ...'

'Och, he wasna weel. He wouldna be thinking right ...'

'His mind was very clear, as you would have known if you'd bothered to visit him.'

'Now don't ye get on your high horse wi' me, woman! If ye ken which side your bread's buttered, ye'll no' be causing any trouble in Don's family. The cottage will need a bit o' decorating, but I expect ye'll manage that.' He looked beyond her and his eyes travelled around the kitchen. 'Aye, ye made a fair job o' decorating this place.'

'I won't move! I c-can't. I promised Don ...'

'Now listen tae me.' Mr Greig's eyes hardened and Lucy shivered at the coldness she saw there. This was the grandfather of her children. 'The cows are mine. Don didna pay for them and ...'

'But he earned them! Six times over! All the work he did for you ever since he left school, and here at Skeppiehill, and you never paid him wages. You promised to set him up in a farm instead. Even then, you took the profits as long as you could get away with it ...'

'That's all i' the past. Remember I'm the tenant here. It's my name on the rent book. I pay the rent.'

'D-Don paid the rent!' Lucy gasped. 'He-he gave it to you ...' Lucy's voice tailed away. She stared at her father-in-law incredulously, shocked to the core of her being. He was nodding his head slowly as he saw understanding dawn. 'That's right,' he said triumphantly. 'The tenancy's in my name. I'll say who lives here, who farms it, and it'll no' be a widow woman. I'll give ye a few weeks to get

219

gathered up, then oor Willie will move in. We'll help ye move your wee bits and pieces o' furniture – the things that belong to you, mind. The likes o' that useless piano …'

Lucy sank onto a stool and buried her face in her hands. There were no tears. Her eyes felt hot and dry. Her whole being was in shock and she began to shake uncontrollably.

'There's nae need tae upset yoursel'. Ye're young and pretty enough. Ye'll be taking another husband before we ken where we are, but I'm damned sure he'll get naething frae this place.' The baby began to cry. 'I'd best be going then. I'll arrange for ye tae rent the cottage. Think on. A couple o' weeks then we'll bring a tractor and trailer to move your stuff.' He turned on his heel and strode away. Lucy was thankful because she had a terrible desire to seize the kettle from the hob and fling it at him. She knew how heartless he had been with Chris and Adam, but she'd never dreamt he would take everything she and Don had worked for.

As she fed the baby, she pondered her situation. It was true she had no claim to the tenancy of the farm. She had nothing to prove that the cows were Don's. All she could claim was the machinery Don had bought. She had receipts for that. But machinery lost its value the moment it was delivered. All she had was the new tractor and trailer and a second-hand buck-rake and a few small tools. She still had £500 in the bank from Grandfather Maxwell. Thank God Don had insisted she must keep it, but it would not last long … Already the new decimal coins were beginning to appear in circulation; a five new pence piece for a shilling and a ten pence piece for two shillings. Soon the new coin to replace ten shilling notes was to be in use: a 50 pence piece. Conan and Fiona were convinced the changes, the threat of more strikes and the high bank rate at eight per cent would render money in the bank almost worthless before long. All day her mind went round and round. This was a problem she must solve herself. She couldn't run back to Fiona for some magic solution this time. Automatically, she attended to the children, washed and cooked, tidied the house, but her mind was seething with problems. Should she try to get a teaching job again? Who could she trust to look after the children? Biddy Norman was too young to be left alone with them. How much would it cost to look after them?

Lucy had barely put the boys to bed when there was a tap on the back door. Christine came in, closely followed by Adam. Wordlessly Chris opened her arms and embraced Lucy, hugging her tightly, rocking her as though she was a child herself.

'Mum told me what he's done! I can't call him Dad any more.'

For the first time that day, Lucy allowed the tears to fall. 'I know it's no g-good crying ...' she sobbed.

'He's a fiend! A miserable, greedy swine!' Chris raged.

'Oh Chris ... P-please d-don't say that. I d-don't want ...'

'Trouble?' Chris laughed harshly. 'He has brought the trouble on himself. When Mum phoned to tell me what he'd done she was all for walking out on him.'

'Oh, no! Don would have hated that to happen, Chris!'

'I know. Anyway, she's worked all her life to keep the farm going and rear my father's beloved sons!' Chris growled sarcastically. 'And she has nothing in her own name. He's controlled everything. I've persuaded her to stay, but she wants you to know, Lucy, that she'll never, never forgive him for the way he's treating you, and the wee bairns – their own grandchildren. She's moved into a different bedroom. She says she'll never sleep with him as his wife again. That's the only way she can show him how disgusted she is – but that doesn't help you.' Chris slumped onto a stool dejectedly.

'Aye, well that's for them to decide,' Adam interrupted gently. 'Listen, Lucy. Chris and I want to help you salvage whatever you can from this sorry mess – for Don's sake, and the bairns, as well as yourself. The bull he bought, he said you gave him the money? You should be able to sell him and claim the proceeds. Do you know how he was registered with the Friesian society?'

'Oh yes, it was my job to do the accounts and register all the pedigrees.' She gave a wan smile. 'And anything else which involved using a pen. It was Don who insisted we should build up the herd together, in our joint names. That's why he chose Donluc for the herd prefix.'

'Good for him!' Adam's eyes lit up, then narrowed thoughtfully. 'So-o,' he whistled softly, 'does that mean the calves from the bull are registered under your own herd prefix?'

'Yes, of course. All the calves and young stock born since we've … s-since we thought we were f-farming on our own … have been registered, including two young bulls Don planned to sell as stock bulls at the next Paisley pedigree sale.'

'Well, well!' Adam sighed with relief. 'That's better than we'd dared to hope, isn't it, Chris?'

'I-I don't know what you mean,' Lucy said dully.

'It means my miserable pig of a father can't claim any of the stock registered in yours and Don's name. Some of the heifers from the bull you bought must be pretty near calving by now. Right?'

'Six of them are due to calve any time now.' Lucy nodded. 'Richard is really good at watching them. I-I had thought of asking him if he would like to stay here, in the house. He's very conscientious. He's getting up at night to see them calved safely, just as Don used to do.'

'Aye, he'll be sorry when he hears the place is being taken over by Will,' Adam agreed. 'It'd be a lot easier for him to stay here, and for you, if you've a spare room?'

'Oh there's plenty of rooms.' Lucy nodded. 'You ask him, Adam, then if he wants to refuse, it will be easier for him.'

'Right then. So the thing to do is arrange a sale of all the stock with your herd prefix, Lucy. Considering the bull's pedigree, plus the way he seems to be breeding, I reckon you'll get a reasonable sum. When folks hear the reason you're selling, that'll add a bit too. Farmers are pretty good at rallying round with support and Don was always popular and willing to lend a hand to neighbours. I'd like to offer for the bull myself. Maybe Bridie would buy a half share with me.'

'B-but ...' Lucy looked from one to the other. 'Your father, Chris ...? He'll never allow ...'

'He can't stop us!' Chris declared firmly. 'The trouble is, it takes time to arrange a pedigree sale. It can't be done in five minutes. There's all the pedigrees and milk records to be assembled, and the auctioneers need to get them printed in the sale catalogue.'

'If we act quickly, we should be in time for the next sale. I could phone the auctioneers in the morning and let them know how many to expect,' Adam offered.

'Good idea,' Chris said firmly. 'And if Richard stays here with you, Lucy, until after the sale, he'll make sure there's none of the calves and stirks slyly find their way to Home Farm, courtesy of Will.' Chris's mouth was set in a determined line.

'I-I don't know what to say ...' Lucy began.

'I know it's not what Don had planned for you, Lucy,' Adam said gently. 'But I promised him I'd give you all the support and help you wanted. This seems to be the best we can do to salvage something of Don's for you and the bairns. But we'll make the most out of what we can get. Some of the neighbours will lend a hand with washing and grooming the day before the sale and I'll come over myself and help Richard milk them very late the previous night so they look their best on sale morning.'

'Y-you're very kind – both of you – but, Chris, your father will be furious with you and Adam ... He'll never stand for it. I can't let you ...'

'Chris's father won't be pleased,' Adam said grimly. 'There's no doubt about that.' He grinned suddenly, a faintly malicious grin for Adam. 'Wait until he sees the prices I'm expecting you to get, Lucy. And there's damn all he can do about it when they're in your name.'

'Serves him right. Don earned every penny you'll get, and more besides. The whole lot should have been yours, Lucy. What did Fiona and Conan say?' Chris asked doubtfully. 'I don't know how I'm going to face them at the christening.' She bit her lip anxiously.

'I haven't told them,' Lucy said. Her voice trembled. 'I-I can't. I have to make my own decisions over this. You've cheered me up a bit though. At least it sounds as though I'll have a bit longer to decide what to do. I-I hate the thought of living so near and having to watch Will making changes here ... D-Don had so many plans ...'

'I can understand that,' Chris said gently. 'Don't think about it. Not until after the sale. Dad will just have to wait a bit longer for his bloody farm. Some other solution might turn up. Just tell him firmly that you'll move out in your own time. Remember you have our support, and Mum's. I can't tell you how much this has upset her.'

Later that night, as Adam and Chris prepared for bed, she said, 'I know I shouldn't interfere, but I think I'll feel better if I can explain to Fiona and Conan what Dad has done. I want to let her know how much we, and Mum, despise him for it.'

'Do you think you should?' Adam asked doubtfully. 'I had a feeling Lucy didn't want them to know until she'd come to terms with yet another change in her life. It's certainly been turned upside down.'

'Yes, it has, but Lucy's family might have other

suggestions – or at least a better solution than that old cottage. I wouldn't be surprised if they want her to move back down to Dumfriesshire when they hear she can't keep the farm on.'

'They might,' Adam said doubtfully, 'but Lucy is very proud and independent.'

'I know, and Fiona realises that. She'll be tactful, I'm sure. Anyway, there may not be anything they can do …'

'Well, if you're telling them, perhaps you should call Bridie too, and see whether she'd be interested in buying a half share in the bull. I think he'll make more at auction than Don paid for him, especially when his progeny will be there to show how well he's breeding. We have to do the best we can for Lucy, even if it means we don't get him ourselves.'

'You're a good man, Adam,' Chris said warmly. 'I know Don would willingly have given you the use of the bull for a season if he'd known you wanted to try him on your own cows.'

# Chapter Eighteen


Fiona's instinctive reaction to Chris's news was shock and indignation on Lucy's behalf. Then, even more so, on Don's. He'd worked so hard and been loyal to his parents. But Fiona had learnt to exercise control over her own feelings, so listened intently as Chris went on to explain how Adam and herself planned to help Lucy gain as much as possible of what was rightfully hers.

'You're proving a true friend, Chris. I understand how hurt and angry you must feel, but I fear it will make things even more difficult for you and Adam with your family. I ...'

'They can't get any worse and I'm ashamed to call him my father. We'll do everything we can for Lucy. I just wanted you to know neither Mother nor I condone what he's doing to Lucy.'

Conan was away overnight inspecting a hotel he hoped to use for one of the tours. When he returned the following evening, she told him what Mr Greig proposed to do. He was furious. He was all set to drive up to Ayrshire and confront him on Lucy's behalf.

'She's in no condition to stand up to a heartless sod like that! I'll speak to him myself. Surely she must have some legal rights?'

'You can't do that,' Fiona reasoned. 'You might spoil the friendship between Chris and Lucy. Remember we're not supposed to know yet. Chris wanted to let us know how she felt herself, but she probably guessed how we would react and is giving us time to come to terms with it. Knowing Lucy as we do, I don't think she'll want a legal battle with Don's family. We must wait until she confides in us. She'll probably tell us after the christening on Sunday. I've been thinking about it half the night.'

'Ah, sweetheart! I'm sorry I was away when you needed me. No wonder you look tired.' Conan was contrite.

'Well, now I've had more time to consider, I can't help wondering if Mr Greig might be right ...'

'Right! He's a miserable, money-grabbing ...'

'Hush!' Fiona put a finger over his lips. 'He's doing it for all the worst possible reasons and he's behaved abominably but, for all that, it may be for the best in the end. It would be a hard life for Lucy, trying to keep the farm going and bringing up three small children on her own. You must admit farming is hard work, even with a husband.'

'We-ell, yes, that's true enough,' Conan conceded with a frown. 'But I still think ...'

'We can't do anything to help until Lucy tells us herself. Meanwhile, we could find out if there are any suitable cottages around here ...? I know it's selfish of me, but now that this has happened ...'

'You mean we should encourage Lucy to move back?' Conan said slowly, as understanding dawned.

'Well, at least we would all be nearer if she does need help. And she'll have to earn a living one way or another to keep three children. She's going to need all the support she can get.'

'That's true. The trouble is Lucy is so proud and independent.'

'And who does she get that from, I wonder?' Fiona teased gently.

'I suppose you're right – she does take after me in lots

227

of ways. But I'd feel happier too if she were living nearer. We could give her a job organising bookings and payments for the tours. She'd be ideal, with her intelligence and integrity ...'

'We could, and it would be to our benefit, but Lucy would never believe us. I doubt if she'd accept. I think the best we could hope for at present is to persuade her to move back down here. Would it be worth ringing Jordon Niven to see if he has any houses coming up for sale?'

'It's worth a try, but I doubt if Lucy would accept help in that direction either. She'll want to wait till she sees how much money she can spare. Even a cottage to rent would do temporarily ...'

'That's true. I – er – I suppose we couldn't ask Jordon if he has anything suitable? I think he'd agree to co-operate with us if there's something affordable, once we explain Lucy's circumstances.'

'How d'you mean?' Conan looked at his wife intently.

'Well, Chris thinks Lucy will easily get back the price of the bull Don bought, and maybe more. She already has £500 in the bank. If there's a house to sell for something like £1,500 to £2,000, perhaps we could ask Jordon to offer it to her for a thousand. We could pay the rest to him and Lucy need never know. We could easily afford that, couldn't we ...?' There was pleading in Fiona's eyes and Conan suddenly realised how much she would love to have Lucy and her children nearer. Come to think of it, so would he.

'You're a witch of a woman!' he chuckled. 'I don't know where you got such a devious brain.'

'I'm not devious! Anyway, when you deal with city slickers, as I used to do, you have to use all your wits and stay one step ahead.'

'All right, I'll telephone your Mr Niven tomorrow,' Conan promised and prayed silently they could reach some arrangement without ever hurting Lucy. At least

Jordon Niven was trustworthy and discreet, and Conan had a feeling he would do almost anything to please Fiona, so long as it was legal.

The following morning, Bridie telephoned Fiona. She sounded unusually diffident.

'I had a phone call from Adam Green, Chris's husband, last night. He ... I ... he says Lucy will be selling the bull and he wants to know whether I would buy a half share,' Bridie said carefully.

'And would you?' Fiona asked. 'Or would you be doing it as a favour to Lucy?'

'Oh, Fiona!' Bridie burst out, unable to keep up a pretence. 'I'm so terribly sorry this has happened after all Lucy has been through recently. Mr Greig must be a monster of a man ...'

'Yes, I think so too. Do you want the bull, Bridie?'

'Oh, yes, but Don knew that before he died, so Lucy would know I'm not bidding as a favour. He has excellent breeding behind him and he's leaving nice young stock. I reckon he'll make at least 800 guineas. That's why Adam thinks he can only afford a half share. We'd have to have him insured and draw up a proper agreement, of course. I shall certainly go to the sale and bid up some of his progeny. I'll rally round some of the other breeders as well. They'll make sure Lucy gets a good sale when they know the circumstances. It makes my blood boil when I think how shabbily Mr Greig is treating her.'

'Yes, I know. We're not supposed to know yet but Chris phoned to explain. I expect Lucy will tell us at the christening, but Bridie ...' Fiona frowned at the phone. 'Perhaps it wouldn't be such a bad thing if you phoned Lucy and told her you would like to buy a half share of the bull, and mention the price you're willing to pay. It might reassure her to know she has at least a thousand pounds, or more. According to Chris, the cottage Mr Greig is procuring for her isn't up to much and Lucy hates the idea of living there. Conan and I would love for her to move down here. She may insist on renting a cottage, of course, but if there was one to sell at an affordable price Conan thinks it'd be more secure, and a good investment for her and the children.'

'Yes, I'd agree with him on that. I wonder whether Lucy would fancy moving back to her old home in Lochandee? Rumour has it that the man who bought it has run short of money. He raised the roof to make bedrooms, knocked out a downstairs wall and took out a fireplace. I haven't seen it, but Carol told me it's been empty for months and she's quite upset about it. She stayed there with Beth, you know, when she first came to Lochandee with Wendy and Joanne as evacuees.'

'I didn't know it was still unoccupied. It has a lovely big garden at the back. Conan thought about buying it the last time it was for sale.'

'Maybe you should mention Chestnut Cottage to Lucy – see what she thinks? She'd certainly tell you if the idea didn't appeal.'

'Yes, she would. I wonder whether we could take a look from the outside before we go up for the christening? It might be cheaper when it needs things doing.' Privately, she thought it might be easier to persuade Lucy that it was cheaper than it really was if it looked half-derelict. At least they knew it was soundly built and had potential. Fiona's heart ached for Lucy and she wondered whether it was sensible to suggest returning to the home where she had spent her childhood.

'Carol would let you see it. She has a key for the tradesmen getting in, but they told her they weren't coming back until they got some money.'

'Oh dear, as bad as that? Still, the owner might be glad to sell in that case. It's an ill wind if it doesn't blow somebody some good. Thanks for that bit of information, Bridie.'

'You're welcome. I'd love to have Lucy living in Lochandee again myself, and I'm sure Mum would. Adam says his brother, Richard, is terribly upset about the upheaval too. He'd been with Don since before he left school. Apparently, he's made up his mind to leave Skeppiehill as soon as Lucy and the children move out.'

'Oh, I didn't know. Chris didn't mention him but it's distressing everyone concerned.'

'I'd offer him a job here, at Glens of Lochandee, but I've no spare room. He'd have to find digs. Of course, I haven't mentioned that to anyone else,' she added hurriedly. 'Frank and Emmie are getting older though and neither of them like the new milking parlour. They preferred it when the cows were in the byre all tied in their own stalls.' She sighed. 'You can't please everyone, but there's always changes. Some folks have a worse deal than others. It makes me think how lucky Nick and I are.'

'I know what you mean. My life with Conan seems like heaven compared with Lucy's.'

'I feel so sorry for her. Do let me know if you think there's anything we can do.'

'Will do. If we do persuade her to move down here I expect we would be glad of Nick and his lorry to move her furniture, but we'd better let Lucy make her own decisions.'

At the christening, Lucy looked pale and drained. Chris and her mother were tense and ill at ease. Fiona knew how difficult it must be for them. The boys' christenings had been celebrations, with the minister and his wife joining the family for a meal. This time, it was a short simple ceremony at home, then the minister took his leave. Kirsten had cried all the way through, but Lucy knew it was not the christening, or the people, which had upset her. She was hungry and fretful all the time and Lucy blamed herself. She was constantly tired and worried, her mind in a turmoil. Baby Kirsten seemed to sense her

231

mood, seeking constantly for her breast whenever Lucy picked her up.

At the last minute, Rachel had decided she would like to be present at her great-granddaughter's christening. Now she rose from her chair and moved across the room to Lucy. Gently, she lifted the crying infant into her arms, rocking her patiently. For a little while she was quiet but soon she was nuzzling into Rachel, clearly searching for food. She caught Lucy's eye and moved into the kitchen. Lucy followed.

'Please don't wear yourself out,' Lucy said wearily. Rachel smiled.

'I may be a great-grandmother, lassie, but I'm only 67 and I don't feel like one.' Then her expression grew serious.

'If Beth had been alive she would have advised you to put this wee bairnie on the bottle, so stop wearing yourself out and fretting over her. I had to put Bridie on the bottle – or at least the nurses at the fever hospital did. They took Conan and wee Margaret away because of the diphtheria, and they had to take Bridie into isolation. It didn't do her any harm in the end. Wee Kirsten will be more content if you give her what you can, then top her up with a bottle.'

'Do you think so? Really?' Lucy stared at her grandmother in disbelief. 'It must have been awful seeing your children being taken away, then … then losing one of them …'

'It was,' Rachel said quietly. 'Now you take my advice; you need to preserve your own health and strength, Lucy. You've three bairns depending on you, not just Kirsten. If you'd like me to come and stay any time, lassie, you only have to say the word. Fiona or Ewan would drive me up. I'd be glad of the company, as well as keeping an eye on the laddies and nursing this wee treasure.' She looked down at the tiny figure, sucking her thumb as though her life depended on it. Lucy looked at them and her eyes filled with unexpected tears. They came too readily these days. She knew it was because she was exhausted.

'I hardly know what I want,' she said, striving for control.

'I can understand that, lassie,' Rachel said softly. 'One minute, all you want is your own company – a wee bit of space, some solitude. The next, you're feeling angry because you're alone and the world seems so unfair.'

'Yes.' Lucy stared at her grandmother. 'That's exactly how I am. You really do understand ...'

'Of course I do, Lucy.' Rachel put her free arm around the thin shoulders and squeezed gently. 'So remember that, when you need help. I'll do my best not to add to your troubles.'

'You could never do that,' Lucy said.

They returned to the room in time to hear Conan and Chris discussing houses.

'I was just telling Chris and Adam that your mother's house is to sell again, Lucy,' he said with deceptive casualness. 'The man who bought it had all sorts of grand plans, but he's run short of money before he finished half of them. I believe it looks pretty awful. I expect it'll be a bargain for whoever buys it though.'

'Have you any idea how much it will make?' Chris asked.

'I shouldn't think it'll make more than £1,000 to £1,200 the way it looks. Of course, it'll cost a few hundred to make it habitable.'

'Would you fancy going back there to live, Lucy?' Chris asked. 'Or if not to the same house, would you like to go back among your friends and all the people you know?' Her mother looked startled and stared at her daughter in dismay.

'Oh, no!' she protested. 'You shouldn't suggest such a thing, Chris.' She sounded hurt, then her mouth trembled at the thought of losing her grandchildren. 'You wouldn't move so far away, would you, Lucy?'

'Now, Mum, it has to be Lucy's decision where she lives,' Chris said firmly. 'And there's nothing to attract anybody to that old cottage Dad's expecting Lucy to rent.' She turned to look Lucy in the eye. 'You know how much I'd miss you, Lucy, if you moved away, but I believe you need all your friends around you, and all the help you can get, while the children are so young.'

'But I'd help if she needed me ...' Mrs Greig began.

'You couldn't, Mum. Things are strained enough for you at home as it is. You'd feel even more torn in two. It's not good for you.'

'If Lucy did decide to move back home,' Fiona said, deliberately using the word "home", 'we'd all be relieved and delighted, of course, but Mrs Greig ...' She reached out and patted the older woman's work-worn hands as they twisted on her lap. 'Adam and Chris would bring you down to visit Lucy and the children. You might even manage to stay for a weekend now and then, if Lucy has a spare bedroom.'

'Even if she hasn't room, there's plenty of us to give you a bed,' Rachel suggested. 'But, of course, it will depend what Lucy decides to do.'

'I expect there'll be other cottages to sell eventually,' Conan said. 'Maybe not such a bargain as Chestnut Cottage, of course. It has such a good-sized garden at the back. Ideal for children.' He smiled reminiscently. 'I seem to remember getting into hot water for trying to climb the old tree then falling into the burn.'

'That's right, you did!' Rachel recalled accusingly. 'You were often late home from school, but that day I remember you were very late and you were wearing somebody else's trousers.'

Lucy listened quietly. All her memories of Lochandee had been happy ones until her mother's death. Even then, Fiona had welcomed her so warmly and she had known everyone in the village. She had never felt alone or left out of things. Not as she did now.

'I'll think it over,' she said quietly, and they all knew the matter was closed. The seeds had been sown. In time, Lucy would make her own decision. Conversation turned to the coming sale, with Bridie and Adam's desire to buy the stock bull, then, inevitably to Ewan.

It was Mr Greig who precipitated Lucy's decision. He arrived at the house two evenings later, clearly expecting to find Lucy alone and the children in bed.

'Oor Will tells me ye're planning tae sell my stock and make off wi' the money,' he accused without any preliminary greeting. Lucy looked back at him. There was nothing in him that reminded her of Don. For a fleeting second she wondered whether he really was Don's father. 'I'll sue ye if ye sell anything!'

'I'll sell nothing that belongs to you, Mr Greig.' Inside she was trembling but outwardly she looked cool and her green eyes held his furious gaze unflinchingly.

'Then what's all this nonsense about entering cattle for the pedigree sale?'

'Don's cattle, you mean? The young stock he bred and reared. I'll not sell any of the milking cows you *claim* as yours.' He saw the contempt in her face and his eyes narrowed.

'They're *all* mine. You can sell the old bull if you like, but ye'll get nothing for him by the time ye've paid the haulage.'

'I expect to get back every penny we paid for him,' Lucy said. 'He's a proven stock bull now and his progeny will show his real value.'

'Somebody's been advising ye!' he growled. 'But I'll make sure ye dinna try selling anything else frae here. I'll ...'

'Good evening, Mr Greig.' Richard came through from the kitchen. He was only 21 but he held himself erect and addressed Don's father with cold politeness. Lucy knew he must have heard their conversation and she was relieved by his appearance. Mr Greig was disconcerted.

'What are ye doing here at this time o' night?' he demanded.

'Doing my job as stockman,' Richard answered levelly. 'I'm lodging here to keep an eye on the stock for Mrs Greig, just as I promised your son I would do.'

'What d'ye mean "keeping an eye?" There's nae need for ye tae be staying here ...'

'I think there is, Mr Greig. We have heifers due to calve. Fine pedigree heifers, registered in Mr and Mrs Greig's names, and with their own prefix.' He paused, letting the information sink in. He saw the anger glinting in Mr Greig's eyes then continued. 'They're too valuable to risk losing any. I'll be staying at Skeppiehill until after the sale but, now that you're here, I may as well tell you I shall be leaving here as soon as Mrs Greig and her children move out.'

This was an exceptionally long speech for Richard and Lucy looked at him in astonishment. He caught her eye and saw a little twitch at the corner of her mouth. Knowing he had her approval, he felt a surge of relief, as Chris had warned him he might need to stand up to her father. The older man stared at him.

'And good riddance I say!' he growled furiously. 'You and that bloody upstart of a brother, ye're nothing but trouble. Ye'll get no reference for another job frae me. I'm warning ye, naebody will want to employ ye.'

'Oh, you needn't concern yourself, Mr Greig. I've had two offers of work already.'

Mr Greig opened his mouth then snapped it shut again. He turned on his heel and strode away without a word.

Lucy went into the kitchen and sank weakly onto a chair. Richard followed.

'Shall I put the kettle on, Mrs Greig? Make us a cup of

tea?'

'Yes, please, Richard. Thank goodness you were here.'

'I'm glad if I was a help.' Richard frowned. 'Do you think they would move any of our young stock away before the sale?' he asked.

'Willie and his father? I don't think they would dare – not now they know you are staying here too – but we'll move the dog kennel round to the yard. Tim will be sure to bark and warn us if anyone comes snooping.'

'Yes, that's a good idea,' Richard said with relief. 'I sleep like a log, or so my mum says.' He grinned.

'You need your sleep when you're up so early to milk. Anyway, I'm a light sleeper, so don't worry. The only problem is, I wouldn't be surprised if Willie stops coming to help us.'

'I'm not bothered. He's more of a hindrance than a help half the time. It's the way he cuts corners. I'll manage with a bit o' help from Walter Blake.'

'Yes.' Lucy nodded. 'I'll be glad if Willie stays away myself. All he seems to do is eat. Chris is buying my hens, with the two smaller huts, so she'll be taking them away soon and that'll be another job less.'

When Richard had gone to bed, Lucy sat on in the warm kitchen, mulling over Mr Greig's visit. He seemed to have no love at all for his grandsons. In fact, he almost seemed to hate her because she would not do exactly as he wanted. Chris was right: there was nothing to keep her in this district now. In fact, it would be an impossible situation. She glanced at the clock. It was late but she didn't think Fiona would be in bed yet. Before she could change her mind she dialled the numbers.

'I'm still not sure what I want to do, Fiona,' she said carefully, 'but I'd like to know what price the man wants for Chestnut Cottage and how much you think it would take to make it habitable – or at least enough room for us to manage. The children could share a room for now, then maybe I could do up some of the rooms when I can afford it.'

'Sounds a good idea,' Fiona agreed calmly, but inside she was cheering madly. She didn't tell Lucy that Conan already knew the price of Chestnut Cottage. 'I'll phone Jordon Niven tomorrow and ask him to send you particulars.'

'Thanks, Fiona. Goodnight.' Lucy slept better that night than she had done since Don's death. Even Kirsten seemed more content now that she was getting supplementary feeds. Perhaps she would ask Grandma Maxwell to come and stay while she helped Richard prepare for the sale. Then there would be the packing to do.

Ewan had increasing worries of his own, but beside Lucy's troubles he knew his problems with Gerda and her spending paled into insignificance. Even so he couldn't put it out of his mind for ever, now he knew he could no longer trust her.

Usually, Gerda opened the mail as soon as the postman arrived. She was diligent about checking the used cheques and the bank statement, mainly so that she could remove the personal ones she didn't want drawn to Ewan's attention. Quite by chance, they had a relief postman. He was not familiar with the rural run so he didn't know the regular postmen had their favourite houses where they stopped for coffee. As a result, he arrived much earlier than usual. Ewan was just finishing his breakfast so he opened the letters while he drank another cup of tea. One of them was the bank statement. He flipped through the used cheques. He sat up, alert now. Paying greater attention, he drew out six. The names of the firms were totally unfamiliar to him. The amounts were not huge, but two of them were nearly £100 each, so not trivial either, when added together.

Gerda came down for breakfast late, yawning, still in her dressing gown. She started when she saw the opened letters and Ewan scrutinising the returned cheques. She tried to snatch them from him.

'I'll check them when I've had my breakfast. Isn't it time you were back at the farm?'

'I'm in no rush. I was up half the night calving a cow. There are some cheques I don't recognise …?'

'Oh? Maybe the bank has sent them here by mistake.'

'I don't think so. They all have your signature on. Who is PM Wilson & Son and what have we bought from them?'

'Oh that. It was just a little household account – paraffin or something, I think.'

'And R Carlyle Ltd?'

'You've been checking up on me!' Gerda accused, her pale face flushing angrily.

'It seems I need to check up on you.' Not for the first time Ewan wondered whether his trust in his wife had been misplaced. His heart sank. She was supposed to be his life's partner, mother of their son. If he couldn't trust Gerda, whom *could* he trust? There was nothing else she was willing to do to help. His father had always left the accounts to his mother as long as he could remember. He couldn't ever recall them falling out over money. After all, they were working to the same end, weren't they? He looked up at Gerda with a frown. Perhaps not. Maybe Gerda wouldn't care if the farm didn't pay, or if there was nothing for Paul to inherit.

'What are you staring at me like that for?' Gerda snapped.

'I wasn't staring exactly, just wondering …'

'Well, stop wondering then and get on with your precious farming. You're always wanting me to help with your bloody bookwork.'

Paul came through, trailing his favourite teddy and

rubbing his eyes.

'Why are you shouting, Mummy? Are you cross?'

'Of course not!' But Paul knew when his mother was angry.

'C-can I c-come with you, Daddy?'

'You're not dressed,' Gerda snapped.

'I'll wait for you, wee chap,' Ewan promised. 'You can have breakfast with Granny. I'm going to be busy moving some calves to new pens.'

'Can I see them?' Paul asked eagerly.

'If Granny will bring you outside. Now get dressed quickly.'

Gerda flounced away, her mouth set. Ewan sighed. It was not the money which bothered him so much. It was the fact that Gerda refused to tell him the truth. She had gone behind his back. It wasn't the first time, and he knew instinctively that her deceit might grow if he did not confront her. He resolved to say no more for the present, but he would make a point of checking the bills from now on so she knew he was not blind to her overspending. He should have remembered her father's warning. He sighed heavily. He really had enough to do outside without wasting time on accounts.

Meanwhile, Gerda sulked. One of the bills had been for a pair of satin sheets at £17 a pair. She knew that was more than any of Ewan's men earned in a week, but she didn't care. She'd taken them to Hubert's house. They were heavenly – sensually indulgent when they made love – and they earned Hubert's total approval.

# Chapter Nineteen

Lucy was glad of her grandmother's help with the children. There was far more work to preparing the stock for a sale than she'd realised and she was extremely grateful to Richard and Adam, together with two of the neighbours, who had volunteered to clip and shampoo the six newly calved heifers.

When she saw them, gleaming black and white in the sunlight, their neat udders clean and powdered, she knew Don would have been truly proud. Tears sprang to her eyes and she brushed them away. Crying helped no one.

'You've worked hard and made an excellent job of them all, Richard,' she praised warmly. His youthful face flushed with pleasure.

'D'you think Mrs Jones will think so too?'

'I'm sure she will, Richard. Are you seriously thinking of moving down to Dumfries to work at Glens of Lochandee then?'

'I'd like to work with a pedigree herd, and with a boss who cares about stock,' he nodded. 'But Mrs Jones says I ought to drive down to see the herd and the place for myself before I make up my mind. If I decide to move she said I could stay with one of the men and his wife for a month until I find digs. Frank ...? I've forgotten his name.'

'Frank Kidd and Emmie. I know them well. I'm sure you'd get on with them. I'm driving down myself the day after the sale, to look at the house where I used to live. I believe it's in an awful mess, but my grandmother says we could stay with her until some of the rooms are ready for us to move in.'

'She's a fine old lady, Mrs Maxwell. Chris says all your family are nice folks – well, all but one.' He flushed guiltily but Lucy smiled.

'Don't worry, Richard, I can guess who Chris had in mind and I don't get on very well with her either.' He looked relieved.

The sale was an even greater success than Adam had forecast. It made Richard proud and pleased to gain his elder brother's approval. Lucy felt overwhelmed. She knew some of the young stirks had made more than their real market value even for pedigree cattle. One or two had been bought by neighbours who were not remotely interested in pedigrees and had bought as a kindly gesture. Even those who had not purchased had helped by adding to the bidding.

The biggest surprise of all had brought some disappointment to Bridie and Adam, but their joy for Lucy was greater. One of the men who selected bulls for the English Milk Marketing Board's bull breeding station had attended the sale specially to see Don's bull, and to inspect his progeny. Adam, with Bridie's full support, had offered to the maximum they could afford but was outbid. The bull had made more than three times what Don had paid for him. Lucy couldn't believe her ears. Ewan was standing beside her. He turned and gave her a spontaneous hug of congratulations, just as one of the farming press photographers clicked his camera.

'Now I'll go and have a word with the buyer and book some semen to inseminate some of my cows.' Ewan grinned.

'Yes, we'll come with you and book some for ours too,' Bridie agreed as she and Adam joined Lucy at the ringside. 'It will be cheaper at first, but if he breeds as I think he will, it'll get dearer, once production figures for his progeny become available.'

It was the report of the sale which enlightened Mr Greig, since he'd refused to attend the market in person. He was furious. He'd never fully appreciated Don's careful stockmanship, or his eye for selection.

Mr Greig didn't come to offer a helping hand on the day Lucy was due to move, much to her relief. She didn't want to see him again but felt tearful when Don's mother came to say goodbye and wish her well. She pressed three ten shilling notes into her hand, one for each of the children.

'I needna have worried about you needing help with the furniture, lassie. I see your family are taking good care o' ye.'

'Yes, they're all very kind,' Lucy sighed, watching Ewan, Nick, Conan and Adam manoeuvring the piano into Nick's lorry. 'Chris and Adam have done everything possible to help me. Christine is a true friend. I'll never forget her kindness, or yours. Please come to see us when we're settled in.'

'I'd like that lassie, though I don't know how you can ever forgive the way you've been treated by the rest o' my family.'

'You've always done your best for us,' Lucy said sincerely, 'and you must get to know Don's children and keep in touch. He would have wished it.'

'Aye, I'll do that,' Mrs Greig said through her tears.

Lucy was dismayed at the state of her old home and her heart sank. Had she been too hasty in her desire to get away from Skeppiehill? It would be several weeks before she and the children could move to Chestnut Cottage. Rachel assured her she was delighted to have their company, but Lucy worried in case the invasion of herself, a young baby and two boisterous toddlers would prove too much for her grandmother. Perhaps she should have stayed with Fiona, but her grandmother had offered first and she would have been hurt.

'I miss Paul now he's started school,' Rachel confessed. 'I expect he'll want Ewan to fetch him to play with Ryan as soon as he gets home in the afternoons. We've always given him strict instructions not to come up the lane and through the farmyard by himself. You can never tell what might distract a young boy's attention and make him wander off. Or one of the tractors could be working and children are almost invisible from a tractor cab. He's always been quite obedient so far.'

'Paul's a lovely little boy. He's like Ewan used to be, don't you think?'

'Yes, he is. And his mind is set on being a farmer, though he might change as he gets older.'

'I must try to teach Ryan his letters and numbers so that he's not too far behind when he starts school at Lochandee,' Lucy said anxiously.

'He'll be fine. He's a bright wee fellow. It's better for him not to have too many changes all at once, although he does seem to have accepted all the upheavals in his young life very well so far. Peter and Billy seem pleased to have him around when it's safe for him to watch them at work.'

When Ewan realised Lucy had been in the habit of sketching the calves, handling the pedigree registrations, and compiling milk records, he was quick to ask if she would take over the Rullion records.

'It'd be a great help to me. There's always things to see to around the farm. I'd be glad to pay you, Lucy, if you could manage to do them.'

'Oh, I don't want any money! Doesn't Gerda take care of all the bookwork?' she asked in surprise.

'She pays the bills then enters them in the book for the accountant but nothing more. She doesn't do the PAYE for the wages and she hates anything to do with animals or the farm.' Lucy saw the shadows in his green eyes and her heart ached for him. She guessed he'd been sadly disillusioned since his marriage to Gerda.

'I'll be glad to help, so long as your mother doesn't mind. I could sketch the calves while Cameron and Kirsten have their afternoon nap and Ryan can come with me as he used to do at home.' Home! She scarcely knew where home was any more. All her furniture was stored at Fiona's. She swallowed hard, banishing the melancholy which threatened to swamp her. 'I'll fill in the pedigrees in the evenings, if you show me where you keep the files and schedules. Do you attach the Register of Merit certificates?'

'No, I keep them separate but write it on each registration. Everything's still at Mum's so there's no problem there. Gerda said she didn't want the filing cabinet cluttering up her house.'

Lucy nodded. At least she'd be doing something useful. She had enough money to pay for the essential renovations to Chestnut Cottage and, thanks to the success of the farm sale, she should have enough to manage until Kirsten was a year old if she was careful. By then, Cameron would also be ready for school so she would look for work. Conan had offered her a job. Business seemed to be growing fast, but she shied away from anything which might be contrived for her convenience. She needed to be independent.

She'd enjoyed teaching and Carol had already volunteered to look after the children when she was settled at Lochandee again. It would be a great relief to know Kirsten was in the care of someone she could trust. Her mind returned to Harry Mason, the man she'd believed to be her father. She had loved him as a father too. He had been so keen that she should train to be a teacher. Neither he, nor her mother, had lived to see her qualify, she thought sadly, but she was grateful for their influence now, and for Fiona's help and generosity. In spite of Don's death, Lucy knew she'd been fortunate in her family and friends. She felt a surge of thankfulness.

Surely Harry and her mother would have approved of her moving back to Lochandee where her early roots began? Everyone else seemed to approve. Everyone except Gerda, she thought. It was unfortunate she had seen the photograph in the paper of Ewan giving Lucy a congratulatory hug at the sale. Gerda had no reason at all to be jealous, yet she always gave that impression. Certainly, her tongue was as spiteful as always whenever they met. Thankfully, that was not often. Gerda seemed to go into town most days, returning just in time to get Paul off the school bus. Since Paul started school Ewan had fallen into the habit of having his midday meal at the farm, along with Billy Smith. Already Ryan and Cameron looked forward to spending lunchtimes with him and Billy. As for herself, Ewan was the nearest she could have had to a brother and it was comforting to slip back into their old easy friendship.

Rachel insisted she didn't need peace and quiet.

'I enjoy having people around and preparing meals. It reminds me of the old days and it keeps me young.' Even so, Lucy and the children spent most Sundays with Conan and Fiona. Bridie's twins often joined them there, but they still pleaded with Lucy to come over to Glens of Lochandee on Saturdays. Alicia and Margaret were 14 now. They both loved children and wanted to teach. Paul usually accompanied them to Glens of Lochandee, where he and Ryan followed Max around the farm whenever possible. At 16, Max's heart was already set on farming and he was reluctant to leave Lochandee, even for agricultural college. He was remarkably patient with his young cousins and often pushed them around in the hay barrow as he bedded the calves, making them squeal with delight when he went fast.

'You're just like your mother, Bridie,' Lucy said pensively. 'You seem to thrive on having people around you.'

'Oh, I enjoy it when you bring the wee ones. Besides, Lucy, you fit in as though you'd never been away. You're never afraid to lend a hand. Your mother was just the same. Actually, I look forward to your visits. It's lovely to have a womanly chat.'

'Yes.' Lucy smiled. 'I know exactly what you mean.'

'As for Paul, he's a grand wee laddie,' Bridie reflected. 'I could love him any time, which is a wonder, considering how peevish Gerda is.'

'He's not a bit like her, but your mum says Gerda's father was a nice man. Of course, Paul reminds me so much of Ewan.'

'Yes, he even has the same green eyes; they sparkle like the devil when he's up to mischief. He has such an impish grin.'

'You should see the list he's made for Santa! It's hard to believe it'll be Christmas in three weeks.' Lucy sighed heavily.

'I don't suppose you feel much like rejoicing,' Bridie sympathised. 'I'm not so sure it's a good idea of Mum's to want us all at Nether Rullion for Christmas dinner. Don't you think it might be too much of an ordeal for you this year, Lucy?'

'No.' Lucy's mouth trembled but she bit her lower lip hard. 'I have to make an effort for the sake of the boys. I'll be glad to be busy. Anyway, your mother has set her heart on having everyone at Nether Rullion again.'

'Mmm, well at least Gerda is near enough home to make her excuses if she wants to leave when the washing up starts,' Bridie said drily.

'Of course! The washing up!' In spite of her own melancholy, Lucy gave a spurt of laughter. 'Gerda was always, but always, like that, even when we were at college. At least she can't make the drama group her excuse on Christmas Day. Exactly what does she do there? Do you know? She seems to go into Dumfries every single day. I asked Ewan but he just looked glum and said she isn't employed by anyone, or at least she doesn't earn any money.'

'No, she just spends it!' Bridie said grimly before she could help herself. She frowned thoughtfully then she looked Lucy in the eye. 'There are lots of rumours doing the rounds about Gerda. You're sure to hear them now you're back. I'm sure they can't all be true, but there's usually something ... I'd hate Ewan to get hurt.'

'So would I. I've always felt responsible for introducing Gerda to Ewan at our 21st birthday party. But, Bridie ...' Lucy bit her lip. 'I got the impression that Ewan is already disillusioned with his marriage anyway. I think the only thing that would really hurt him would be if she ever took Paul away from him.'

'Took Paul away!' Bridie scoffed. 'She could never look after him. She doesn't even like children. He's spent more time with my mother than he has ever spent with Gerda. She seems to think it's a grandmother's duty. Mind you, Mum loves Paul's company.'

'I know and he adores her – and Ewan, of course.'

'Let's change the subject.' Bridie shuddered. 'Gerda's bad news. What did you say to Conan's proposition for Chestnut Cottage, Lucy?'

'A-ah!' Lucy pursed her lips. 'I haven't decided yet.'

'I thought it was a splendid idea, if Conan can loan you the money, but then it would be to my benefit too.'

'Your benefit, Bridie?' Lucy glanced up in surprise.

'We-ell yes, though it was Fiona's idea originally,' she added quickly. 'She thought if you added a downstairs cloakroom – in the alcove between the hall, and the room that used to be your grandfather's shop – you could let out that room without a lodger disturbing you too much. I'd hoped you might agree to take Richard in ... I mean, you do know him. And he is looking for digs. I'd hate to lose him now. He really is a grand young stockman. He and Max get on really well.'

'Yes, I can believe that. He's very conscientious.' Lucy frowned. 'Isn't he getting on with Frank and Emmie, then?'

'Oh, yes. Emmie says he's a really pleasant lad to have around and always thanks her for his meals. But the arrangement was only meant to be for a month and that's passed already.' Bridie looked thoughtful. 'To tell you the truth, Lucy, I don't think it's a good thing having two men working together and sharing the same house. Frank and Emmie are excellent workers, as you know, but Frank's very set in his ways. Richard could almost be their grandson and he has more modern ideas – both for work and for leisure. Did you get on all right with him when he lodged with you at Skeppiehill?'

'Oh, yes. He's easy to feed, and clean and tidy around the house. He was really good with the boys too ...'

'Well then? Wouldn't you consider doing up that room and giving it a go?' Bridie pleaded. 'The going rate for board and lodging is about three pounds to three pounds ten a week, according to the Agricultural Workers' Schedule. Of course, he gets his two quarts of milk a day and a dozen eggs a week. I usually have more chipped eggs than I can use myself so you could have as many as you like. I'd be really pleased if I thought Richard was happily settled.'

'I hadn't thought about it like that,' Lucy said slowly, wondering whether this was a family conspiracy of some sort. Then she tossed her head in annoyance. She was becoming paranoid about keeping her independence. It was all because of Don's father. She had vowed she would never allow herself to be in anyone's power again. 'I jibbed at the idea of borrowing the money,' she confessed. 'Conan and Fiona paid all the legal fees, you know. They've done so much already.'

'Well, Conan should help you! It's still hard to think of him as being your real father, Lucy, but he is. Even so, he wouldn't offer you the money if he couldn't afford it. I think he and Fiona are making a real success of the buses and all the tours they organise. Fiona has such a good sense of business and she's so efficient. I've never known her make a bad suggestion.'

'I know you're right, of course. It's just that I hate being beholden to anyone. I'm hoping to have enough money to keep us until Cameron starts school and Kirsten is a bit older. It would probably make things a bit easier if I had Richard as a lodger, especially with the free eggs and milk.'

'Well, I don't suppose Conan's in a hurry for you to repay the small loan it would take to make a cloakroom and decorate the downstairs room. I'll bet Richard would do the decorating for you when it's for his benefit. He could let himself out by the side door so he wouldn't disturb you or the children when he leaves early in the mornings. He has his breakfast with Nick and me anyway, after we've finished milking.'

'I see.' Lucy wrinkled her brow. 'I'll think about it and let you know. Richard would need to buy a bike if he was living in the village though ...'

'Oh, he's got one already. He's eager to explore the district. He met up with Billy Smith one Saturday night in Dumfries. Billy has introduced him to some of the local folks and promised to meet up with him for the Christmas Eve dance. I'm really hoping he'll settle down here.'

It was a beautiful afternoon in May but Lucy felt unusually depressed. Last year she and Don had been together. Never in their wildest dreams had they thought his tiredness had a sinister cause. She longed to share all the small achievements of their children with him, the trivial anxieties, the joy of spring. Half her life had been cruelly torn away. She didn't believe the ice around her heart would ever melt completely, in spite of the warmth and kindness of her friends and family.

Almost as though she was telepathic, Rachel called to see her that afternoon and Lucy welcomed her grandmother with real gratitude. Now, Rachel sat in a wooden armchair in the tiny back porch sleepily watching the boys, while Kirsten sat up in her pram, waving to the birds or to anyone in sight.

Richard had become almost a part of the family by now and he had set himself the task of making a vegetable plot in part of the long-neglected garden. Frank Kidd had been delighted to advise the younger man on double digging, getting some manure into the ground, making drills for potatoes and generally supervising. Richard surveyed his long straight rows with pride and moved across to help Ryan dig his own small patch to plant some radishes and carrots, while Cameron insisted on having a plot to plant pretty flowers for Mummy.

'I'd forgotten what a lovely big garden this is for children,' Rachel said, when Lucy brought out a cup of tea with a plate of newly baked shortbread.

'Yes, it is. I never played in it much myself though. I spent most of my time with Ewan at Glens of Lochandee.'

'Did I hear someone using my name in vain?' A deep voice called from the corner of the path leading from the front of the house and the main street.

'Ewan? What are you doing here?' Rachel asked in surprise. A small figure darted from behind Ewan.

'Boo! I made you jump, Aunty Lucy. Can I play with Ryan and Cameron? Mum didn't come home, did she, Daddy?' Without waiting for a reply from his smiling elders he ran off to where Richard was showing his young assistants how to clean their tools before putting them in the shed.

'I'm going to the farm to milk now, boys, so you can play Cowboys and Indians, but don't you dare run over my vegetables!' he growled fiercely.

'We won't!' they all shouted, grinning mischievously.

'I must get back to the milking too,' Ewan said. 'Gerda promised to be back by 1.30 p.m., but it's after three and she's still not home. Is it all right if I leave Paul here?'

'Of course it is, Ewan. The boys will be pleased to have him to play,' Lucy assured him.

'And will you bring him back with you, Mum?'

'Of course I will.'

'You look deadly tired, Ewan,' Lucy said, eyeing him with concern. 'I've just made some tea. Come on in and have a cup with Richard before he goes to Glens of Lochandee.'

'Thanks. I could do with a cup to wake me up.'

'Peter said you'd been up half the night,' Rachel remarked. 'He mentioned a bad calving?'

'Yes, we lost the calf. I'm hoping the cow will be all right. The calf was coming hind feet first – big too. I think the cow may have hurt her back, but she was on her feet and drinking when I looked in after dinner. She's one of our best animals too.' He grimaced wearily.

'Aye, that's farming though,' Rachel sympathised. 'It's not all straightforward. Away and have a cup of tea, laddie. I'll look after Paul.'

Ewan's pick-up truck was parked on the side of the village street, outside Chestnut Cottage. Lucy walked beside him to the front of the house.

'You really do look exhausted, Ewan.'

'Nothing a good night's sleep willna cure,' he said wearily. 'I meant to rest this afternoon but Paul didn't believe in giving me any peace.'

'You should've brought him over earlier ...' Lucy

broke off at the sound of car tyres screeching to a halt.

Gerda didn't usually drive home through Lochandee, but there had been a minor accident on the main road and she hated waiting. Having made a detour, the sight of Ewan's truck outside Lucy's home came as a shock. She drew to a furious halt.

'I might have known you'd be here!' she called angrily. Ewan's eyebrows rose in surprise.

'I've just brought Paul. It's time I was at the milking, but you didn't come home to look after him.'

'Where d'you think I'm going now? Timbuktu!'

'You promised to be back more than two hours ago. I'd no way of knowing when you would come.'

'Oh that's right, blame me!' Gerda sounded bitter. 'You just can't wait to come round here to see *her* at the first excuse!' She glared at Lucy.

'I-I ...' She stepped back, shocked by Gerda's inference.

'Just ignore her,' Ewan said quietly. 'She always gets unreasonable when she knows she's in the wrong.' He squeezed her shoulder reassuringly. 'You go in now.'

'Don't you dare stand there whispering to your beloved Lucy in front of me!' Gerda almost screamed.

'For heaven's sake, calm yourself!' Ewan muttered, glancing up and down the street, knowing how swiftly gossip travelled in any village. 'I'm on my way home. If there's anything to say, then say it there.' He strode to the truck and drove quickly away. Lucy had already disappeared and Gerda was left open-mouthed in frustration. But she wasn't finished yet. She had more to say about her husband paying secret visits to his little widow. He would never expect her to see his truck outside Lucy's cottage.

Gerda was moody and taciturn when Ewan returned to the cottage after the milking was finished that evening. He felt too tired to humour her.

253

'Lucy is the last person you should be jealous of,' he said in a sharp retort to her stupid innuendoes. 'If you'd come home on time, I'd never have been there.'

'I've every reason to resent her. You all treat her as though she's made of delicate china and ...'

'For goodness sake, Gerda. She's lost her husband. She needs her family ...'

'A-ah, and you're not slow to get in there now she's a widow, are you? You can't wait to get your hands on her now she's free, can you!'

'Don't talk filthy rubbish!' Ewan muttered. He was tired and fed up with her carping.

'It's not rubbish. You've always loved Lucy ...'

'Of course I have. She's one of the kindest, nicest people you could find – which is why she befriended you.'

'So! Now we're getting to the truth. You admit you love her!'

'Of course I do. We were brought up together, almost like the twins ...'

'Don't take me for a fool, Ewan Maxwell.'

'Well, that's what you are!' Ewan jumped to his feet. 'I'm going to bed.'

'No you don't!' Gerda grabbed his arm. 'Don't walk away from me! If you and Lucy ...'

'Lucy is my niece, for heaven's sake!' Ewan forgot caution. He was irritated and exhausted. 'There's little enough to keep me here with you, but Lucy would be the last person I would go to if I wanted to commit adultery.'

'She's what? What did you say? Y-your niece ...?'

Ewan rubbed a weary hand across his eyes. 'Paul's nearly asleep in the chair. Get him ready for bed and stop acting like a fishwife.'

'Your niece, you said! How can she be your niece ...?' Gerda's eyes narrowed. Suddenly she knew – knew what she should have guessed all along. 'Conan! He's her father, isn't he, her real father?'

'Yes, yes, yes. Are you satisfied now?'

'No, I'm not bloody well satisfied.'

'Well, you'll have to be. I'm going to bed.' He left her fuming and frustrated.

Well, well! The *perfect* Maxwells were not so perfect after all. Ewan had just provided her with another weapon, as well as the son he adored. Why should she worry about sullying their precious name? They had done that already. From now on, she would consider nobody but herself.

# Chapter Twenty

Even after four years of clandestine meetings with Hubert Boyd-Hill, Gerda still felt the same excitement whenever they were together. She told herself she'd done her duty to Ewan when she gave him an heir to take over his farm and his beloved cows.

Hubert moved from his dingy digs into a delightful small cottage on the outskirts of the town. They had more privacy and they spent a lot of time there whenever Hubert was not making one of his trips to London. The disadvantage was that Hubert constantly told her he'd bought the cottage for her sake.

In his own mind perhaps he had, she conceded, but she was the one who was finding payments for the mortgage. She'd paid for the furniture and the furnishings too. Hubert had good taste, but it was expensive. He seemed to think she could get her hands on an unending supply of money. He thought farmers reaped gold from their fields instead of grain.

Neither he nor Ewan had any idea of the debts piling up with stores in Dumfries and Carlisle, and even farther away – not to mention all the mail-order companies which had grown in number and popularity, selling everything from jewellery to shoes, and clothes to furniture. Gerda found mail-order catalogues irresistible and nearly all offered credit.

Ever since Ewan had discovered the discrepancies in

the firm's bank statements he had checked them frequently. He could barely summon the energy to quarrel with Gerda unless the sums were large and she'd learnt to mask her more lavish purchases when using the farm account. Cunningly, she often asked stores to make out invoices for two, and sometimes three, smaller amounts, instead of one large one which would draw his instant attention. The payments were becoming more and more numerous and Ewan knew they could not go on. Every month now he queried the number of items on the bank statements. They quarrelled bitterly when he criticised her extravagance.

Ewan was no longer the easygoing boy she'd married and twisted around her finger. He had grown stern, almost grim, and his responsibilities were heavy. In defending herself, Gerda always resorted to sniping at his family, or accusing him of lavishing all his time and attention on the farm and cattle. Illogically, she always ended up venting her resentment and spite on Lucy, sensing this provoked Ewan even more than criticism of his mother or Bridie.

It had been a shock, seeing him with Lucy, so friendly and affectionate. It was a long time since she had seen that look of tenderness on her husband's face, except when he talked to Paul. Gerda could not forget the shaft of anger and jealousy she had felt. She didn't love Ewan, but she was determined no one else would have him. Even if Lucy were related, she was young and pretty and a widow now. More importantly, she shared all Ewan's interests in the farm. Even Paul had learnt to love her. A combination of jealousy and anxiety made Gerda more vicious and unreasonably demanding than ever.

'I've an appointment in town at five o'clock,' she said on Monday morning when Ewan came in for breakfast. 'I'll be leaving here by 4.30 p.m. You'll have to look after Paul yourself.'

'You know very well that's the worst possible time,

Gerda! I'll be right in the middle of milking. Couldn't you change your appointment? Is it with the dentist?'

'No, I could *not* change it. You alter your routine for once. I *always* have to be here when the school bus brings him back,' she grouched. 'He's your son. You look after him.'

'Oh, very well,' Ewan sighed wearily. 'I'll come down and collect Paul before you leave. He'll stay with my mother until I finish milking. In fact you could take him to Mum's yourself, for once. It would save me having to leave the milking parlour in the middle of milking?' Gerda turned away, ignoring the weariness on Ewan's face, the shadows in his green eyes.

'You know I never go near the farm, or the house, if I can help it. You'll have to fetch him yourself. Half past four. Don't be late.'

Gerda's appointment was only with Hubert. He had returned from a trip to London and they were going out for a meal, before seeing a film but there had been no specific time. Gerda simply wanted to assert her own importance. As it happened, Hubert arrived in the early afternoon. Gerda was surprised and pleased until she realised he was in one of his irritable and impatient moods.

'I can't leave until Paul gets home,' she protested. 'Ewan's coming to take him to his granny at 4.30 p.m. I'll make some tea, shall I?'

'Tea! I need something stronger than tea! Surely he can wait here on his own? Lots of kids do. He's six years old, for God's sake. Don't pamper him.'

Gerda bit her lip doubtfully. Hubert was angry about something and she hoped it was nothing she had done, or forgotten to do, like paying one of the many demands for money he kept receiving.

'I suppose he'll be all right,' she said doubtfully. 'I'll leave the door unlocked so that he can get in out of this horrid rain.' She snatched up her raincoat. 'I expect he'll be fine, this once.' She slammed the door and ran after Hubert. 'It's been a filthy day.' She panted. 'You'd think it had turned from spring back to winter overnight the way it's raining.' She stopped short, her pale blue eyes widening. 'You've changed the car! It's lovely but …'

'Had a bit of a smash when I was in London,' he said curtly. 'I need a car of some sort if I've to live in this godforsaken place.' He had no intention of telling her the other car had been hired and had been called in because he was so far behind with the payments. It had taken him all his time to raise the first payment for this one from another company. Things were getting tight all round.

Back at the farm Ewan and Peter gently guided a cow into the milking parlour. She'd had milk fever and he had given her calcium into her blood.

'We'll get her in first so that the rest don't push her around,' Ewan said.

'Aye, she's certainly needing some relief,' Peter agreed. 'It's fairly streaming from her udder.'

'Bella is one of the best milkers we've got. We'll take off enough to ease her.'

The cow obviously appreciated their ministrations, not to mention the cake in the parlour trough. Suddenly, the cow behind gave a violent push. She'd finished her own ration of cake and was determined to shove past Bella to eat from her trough. The weakened cow had no resistance against the strength and determination of the one behind. Her feet slipped, legs buckled. Down she went with a sickening thud. Ewan rarely swore but he did so now. The concrete of the parlour floor was kept spotlessly clean for the sake of hygiene, but on a day like this he could have wished for a thick soft layer of manure to protect Bella. Swiftly, he opened the rear gates of the parlour and drove the other cows backwards until the run was empty, except for the prone animal.

'That'll give her as much space as we can manage,' he said to Peter but, as she struggled and slipped, he knew she would never get up on her own.

'She's not going to manage it, poor beast,' Peter said glumly. 'What'll we do? We can't milk the rest of the cows until we get her out of the parlour.'

'No, you're right.' Ewan frowned and bit his lip. The space was so confined. 'Bring Billy. Between the three of us, we'll have to drag her clear of the parlour, then lift her on a wooden pallet with the tractor forks and get her into the shed with plenty of straw.'

It took a tremendous effort for the three men. Bella was a heavy cow and she did her best to struggle to her feet, but that only made the operation more difficult. Ewan received a nasty kick on his shinbone from one flailing leg. At last, they pulled her clear of the passage. Billy ran to bring the tractor. It was a slow job to manoeuvre the cow to the loose box with Peter and Ewan holding her safely on the wooden pallet. They managed it eventually and breathed a sigh of relief. It was only when they turned to go back to the milking parlour that Ewan remembered the time.

'Heavens, it's nearly five o'clock already. I was supposed to fetch Paul at half past four. I expect Gerda will have brought him up to Mum's by now, but I'd better check. Take over the milking, will you, Peter? Just until I get back.'

He ran to the farmhouse but Rachel had seen nothing of Paul. Head down against the driving rain, Ewan ran to the pick-up truck. Before he could drive out of the yard he saw two bedraggled figures plodding up the narrow lane from the cottages. One was Mr Smith, Billy's father. Clinging to his hand was Paul. Ewan jumped from the truck and ran to meet them but, even before he got close, he could see Paul was crying. Shuddering sobs were shaking his small frame. Mr Smith's face was grim.

'I've just got home frae work. I was early today on account o' the weather. Good job tae!' He looked down at Paul. 'This poor wee bugger was huddled on't doorstep. He couldna reach up tae the latch tae open the door.'

'But ... but isn't ...? Paul? Surely Mummy didn't put you outside to wait in the rain?'

'She's not at hame,' Mr Smith said abruptly. 'Door's unlocked. I shouted in. The hoose is empty. Thought I'd best bring the wee fellow up here. Sodden, he is. Cold tae. He must hae bin cowering there for twae hours or more – ever since he got off the school bus, I reckon.'

'B-but ... thank you for bringing him up.' Ewan was bewildered. Surely Gerda had not left the house before Paul arrived home at 3.15 p.m.? She must have known he was not tall enough to reach the old-fashioned door latch himself. His overalls were filthy from working with the cow, but he lifted Paul's shuddering little body in his arms and hugged him close. He felt like crying himself as he felt the soft cold cheek against his own – saw the frightened, tear-drenched eyes and fine wet hair plastered darkly against his small head.

'Will you come on inside for a hot drink, Jon? I can't thank you enough for bringing him.' He turned towards the house.

'I'll get awa' hame, but thank ye anyway.'

'Oh, but ...' Ewan turned, pushing the door ajar with his shoulder just as Rachel appeared. He set Paul on his feet. He ran into his grandmother's arms, sobbing unrestrainedly now.

'M-mummy wasn't there. Nobody was there ... C-couldn't open the d-door ...' Rachel drew him inside, soothing him gently as she peeled off his wet clothes. Ewan looked at Jon Smith.

'It was partly my fault,' he said. 'I knew my wife was going away at 4.30 p.m. but we've had a problem with ...'

'She must hae left the house long since, before the wee fellow got off the bus. He said she wasna there to meet him. The puir wee devil said he shouted and shouted but she didna come. Scary for a wee laddie, and worse on such a day. He'd tried dragging a log to the door to stand on but it had wobbled. He fell and scraped his knee.'

'Thank you for rescuing him,' Ewan said gratefully, but he was trying hard to control his anger with Gerda. He was not blameless either and guilt made him feel worse than ever. But even if he had gone promptly at 4.30 p.m. Paul would still have been waiting in the rain, cold and alone, for nearly two hours. He hoped fervently that his small son would not catch a chill or, even worse, pneumonia. Panic claimed him and he dashed back to the house.

Rachel already had Paul in a warm bath. She reassured Ewan as best she could.

'He's a sturdy wee fellow. I think he'll be all right as far as chills go.' Her eyes met Ewan's. 'I'm not so sure what other effects it might have on the wee soul though,' she said in a low voice, her eyes grave. 'Even now, he keeps giving little shuddering sobs. He thought everyone had run away and left him all alone.'

Rachel was right. Physically Paul was a sturdy, healthy boy and he was none the worse for his soaking. Unfortunately, Gerda had already sown many seeds of doubt in his young mind about his security with her frequent rages. He had often heard her shouting she had never wanted a child, and why did she have to stay home and look after him. As he waited alone in the pouring rain, growing colder and hungrier, his childish imagination had grown into a conviction that no one wanted him and he had been left to starve like the boy in the fairy story. He could find the way to the farm and Granny Maxwell, but he had promised her he would never go there alone.

Rachel succeeded in distracting his attention from his

ordeal. It was later than usual before Ewan finished milking and he stayed to share the hot meal which his mother had prepared for himself and Paul. But when it was time to go home to bed Paul refused to return to the cottage. Eventually Rachel agreed he should stay the night with her until Ewan had sorted out his problems with Gerda and extracted a promise that she would never neglect Paul again.

There was nothing she could do to prevent the nightmares which haunted her grandson's sleep and kept her awake for long hours during the night. When Ewan arrived to drive Paul to school the following morning, he saw at once that both his mother and his son were pale and tired.

'I think he should have a day away from school today,' Rachel said.

'A day off!' Ewan stared at her. His mother had never believed in giving in to weakness. Was she going soft with her grandson?

'We both need a quiet day after the night we've had,' she said firmly. 'I think Paul's going to take a lot of reassuring. It's more than just being left out in the rain. A lot of other fears surfaced during the night. He's a very troubled wee boy and has a vivid imagination which makes his fears worse.'

'I don't want to go back there!' Paul whispered hoarsely. He clung to Rachel in a way he'd never done before, his small chin wobbling, his green eyes dark with nameless fears. 'I want to stay with Granny for ever and ever.' Rachel gave him a reassuring squeeze then sent him outside to feed one of the kittens. She turned to face Ewan. 'Did Gerda say why she'd left him?' she asked sternly.

'Not exactly, but I have a fair idea of the reason.' Ewan sat down and stared at the floor, then raised his head and looked his mother in the eye. 'My marriage to Gerda has been a failure,' he said dully. 'I can't give her the sort of life she craves. The only good thing to come out of it is Paul.'

'Oh Ewan ...' Rachel looked helplessly at her son's bowed head and her heart ached for him. But it was not her way to pretend. She'd suspected for a long time that things weren't right between him and Gerda. She had known he was unhappy, but it had never been her policy to ask questions or interfere. She'd done her best to talk to Gerda – to be friendly – but there had never been any response.

'She's been seeing some actor fellow for a long time. When I talked of a divorce, she threatened ...' He bit his lip.

'Wh-what did she threaten?'

'She said she'd take Paul with her and make sure I'd never see him again.'

'Oh Ewan! B-but ...'

'I know, I know,' Ewan said wearily. 'I've put up with a lot from her for Paul's sake. It would be bad enough if she took him away because she loved him – even wanted him – but it's even worse to know she doesn't like children – even her own son. She would have done it purely for spite. I'm convinced she would have neglected him.'

'She's certainly never cared for him much,' Rachel said slowly. 'So what can you do?'

'Last night I told her Mr Smith was a witness to her conduct and her neglect of Paul, and that I would fight for him in the courts, if necessary. I think I've shaken her conviction that she holds the trump card, but I wouldn't like to put it to the test, at least not yet. If you're willing to keep Paul here for a few weeks I thought we could see whether he changes his mind and wants to return to his mother?'

'Of course, he can stay for as long as he likes, but ...'

'I'll ask the bus driver to drop him at the farm road end. There's just one thing though, Mum: if you have Paul to care for, I insist on getting you some help.'

'Oh, but ...'

'It could be an indefinite stay. I'm fairly certain Gerda won't leave of her own free will, if only because she wants the money,' he added bitterly. 'So I shall leave the cottage. If you have both Paul and me to look after, would you consider having Joanne to help?'

'Joanne?'

'Carol's daughter, Joanne Williams. You knew she nearly had a nervous breakdown after she was jilted?'

'Yes, I knew that, but it wasn't only because he left her for a young girl. She'd helped him build up his business from nothing. It was her whole life and she was left with nothing.'

'Well, Lucy says she's much better now and she's thinking of doing something entirely different, even if it's only temporarily. When Lucy starts teaching again, she'll not have time to help me with the pedigrees. She thought Joanne might take it on. I'm going to stop Gerda paying the bills and doing the accounts too. She's cost me far too much already. Keeping the peace at any price will not be important if Paul isn't in the house.' Ewan was speaking as much to himself as to her, Rachel knew. She noticed how grim he looked when he mentioned his wife. 'Anyway, can I ask Joanne if she would work two days a week helping you and another day doing the farm office work? Lucy thinks she'll find it well within her scope after running the business for her ex-fiancé, and Joanne wants something easy until she gets her confidence back.'

'Well, I certainly like Joanne, and her sister Wendy,' Rachel said slowly. 'I remember when they came to Lochandee as evacuees with their mother. Carol's husband was lost at sea not long after. They've not had an easy life. If you're sure Joanne won't mind housework then we could give it a trial.'

'I'll have a word with her this afternoon,' Ewan promised. 'I expect Gerda will kick up a fuss when I take the farm accounts out of her keeping. Well, the chequebook anyway.' He grimaced bitterly. 'But that's just too bad. I've had enough.'

Ewan's look of resolve reminded Rachel poignantly of his father.

Afterwards, she wondered whether she should have tried to influence him. Should he have given his marriage one more chance? Would things have turned out better if he had?

# Chapter Twenty-one

Ewan had tolerated four years of Gerda's neglect, so he decided a few more weeks made little difference to him now. His main concern was to make certain Paul would not suddenly change his mind and want to return to the cottage and his mother. Strangely enough, he rarely mentioned Gerda and he didn't seem to think of the cottage as home.

Was it possible she'd made so little impression on his young life? Ewan found it even more extraordinary that Gerda never expressed the slightest desire to see her own child.

Without his son, Ewan found the cottage held no attraction for him either. He spent more and more time at the farm, usually only returning to the cottage after he had read Paul a bedtime story and tucked him up for the night. Gerda was rarely at home.

So far, he'd not made any other changes, but Joanne seemed more than willing to help his mother and it soon became apparent they got on well together. Lucy had shown her how to deal with the birth registrations for the calves. Once she was used to donning Wellingtons and trousers before going into the pens, she was very efficient. She didn't seem to mind the calves trying to suck her fingers and understood how important it was to observe even the smallest marking. She began to take an interest in the animals as individuals too, asking questions about the various cow families and their records. Ewan was delighted and relieved.

'I've been invited to judge some herds in Ireland for a competition, Joanne. I'd begun to think I ought to cancel because I'd be away for several days, but I do believe you and Peter will probably manage perfectly between you.'

'We'd certainly do our best, and Billy Smith is very conscientious too, if he has some responsibility.' Joanne nodded. 'It would do you good to get away, Ewan.'

'Yes, I believe you're right. About the accounts – will you be ready to cope with them when I return?'

'That'll be no problem.' Joanne smiled. 'After all, I was used to that sort of work …' She was amazed to find she could talk about it without flinching now. Lucy was right. She was making a new life and putting the past behind her. Mrs Maxwell's soothing presence and cheerful manner had helped enormously, as had the complete change of environment. She enjoyed walking around the farmyard, seeing the animals and poultry and often taking Paul with her when he was not at school. His questions were endless.

'You'll find a few discrepancies between the bank and the accounts to begin with, I expect,' Ewan said. He met her eyes squarely and gave a wry grimace. 'Gerda's been making use of the business chequebook. She's taken advantage and I've let her get away with it for too long.' He sighed. 'It seemed worth it for Paul's sake. Recently the amounts have grown in size and number, so it's got to stop …'

'Oh, I see.' Joanne nodded uncomfortably, but she gave him a sympathetic glance. She was not the only one who had been disappointed in her choice of partners, she realised. It must be worse to have been married, only to find it was all a dreadful mistake.

A few evenings later, Ewan waylaid Gerda on her way out.

'Perhaps you'd like to move in permanently with Hubert Boyd-Hill?' he suggested. 'You spend so little time here anyway.' She looked at him sharply but she was dismayed to find he was neither bitter nor upset. He was quite matter-of-fact. She realised it was what he wanted her to do. He no longer cared. She stared at him.

'You can't get rid of me so easily,' she snapped. 'This is my home.'

'In that case, I'll move out myself,' Ewan said evenly. He was determined to remain cool and unprovoked. He knew exactly what he wanted to do now and the sooner he could get Gerda out of his life – and Paul's – the happier he would be.

'Makes no difference to me.' Gerda shrugged. 'You're hardly ever here anyway.'

'Then that makes two of us. We'll agree to go our separate ways. You can keep the contents of the cottage. They're all your choosing anyway. Just one thing ...' His green eyes narrowed. 'Don't imagine I'll put up with Boyd moving in here. I've subsidised you both long enough. As soon as enough time has passed, we'll get a divorce.'

'Divorce!' Gerda's voice rose. 'I never said anything about divorce. I'll not agree ...'

'My dear Gerda.' It was Ewan who showed his contempt now. 'You can't seriously believe I want to keep you as my wife, the way things are.'

'We can go on as we are ...' she began.

Ewan thought he detected something like fear in her pale blue eyes, but there was hardness too. 'I think not. I only put up with you playing around with your fancy-man, and helping yourself to money, for Paul's sake. But you're the most unnatural mother I've ever come across.'

'You never met *mine*!' Gerda snorted. 'At least I stayed. She didn't!'

Ewan didn't answer. There was no point in prolonging things.

'I'll get the rest of my things from my room, then I'll collect the box with the accounts and the chequebook, to take them with me up to the farm. Joanne Williams will handle all the books from now on.'

Gerda stared after his retreating figure, her face paling. The chequebook! He was taking it away with the accounts. What would she do? What would Hubert say when she couldn't get the extra money he kept demanding?

She had never been able to manage on her allowance, though she knew it had been a generous one, after she gave up teaching. Would Ewan even continue to pay it? Swiftly, without any clear thought, she slipped the new chequebook under a cushion. The old one had only a few cheques left and the postman had brought the new one yesterday. She would say the bank had forgotten to send a replacement, if Joanne asked.

She would probably never notice a few extra cheques so long as the amounts were inconspicuous. Even if she did, Ewan might ignore them. She slumped in a chair. He was not a bad man ... He had been more tolerant than she deserved, even though it was only for the sake of his brat. Had she ever loved him? Truly loved him. In her heart Gerda had to admit she had not. All she had wanted was his adulation. That, and someone who could keep her in pretty clothes and buy her jewellery.

The sound of a car horn brought her to her feet. That would be Hubert. She would not tell him tonight.

Ewan set off for his trip to Ireland with a lighter heart than he had felt for some time. He knew he'd reached a major turning point in his life. He'd made mistakes but had a lot of life ahead of him and would make the best of it, principally as far as Paul was concerned.

He signed the cheques ready for Joanne.

'Pay the biggest bills first and, if you see Gerda, ask her if the bank has sent out the new chequebook. I'll sign the rest when I return and tell them to send all communications to this address from now on. I must ask them to cancel Gerda's signature on the business account too ...' He frowned. He hadn't thought about that. Still, he had no time to do anything about it until he came back from Ireland and Gerda would have no access to his account anyway without cheques.

Joanna did as he asked and posted off the cheques to the various businesses. Resolving to have everything up to date and ready for Ewan's return she decided to walk down to Gerda's cottage and ask whether the new chequebook had arrived.

Gerda frowned at the sight of Joanne and did not invite her in. Joanne was pleasant and businesslike. It never occurred to her that Gerda would be totally dishonest in her dealings with Ewan.

'Oh, I did fill in the form for the new one, but the bank will have forgotten to send one. They often make mistakes,' Gerda said airily. 'You'll have to go in and ask for it next time you're in town.'

Joanne thanked her and turned away unsuspectingly. She was just turning away from the cottage when a gleaming Jaguar car drew up. Joanne's eyebrows rose and she eyed it appreciatively.

'Who was that?' Hubert Boyd-Hill asked abruptly. Gerda frowned but she explained why Joanne had called. He had been furious when he heard Ewan had left the cottage, taking away the accounts and chequebook.

'You should have played him along better. Surely you could have used your feminine charms on him?' Gerda had remained moody and silent. He obviously didn't mind sharing her with another man so long as she got her hands on plenty of spare cash for his benefit. She hadn't told him then that she had kept the new book, but she told him now.

'Well, well!' he chuckled. 'My clever little goose!' Then he sobered. 'It's only a matter of time before they find out you have it. I think we'd better put it to use right away.'

'There's no hurry ...'

'Of course there is. Your husband will cancel your signature – if he hasn't done it already,' he said, jerking upright at the possibility. 'You should have told me. The sooner we clear him out the better.'

'Clear him out?'

'How much does he usually keep in his business account?'

'He always likes to make sure there is enough to pay the monthly bills, cattle cake, the vet, tractor fuel, the wages, things like that ...'

'How much spare does he keep, for God's sake?'

'He's trying to accumulate enough to change one of his big machines just now. I suppose he could have about £5,000 if the milk cheque is in and the bills aren't paid yet ...'

'Five grand!' Hubert's small eyes gleamed. 'Right, make out a cheque to yourself for that amount and we'll go in right away and cash it ...'

'We can't do that!' Gerda gasped.

'We have to, before that woman goes in and alerts the bank, and before the firms present the cheques she's sending out. You always paid the bills at the end of the month, didn't you?'

'Y-yes. But in any case they would never give me that much in cash. We only ever drew about £100 to pay wages and petrol.'

'All right, make it two grand then. I'll drive you in right away. And while you're at it you can make out a cheque to me for the other £3,000. I'll put it into my account until we need it ...'

'I c-can't ...' Gerda stared at him. The amounts she had fiddled herself had been hundreds but never thousands – apart from the fur coat. She frowned. If she added up all

272

her debts, though, it would take £2,000 to pay them off. She had no idea how much Hubert's own debts might be. She was pale and irritable. She had not slept for thinking about them since Ewan left.

'Can't or won't?' Hubert demanded angrily. 'Either you do it now while we have the chance or that's the end for us.'

'You don't mean that, Hubert ...' Gerda stared at him. She felt like bursting into tears. He looked back at her and turned on his old charm, speaking softly, persuasively. He knew she would do as he wanted in the end and, once the money was in his possession, Maxwell would never get his hands on it.

It was two days later before Joanne was in town. She called at the bank but, as she had anticipated, they refused to hand over Ewan's chequebook without his authority. He would be home by midnight if he caught the evening ferry. He would sort things out in person.

There was a small pile of letters waiting for Ewan the following morning but he pushed them aside until he had eaten his breakfast.

'Joanne couldn't pay the rest of the bills, but she said she would call in tomorrow morning and do them after you have had time to go to the bank for a new chequebook,' Rachel said as she sipped a cup of tea.

'Mmm, all right. Did she ask Gerda if it had been delivered to the cottage?'

'Yes, she did, but Gerda told her she'd have to collect it. She said the bank often made mistakes, but I don't remember them being careless.'

'No ... yes! What the ...' Ewan swallowed the last of his tea in a gulp and waved a letter at his mother. 'They've made one now! This says my account is overdrawn!'

'Overdrawn!' Rachel looked at him in concern. 'Could Joanne have made a mistake, do you think?'

'I don't know ...' Ewan scraped back his chair and

273

went towards the bureau. He frowned as he looked at the invoices Joanne had just paid and then at the chequebook stubs, all neatly filled in and in order. 'I can't see any mistake here. Joanne's meticulous. I'll phone the bank.'

He returned a few minutes later, his face pale and strained.

'They put me through to the manager. I'm going in to see him. Now. As soon as I've washed and changed.'

'But ...' Rachel shook her head. Ewan was already taking the stairs two at a time. She went into the hall and brought out his mackintosh and fine leather boots. It had poured all night and was still raining heavily.

'Ewan ...?'

'I'll tell you all about it, Mum, when I know myself.'

'Yes, I know that. I was going to say concentrate on your driving and forget about the bank ...'

'Forget! There was more than £6,000 in my account – more than enough to pay all this month's bills and change the combine harvester!'

'Think about that when you get there. There'll be floods on some of the back roads after the rain we've had.' Rachel frowned and bit her lip. Ewan had already closed the door behind him. He was so worked up about it, but surely the bank would soon put matters right.

Ewan stared across the desk incredulously.

'You paid out £2,000? In cash?'

'Well, your wife does have your authority to sign the cheques, Mr Maxwell,' the bank manager said levelly.

'Not any more she doesn't!'

'I – er ... I see. You mean, you want us to cancel that authority.'

'Certainly I do. Even so, there was more than £2,000 in my account. So why is it overdrawn?'

'One moment, while I get particulars of your account and recent drawings, please.' Ewan waited, drumming his fingers impatiently. He could barely control his agitation, or his fury. He might have guessed Gerda would do something like this. He should have cancelled her authority immediately. If he'd had any sense, he'd never have given it in the first place ...

'Here we are, Mr Maxwell ...' The man was frowning down at the papers in his hand. He read out one or two of the amounts – cheques which Joanne had paid and which Ewan recognised as legitimate monthly accounts for cattle cake, another for detergents and sundry dairy items. 'Aah, this is the one which made you overdrawn. £3,240, ten shillings and sixpence ...'

'£3,000! Then it's definitely a mistake.'

'A new tractor? A car ...?'

'No! Who is the cheque made out for?'

'Messrs H. Boyd-Hill.'

'What! Why the ... stop the cheque! You must stop the cheque!'

'It's too late for that, Mr Maxwell.' The manager's sandy eyebrows rose. 'The cheque was dated more than a week ago.'

'That doesn't mean anything. It could have been backdated. It probably was. Has it gone through?'

'Yes. It was presented four days ago.'

Four days, Ewan's mind calculated furiously. That must have been the day after he left for Ireland.

'Do you wish me to see who signed the cheque?'

'No.' Ewan slumped in his seat. 'The man's a swindler! And she's just as bad. Can't you get the money back? Is there nothing you can do?'

'I'm afraid it's too late for us to do that.'

'I see. Thank you.' Ewan rose, his face grim, his mouth set. At the door he turned back to the bank manager. 'Be sure to cancel my wife's authority and, to make doubly sure, you cancel my account and open a new one.'

'We can certainly do that, Mr Maxwell, but meanwhile

you are over ...'

'Set up the new account. I'll come back tomorrow and sort this mess out. Meanwhile, if you could arrange an overdraft to cover this month's cheques ...?'

'We-ell, very well, I'll see what I can do, Mr Maxwell. I shall need your signature and ...' He looked at Ewan shrewdly. 'Your family have dealt with us for many years and we have never had anything like this happen before.'

'Nor ever again, I hope!' Ewan muttered as he went out.

In that moment, if he had known where to find Hubert Boyd-Hill, he knew he would have been capable of murder. As it was, he did know where he'd find Gerda at this time on a pouring wet morning. She was probably not even out of bed. He yanked on his mackintosh and ran across the street to his car.

He was seething, his mind racing to think of some way to make the two of them pay for their treachery. It wasn't just money. He was a fool. He had been tolerant too long, overlooked too many things for the sake of peace in his home.

He would turn Gerda out of the cottage. She could live with her actor. She could starve by the roadside for all he cared now. What a fool he'd been ... His thoughts went round and round. His brain made plans then, just as quickly, rejected them. He had to keep within the law.

In front of him, a car drew to a halt. Ewan stood frantically on the brakes. Tyres squealed on the wet road.

For the next mile he concentrated his attention on the traffic but, once out of town, he put his foot down automatically, his jaw clenched.

Mentally, he pulverised Hubert Boyd-Hill's cunning face.

Ewan knew the road like the back of his hand. Had he been thinking, he would have remembered the hollow between Waterside and Stoneybrae would be flooded in this weather. His thoughts were far from the roads, or driving.

The car hit the water at speed. It skewed out of control.

# Chapter Twenty-two

Gerda heard the knocking on the cottage door. She groaned and turned over, snuggling even further beneath the blankets. She was not expecting anyone and she never answered the door looking a mess, still in her nightgown and without makeup.

The knocking ceased. The two people conferred and decided to drive on up to the farm.

Rachel stared in shocked silence at the policeman and woman. Afterwards, she couldn't remember inviting them in, or the kindly policewoman making tea for her. She must have given them Bridie's number, and Conan's.

'We think the car must have spun out of control when it hit the water,' the policeman was explaining to Conan. 'It appears to have rolled over the banking into the field. The doctor believes your brother was killed instantly.'

Rachel was only vaguely aware of the burr of voices. She couldn't take in the meaning of the words. Ewan! Her son. The youngest of her family. Paul's father. He couldn't be dead. He couldn't!

It was Bridie who stayed to care for her mother and look after Paul in the days which followed. The little boy couldn't understand that he would never see his daddy again. His earlier nightmares returned.

'Let him stay with us for a few nights,' Lucy suggested the second weekend after the funeral. 'It might take his mind off things and it'll be good for both Paul and Ryan to play. 'Besides, Bridie, you look all in. You can't go on helping Peter at Nether Rullion and running Glens of Lochandee, as well as having broken nights with Paul. You've all helped me such a lot. I'd like to do something in return.'

'Thank you, Lucy,' Bridie agreed gratefully. 'There's worse news though. I haven't told Mum yet. She's been so quiet and withdrawn. Not at all like herself. The doctor thinks it's the shock of hearing of Ewan's death so unexpectedly, and from the police. I don't want to add to her troubles.'

'Yes, it was a terrible shock for all of us and it must have been far worse to find the police at the door. Surely things can't get any worse?'

'Mr Niven asked me to go into his office. Conan too. You'll not believe this, b-but Gerda went to see him the day after the funeral and instructed him to sell Nether Rullion immediately, and everything connected with it. She told him she'd arrange for the cows to be sold at the local market next week.'

'But she can't do that, surely! Even if she could, it'd be a stupid thing to do!'

'She seems to think pedigrees are just worthless bits of paper ...'

'I can't believe even Gerda could be so foolish!' Lucy gasped. 'In a fine herd like Nether Rullion, they'd treble the value, and more. I can't believe even Gerda could be idiot enough to want to sell a herd like this as ordinary commercial cattle. How could she possibly throw away everything your father and Ewan have worked for all these years?' Lucy felt anger boiling up in her on Ewan's behalf. 'Joanne and I could find all the information for a catalogue if the herd has to be sold. But does it? Has she the authority? Had Ewan made a will? What about Paul's inheritance? He must have rights too?'

'Ewan hadn't made a will but, yes, Paul does have legal rights. Gerda insisted she had the right to handle everything. She's his mother and responsible for Paul.'

'Responsible!' Lucy gasped in disbelief.

'Mr Niven said his meeting with her was the most unpleasant he has ever experienced. She insisted he put the houses on the market immediately – Mum's, as well as Peter's, and the cottage ...'

'Surely she wouldn't ... She can't do that! Can she? Ewan was intending to apply for a divorce once they'd been apart long enough. He-he told me so himself.' Lucy took a deep breath to steady the welter of emotions she felt. 'I know it's unchristian of me to say so, b-but all that show of a grieving widow, dressed impeccably in black from head to toe ... it was all a pretence. Sh-she never loved Ewan.'

She couldn't bring herself to tell Bridie the words Gerda has hissed in her ear at the funeral. Lucy had just given her grandmother a comforting hug and stepped away. Gerda leaned towards her on the pretext of exchanging sympathetic platitudes. Instead she hissed, 'You needn't pretend. I know now you're Conan's bastard.' Lucy knew she would never forget the venom behind the words, nor the look of triumph in Gerda's pale eyes as she muttered, 'The Maxwell money is mine now. You're nothing!' She couldn't suppress a shudder as she recalled the look on Gerda's face.

'Are you all right, Lucy?' Bridie said in concern. 'You're terribly pale.'

'Y-yes, I'm fine. It was just talking about the funeral and r-remembering ...'

'Well, Nick would certainly agree with you about the grieving widow bit. He thinks Gerda is the biggest hypocrite on earth. He thought she was trying to imitate Jackie Kennedy.'

'He may be right.' Lucy nodded with a wan smile.

'Mr Niven thinks there's someone advising Gerda, or at least influencing her. He got the impression she wants money in a hurry. Whoever it is, he says neither of them understand much about the ways of business, particularly farming, or about the legal aspects.'

'I can imagine.'

'Apparently she was dismayed, almost alarmed, when Mr Niven told her it could take 12 months or more before Ewan's affairs were settled. That was bad enough, but when she heard the provisions Dad had made before his death, she flew into hysterics and cursed him. He threatened to put her out of the office.'

'That's typical of Gerda when she doesn't get her own way.'

'I thank God Dad had the wisdom to seek Jordon Niven's advice, and to act on it. Not long before he died he gave instructions for Nether Rullion to be put in trust for Paul. He made provision for Mum and Peter Forster to occupy their respective farmhouses for as long as they live.'

'Oh, thank goodness for that!' Lucy let out a long breath she didn't know she'd been holding. Again, Gerda's venomous words echoed in her head. 'What a shock she would get. Obviously, Ewan must never have told her what your dad had done.'

'It was certainly a shock. She threatened to get another lawyer. Jordon told her she'd be very welcome to do so, but he would carry out his duties and there was nothing she could do to get her hands on any of the land or property, including the cottage. She could live in it, but it belongs to the farm so she can't sell it.'

'Gosh, I'll bet Gerda was furious.'

'Shocked speechless, Mr Niven said. Then she flew into a furious rage. Before she left the office he got the impression she was almost afraid – though I can't think why.'

'Perhaps she's in some kind of trouble? Maybe in debt? She used to overspend when we were at college, but her father always came to the rescue then.'

'I never thought of that. She ran up big debts before Paul was born. I remember she bought a mink coat and the firm was going to sue her for the money.' Bridie frowned suddenly. 'I wonder if that has anything to do with Mr Niven having difficulty with the bank ... As executor, he was arranging for the business to carry on as usual until everything gets sorted out, but they're refusing to give permission for anyone to sign cheques. Apparently, Ewan had been in and given instructions to that effect, just before he was killed. I think they're going to open a new account. All the bills will have to go through Mr Niven. As you'll know, Lucy, the existing bills have to be paid and new ones keep coming. I ordered a load of cattle cake yesterday – we have to keep the farm running. The cows don't suddenly stop eating.'

'No, of course they don't. Do you think Peter will be able to carry on here with Billy Smith, if you hire another man? I know no one can replace Ewan and everything he did, of course ...'

'I think Peter would manage most things. Joanne seems very competent with the pedigrees already and she was just taking over the accounts. I can't understand why there should be a problem.' Bridie frowned.

'It does seem strange that the bank should stop all the payments,' Lucy agreed. 'That will certainly worry your mum, if she finds out.'

'I hope she doesn't hear about it until we get things sorted out. Peter is a conscientious stockman. He knows we'll all be working for Paul's sake and he thinks the world of him. I think we shall manage until Paul is old enough to decide if he really wants to farm.'

'He's so young.' Lucy sighed sadly. 'But he does love animals.'

'Well, I'll do everything I can to give him his chance, poor wee soul,' Bridie said. 'One thing's for sure, we must never let Mum know Gerda was planning to turn everything into cash, even the house.'

'You're right.' Lucy shivered. 'She'd take Paul away without a second's thought, if it meant she could get control of his inheritance.'

'Lucy! I hadn't thought of that aspect! It'd break Mum's heart to lose both Ewan and Paul! That'd be worse than losing her home.'

'We can't let that happen, Bridie.' Lucy's usually gentle expression hardened. 'I know Gerda's attitude to children. She'd never love and care for Paul as a mother should.' Nor even as any normal compassionate human being, she thought silently.

'I pray it'll never come to that,' Bridie said anxiously. 'Ewan was chief trustee but it's Conan and myself now, with Mr Niven. Dad must have had some sixth sense that Paul might need protecting from his own mother.

Gerda was nervous about seeing Hubert after her interview with Mr Niven. He had known she was going to the lawyer's office and couldn't wait to hear how quickly she could get her hands on Ewan's fortune, even if it meant having the brat tagging along with them.

He was waiting for her at the cottage, pacing the floor and smoking. He had already arranged for her furniture to be removed and sent to the saleroom in two days' time. Some of his own items were antiques, although it was her money – or rather Ewan's – which had paid for them. They were going to a specialist sale. Sometimes, she felt resentment at Hubert's high-handed actions, but he always seemed to have good reason for them and the words to lift her out of her moods.

The question now was, could she keep his attentions without the regular cash handouts he had grown to expect?

Could she soothe his temper when he heard her news? In spite of his charm, Gerda was aware of his faults, but many of them were hers too, so she understood and forgave them.

'We're two of a kind, you and I,' he'd often remarked and she knew he was right.

Now, she faced him across the living room of the cottage. She reported the steps Ross Maxwell had taken to protect his grandson's inheritance but Hubert seemed unperturbed.

'You're the boy's mother. You'll have control of him and his fortune. You must tell them all you're selling the property in the boy's best interests. Once you have the cash ...'

'No! You don't understand, Hubert. I can't touch any of the property, not even this cottage. Oh, I can live in it,' she said bitterly, 'for as long as I like, but I can't sell it. Bridie and Conan are the trustees, now that Ewan is dead. I can't even have the chequebook to go on paying the bloody bills!'

'That's ridiculous!' Hubert swore profusely. 'Somebody will have to pay out the money!'

'The lawyer says it could be a year or more before Ewan's affairs are wound up because he was in business. Meanwhile I get the same pitiful bloody allowance. I can't even have that until he has sorted out "problems with the bank". We both know what the problems are! There's no money left in the account to pay the monthly bills. I shall get nothing!' she wailed. 'What am I going to do? I've had two letters threatening to take me to court. I haven't enough money to pay a fraction of what I owe, even if I use all the £2,000 I drew in cash. Can't you lend me some? I don't want to go to jail, Hubert. Hubert!'

She watched as his face paled. He slumped down onto the nearest chair.

'This is a fine bloody pickle we're in! I thought

284

spouses got a better deal these days when husbands died without a will.'

'That's what Mr Niven said. Scottish law changed in 1964. God knows how bad it was before that! I could have inherited up to £5,000 of moveable assets if I hadn't had the brat. As it is, I'm only entitled to £2,500. If the cottage had belonged to Ewan, instead of his father tying the deeds into the bloody farm, it would have been mine. I could have sold it, so long as it was not worth more than £15,000! Imagine what I could do with £15,000 ...' She sank down onto the settee and closed her eyes.

'You thought there'd be no problem,' Hubert said accusingly. 'I've already sent for the airline tickets, but we both know the cheque will bounce unless you put some money into the account.'

'You'll have to use some of the £3,000 I gave you. Have you cashed the cheque?'

'Of course I have!' he said scornfully. 'Your dearly beloved husband would've stopped it the minute he returned from Ireland.'

'Yes. I think he'd probably been to the bank. He must have been on his way back when he was killed.'

'And we thought we were home and dry! I thought we'd be better off when we heard he was dead, but we're going to be a hell of a lot worse off. Unless we think of something pretty quickly ...'

'I've already used some of the £2,000 I drew in cash – don't look at me like that! I had to, to keep the local shops quiet until we got out of the area. You'll have to draw the money from that cheque I gave you.'

'Not on your life! I've banked that in the new name we agreed to use once we get abroad. Mr and Mrs Fritz. You said that was your mother's maiden name.'

'It was, and much good it ever did me,' Gerda muttered bitterly.

'Never mind the past,' Hubert said irritably. 'Who is

285

handling the creditors? Paying the bills for the farm to keep going?'

'Mr Niven is the executor. He said something about paying creditors being the first priority. Only after that can I get anything. I should be due up to £2,500 of the moveable estate. But don't you see? We took all the cash out of the account. I think that's what he meant by "moveable estate"! There won't be any. There isn't even enough to pay this month's bills! Ewan would probably have sold some cows or something if he'd been alive. He'd have been furious when he found out, but I knew he'd find the money to pay the bills somehow. That's the Maxwell way – pay what you owe.'

'To hell with the Maxwell way!'

'I'm afraid, Hubert. The bank is sure to be looking into things to find out what happened to Ewan's capital. Mr Niven will find out who drew the cheques ... They might even think we killed Ewan to get his money!'

'It was an accident, for God's sake. Calm down, Gerda. Niven won't know anything until he starts poking his nose in and lawyers always take for ever.' Hubert's small eyes narrowed as he considered various plans and rejected them.

Eventually, he said, 'I'll tell you what we'll do – you said the first priority was for Niven to pay the creditors, didn't you?'

'Yes, but ...'

'Listen, you goose! You're still Maxwell's wife, or rather his widow. Your creditors are his responsibility. This is what we'll do. Listen carefully, and don't argue. It's the only way.'

# Chapter Twenty-three

'Gerda, make a list of all the firms who are demanding money from you,' Hubert ordered. 'Then, you'll have to use my old typewriter. I'll help you compose an official-sounding letter. It will inform all creditors of Mr Ewan Maxwell's death and instruct them to send their accounts to his solicitor for settlement.'

'We can't do that! Mr Niven will ...'

'He'll not know. We'll post the letters when we're ready to leave here, and preferably on our way to leaving the country too, if we play our cards right.'

'But some of them are threatening to take me to court now. *Now*, I tell you!'

'I'm not intending we should hang about! It'll keep them quiet for a few days if they get a response to their demands, and some hope of eventual settlement. By the time they all send their demands to Niven, we'll be long gone.'

'But what about your own bills?'

'Don't you worry your head about them, my sweet,' Hubert said smoothly. 'You don't think I use my own name all the time, do you? The most recent bills are already in Maxwell's name. Things like the car and the London tailor who made my suits.'

'Hubert! How ... how ...' Gerda was lost for words. 'Supposing Ewan had found out?'

'I only used his name after things were getting pretty

hot for me. I knew the crunch was coming – one way or the other. Now, let's get going. I've another little plan, if I can contact the man we need to carry it out. I'll need to pay a few calls around the pubs to find him though.'

'What sort of plan?' Gerda asked suspiciously.

'I'll tell you when I find out whether it can be done. By the way, does Mrs Maxwell still go to church every Sunday? Back to Lochandee?'

'Yes, but why do you want to know that?' In answer, Hubert tapped the side of his nose, a gesture which always infuriated Gerda, but she was too tense to tell him so right now. She was in a mess. They both were. She didn't know how to get out of it on her own. She didn't even know where her own father was living now, she thought bitterly. He should be here to help her. Typically, Gerda managed to blame everyone except herself for her predicament.

It was two nights later before Hubert managed to contact the man he believed would help them carry out his plan. The cattle dealer gave every indication of being a slow, simple sort of fellow. Smugly, Hubert thought he handled the whole thing pretty smartly himself.

He related a fine story about Gerda's pathetic state since being widowed and the unfair treatment she was receiving at the hands of the Maxwells, but he knew nothing about the world of farming – a fact which the cattle dealer had been quick to grasp.

'Is the herd free frae brucellosis?' he asked gruffly.

'Brucellosis?' Hubert frowned. 'I expect so. They're all pedigree anyway.'

'Brucellosis is a disease, man! Nothing tae do wi' the way the animals are bred. They're worth more all round if the herd's accredited.' He eyed Hubert shrewdly from under the shadow of his cap and smothered a smirk of satisfaction. 'Ye'll need a permit for each animal ye're wanting to sell. Take the ear numbers to the government offices. They'll fix you up with the paperwork.'

'I-I can't do that!' Hubert frowned. He had no idea what ear numbers were, or where to find them. 'I told you this whole operation has to be carried out as soon as possible and with the minimum of fuss. We don't want everybody knowing ...'

'I see ... Right ye are, guvnor.' The dealer's eyes narrowed, watching the suave man closely, seeing the nervous way he fiddled with his beer glass. 'Ye'll understand the cattle are worth a lot less, then?' he suggested slyly. 'If ye can't sell them on as accredited – free frae tuberculosis and brucellosis?'

'Oh, but they will be. It's one of the best herds in Scotland!'

'Maybe it is, but man, ye must ken even the best herds get breakdowns in health. Then they have to dispose of their reactors. Naebody's going to take your word, or mine, that they're free o' disease, not without all the bits o' paper frae the government.'

'B-but you can still sell them ...?'

'Aye. I'll send them down to a dealer pal o' mine in Cheshire. There's still demand for cattle down there after the bad outbreak o' foot-and-mouth. As I said, I canna pay ye as much for them without the permits.'

'We'll take what we can get,' Hubert declared, unused to the way dealers operated and bargained over the last sixpence. The man raised his eyebrows and bit back a grin. 'But you have to move them on a Sunday morning while the womenfolk are at the church,' Hubert reminded him. 'We don't want to cause them more – er ... distress than they've suffered already,' he added smoothly.

'You said they were pedigree cattle. I'll need the registrations.'

'Oh, forget about the formalities, my man,' Hubert said, haughtily waving his hand, totally unaware he was brushing aside more than half the value of most of the cows, or that well-bred pedigree animals from an attested herd would bring four times what a dealer would pay if they were sold at a pedigree auction sale.

'But you did say they were pedigree? I've heard o' the Rullion herd. They're pretty good, by all accounts.'

'Oh, they are. They've won at some of the agricultural shows ...'

'Pedigree breeders dinna need the likes o' me tae sell their cattle as a rule ...' the dealer said drily. He looked searchingly at Hubert. There was something fishy about this transaction. It was like taking sweets from a baby. So long as no one accused him of stealing the cattle it was all right by him. He could make a pretty sum out of men like this Mr Fritz, if that was his real name. 'Ye dinna have the pedigree registrations to hand then, I take it?'

'Er ... no. The paperwork has been, er ... neglected.'

'Well, so long as ye understand they're only worth the price o' commercial cattle without them?'

'Very well. How many could you load in an hour and when can you remove them?' Hubert asked eagerly – too eagerly.

'Let's see,' the dealer lifted his cap and scratched his head as though wrestling with a major problem. 'I could send my two big lorries. Say 20 animals in each ...' He frowned at Hubert, eyeing his well-polished brown shoes and the cut of his jacket. 'I take it ye'll no be there tae help load them on to the lorry.'

'Oh no!' Hubert stared back at him. 'Don't you send a man with the lorry?'

'Well, it doesn't bloody well drive itself!' he retorted sarcastically. 'But two drivers canna load 40 cows on their ain! Not in an hour.' He was dealing with a right ninny here. He frowned. 'I'll need a letter o' authority frae the widow who wants tae sell them. Ye'll need tae hand it over before any o' the cows are loaded on to my lorries.'

'You will have it.' Hubert assumed an air of superiority. The dealer was hard pressed not to burst out laughing. 'In return, I request payment in cash.'

'What! For the whole bloody lot?' The man's eyebrows almost disappeared beneath his cap.

'That's what I said.' Hubert nodded officiously.

'Proper cocky wee feller he was,' the dealer remarked later to one of his drivers, 'and as ignorant as a pig in a sty about selling livestock. If the cows are as good as I've heard then we'll try and squeeze an extra one on each lorry. If I'm any judge o' silly buggers, he'll be none the wiser. We'll tell him we could only load 39 and that's what I'll pay him for.'

He'd promised Hubert he would send extra men to load the animals and certainly kept his word on that score. Instinct told him the sooner he had his cargo loaded and off the premises, the better it would be.

When Bridie came out of church the following Sunday morning, she was astonished to find Peter Forster waiting for her. She could see he was agitated even before she reached him, and his face was white. Her first thought was for the sick cow he'd been attending. She knew he'd been up most of the night with a difficult calving, but they'd both thought the cow would survive, even though the calf had been born dead. That was one of the hazards of farming and had to be accepted. It was not something to get so worked up about. Her own philosophical attitude deserted her when he greeted her.

'I never go to bed in the daytime! They came while I was sleeping! They've taken half of the milking herd! Maybe more. They said they had written authority ...'

'Peter ...' Bridie said faintly. 'I don't know what you're talking about.' She took his arm and gently steered him out of the churchyard, away from curious glances. Nick, her mother and the children were talking to Lucy as they came out of church but, seeing Bridie with Peter, they all moved to join her before she could get Peter to explain coherently.

'This is not the place to discuss things,' Nick frowned, seeing the groups of people eyeing them.

'Come to my house,' Lucy suggested. 'It's only up the street, Peter. Whatever is wrong, you look as though you need a drink of something.'

'But, Mrs Jones!' Peter almost wailed, snatching at Bridie's arm. 'The longer we wait, the further away the lorries will be ...'

Once inside Lucy's house, the children obediently went to change out of their Sunday clothes and scampered outside to play.

'Now, Peter, start at the beginning,' Nick said quietly while Lucy brewed a pot of strong tea.

'I never go to bed during the day ...' Peter looked pleadingly at Bridie.

'You must have been tired out after last night.' She nodded. 'And it is Sunday after all. No one could blame you for that. Go on, Peter. You said there were two lorries ...?'

'Yes. I did not hear them come. I was sleeping deep. I heard cows making much noise. Looked out of the window and I saw men rounding them into the yard. Bringing the cows in from the field! So early in the day. Other men were chasing them into a lorry – the biggest lorry I have seen. Another big lorry was in the yard. I dress quickly and run downstairs. Pull on my boots and outside. I ask, "What are you doing?" One man – he seemed to be boss – he said he had instructions to remove the cows. "Whose instructions?" I say. "Mrs Maxwell," he tell me. I say he must stop until I bring you, Mrs Jones. He laugh. They filled the first lorry, moved it away and start filling the next lorry. I note down the numbers and come straight for you.' That was the longest speech Peter had ever made and he paused for breath, then added urgently. 'We must get back the cows! We must go after the men!'

'I can't believe this!' Bridie hadn't realised she was standing over Peter, willing him to tell them exactly what had happened, yet not wanting to know what her brain was telling her. She flopped onto a kitchen chair. Her eyes moved to Nick, silently beseeching him to find a solution. Then her gaze settled on her mother's face. Rachel looked white and drawn. She caught Bridie's eyes on her.

'This must be Gerda's doing,' she said. 'She's determined to get what she can, while she can. I've known for a long time that she's been spending more money than she should. Ewan put up with it for Paul's sake. Now he's dead and she knows there must be an end to the money. The day he was killed he'd been at the bank. I overheard him speaking on the telephone before he left. I-I think his account was overdrawn. He said that was impossible. There should have been at least £5,000 in it.'

'Mum! You never mentioned this before ...' Bridie stared at her mother in dismay. They had believed they were protecting her and she had guessed how things were all along.

'It was money,' Rachel said dully. 'Ewan is dead. Dead.' She suppressed a shudder. 'All the money in the world can't bring him back.'

'Oh, Mum.' Bridie moved to her side and put an arm round her shoulders. Suddenly, even the theft of their cattle seemed relatively unimportant beside the enormity of Ewan's death. 'Drink your tea. Please, Mum? All this time, you've been trying to protect us and we've been trying to shield you. Mr Niven said there were problems with the bank. But why should Gerda instruct someone to remove the cows? And who? Peter's right, we must try to get them back. Shall we inform the police, Nick?' She looked helplessly at her husband.

'I think that's the only thing we can do. At least Peter got the numbers of the lorries involved.' He gave Peter a reassuring pat on the back.

'You're sure the man said he had Mrs Maxwell's authority to remove the cows, Peter?' Bridie asked.

'He said so. He waved a letter at me. He did not let me read it though.'

'Could it be that Gerda believes the cows are hers now, to dispose of how she likes?' Nick asked with a frown.

'She knows they're not!' Bridie said. 'I told you she'd been in to the solicitor's office the day after Ewan's funeral. She couldn't wait to get her hands on everything! He told her she had no claim to anything until all the creditors had been paid. If it's true the money had all been taken out of the farm account without Ewan's knowledge it must have been Gerda who withdrew it. She'd know there was none of the moveable estate which Mr Niven talks about. She'd know there was nothing to pay the creditors or her.'

'I'll phone the police. They'll track down the owner of the lorries,' Nick said.

'Use my phone,' Lucy said, indicating the door to the hall. 'It'll save time.'

'I suppose we should notify Mr Niven, but that'll have to wait until his office opens tomorrow. Gerda should be charged with theft.'

'She has left her home,' Peter announced suddenly. 'It is empty since a few days ago. Billy Smith told me. A furniture lorry came and removed everything. The removal men said they were taking it to the salerooms at Carlisle.'

Bridie stared at him in disbelief.

'I didn't know that. But where will she live …?'

'The postman told Billy's father he had brought a letter from the office of – er … passports, is it? It was addressed to Mrs Fritz, but it had the address of Mrs Maxwell's house on the envelope. Mr Smith promised to hand the letter in to Mrs Maxwell. She laugh when she take it from Billy's father. She said the government office was stupid to put wrong name on the envelope.'

'Perhaps she's going abroad for a holiday.' Bridie frowned. 'Maybe she's going to see her father.'

Rachel sat up, suddenly alert. 'She doesn't know where her father is. He specifically asked me not to pass on his address to Gerda. He didn't want her to cause trouble for his new wife. Twice each year he sends a gift for Paul and asks for news of him. I send the reply to a post office box but I know it's in Portugal.'

Bridie stared at her, amazed that her mother managed to share so many confidences, yet always keep them to herself.

Nick came back into the kitchen.

'The police say it will be easy enough to find out who owns the lorries and to track them down. They praised your prompt action, Peter,' he added, giving the still-agitated Peter a reassuring smile. 'Apparently, if Gerda has authorised the sale of the cows and she is not the rightful owner, then it's tantamount to theft.'

'It's Paul's inheritance. She's stolen from her own son!' Bridie said indignantly. 'And it seems she has already claimed all the available cash from Ewan's account.'

'What good would his inheritance be if Gerda took him away from here ...' Rachel said. Her voice trembled and sank to a whisper. 'It was bad enough when she neglected him at the cottage. I couldn't bear what it might do to him.'

'Oh, Mum,' Bridie said gently. 'Is that what's been troubling you? Is that why you've been so quiet – so withdrawn?'

'It's my greatest fear,' Rachel said clearly. 'To lose Ewan, and then for his mother to claim Paul ...' She shuddered. 'She threatened to take him away from Ewan once before, if he divorced her. Ewan told me so himself. Since Gerda had neglected Paul more and more, Ewan was prepared to leave her and to fight for his own son. With

Ewan gone, who but his own mother would have charge of him, if she wants him? Let her take the cows. If that'll get her away from here, she'll leave Paul in peace, here where he belongs. Don't you see?' Rachel pleaded, looking round the circle of faces. 'If Paul inherits anything of value, Gerda would claim him so that she could control whatever he has. She would turn everything into cash, and she would spend it. Her father warned us. It's a weakness with her, a flaw in her character. I'm 67 now. I may not be here long enough to see him grow to manhood, but I'm not thinking of myself. I c-couldn't bear what it might do to Paul if Gerda took him away. He never asks for her, or wants to go to her. If he has nothing, she'll not want him. He would be a burden to her.'

'I see ...' Bridie looked up and met Lucy's troubled eyes. Lucy gave a faint nod.

'It seems dreadful to steal from her own son, I know, but your mother is probably right about her motives, however harsh it sounds.'

'But she'll have no idea of the real value of Ewan's cattle,' Bridie said glumly. 'A dealer would never pay their true worth. Should we really let her get away with it, Mum? I-I don't know whether we can afford to. Mr Niven seemed to think we should have to sell some of the stock just to settle creditors, and there's no wonder, if all the capital has been taken from the bank. Obviously, he must have discovered that already. Now we know why. Perhaps we should see what he says – and Fiona and Conan too. Conan is a trustee, after all. He must be consulted.'

'Then I must speak to Mr Niven too,' Rachel said. 'I'd do anything – make any sacrifice – to keep Paul here, with us. Not all the cows or money in the world are worth a little boy's happiness – and safety.' She shuddered.

Bridie looked at her mother doubtfully.

'What she's done is – is criminal ...'

'I know it is. I know it's wrong to take the cows like

that, and such a waste of fine animals too. She'll pay for her sins one day, I'm sure of it. All I ask is that Paul is not made to pay too.'

# Chapter Twenty-four

The police tracked the cattle to three farms in Cheshire, all belonging to the same farmer and cattle dealer. He had purchased them quite legitimately and readily gave the particulars of his Scottish contact. There again the dealer had proof that he had been given authority by Mrs Gerda Maxwell to remove the cattle from her premises. The deal had been initiated by a Mr Fritz and he had requested payment in cash. The dealer had insisted on having a signed receipt and proffered this to the police as proof that he had conducted the transaction in good faith. All this they reported to Conan and Mr Niven and Bridie.

'But so far they haven't been able to track down either Gerda or this Mr Fritz,' Bridie reported to her mother. Rachel looked white and strained. She couldn't rid herself of the terrible fear that Gerda would retaliate by taking Paul away if she found herself trapped in a nasty situation.

'I expect they've moved to another house ...'

'You've kept Paul away from school again, Mum?' Bridie frowned as she watched the little boy walking across the farmyard, his hand in Peter's as he chattered happily about the animals.

'Yes. I know it's wrong, but I'm afraid Gerda might steal Paul away like she did the cows,' Rachel said tensely. 'I couldn't bear to lose him too, Bridie. Or at least I would bear it, if I believed he'd be better off with his own mother. Gerda resented him from the day he was born. She never made any effort to care for him. It would break his heart to leave Nether Rullion and all his family. He often talks about Ewan, even though I explained his daddy had gone to live with the angels.'

Bridie nodded, unable to reply for the lump in her throat. So far, she hadn't told anyone except Nick, but Mr Niven was becoming seriously concerned about the growing list of creditors. He felt many of them were not genuine business ones. He was requesting more details from the firms concerned. Some of them were long overdue and demanding immediate settlement. If the missing capital could not be replaced soon, he could see no way out, except to sell the remaining cattle. It was up to her to prepare her mother but she scarcely knew how to begin.

Mr Niven felt strongly that Gerda should be traced and made to repay the money she had taken from Ewan's estate, both in cash and by selling so many of the dairy herd, since it was impossible to generate income from the farm without them.

'You must make your mother understand that many of these later accounts are for expenses incurred by your brother's widow,' Mr Niven had said that morning when Bridie kept her appointment at his office.

'I-I'll try to explain and get her to change her mind.'

'I can understand her reasoning,' Jordon Niven sighed. 'If the child is happy where he is it would be cruel to take him away, especially if, as you say, his mother does not look after him well?'

'She never has! There's no place in Gerda's life for a child – except to use as a pawn,' Bridie said angrily. She was thoroughly frustrated. She felt Gerda should be made to pay, and that could mean going to jail, but knew she could never go against her mother's wishes. It was true – it would probably break Paul's heart to leave Nether Rullion, all the animals and the people who loved him and cared for him.

'If we leave things the way they are now,' Jordon Niven said slowly, making his fingers into a steeple, as he always he did when he was considering a serious situation, and finding no satisfactory solution, 'the way things are, it looks as though the boy is going to lose his inheritance whatever we do. Only today, we have had two creditors contact us – one from London demanding payment for a car, supposedly hired by a Mr Maxwell and never returned. The firm has reason to believe the car has since been sold. It is clear to me your sister-in-law is not alone in this – this treachery. If we settle all these additional creditors, there will be nothing left to run the farm as a viable business.'

'B-but surely …' Bridie's face went white as she stared across the desk.

'It is true.' He tapped a sheaf of papers with a long finger. 'Some of these accounts have been accumulating over several years. It looks as though Mrs Gerda Maxwell has never paid her way. Then again, if we do manage to trace her and to press charges, would she still have the cash she withdrew from the bank? And supposing we sue her, if she claims legal custody of her son, as you fear, she'll no doubt use whatever meagre income can be raised from Nether Rullion on his behalf. All in all, it would appear the child would reap no benefit from renewing his relationship with his mother.'

'No, he would not!' Bridie said robustly. 'She must have been bleeding Ewan dry for years. He'd have done anything to protect Paul, I know he would.'

'He had made an appointment to see me to discuss divorce proceedings,' Jordon Niven said thoughtfully. 'I am not breaching client confidentiality by divulging that information. Your brother is dead and the knowledge that he had reached such a decision may help us all decide what is best for his son. If you don't mind, Mrs Jones, I think I would like to call to see your mother tomorrow afternoon. I have always found her a woman of wisdom. Will you make sure it is convenient, please? After that, I will arrange to see yourself and your brother again as trustees for the land and buildings. Fortunately, the creditors would have no claim on them – only on the stock and the machinery.'

Bridie frowned. What good was the land and buildings if there were no cattle and no capital to replace them? Land, labour and capital – her father had always declared they were the three limiting factors to successful farming. Paul would inherit the land, but there was no capital to buy the stock or to pay the wages, and without wages there'd be no labour. She brushed away sudden tears as she thought of all the years and hard work her parents had put in to buy and improve Nether Rullion, and to build up the dairy herd. Maybe she should drive over to the garage later and discuss everything with Conan and Fiona. They all owed it to Ewan to do whatever was best for his son, and Paul was such a lovely little boy.

Jordon Niven was surprised to find Rachel looking calm and dignified, but with a determined set to her soft mouth. Ross Maxwell would have told him that meant there was no way she would change her mind. He noted the lines of strain and her unusual pallor. Even since he had seen her last her thick dark hair seemed to have turned almost white, but her green eyes held a resolute gleam as she set a tray of tea before him and pulled up a small table.

'I must tell you, Mr Niven, nothing you can say will persuade me to pursue my son's widow and to raise a court action against her. If cornered she's capable of retaliating ruthlessly and viciously. I won't allow my grandson to be sacrificed in the name of justice.'

Jordon Niven sipped his tea slowly, regarding Rachel over the rim of the china cup. He set it carefully in its

301

saucer.

'Did your daughter explain how deeply in debt your son's estate is?'

'Ewan was never in debt!'

'No, not personally, nor his business, but with the bank account depleted and the addition of creditors we knew nothing about ...'

'Yes, Bridie explained all of that.' Rachel leaned forward. 'It's a nasty business to be landed with someone else's debts. I agree it's most unjust and that the persons responsible should be punished, but ...' She shook her head vigorously. 'Not at any price. Not all the money in the world is worth my grandson's happiness and peace of mind, Mr Niven.'

'I understand your point of view, Mrs Maxwell, but I firmly believe some of the creditors were not even your daughter-in-law's. Do you know the name of her – her friend?'

'Ewan mentioned a Mr Hubert Boyd-Hill ...'

'But no one called Fritz?'

'Fritz was the name of Gerda's mother. And Gerda's maiden name was Fritz-Allan.'

'A-ah! I see. It seems to me that our Mr Boyd-Hill used several different names. The police appear to think a Mr and Mrs Fritz travelled to Portugal by air the day after the cattle were stolen. According to your daughter, Mr Fritz was the name of the man who negotiated the trumped-up sale with the cattle dealer.'

'Yes, that's correct but, Mr Niven, before we go any further, there's a question I'd like to ask you.'

Jordon Niven bit his lip. He had a growing feeling that Mrs Rachel Maxwell was increasingly taking charge of this interview. 'Go ahead. What do you wish to know?'

'Supposing we settle the farm creditors, plus the debts which Gerda and her – her friend have accumulated ...' She held up her hand to brook any interruption. 'Once my son's estate is settled, finally settled, is there any way that dreadful pair could use the Maxwell name again to run up more debts for us, or later for Paul, to settle?'

'There are ways of preventing such a situation occurring again, but ...'

'And if we decide not to pursue Gerda for theft of the cattle, is there any way we can make sure she cannot claim custody of Paul? The child's welfare, Mr Niven, is my overriding concern.'

Again, Jordon Niven sipped his tea, giving himself time to decide the best course of action and the best advice.

'Let me get this straight, Mrs Maxwell. Even if it means selling off the remaining cattle to pay all – I do mean all – the people claiming from your son's estate, you would be willing to do that so long as the boy's mother had no claim on him?'

'Exactly that. Gerda must *never* get custody of Paul.'

For the first time, Jordon Niven allowed himself a small smile.

'I think we could make sure of that, Mrs Maxwell. If the Fritzes have gone abroad to live, we could issue a warrant in the various names they are known to have used ...' Now he held up a hand to prevent Rachel's protest. 'This would not be a view to pursuing them for the money at all costs, so much as making them less likely to risk returning to this country and possibly going to jail. In view of her past neglect, I believe we could also make a case ensuring Mrs Gerda Maxwell cannot claim custody of Paul, so long as yourself, or other family members, are prepared to take on that responsibility.'

'I am, but I realise at my age I may not live for as long as he needs me. I will discuss it with my family, but I am sure Bridie or Lucy would care for Paul.'

'In that case, Mrs Maxwell, I think I can handle things to your satisfaction. But that still leaves the creditors. How could you continue to live here, and to feed, clothe and educate your grandson if there is no income from the dairy herd?'

'Ah …' For the first time Rachel's eyes clouded and her expression was one of deep sadness. 'It's not what I would have wished for Paul, and certainly not what my husband would have done, but during the night I decided on a solution which will suffice until Paul is of an age to take over the running of Nether Rullion himself and decide his own future. It will not be as easy for him as my late husband had intended, but at least it should protect the land.'

'May I ask what this solution might be?' Jordon Niven asked curiously and with some unease. After all, Mrs Maxwell was an elderly woman now. Was she capable of making such major decisions on behalf of her grandson?

Almost as though she read his thoughts, she said, 'I'm 67, Mr Niven. I will admit that recent events have rather shaken me, but now there's a challenge to be faced for Paul's sake.' She gave a faint smile. 'My late husband would have told you I thrive on challenge. I hope to live at least another ten years, but that is in God's hands. Since the rest of the stock must be sold we must prepare for the best pedigree sale we can arrange. That should clear the creditors, I believe? After that, most of the arable fields will be sown with grass and all the fields will be let for seasonal grazing. It's not ideal,' she said sadly, 'or what any of us would have wished, but I know several of our neighbours will be glad of the opportunity to rent extra grass so close to home. Renting grass parks we call it around here.

'My daughter will no doubt rent some of it to supplement Glens of Lochandee land. I believe she'll also supervise the cropping of two or three fields each year to keep the grass in rotation, with the help of Peter Forster. We employ three men and I'll be sorry to lose Billy Smith,

304

but one man will be sufficient to take care of the farm in its new form. Peter won't be happy either, but I think he'll prefer to stay here. He'll check the cattle belonging to neighbours each day and fertilise the grass, mend the fences, drains and ditches. Yes, there'll be plenty for him to do.' She sighed. 'He'll still be able to keep a couple of pigs and I'll have my hens. We may even be able to keep two or three calves for Paul in the small paddock beside the house ... As far as the cottage is concerned, it could be sold, if the debts aren't settled by the sale of the cattle. Otherwise, we'll rent it out to give a little extra income.'

'It sounds to me as though you have got it all worked out, Mrs Maxwell,' Jordon Niven said with a note of respect.

'Yes, I lay awake most of the night, thinking things through.' Rachel sighed, feeling suddenly very tired. 'I believe income from grass lets is treated differently for tax purposes but Fiona will advise us about that.'

'She will indeed,' Jordon agreed readily. 'Fiona and Conan have built up an excellent business with their coach tours. Did I hear they have taken over a hotel too, somewhere on the south coast? You must be very proud of them.'

'Yes, I've been blessed with a good family.' Rachel nodded, but she gave an unconscious sigh of weariness and Jordon Niven rose to take his leave. He hoped everyone would agree to this new strategy for Nether Rullion. It was not at all what Ross Maxwell had planned when he tried so hard to protect his life's work for his son and grandson. It seemed to be the best that could be salvaged under the circumstances. Paul was luckier than many to have such a family to love and support him. Jordon hoped with all his heart that Mrs Maxwell would be blessed with many more years to guide her grandson towards manhood.

# Chapter Twenty-five

Rachel remained firm in her decision to sell off the remaining cattle, pay off all the debts and clear the Maxwell name once and for all. In her heart, she knew she would make almost any sacrifice to protect Paul and keep him among those who loved him.

Inevitably the day of the sale came round and Rachel's courage and determination almost failed her when she saw how it upset Paul. Had she made the wrong decision? Yet what alternative had there been? None that she could have explained to a six-year-old boy. She could never tell him his mother had run away with all the available cash and stolen the animals which would have brought in an income. No, it was enough to have Mr Niven's assurance that Gerda Maxwell would have no claim on her son, or his inheritance in future.

Bridie had explained as gently as she could that the remaining animals would have to be sold, but it had taken three months to finalise the arrangements, fix a date for a pedigree sale on the farm, and to get all the milk records and pedigrees ready for the auctioneers to print the catalogue. Perhaps it had been a mistake to hold the sale at Nether Rullion, yet she knew it was better – most of all for the animals. It would have been a mammoth task transporting the young cattle to the auction and they would have had a second journey by lorry to various parts of the country after the sale.

Paul simply couldn't understand why they had to go anywhere and he sobbed into his grandmother's lap.

'I'll keep him indoors,' Rachel whispered above his head, but her eyes were troubled as they met Bridie's stricken gaze. Both Bridie and Lucy had done their utmost to make this sale a success. Every spare minute had been taken searching out records and pedigrees, getting the animals into the very best condition and, over the past few days, washing and grooming them for the big day. Peter Forster and Billy Smith had worked hard too. They had spent intervening weeks cleaning and painting the surplus machinery which would no longer be needed. After the sale, even the milking parlour would be dismantled and sold. This had been Nick's suggestion.

'There'll be no use for it without cows. It'll deteriorate and the rubber parts will perish. There are more modern systems being developed too. It's better to get whatever cash is available now.' Reluctantly, Rachel had agreed, knowing that Nick spoke good sense.

There was as much bustle inside the house as there was outside. A small room near the back door had been cleared for the buyers to come and pay their money to the auctioneer's clerks. The dining room had been cleared and set with trestle tables to feed the people attending the sale, particularly those breeders who had travelled several hundred miles to buy some of the Nether Rullion bloodlines. Rachel worried whether there would be enough cold meats to feed them all when she saw the crowds in the yard.

'Don't worry,' Fiona said calmly. 'If you think we're running short just give me a signal and I'll pop into town to the butcher's.'

'There's piles of food,' Lucy said reassuringly. She had hired the tea urns from Lochandee Village Hall, and Joanne and her mother had volunteered to help keep the teacups filled.

'I've never seen so much food in a house before!' Carol exclaimed. Although she had lived in Lochandee ever since the war, her roots were in the city and she had never got into the habit of having a big baking day every week as most of the country people did. Bridie and Lucy had baked pies and scones, while Rachel had been baking fruit loaves for the past few weeks. It was a tradition to give the purchasers a good feed at a farm sale, though Nick had told them the farmers' wives often refused to cater these days. Many of the farm sales arranged for a van to come and sell food to those who needed it.

'We'll cater the old way,' Rachel said with quiet determination. 'I would hate the neighbours to think we were mean, or so short of money we couldn't feed them.' She was well aware of the rumours circulating in the district. The sales representatives travelled from farm to farm selling machinery, feedstuffs, seeds and fertilisers and dispensing the gossip of the countryside along with their sales patter.

It had often amazed her that news spread so rapidly. Most of the salesmen would have known Gerda was seeing another man, even if they didn't know who he was. They would also be aware that following Ewan's death there was insufficient cash to pay for all the products their respective firms had supplied to Nether Rullion. Jordon Niven had reached agreements with the major farm suppliers, assuring them their accounts would be settled in full if they would agree to wait until after the sale. The Maxwells had a good reputation for prompt payment as a rule so there had been only one firm which had raised objections. Rachel felt saddened and embarrassed by the whole affair.

As the buzz and air of excitement increased, Paul ran upstairs to his bedroom. Alicia promised to keep an eye on him. The twins were almost 16 now and they had pleaded with Bridie to take a day off school to help Granny at the sale. Rachel was glad of their young legs to fetch and carry, and keep the teacups and saucers washed and replaced ready for the constant stream of hungry farmers.

Now Alicia said quietly, 'Paul has cried himself to sleep, lying face down on top of his bed.'

'It'll be a blessing if he sleeps until most of the business is by,' Lucy said, overhearing.

Having arranged for Kirsten to stay with an old friend in Lochandee, she'd insisted Ryan and Cameron should go to school as usual, much to their disappointment. She needed to be free of parental duties if she was to help her grandmother today. She knew Paul was to have gone to school too, but the auctioneer and his clerks had arrived early and shortly afterwards the cars of early viewers began to arrive. Peter, Nick, Max, Alicia and Margaret had been at Nether Rullion since the crack of dawn getting animals fed and bedded and giving a last-minute brush up. They were gathered around the kitchen table eating a big breakfast, preparing for the long day's work ahead. The air of tension and excitement increased. Paul could sense it. He looked at the strangers. He listened intently as the auctioneer discussed the arrangements for getting the cattle into the sale ring. In dawning horror he began to realise what his elders really meant when they had talked about a sale.

Already dressed in his school shoes and uniform, he had dashed out of the house and into the yard, narrowly missing a car full of prospective buyers which was edging its way to the field where the cars were to park. Rachel panicked, fearing for his safety.

'Wait here, I'll get him, Mum.'

Bridie found Paul in one of the calf pens with his arms around the necks of two small calves. They were twins and had been very small when they were born. Paul had helped to care for them. Although they were two months old they were still small for their age. They were his favourites. His teeth were chattering and racking sobs shook his small shoulders as he whispered into their ears. Bridie's heart ached for him. A memory of herself as a child flashed into her mind. She had felt ill with grief when the dreaded foot-and-mouth had come to Lochandee and her father had tried so hard to explain why all her beloved animals had to be slaughtered. But these animals were not being killed. She tried to tell Paul they would be going to a lovely new home. Nothing she could say would comfort him. Bridie remembered the awful silence in the farmyard at Lochandee when all the animals had gone. It had felt eerie and deserted, so empty ... lonely ...

Against her better judgement, Bridie found herself kneeling beside Paul, promising to keep these two small calves out of the sale. For a moment his sobs ceased. He looked searchingly into her face, but then his face crumpled again.

'B-but their friends will be l-leaving. They'll be l-lonely ...'

'No, they won't. They'll have each other. And they'll have you.' She stood up. 'Come back to the house with me, Paul. I promise to keep these two calves specially for you, but I do have a lot of work to do today.' Silently Paul shook his head and buried his wet face against the neck of one of the calves. It tried to lick his hair. In desperation, Bridie picked him up and carried him back to the house, still sobbing as she handed him over to her mother for comfort.

Bridie made a large card saying "Withdrawn from sale" and went out to find Peter. He had promised to organise the animals ready for going into the ring. He was as pleased as any small boy himself when Bridie told him what she had done.

'I'll look after them with Paul,' he said solemnly. Bridie knew how upset Peter had been when he first heard about the sale, but he had been relieved to learn he would still have a place at Nether Rullion, albeit not so interesting to him. Billy Smith had been upset too, but Bridie had given him an excellent reference and he had got a job on a farm near enough for him to continue living at the cottage with his father. He was to start immediately after the sale.

A fortnight earlier, Chris and Adam had come down to visit Lucy and get a preview of the Nether Rullion stock. Bridie had shown them round, telling Adam which animals she would like to buy for her own herd at Lochandee.

'I shall have to stand beside the auctioneer, to answer his queries as the animals come into the ring,' she said. 'I wondered whether you'd bid for me, Adam? I want it to be all fair and honest.'

'I'll be pleased to do that, Mrs Jones,' Adam said, regarding Bridie with respect. He knew lots of breeders would have taken advantage of the relationship and taken their pick before the sale.

'As a matter of fact, I'd like to keep two or three of the cow families going with the Rullion prefix. One day I hope they'll provide a small nucleus for Paul to build up a herd of his own, if he decides farming is what he wants to do. These are the ones my father started with ...' She indicated the names in the catalogue. 'And I know Ewan was pleased with the way the Ruby family was breeding, so perhaps you could put in a bid for either of these two. Adam grinned as she pointed to the lot numbers.

'I have a fancy for one of them myself. Now I know I'm really on the right track.'

When Paul woke, the actual selling of the animals was almost over but the house was full of strangers phoning for cattle lorries to transport their purchases. Nick's two lorries were fully booked and so were several others which had come to the sale in the hope of getting work. The dining room was full of men, all discussing their

311

purchases.

'It's almost time for me to meet Ryan and Cameron from school,' Lucy said to Rachel. 'Shall I take Paul with me and keep them all at Lochandee until the lorries get loaded and on their way?'

'Oh, Lucy, if you would!' Rachel agreed, with relief. 'It might take his mind off things if he and Ryan can play together.'

'Yes. They're in the same boat now,' Lucy said sadly. 'Neither have a father or a farm. Well, Paul will have a farm, but he'll still have to struggle to buy the stock and make it a proper farm again.' Her tone was wistful. Conan gave her a speculative look, biting his lip as thoughts went round and round in his head.

At this stage, he decided, there was nothing he could do to help his grandsons. They had the love and care of their mother and that was what they needed most. In a few weeks, Lucy would be starting teaching full-time in one of the local village schools a few miles from Lochandee. She seemed to be looking forward to it. She already had several pupils for piano lessons. She could have had more, but preferred to spend some time after school with her own children. She continually assured Fiona they were all right for money, but Conan knew and approved of his wife's generosity with little gifts of shoes for the boys or a dress for Kirsten.

He smiled as he looked across at Fiona now, calmly refilling plates of scones for the hungry men and returning their quips with a wit and humour of her own. Neither of them would have wanted Lucy to be widowed so tragically young, but Lucy's loss had been their gain. It was lovely having her live so near. They truly enjoyed their grandchildren. Fiona was inordinately proud of Cameron's way with numbers although he hadn't been at school very long. Ryan was different. Already he was reliable and steady, not as quick to learn as his younger brother, but acutely observant and he had an excellent memory. As for Kirsten, Conan thought she was the most beautiful little girl in the world with her green eyes and red-gold hair – not to mention the wide, toothy smile which could charm the heart out of him. Lucy was always remonstrating with him for spoiling her.

Rachel came and sat in an empty chair beside him.

'You're looking pleased with yourself, Conan.'

'Am I?' He looked startled. 'I was just daydreaming and thinking how lucky we are to have Lucy living near us now.'

'Yes, she's a grand lassie. Ever ready to lend a hand, and full of sound common sense.' She sighed heavily. 'It's an ill wind if it doesna blow some good to somebody, I suppose.' She bit her lower lip hard and her voice held a faint tremble. 'Though I find it hard to see what good can possibly come out of this day's toil.' Conan looked at her sharply.

'But Bridie said it had been an excellent sale. Better than her expectations.'

'Oh, yes, it'll pay off all the creditors, and a bit besides. But just think what a waste it was to sell the very best of the dairy herd as commercial stock – and maybe not even a fair price even for commercial cattle. Gerda knew nothing about cows. It was criminal really ...'

'Mum! You're not regretting your decision not to prosecute, are you?' He looked at her in consternation. She had been so certain.

'No ... No, I'd have sacrificed anything – everything – just to make sure Paul is loved and cared for. There was no telling what Gerda might have done with him; maybe even put him in a home if she felt he was preventing her enjoying her life.'

'I'm glad to hear you've no regrets!' Conan said, in relief. 'If it's any consolation to you, Fiona thought you'd made the wisest decision possible and Lucy most certainly did. She knew what Gerda was like when it came to caring for children.'

'Oh, well, I'm glad they both agreed with me. Your father had great faith in Fiona's advice, you know. I've often wondered if she had anything to do with him putting the land into a trust for Paul, and making all those provisions for Peter and for me to stay in the houses. That must have been a shock to Gerda when she found out.'

'I'll bet it was, but then Dad would never have done it if he had not mistrusted her motives. He was pretty shrewd himself.'

'Yes. He certainly did his best to provide fairly for each of you, but I don't know what he'd have thought to this day's work. I shall feel as sick at heart as Paul does when I go out in the morning and see all the empty sheds. It won't feel like a farm at all.'

'Did Bridie tell you she had kept back twin calves for Paul to rear? And one of the heifer stirks hurt its leg trying to jump out of the sale ring so she withdrew it as well.'

'Ah, I didn't know that.' Rachel's face brightened a little.

'Then Peter has his pigs and you have your hens, and the old collie,' Conan comforted. 'I know it won't be the same as before, but at least the fields are still yours and soon there will be other cattle to graze them. Bridie said she was bringing some from Glens of Lochandee.'

'Aye, you're right, laddie. We should be thankful for what we have left, and most of all that Paul will be safe and loved.'

# Chapter Twenty-six

'You know, Mum, you look really smart in that new outfit. I can't believe you're 79,' Bridie said in all sincerity as she eyed Rachel's emerald green dress with the matching jacket and a hat which toned in as though it had been made for it.

'Hush!' Rachel's green eyes sparkled with humour. 'I don't feel a day above 50 so don't tell anyone.'

Bridie smiled back at her and sat down on a vacant chair. 'I hope I look as well when I'm your age.'

'I think you make an exceedingly lovely mother of the groom,' Rachel assured her. 'Indeed, I heard Nick telling you so, and he's still a handsome man himself. I'm sure Max is very proud of you both, but then he always has been.'

'Yes, we've been very lucky in our children. It was a surprise 18 months ago, though, when Alicia and Margaret told us they both wanted to get married and have a double wedding.'

'Well, they seem idyllically happy and now nature has conspired to keep them doing things together. They've each given you a lovely wee granddaughter.'

'They have indeed, and now we have Megan for a daughter-in-law. She is a lovely girl. She shares all Max's interests in the farm and the cattle. I'm looking forward to taking things a bit easier once they come back from their honeymoon.'

'Yes, Nick was telling me he's booked a holiday abroad on one of Conan's tours. You'll need to get passports ...'

'Did I hear someone mention my name?' Conan chuckled as he joined them and took a seat on the other side of Rachel. 'My word, Mum, you get younger every day!'

'And you've inherited your dad's silver tongue, laddie. Are you wanting to ask a favour?'

'Not at all!' Conan said indignantly, then he saw the twinkle in her eye and grinned. 'I imagine you're very proud of all your grandchildren today?'

'I am indeed – and my great-grandchildren.'

'Yes, the two wee flower girls almost stole the show. Alicia and Margaret needn't have worried about their offspring misbehaving. They looked and acted like wee angels.'

'I'm sure you're very proud of your own granddaughter too. Kirsten makes a beautiful bridesmaid, and she's so patient with the little ones. You and Fiona must count your blessings, Conan.'

'We do,' Conan said simply. 'Lucy's made a good job of bringing up her family on her own. I often wondered whether she'd get married again when she was widowed so young but I don't think she will now.'

'No, I don't think she'll ever love anyone but Don. Conan ...?'

'I know what you're going to say, Mum.' Conan smiled down at her.

'You do? You always were a mind-reader. Maybe that's why you've done so well in that business of yours. It's not everyone who can deal with the public. Someone told me you make them feel you are doing them a real favour by organising a wonderful holiday; they quite forget you're relieving them of their money while you're doing it.'

'Well, that's part of the secret of running a successful tourist business.' Conan grinned, then his green eyes grew serious. 'I couldn't have done it without Fiona though. We've been a team in every way from the very beginning.'

'I know. You were very fortunate. So, does Fiona approve of the offer you've made to Ryan? And are you sure about it? It'd be a dreadful disappointment to him if you changed your mind after he gets through agricultural college. He reminds me so much of your father ... and yet he's like Don too. Bridie says you couldn't get a better stockman anywhere.'

'Yes, she said the same to us, but we accepted years ago that all Ryan wanted to do was farm. He's never shown any interest in the buses.'

'Not like Cameron does.' Rachel smiled.

'Fiona agrees we should give all three of our grandchildren an equal chance and Cameron has already decided for himself. He wants to go to university and then join us in the tourist business. Fiona is pleased but she does understand how desperately Ryan wants to farm.'

'It's bred in him, on both sides.'

'Yes, I realised that when he and Paul were quite small. Mentally, I think I made plans to help him a long time ago. I always knew it was Lucy's deepest regret that she would never be able to help him into a farm as Don would have tried to do. I wouldn't have suggested putting up the capital for Ryan and Paul to go into partnership at Nether Rullion though without getting Bridie's agreement first. That's right, isn't it, Bridie?'

'It is. Of course, we're both trustees for Paul so it's a big responsibility. Now, I think I'd better circulate among the wedding guests.' Bridie smiled. 'I'll talk to you again later, Mum.' Rachel and Conan watched her go towards another group of wedding guests, her feet light, her figure still neat in her dusky pink suit.

'Fiona has agreed to draw up a proper legal partnership

for the boys,' Conan said, 'so you have no need to worry, Mum – and Bridie will supervise the farming side of things until they are 25.'

'Yes.' Rachel nodded seriously. 'It is better to have an agreement in case they decide to split up, as you and Nick did.'

'Well, Paul will have the Nether Rullion land out of trust by then and, if we provide Ryan with the capital to stock it and install a modern milking parlour, they should have a good start. After that, it'll be up to the pair of them to work hard and make a success of things. Neither Bridie nor I expect them to farm in partnership for ever. They're both ambitious. I think they'll expand until they can afford a farm each. At least they'll have a decent start.'

'Yes, that's more than I dared to hope when Ewan was killed,' Rachel reflected. 'I'm sure they'll both work hard.' Her eyes moved to Paul, tall and slim-hipped, with an infectious smile and thick blond-streaked hair. 'Meanwhile, having something to work for will give them an incentive to get through their course at agricultural college,' Rachel agreed.

'Yes.' Conan grinned. 'They both thought they should rush into farming straight away, but Bridie has insisted they must work on another farm for a year at least to broaden their experience before they go to college. I agree with her. After all they're only 19,' he added sternly.

'Oh, yes.' Rachel smiled at his tone. 'And you and Nick were fighting a war at their age. Remember?'

'So we were. Our view of the world changed completely. No doubt theirs will too.'

'You think one of them might decide to do something else? Other than farming?' Rachel asked in surprise. Ever since they were old enough, Ryan and Paul had spent their weekends and school holidays at Glens of Lochandee, trailing after either Max or their Aunt Bridie. There was only six months between them and they had always been the best of friends.

'They probably both know more about livestock and breeding than their college lecturers will ever know,' Bridie had said, 'but farming's changing rapidly since decimalisation came in, and after all the strikes we had, the price of everything seems to have doubled. Then the Common Market has brought so many new regulations. I can't teach the boys everything and I can see great changes ahead.'

The boys had protested vigorously.

'You can teach us all we want to know, Aunt Bridie,' Paul said, and Ryan had heartily agreed.

'No, I can't. You need to learn about economics and the science behind animal diseases and hygiene. Bacteriology can be very interesting and it helps you understand why I make you do some of the things when you think I'm fussing.' She grinned at them. 'Oh yes, I know what you think! Anyway, there's accounts to do, and a lot to learn about seeds and managing grass, making silage, using the correct fertilisers and getting the soil analysed. I know lots of people think nature sees to all these things, but you two should know better and you need to learn to combat the problems as they arise, and even see them coming. You might both decide to be arable farmers ...'

'We shan't!' they had echoed in unison.

'Well, I often think it must be easier than milking cows seven days a week. But if you go to college, the choice will be yours.'

Conan and Fiona had agreed with Bridie on this and reluctantly the boys had agreed.

'Look, Max and Megan are starting the dancing,' Conan said, drawing Rachel's attention back to the wedding reception. 'They make a lovely couple, don't you think?'

'I do indeed. I pray with all my heart they'll be happy

together at Glens of Lochandee.'

'I think they will. They seem well-matched. Would you like to dance, Mum?'

'Won't Fiona be waiting for you?'

'She's too busy chatting to Mrs Greig. Now *there's* a woman who looks ten years younger since she was widowed.'

'She does look well,' Rachel agreed. 'But no wonder. Mr Greig was such a crotchety old man. Christine's like her mother. She and Lucy have remained close friends over the years. Look, there's Cameron asking one of the bridesmaids to dance!' Rachel said in delight. 'He's just like you, Conan, with his green eyes and roguish grin. He has your build too – tall and slim. Ryan's more like Don was – sturdier built. Is Fiona pleased Cameron will be joining you in the business?'

'Yes, she is, and she's delighted he's studying accountancy. She feels we'll need one in the firm when she retires, and I think she's right about that. Cameron is already pretty useful around the office, and he doesn't mind getting his hands dirty either, if one of the buses needs attention. I thought at one point he was going to be a mechanic, but I believe he'll be more useful as an administrator, if he takes over the business someday.'

'And Kirsten ...?'

'She's like Bridie. And Fiona says Lucy was the same – excels at languages. She's only 15 yet, but she talks about going to university. Fiona has already told her we could use someone who can speak a couple of foreign languages to deal with some of the problems we get now we send tours abroad. Whatever she decides, we'll see she gets a share in the business too. Fiona has already put some shares in Lucy's name. We want to keep it in the family.' He grinned down at Rachel. 'I'm getting as bad as Dad, except that he wanted to make us all into farmers at Glens of Lochandee.'

'Yes ...' Rachel sighed. 'But you each made your own way in life in the end.' Conan saw the shadow which passed over her face.

'You're thinking of Ewan?' he said softly.

'I was. He thought Gerda was the love of his life. He was so young. We should have been firmer – made them wait ...'

'Things might have been worse if you had. I suppose we were both a bit headstrong – each in our own way,' Conan reflected.

'You were indeed!' Rachel agreed. 'You can't imagine how we worried about you when we knew you'd joined the RAF.'

'I think I can understand now,' Conan said, leading her back to a seat as the dance finished. His eyes moved to Lucy, and then to her children, his own grandchildren. He hoped and prayed their paths through life would be happy. His gaze moved to Paul, his nephew.

'Paul looks just like Dad,' he said involuntarily.

'I've often thought so too.' Rachel smiled. 'Except he has green eyes, like yours, and mine. He has a lovely nature and that's the biggest blessing of all. He and Ryan could almost pass for brothers. I'm sure they'll make a great success of bringing Nether Rullion back to the farm it used to be.'

# The Lochandee Series by Gwen Kirkwood

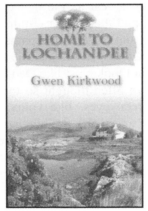

Please visit
**www.gwenkirkwood.co.uk**

For more information on **Gwen Kirkwood**
and other **Accent Press** titles, please visit

**www.accentpress.co.uk**

Lightning Source UK Ltd.
Milton Keynes UK
UKOW06n0406061215

264117UK00001B/11/P

9 781786 151469